PANAMA

PANAMA

a novel

Carlos Ledson Miller

ISBN   1-4196-7621-0
ISBN-13   978-1419676215

Front cover photo by Bernard Cloutier
          (http://bernardcloutier.interspeed.com)

This book was printed in the United States of America.

CONTENTS

PROLOGUE: EL NIÑO 15

1. BIENVENIDOS 46
2. LOS DOBERMANS 57
3. BATALLON DE LA DIGNIDAD 67
4. PORTOBELO 85
5. LA SAN BLASA 100
6. LOS MACHOS 109
7. COLON 116
8. EL CIMARRON 130
9. NORIEGA 149
10. LA PREVENTIVA 163
11. LA VISION 175
12. LA GRINGA 183
13. LOS ESTUDIANTES 212
14. LOS RABIBLANCOS 224
15. EL CUARTELAZO 244
16. EL NECROCOMIO 273
17. VENGANZA 293
18. CAUSA JUSTA 308

EPILOGUE: PANAMA 2000 323

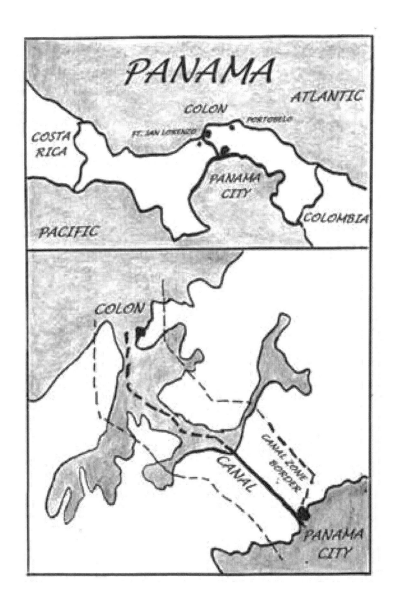

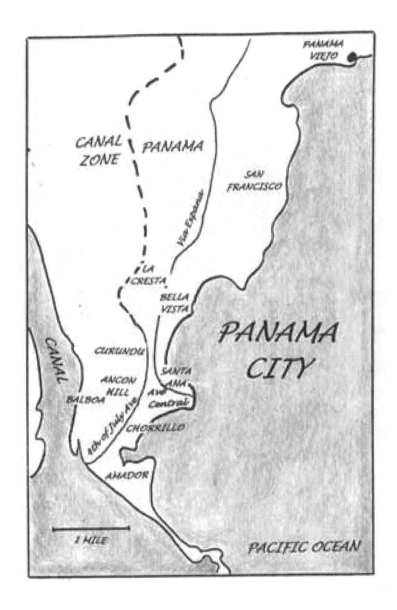

AUTHOR'S NOTE

Throughout most of the 20th Century, the United States claimed sovereignty over a wide swath of land that bisected the isthmus of Panama. The "Canal Zone" extended five miles on either side of the fifty-mile canal. In Panama City, the border between the nations was delineated by a major thoroughfare: *Fourth of July Avenue.*

In 1964, after sixty years of turbulent coexistence, a bloody riot erupted between Canal Zonians and Panamanians. The catalyst was a Canal Zone student raising an American flag in front of his high school, in defiance of an agreement between the United States and Panamanian governments. Aftershocks of the disturbance continued into the following decade, and eventually prompted President Jimmy Carter to pledge that the United States would cede all claims of sovereignty in Panama at year-end, 1999.

This book is a work of fiction. Although it is set during pivotal periods in Panamanian history, the characters are fictional, except for cameo appearances by a few historical figures. The dialogues and the specific incidents involving all characters—fictional and historical—are products of the author's imagination or are used fictitiously.

This novel is dedicated to the people of Panama: Panamanians, Canal Zonians, and those who, like the author, lived on both sides of *Fourth of July Avenue.*

RELATIONSHIP OF PRINCIPAL CHARACTERS

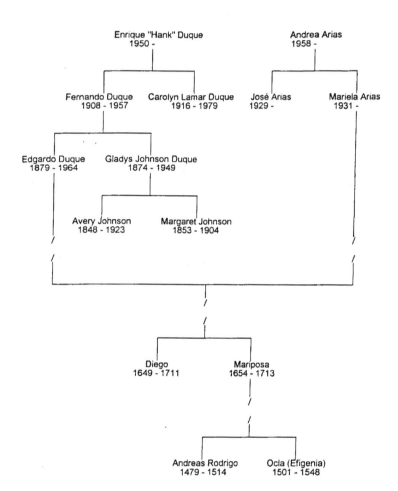

PANAMA

PROLOGUE: EL NIÑO

. . . ask what you can do for your country.
—John F. Kennedy

January 1964

A seagull's shrill cry awoke Hank Duque from a sound adolescent sleep. The woven cord hammock rocked as he struggled into a sitting position. He stretched, then rose unsteadily and stepped to the veranda railing. To his left lay the Pacific Ocean, undulating in the morning breeze. To his right, a mile away, stood the butte known as Ancon Hill. The sun illuminated the Canal Zone hillside, while shadows still encased Panama City.

Hank turned and hurried across the veranda and into his grandfather's apartment. The polished tile felt cool against his bare feet as he padded down the narrow hall. He paused in the kitchen doorway. His grandfather sat hunched at the breakfast table, reading a book through a magnifying glass.

The old man looked up and smiled. *"Buenos días, Enrique."*

"Good morning, Grandpa."

"Enrique, you must use your Spanish if you are to learn it."

"What time is it?"

"En español," his grandfather said, insisting on Spanish.

"¿Uh . . . qué hora es?"

His grandfather nodded approvingly, then checked his watch. *"Son las siete y media."*

"Seven thirty? Jeez. I'm supposed to be in Curundú at nine."

"But why? Today is Saturday."

"I've got a tennis tournament. We're playing Cristobal High. I'm in the freshman finals."

His grandfather frowned. "But how will you get there? Miguel won't be here until noon." At eighty-five, Edgardo Duque could no longer drive the congested Panama City streets. The university, where he had taught for more than forty years, provided him with a driver.

"I can make it on my bike," Hank said, "if I hurry."

He left the kitchen and entered the bathroom. His clothes lay neatly stacked on the bottom towel shelf. His grandfather's maid had unpacked his overnight bag when he arrived the previous evening.

Hank pulled on clean cotton briefs, then grabbed a pair of white tennis shorts. Preoccupied with thoughts of the upcoming match, he lowered the shorts to knee level, inserted one leg, then the other. Something lighted on his lower left shin. Hank looked down in terror. "Grandpa! Scorpion!"

The old man appeared in the doorway, holding a broom. "Don't move!"

Hank released his grip on his shorts; they fell in a heap about his feet. The two-inch scorpion raised its front pincers and flexed its upturned tail, the venomous stinger coming dangerously close to Hank's skin. It turned slowly, then started down Hank's leg.

"Do something, Grandpa!" Hank begged.

The scorpion lowered its pincers and disappeared inside Hank's left pant leg. Hank began to shake.

"Keep still," his grandfather said.

"I can't," Hank said, fighting back tears.

"Enrique," his grandfather said softly, "please, you must remain still." He placed the bristled end of the broom near Hank's feet. "Show courage, *Nieto.*"

Hank took a deep breath.

"Can you feel it moving?" his grandfather whispered.

"I don't know . . ."

"Be still . . . I think I see it . . . there!" The old man raked the broom across Hank's feet.

Hank screamed and jumped backward, landing on his backside.

His grandfather trapped the angry scorpion against the side of the bathtub and crushed it, first with the broom's bristles, then with the handle. He carefully picked it up by its pincers and flushed it down the toilet.

Hank got to his feet and pulled up his shorts. A shudder ran down his spine. "Jeez, Grandpa . . ."

"Enrique," his grandfather said sternly, "I have told you to always shake out your clothes and shoes before you put them on."

"I know, Grandpa. I forgot. We don't have scorpions in Ancon."

The old man shook his head, but a smile formed. "Ah, yes, you Americans forbid them to cross Fourth of July Avenue."

Hank laughed with relief. His Panamanian grandfather liked to tease him about the rigid discipline that Americans imposed on their side of the border.

"Finish getting dressed," his grandfather said. "I will fix your breakfast."

"I don't have time, Grandpa."

"You must eat."

A few minutes later, Hank sat at the kitchen table, bolting down papaya, scrambled eggs, and toasted *micha* bread.

"Will you be staying here again tonight?" his grandfather said.

Hank nodded, his mouth full. "The hospital's got Mom on the night shift all week."

"Good. We will have more time together."

Hank carried his plate to the sink, then headed for the living room. The shiny red racing bicycle his grandfather had given him for Christmas stood near the entryway. Hank opened the front door and rolled the bike onto the tiled front stoop. As he reached back to close the door, he called out, "Goodbye, Grandpa!"

He carried his bicycle down the steps, then pushed it through the lush tropical plants that lined the cracked, concrete walkway.

"Enrique!" his grandfather called out from the stoop.

Hank turned. "Yes, Grandpa?"

"Did you say you will be in Curundú this morning?"

"Yes, Grandpa."

"When Miguel arrives, I will have him bring me over so I can watch you play."

Hank forced a smile. "Okay, Grandpa." His Panamanian grandfather always seemed so out of place when he visited the American Canal Zone.

The old man waved, then reentered his apartment. Hank climbed onto his bicycle, dropped it into low gear, and started up the palm tree-lined hill.

Two Panamanian youths Hank's age strolled down the sidewalk on the opposite side of the street. "*¡Gringo!*" the taller one shouted. Both boys stepped off the curb and started toward him.

Hank stood up and pedaled hard. He heard another derisive shout in Spanish as he pulled away, but only understood the word *pantalónes*. Apparently they were making fun of his short pants. He glanced over his shoulder. A half-block down the hill, the boys stood with hands on hips, taunting him. Hank extended his middle finger. The boys cursed, and started after him, but Hank had too much of a lead. Laughing, he turned onto *Vía España*, Panama City's busiest thoroughfare.

He cut across the street to the far curb, passing in front of a brightly painted *chiva*. The driver of the minibus leaned on his horn and shouted out the window, "*¡Cuidado, niño!*—Watch out, boy!"

Hank grinned and waved. The driver returned his wave and roared past.

Traffic was heavy on *Vía España*, but not as bad as during the week. Hank leaned low over the swooped handlebars to reduce wind resistance and kept pace with most of the southbound traffic. He spotted several rotting oranges in his path and swerved to avoid them, drawing another horn blast. The morning sun beat against his back; he broke a sweat and began to breathe hard.

Momentarily clear of immediate traffic, he lifted his head.

Ramshackle dwellings and rundown shops lined both sides of the thoroughfare. He sped past an open market and caught a glimpse of vendors setting up stands. The aroma of fresh produce saturated the air.

A few blocks farther, the street pinched down between rickety three-story buildings. Ahead on the right lay *Parque de Lesseps*. He swerved into the park and crunched along the gravel footpath that bisected it. The dense tree canopy provided momentary relief from the sun. Several park benches were already occupied by women tending small children.

Hank braked at the far side of the park in front of a steep flight of concrete steps. He lifted his bicycle onto one shoulder and started up. At the top of the steps, lay Fourth of July Avenue. Sprawled across the hillside was his home, the far-flung American community of Ancon.

"Move up!" Hank's florid-faced tennis coach bawled, after the Cristobal High School player's first serve hit the net.

Hank edged forward. He was ahead 5-2 in games, but had misplayed the last two championship points. Heat waves radiated off the Curundú tennis courts. Hank crouched forward, and sweat poured from his forehead and splattered on the gray concrete between his feet, evaporating immediately.

His gangling redheaded opponent hit his second serve, looping it tantalizingly over the net. Hank set himself and slammed it with his forehand. Too low! he thought, but his top-spin caught the tape and pulled the ball over for the win.

A scattering of applause rippled through the small group of parents watching the match.

Hank jogged to the net and extended his hand. "Good game, man."

His freshman opponent reluctantly shook hands, saying, "You lucky son of a bitch."

"Screw you," Hank said with a grin, and jogged over to the sideline.

"You got lucky on that last one, Hank," his coach said, then turned his attention to the sophomore who would be playing the next match.

Hank stifled another, "Screw you."

His two closest friends, Jeff and T.J., rode up on their bicycles. They had lost their matches earlier that morning.

"Hey, Hank," Jeff said, "still wanna go swimming at Fort Amador?"

Before Hank could answer, he noticed his grandfather shuffling toward him.

"Congratulations, Enrique. You played very well today."

"Thanks, Grandpa."

"Are these your friends?"

"Yeah. This is Jeff, and this is T.J."

As his grandfather shook hands with each of the fourteen-year-olds, he bowed slightly and said, *"Mucho gusto."*

Jeff made a poor effort at concealing an adolescent smirk, and Hank felt himself flush. For reasons he didn't understand, his grandfather, with whom he was so comfortable in Panama, was an embarrassment here in the Canal Zone.

"Are you coming home with me?" his grandfather said. "We can put your bicycle in the back of the car."

"I gotta stay around here," Hank lied.

His grandfather nodded. "If I am not at home when you arrive, I will be at the university library."

"Okay, Grandpa."

"Bueno, Enrique," the old man said with a smile, then shuffled toward his ancient Packard that was parked at the curb. Hank waved at Miguel, the university student who drove for his grandfather.

"So, what's it gonna be . . . 'Enrique'?" Jeff said. "You coming with us?"

"Screw you, Jeff," Hank said. "Lemme get my bike."

On their way from Curundú to Fort Amador, the boys rode through Ancon. The manicured boulevards that ran through the neatly aligned beige duplexes were nearly deserted. Hank led the bicycle procession; his English racer easily outran the other boys' heavy, American models.

They passed the Ancon clubhouse, then turned onto a tree-lined side street that ran alongside the elementary school they all had attended. As they coasted down Ancon Hill, they watched a kickball game in progress on the playground.

"Let's stop and challenge 'em!" T.J. shouted.

"Naw, that's kid stuff," Jeff yelled back.

They turned right onto Fourth of July Avenue, and Hank signaled he wanted to stop at the Kool Spot, a small eatery on the Panamanian side of the thoroughfare. As they threaded their way through the traffic, several motorists angrily blew their horns. The boys made it across and pulled their bicycles onto the sidewalk.

"Why are we stopping here?" T.J. said.

"I'm thirsty," Hank said. "Leave your bikes in front of the window, so we can keep an eye on 'em."

"Why didn't we stop at the Ancon clubhouse?" T.J. complained.

"Cokes are a dime there," Hank said. "Here they're just a nickel."

T.J. looked around uncertainly. "But I'm not supposed to be over here."

"Pussy," Jeff said.

"*Who* says you're not supposed to be over here?" Hank said.

"My dad. *I've* got one, you know."

The gibe didn't phase Hank. His father had died of tuberculosis seven years earlier; Hank hardly remembered him. From what he saw of other kids' fathers, like T.J.'s, all they did was keep you from doing things.

"Wait for us across the street then," Hank said, pulling open the rusty screen door. He and Jeff entered, and T.J. reluctantly trailed after them.

Inside, the dimly lighted Kool Spot was anything but cool. The sun shining through the grimy front window was the only source of light, and a single ceiling fan circulated hot, humid air. A lunch counter ran along one side; five mismatched tables lined the other. There were no other customers.

A heavyset black proprietor, clad in a dirty T-shirt, sat on a stool behind the counter, reading a newspaper. He looked up as the boys entered and called out, *"Qué tal, niño."*

"Qué tal, señor," Hank said.

"You haven't been here for a while," the proprietor said in Spanish.

"I go to school in Balboa now, señor," Hank replied in Spanish. Jeff and T.J. stood quietly beside him during the exchange. Like most Canal Zonians, they didn't speak Spanish. On this side of the border, Hank's friends respected his dual nationality.

"Quiero una Coca Cola de cereza, por favor," Hank said to the proprietor. To his friends, he said, "You want cherry-Cokes too?"

"Yeah," they both responded.

"Tres, por favor," Hank said.

The proprietor shooed the flies off two syrup bottles and poured the thick liquids into three glasses. He dropped in three handfuls of ice, then added carbonated water. Behind the proprietor's back, T.J. made a face at the unsanitary preparation.

When they received their drinks, Hank and Jeff drained theirs. T.J. hesitated.

"Come on, T.J.," Hank said, "we don't want to spend the whole day here."

"I'm not thirsty," T.J. said.

"Drink it, you pussy," Jeff said.

The proprietor scowled. *"¿Qué pasa?"*

T.J. grabbed his glass and tried to down his drink in a single swallow. Much of it ran down the corners of his mouth and onto his T-shirt.

"¿Más?" the proprietor said.

"How about it, T.J.?" Hank chided. "Want another one?"

T.J. put his nickel on the counter and hurried outside.

"No más, señor," Hank said. He and Jeff also paid, and started toward the door. *"Adios, señor,"* Hank called back.

"Adios, señor," Jeff parroted. Outside, he said to Hank, "Didn't know I could talk that shit, did you?"

The boys pedaled up to Fort Amador's main gate. An American military policeman, wearing a polished white helmet, waved them over.

"The bubble-head wants to see us," Jeff muttered.

"Oh, no," murmured the ever-worried T.J.

"Shut up, and let me do the talking," Hank whispered.

They stopped at the gate. "Y'all live here?" the M.P. said.

"Yes, sir," Hank lied. "Don't you remember us?"

The guard shook his head. "Lemme see some I.D."

Hank handed over his Ancon identification card, hoping the M.P. wouldn't check it too closely. Jeff followed suit. T.J. dropped his, and had difficulty picking it up. Finally, with a shaking hand, he gave it to the M.P.

"Says here, y'all live in Ancon," the M.P. said.

"Naw," Hank said, bluffing. "That just means we *go to school* in Ancon. We live here in Fort Amador. You remember us."

The guard hesitated, then said, "Uh . . . okay."

Moments later, the boys pedaled down Fort Amador's manicured main boulevard. Regimented tan stucco quadruplexes lined both sides of the street. They passed the post movie theater, where a line of kids, mostly girls, waited to see the matinee showing of *Love with the Proper Stranger.*

"Hey!" Jeff said to Hank. "Did you see that chick in the green dress?"

"Yeah, I saw her," Hank said, feigning disinterest.

"Oh, I forgot," Jeff said, "you prefer dark meat." Then in dramatic falsetto, he sang, "I just met a girl named Maria . . ."

"Screw you, Jeff," Hank said. He put his racer in high gear and pulled away from Jeff's rendition of *Westside Story.* Jeff was right this time, however. Hank had a crush on María Ramírez, one of the few Panamanian kids who attended school in the Canal Zone.

They rode past the post golf course, then out onto a narrow causeway that linked three small islands, miniature hills actually, which rose out of the Bay of Panama.

They pulled up to a thatched pavilion on the first island. Due to the midday heat, the beach was deserted. The boys stripped down to their tennis shorts and headed for the water.

For the next hour or so, they raced back and forth between the beach and a wooden raft that was anchored twenty-five yards off-shore. In the final race, Jeff feinted a dive from the raft, then stood laughing as Hank and T.J. raced ashore without him.

From the beach, Hank shot Jeff the finger. Jeff returned the gesture, still laughing, then stretched out on the raft. Hank sat down in the sand.

T.J. dropped down beside him. They sat in silence for a few moments. Then T.J. said, "Do you really like Maria?"

Hank ignored him.

"I think she's pretty," T.J. said shyly.

"T.J. . . . ." Hank said, fending off what sounded like the beginning of a personal conversation. Then something caught his eye, and he pointed over T.J.'s shoulder. "Hey, look."

"At what?"

Hank jumped to his feet. "C'mon." He started off in the direction of the nearby hillside.

"Where we going?" T.J. said anxiously, stumbling after him.

"See that opening?" Hank said, pointing near the base of the hill. An iron-barred door, almost hidden in the underbrush, hung partially open. The top hinge appeared to be broken.

"What is it?" T.J. said.

"My grandfather told me the Army dug tunnels in these hills during World War II."

"Tunnels?"

"Yeah. Then after the war, they closed 'em off."

They arrived at the base of the hill. Barefooted, Hank picked his way through the prickly underbrush.

T.J. stayed behind. "Hank, you're going to step on something."

"Ouch! Damn it," Hank muttered, but kept going. What was it Grandpa had said about snakes around here? He'd called them fer-de-lances. Hank was almost to the door. He stretched and was able to grasp one of the rusty steel bars. The door creaked open a bit more. Using the bar for leverage, he pulled himself up to the entryway.

"Don't go in there!" T.J. implored from the beach.

Hank squeezed between the concrete door jamb and the steel bars. "It's not a tunnel," he shouted back to T.J. "It's a stairway." Mud and moss covered the bottom steps. Above, the stairs disappeared into darkness.

"Hank!" T.J. shouted.

Hank hesitated a moment, wondering if snakes could climb stairs, then started his ascent. His foot hurt from whatever he had stepped on. The mud and moss gave way to a thick layer of dust, and the walls were covered with graffiti, including several Kilroy caricatures. A pungent odor, similar to ammonia, grew stronger as he climbed.

"Hank!" came a faint cry from outside.

Hank stopped, straining to see up the long stairway. He thought he could make out a landing, but wasn't sure. He heard a rustling sound above, perhaps the flutter of wings. Bats? he wondered. Screw this! He turned and hurried down the stairs.

When he arrived back at the entryway, T.J. was gone. Hank looked through the bars and saw him standing at the water's edge. Jeff was swimming toward him.

Hank squeezed through the tight opening and worked his way back through the underbrush to the beach.

"What's in there?" Jeff shouted, running toward him.

Hank sat down in the sand. "A stairway. It probably goes to a tunnel. The Army dug 'em a long time ago." With a grimace, he went to work on a large splinter embedded in his foot.

"Let's go see," Jeff said.

"It's too dark," Hank said. "We'll have to come back with a flashlight." He managed to get hold of the splinter and pull it out. After he squeezed the wound to flush it, he rubbed his foot in the sand to stem the bleeding.

Jeff looked at the entryway, obviously wanting to explore it himself.

"I have to go home," T.J. said.

"Okay," Jeff said reluctantly. "Let's take this pussy home. Me and you'll come back next weekend."

The boys started across the sand for their bicycles and the return ride home.

An hour later, Hank arrived at his grandfather's apartment house. He turned into the driveway and rode around to the rear of the building. His grandfather's Packard wasn't there; Hank guessed he was still at the university.

Hank returned to the front of the building and stopped at the sidewalk. Down the hill lay the ocean; a freighter rode at anchor a hundred yards offshore. Hank pushed off and coasted across an intersection and into a shady neighborhood park. A young Panamanian governess pushed a baby carriage up the brick pathway. She moved to one side and gestured for Hank to slow down. He braked and was barely rolling as he approached her. *"Hola, bonita*—Hi, beautiful," he said, boldly flirting with her, as he had seen the men of the neighborhood do.

She gave him a look of surprise, then smiled and said, *"Cuidado, joven*—Watch out, young man."

Her smile made him feel older, confident. He wished María Ramírez lived around here.

On the other side of the park, he pulled up to the window of a refreshment stand. *"Un raspado, por favor."*

The old man who operated the stand removed a burlap cloth from a block of ice. He shaved the ice with a metal scoop until he had enough to fill a paper cone, then drenched it with thick purple syrup. He reached for a punctured can of condensed milk and shooed away the flies.

"Sin leche, por favor," Hank said.

The vendor shrugged and handed him the *raspado* without milk.

"Gracias, señor," Hank said. He paid the vendor with a U.S. nickel, and walked his bicycle over to the nearby seawall. He leaned

against the concrete rail and quickly ate the *raspado* before it melted in the sweltering afternoon sun.

Then he looked out to sea. The freighter anchored offshore was a cattle boat he had watched unload before. Hank turned to see if the corral down the street was being readied. Instead, he saw the two Panamanian youths from the morning confrontation swaggering down the sidewalk toward him. Shit! He wished he hadn't shot them the finger.

"*¡Hola, gringo!*" the taller boy said as they approached.

Hank set his jaw and returned the boy's gaze, trying to look tough.

They stopped in front of him. The taller one said in accented English, "Want to ride the bulls with us?"

Hank shook his head.

The boy turned to his companion and said with a sneer, "*Ese gringo no tiene cojones*—This American has no balls.*"

They filed past Hank and down a concrete stairway that led to the beach. They paused at the base of the seawall long enough to strip down to swim trunks, then jogged toward the ocean.

The freighter began to unload. Two booms, equipped with wide straps, lifted cattle out of the hold, swung them over the side, and lowered them into the water. The bellows of the terrified animals carried to the shore.

Two *vaqueros* on horseback rode out of the corral and onto the beach. They stopped at the water's edge and waited to round up the cattle when they swam ashore. One of the *vaqueros* waved for the boys to move away, but they ignored him. Instead, they dived into the next swell and swam out to meet the cattle.

A few minutes later, they each climbed onto the back of a bull. They shouted exuberantly as the animals struggled through the waves, trying to reach the shore. Finally, the bulls were able to touch bottom, and began to lunge and buck. The *vaqueros* waited in the churning the surf, cursing the riders. The boys, laughing, slid off the exhausted bulls and swam back out for their next ride.

Hank smiled. No *cojones*, huh? He rolled his bicycle over to the stairway, lifted it onto one shoulder, and carried it down the steps. He leaned it against the base of the seawall, then pulled off his shirt and tennis shoes. As he jogged toward the ocean, one of the *vaqueros* saw him and galloped in his direction. Hank broke into a run and high-stepped into the knee-deep surf. He dived into the next breaking wave and swam out to meet the incoming cattle.

After a few minutes of swimming into the three-foot swells, Hank lost some of his exuberance. Then he saw the two boys, now on their second mounts.

"*¡Hola, gringo!*" his antagonist shouted, this time grinning.

"*¡Hola, spic!*" Hank shouted back, laughing. A wave caught him in the mouth, choking him. When he recovered, the boys were out of sight, hidden behind the receding swells.

An animal swam toward him, but it had no horns, so Hank moved out of its path. Then, coming up on his left, he saw a bull. He broke into a furious crawl stroke to intercept it. The fear-crazed animal snorted; mucous poured from its flared nostrils. Jeez! The bull swam by, and Hank swam after it. He managed to grab its tail. How had the other boys climbed on? Hank released the tail, swam up close to the head, and tentatively grabbed a horn. The bull paid him no mind. Hank pulled himself onto its back and wrapped his legs around the animal's middle. This thing was huge! Snorting and bellowing, the bull struggled toward shore.

As Hank entered the churning surf, he checked for the *vaqueros*. One had a taut rope tied around a lifeless cow, and was dragging it across the sand. Apparently, it had drowned. The other *vaquero* was down at the far end of the beach, chasing a runaway. Hank decided it was a good time to get off. He relaxed the pressure of his legs and allowed the bull to swim out from under him. Treading water, he looked around for the other boys, but couldn't find them. He hadn't seen them swim back out . . . He shifted his gaze to the seawall. His bike was gone!

Hank was seated at the rear entrance of the apartment building when his grandfather's old Packard pulled in. The student driver helped the old man out of the car, then said, *"Hasta mañana, Profesor."*

"Hasta mañana, Miguel."

The student gave Hank a quick wave and took off on foot up the driveway.

"¿Qué pasa, Nieto?—What's the matter, Grandson?" the old man said, approaching with an armload of books.

Hank mutely shook his head.

"Have you been crying?" his grandfather said, bending down with concern.

"No," Hank lied.

"What is the matter?"

"They stole my bike," Hank said angrily.

"Who stole your bike?"

"Some spics."

"Come in the house," his grandfather said sternly.

Hank followed his grandfather into the kitchen.

"Sit there," his grandfather ordered, gesturing to the breakfast table.

Hank dropped into a chair. He looked down at his feet, his face contorted in an angry scowl.

His grandfather sat down opposite him. "Look at me, *Nieto.* Who are you calling 'spics'?"

Hank looked up. "Kids from the neighborhood. They stole my bike."

"You call the children who live here 'spics'?"

Hank looked down at his feet again.

"If they are 'spics'," his grandfather said, "then what am I?"

Hank raised his head and saw hurt etched into the old man's weathered face. Tears rolled down Hank's cheeks. "I didn't mean you, Grandpa."

"Do you know where that word comes from?"

Hank shook his head.

"Americans gave it to us, when I was a boy your age. They would talk to us, and we would try to explain that we did not speak English. They would mock us, saying, 'He no spiggoty English.' Spiggoty—Spic. Do you understand?"

"Yes, sir."

"Does my Spanish accent bother you, *Nieto?*"

Hank shook his head.

"Look at me," the old man said.

Hank raised his head and met his grandfather's steely gaze.

"My blood is in your veins," his grandfather said. "And, like it or not, it will be there all your life."

"I'm sorry . . . for offending you . . . *Abuelo.*"

The old man studied him for a moment, then gave a grudging nod. "Now, tell me what happened to your bicycle."

"Some . . . boys stole it while I was . . . swimming."

"Swimming where?"

"In the ocean."

"With all the beautiful swimming pools in the Canal Zone, why were you swimming in that filthy ocean?"

Hank looked down again. "I . . ."

"Yes?"

Barely audibly, Hank said, "I was riding the bulls."

His grandfather didn't respond. Finally, Hank looked up. The old man's frail frame shook with suppressed laughter. Hank frowned. "You're . . . not mad?"

"No, *Nieto*," his grandfather said, letting the laugh escape. "As I was not mad at your father."

"My father?" Hank had no personal recollection of his father, only the image of the solemn school teacher, whose photographs still adorned his mother's dresser. "You mean . . . my father rode the bulls too?"

The old man chuckled. "Three generations, and I am the only one able to keep the secret from his father."

"You, Grandpa!"

"It is like I told you, *Nieto*. Like it or not, you have my blood."

Most Balboa High School students had already left for the day.

Hank exited the building through a side door, having delayed his departure to avoid the embarrassment of being seen without his prized English racer.

As he walked past the empty bicycle rack, a voice called out "Hey, Hank!"

Darn! Hank thought.

Jeff rode up beside him. "Where's your bike?"

"Stolen," Hank said sullenly, continuing toward the front of the building.

"Who stole it?"

"Some kids."

"What kids?"

"Some kids in my grandpa's neighborhood."

"Spics?"

Hank hesitated, but then said, "Yeah."

"Let's get some of our kids together, and go get it back."

"I don't know where they live," Hank said glumly.

"Those thievin' spics—"

"What's goin' on over there?" Hank interrupted.

Five upperclassmen were gathered around the school's flag-pole, which hadn't been used for three years. There seemed to be a disagreement of some sort. Hank and Jeff approached the group.

Randy Lindeman, a bespectacled senior class officer, stood with his back to the flagpole. "It's against the law!" he protested.

"I don't give a shit," retorted a thick-necked youth, holding an unfurled United States flag. He was Sam Raguso, a lineman on the football team.

"What's goin' on?" Hank said.

"Get out of here, punks," Raguso said.

"We're not allowed to fly our flag," Lindeman continued to Raguso, "unless we fly the Panamanian flag beside it."

"Says who?" Raguso snarled. "You?"

"No," Lindeman replied. "Said President Kennedy, in his agreement with *Presidente* Chiari."

Hank piped up sarcastically, "Haven't you heard? Kennedy's dead. He got shot two months ago."

"Stay out of this," Lindeman said.

"The kid's right," Raguso said, giving Hank a nod of approval. "Any agreement Kennedy made don't mean shit now. He's dead." The other three boys muttered their concurrence.

"C'mon, Hank," Jeff whispered, "let's get out of here."

Hank shook his head.

"I'm gonna get the principal," Lindeman said. He headed for the front door of the school building.

The four upper classmen looked at each other uncertainly. Raguso muttered something about "God damn spics".

Hank thought of the two boys who had stolen his bicycle, and reached for the flag. "Lemme have it. I know how to do it. I used to raise the flag at Ancon Elementary."

Raguso smiled and handed it to him. Then he and the others stood back and watched as Hank secured the lanyards and hoisted the flag to the top of the pole. They let out a cheer as the Stars and Stripes unfurled against the afternoon sky.

Lindeman came back out of the building, alone. "The principal's already gone."

Raguso pointed to Lindeman. "You touch that flag, and I'll break your God-damned neck!"

Lindeman gave a resigned shake of his head, then turned and walked away.

Raguso said to the others, "Let's go over to the clubhouse. You too, kid. I heard you're some kinda pinball wizard, or something."

Hank smiled, and walked away with his new friends.

That evening, Hank's mother entered their modest kitchen, where Hank was finishing a bologna, lettuce, and tomato sandwich. "Hank," she said, handing him a plastic nameplate, "pin this on for me, honey. I forgot to do it before I dressed."

Hank carefully pinned the nameplate onto his mother's white uniform blouse.

"It's not upside down, is it?" she teased.

"No, ma'am," he said, double-checking. It read: "Carolyn Lamar Duque, R.N.".

"I'm *so* tired," she said, pouring the last half-cup of coffee from the pot. "Sleeping during the day just isn't the same as sleeping at night." She joined him at the kitchen table. "So how was your day?"

"It was okay."

"Honey, I know you feel bad about your bike. Maybe it'll turn up."

"Sure it will," he said sarcastically.

"Hank, *you* are the one who left it unattended."

"I know that, Mom," Hank said morosely.

"I didn't mean to snap at you, honey," she said, forcing a smile. "These split shifts at the hospital make me irritable."

"It's okay," he said, then got up and took his plate to the sink. "I'm going over to the school. We've got some stuff going on tonight."

"Tonight? What's going on tonight? With my schedule, I can't keep track of anything."

"It's . . . about football."

"Football?"

"Yeah. I won't be out late."

"But I thought football was over?"

"It's . . . about next year," Hank lied. "I'm thinking about going out for the team."

"Honey, you know football is very popular in Houston. When I was a girl—"

"Mom," Hank interrupted, sensing what she was leading up to, "all my friends are here."

"You'd make new friends in the States."

"But you said the schools aren't as good there as they are here."

His mother smiled and slowly shook her head, letting him know she recognized his ploy. "Y'all are at least two years ahead of them. But I'm sure somehow you'd cope with being the smartest boy in the class."

Jeez! First his bike gets stolen, and now his mother was talking about moving again.

"Just give it some thought, honey," she said. "Houston's a good place for nurses, and with your father gone . . ."

"But what about Grandpa?" Hank said desperately.

His mother sighed. "This is where we always wind up this discussion, isn't it?" She studied him for a moment, then smiled. "You two would certainly miss each other. I guess we'd better stay on a while longer."

Hank arrived back at the school at dusk. Hundreds of students and their supportive parents camped around the flagpole in small groups, talking and laughing. Occasionally, they looked up at the Stars and Stripes flapping in the evening breeze. Mountie-hatted Canal Zone policemen patrolled the area; Panamanian radio stations had carried reports of the solitary flag raising.

Hank saw Sam Raguso and the three other football players, and walked over to them.

Raguso gave him a nod of recognition. "It's still up there, buddy."

Hank smiled as he looked at the flag, feeling good at being treated like an equal by the toughest kid in the school. Nearby, someone shouted something about "spic kids". A general murmur went through the crowd, and everyone turned in the direction of the Prado, the wide esplanade that led up to the Canal Commission Administration Building.

"C'mon," Raguso told his three friends. They pushed their way to the front of the crowd. Hank followed in their wake. Marching down the street in an orderly procession, came hundreds of university students, neatly attired in white shirts, ties, and slacks. Four youths at the head of the procession carried a large, unfurled Panamanian flag. The Americans, both students and parents, greeted their arrival with jeers and catcalls.

"Go . . . home . . . spics!" boomed Raguso. His three friends chanted his words. Others in the crowd picked up the cry. Raguso looked down at Hank, who reluctantly joined in.

The Canal Zone police moved between the two factions. They spoke with the Panamanian students for several minutes. The Americans began to sing their national anthem. The singing abruptly stopped, however, when six Panamanian youths stepped forward with their flag.

"C'mon," Raguso said, and led his juggernaut forward. They broke past the policemen and rushed the Panamanians. Hank hung back uncertainly. A shoving match ensued. Raguso grabbed one end of the silk Panamanian flag and ripped it nearly in two.

Finally, the policemen separated the angry youths and escorted the now-disheveled six Panamanians and their torn flag back to their main body. Then they herded the entire contingent off in the direction of Fourth of July Avenue.

"Where were you?" Raguso said to Hank, his eyes blazing with excitement.

"Uh . . . the cops stopped me," Hank lied.

"C'mon, kid," Raguso said, draping an arm over Hank's shoulder. "I've got my parents' car and another flag in the trunk. We're gonna go raise it in front of the Tivoli."

Sam Raguso turned his parents' Chevrolet sedan onto Portobelo Street, which ran behind the venerable Tivoli Hotel. "Shit," he said, applying the brakes. "Soldiers."

Hank sat in the rear seat, crammed between two upperclassmen. Through the front windshield, he saw a detachment of Marines in full combat gear pile out of a large truck.

Raguso stopped the car near the hotel driveway. They watched the Marines file into the service entrance. Then Raguso said, "They'll probably give us some shit here. Let's go raise the flag at Shaler's Triangle instead."

"Uh . . . I need to get out," Hank said.

"What?" Raguso said, twisting around. "Where you going?"

"My mom gets off her shift at Gorgas Hospital in an hour. I gotta be home when she gets there."

"He has to go home to his mommy," the boy on his right jeered.

"Let the punk out," Raguso said.

As soon as Hank was clear of the car, the boys roared off in the direction of Shaler's Triangle. Hank headed up the drive toward the hotel. Actually, his mother wouldn't get off work for three more hours. He simply had decided he had done enough protesting for one day.

As he approached the truck, he noticed the driver-side door was open and a Marine was seated inside, smoking a cigarette. "What's goin' on?" Hank said.

"H.Q. thinks there might be some fireworks here tonight," the Marine said with affected nonchalance.

"Fireworks?"

Before the Marine could reply, a squawking voice on his two-way radio demanded attention. Hank continued up the drive.

The Tivoli Hotel was a landmark in the Canal Zone, dating back to Theodore Roosevelt's time. Like most youngsters in the community, Hank had grown up attending functions in its paneled rooms and playing on its landscaped grounds. Now, he stepped off the drive and followed a familiar dirt path that led around the side of the building, through dense tropical shrubbery.

As he approached the front of the hotel, he passed a noisy portable generator that had never been there before. Emerging from the bushes, he was blinded momentarily by two temporary floodlights that had been rigged to illuminate the grounds. A voice challenged him. "Whatcha doin' here, boy?"

Hank turned and raised a hand to shield his eyes from the harsh light. Standing in front of him was a black Marine. "Just lookin'," Hank said. "What are *you guys* doin'?"

"What's it look like?"

"Looks like you're diggin' foxholes."

"You got it, boy. Where's your folks?"

"Inside," Hank lied. "They said it was okay for me to be out here."

The Marine shrugged, then picked up his shovel and resumed digging.

Six stories high and perched on the side of Ancon Hill, the old wooden hotel offered a commanding view of Panama City. The thoroughfare that served as the American-Panamanian border was less than fifty yards away. The night traffic seemed unusually heavy. *Parque de Lesseps* lay off to the right. Hank noticed an unusually large number of people in the park.

"Excuse me, sir," he said to the Marine who had challenged him. "What's goin' on down there?"

"Don't 'sir' me, boy," the Marine said. "I'm just a PFC." The name stamp over his left shirt pocket read "L. L. Witherspoon".

"Okay. But what's goin' on? I go through that park all the time, and I've never seen it like that."

Witherspoon looked down the hill and frowned, then said, "C'mon with me."

They walked across the grounds to where a black gunnery sergeant stood. His starched fatigues were sharply pressed; the floodlights reflected off his polished boots. He had a rifle slung over one shoulder, and his name stamp read "H. G. Taylor".

"What you want, 'Spoon?" the sergeant said gruffly. "And who's this boy?"

"His folks are in the hotel. He says he knows the park down there, and it don't look right to him."

"What don't look right, boy?" the sergeant said.

"There's too many people . . . and something else."

"What else?"

"I don't know. Something . . ."

"Here, look through these," the sergeant said, handing Hank a pair of field glasses.

Hank had trouble orienting the magnified view. "I can't see anything. The trees and bushes are in the way."

"C'mon," the sergeant said.

Hank followed him down the hill to a small clearing. When he peered through the glasses again, he had a clear view. Then he knew what seemed so strange. "Sir, those people down there, they're all men. Usually there's a lot of women, but tonight it's just men."

"Lemme see those glasses."

But instead, Hank panned to a nearby building. "There's a lot of men in front of the Pan American Building too. It looks like there's a fire!" At that moment, he heard a high-pitched whizzing sound, followed by dull smack.

"Incoming!" the sergeant shouted. "Incoming! Kill the lights! Kill the lights!"

Hank lowered the field glasses and looked around in confusion. Another whiz-smack. The sergeant dived at him, knocking him to the ground.

"Stay down, boy!" the sergeant ordered. Then over his shoulder he shouted, "God damn it! Kill those fuckin' lights!" The whiz-smack of incoming fire now filled the air. Taylor brought his rifle into the firing position, aiming toward the hotel. There was a roar, and one of the floodlights slowly extinguished. He turned slightly, and aimed again. Another roar, and the hotel's grounds plunged into darkness.

Taylor grabbed the back of Hank's shirt and dragged him behind a nearby tree. "Stay here, boy. Stay flat on the deck, behind this tree. As long as you do as I say, you'll be okay. Stick your head out, and you'll get it blown off. Now I've gotta get back up there to my men. You stay here."

"Don't leave me!" Hank cried.

Taylor crawled up the hill, into the darkness. Hank froze in the position in which the sergeant had left him, flat on his stomach, with his face pressed into the rough tree bark. Suddenly there was a deafening roar, as the Marines opened fire on the Republic. The outgoing fusillade ripped through the trees, showering Hank with debris. He rolled onto his side and drew his knees up to his chest, then clasped his hands behind his head, covering his ears with the insides of his forearms. Eyes squeezed shut, he quaked in terror.

He lost all sense of time; it seemed the battle would never end. Then he was aware of someone shaking him. Fearfully, he opened his eyes. It was Sergeant Taylor. He'd come back! Hank tried to sit up, but the sergeant pushed him down. The shooting was only intermittent now. Hank wanted to go home.

The sergeant moaned. Hank felt something warm spreading down his arm. No! He scrambled out from under the sergeant's weight. Taylor lay face down, eyes closed, blood flowing from a gaping wound in his neck. Hank grabbed the sergeant's starched collar and futilely tried to stem the flow. "Sergeant! Get up!"

Taylor said something. Hank put his ear next to the Marine's mouth. It sounded like a prayer. "U.S. rifle . . . caliber 30 . . . M-1 Garand . . . gas-operated . . . air-cooled . . . semiautomatic . . . shoulder weapon . . ."

"Sergeant!" Hank screamed into his ear.

Taylor's eyes opened. "Get out of here, boy," he gasped. "Don't go up the hill . . . my men might shoot you . . ." His eyelids drooped.

"Sergeant!"

Taylor's eyes opened. "Sneak down the hill . . . take my rifle . . ." Then his eyes closed and he began to pray again. "U.S. rifle . . . caliber 30 . . . M-1 Garand . . ." The Marine expelled a deep sigh, then lay motionless.

Another fusillade poured down from the hotel. Hank grabbed the sergeant's rifle and scrambled down the hill toward the chain-link fence that stood at the edge of the hotel property. The gate was locked, as it always was. He crawled along the fence, groping beneath it for the washout he and his friends used for a shortcut. He found it, and slid feetfirst under the sharp chain-link and into the overgrown ditch on the other side. He froze, uncertain what to do next.

Only occasional shots were being exchanged across the border now. Hank considered trying to get back up to the hotel. But then, remembering the sergeant's instructions, he crawled into the tall weeds. The nearby thoroughfare was only two lanes wide.

The street lights had been shot out, but the moon still illuminated the concrete expanse. If he could make it across, then through *Parque de Lesseps*, he could catch a *chiva* to his grandfather's house.

His hand touched something alive. A woman screamed. Hank rose to a kneeling position. A dark shadow appeared in front of him, and he felt a sharp pain across his left cheek. Someone pulled at the rifle. Hank jumped to his feet, kicking blindly. He regained control of the rifle and swung it like a baseball bat. He hit something and heard a woman's anguished moan, then the sound of someone frantically retreating through the tall weeds. A moment later, he caught sight of a dark figure running across the street toward the park. On impulse, Hank pulled the rifle sling over his shoulder and high-stepped out of the weeds. Shots rang out as he raced across the street. He leaped the far curb, then ran down the wide concrete stairway that led into the park. The heavy rifle pounded against the back of his thigh.

Enormous trees formed a dense canopy, blocking out the moonlight, but not the incoming rounds. He ran up the gravel footpath; the park seemed deserted. The sniper fire directed at the Tivoli came from the nearby tenements. The lights of *Avenida Central* shone up ahead. He drew closer, and saw several people using a row of parked cars for cover. They'd help him.

As he darted between two cars, the rifle stock slammed into the fender of the one on his right. He skidded to a stop and scrambled back for cover. He pressed against the side of the car and slid down to a sitting position, gasping for breath. The rifle lay across his lap.

"*¡Gringo!*" an angry middle-aged woman cried.

A young mestizo jumped on him and pinned his arms against the car. A black youth grabbed the rifle away from him. Both young men wore filthy white shirts and ties. They apparently had been members of the student contingent that had been driven from the Canal Zone earlier that evening.

The woman bent over Hank and pointed to the scratches on the side of his face. "He is the one who beat me," she said in

Spanish, then pulled up her sleeve to show the students a swollen red welt on her upper arm.

The black student brandished the rifle muzzle in Hank's face. "*¡Gringo hijo de puta!*—American son of a whore!"

"*¡No soy gringo!*" Hank lied. "*¡Soy panameño!*"

The students and the woman momentarily looked taken aback. Then the woman began firing questions at him in Spanish.

Hank couldn't understand what she was saying, and tried to bluff in faltering Spanish. "I am a Panamanian. I just go to school in the Canal Zone."

The black student grabbed him by the throat and slammed his head against the car. "Lying gringo," he snarled in Spanish.

"No," Hank pleaded. "I am Enrique Duque. My grandfather is Professor Edgardo Duque. He teaches at the university."

The student froze. "Your grandfather is Professor Duque?" He relaxed his grip on Hank's throat.

"Yes. I am trying to get to his home in *Bella Vista.*"

The students exchanged glances. "Keep him here," the mestizo said. "I will call the professor." As he rose, he said to Hank, "You had better not be lying."

"Do not believe him," the woman said, glaring at Hank. "Beat him."

"No, señora," the mestizo said. "He may be telling the truth. Professor Duque is a man of the people—an Arnulfista." He took off down the street. The others settled back to wait.

The mestizo had been gone for half an hour. The shooting had stopped altogether. When he finally returned, he was carrying two *raspados.* He handed one to the black student. "Professor Duque will be here in a few minutes. He thinks this is probably his grandson."

The woman shook her head in disappointment. "I go home, then."

"*Perdóneme, señora,*" Hank said.

She shook her head that she didn't accept his apology, then trudged off.

A dark green bus pulled up near the train station across the street. A detachment of Panamanian National Guard troops unloaded and leisurely fanned out along *Avenida Central.*

An officer walked over to where Hank was being detained by the students. "What is going on here?" the officer demanded.

"We caught this gringo running from the Canal Zone," the mestizo student said.

"Oh, yes?" the officer said. With a quick motion, he snatched the rifle away from the black student. "And where did you get this?"

"He had it with him," the black student said sullenly. The antagonism between the students and the soldier was unmistakable.

"Do you see that balcony?" the officer said to Hank, pointing to a tenement overlooking the park. "A little girl was shot and killed up there about an hour ago. Did you do it?"

"No, sir!"

"I will take you to *La Comandancia,*" the officer said with a malevolent smile. "You will have more to tell me there."

"But I don't know anything about a little girl," Hank pleaded.

"*¡Enrique!*" called a familiar voice.

"*¡Aquí, Abuelo!*" Hank called back.

The old man approached, accompanied by the student who drove his car. "Get up," his grandfather said. He ran his shaking fingers over the scratches on Hank's face. "What has happened to you?"

"There was some trouble in the Canal Zone, Grandpa. I was trying to get to you."

The old man studied him for a moment, then said, "Get in the car."

"Wait!" the officer said in Spanish. "Your grandson was carrying this." He held out the rifle.

"So?" the old man demanded.

"A little girl was shot in that building. Your grandson may have done it."

"I am Professor Edgardo Duque," the old man said, fixing the officer in his steely gaze. The students who had detained Hank, now moved beside the old man, showing their support. The driver also joined them.

The soldier grew wary. "I know who you are, Professor."

"Your accusations are nonsense," the old man said. "The boy lives with me. See me in the morning." Without giving the officer a chance to reply, he shoved Hank toward the car. When they were inside, he told his driver in Spanish, "Shaler's Triangle. Hurry!"

"But, Professor," the driver protested as they pulled away, "the Canal Zone is closed to us."

"Go," the old man ordered. Then he turned to Hank and said in English, "I called your mother and told her to meet us there. Now, were you involved in the disturbance over the flag today?"

Hank looked down, unable to respond.

"Were you?"

Tears welled in Hank's eyes. "I raised the flag," he whispered.

"What?" his grandfather exclaimed.

Hank looked up. The tears burst forth, burning his face as they flowed across the claw marks. "I was the one who raised the flag, *Abuelo.*"

"You?" The old man stared at Hank in disbelief. Finally he said, "The little girl, what do you know about her?"

"Nothing, *Abuelo.* I don't know what he was talking about!"

"What about the gun?"

"A Marine gave it to me. He got shot in front of the Tivoli, and told me to take it and run. I didn't shoot anybody!"

His grandfather gazed at him again, and finally gave a nod of acceptance. He closed his eyes for a moment. Then he looked at Hank with profound sadness. "Late last night, the boys brought back your bicycle."

Hank stared at his grandfather, dumbstruck.

"They were just playing a joke on you," his grandfather said.

"But I thought . . ." Hank couldn't finish. Full comprehension of what he had done hit him like a blow to the chest.

"We are here, Professor," the driver announced in Spanish.

Shaler's Triangle was a small public area, just inside the Canal

Zone border. The driver stopped on the Panamanian side. As Hank climbed out of the car, he looked up at the flagpole. No flags were flying.

"Hank!" his mother cried, rushing toward him from a nearby kiosk. She threw her arms around him. "What has happened to you?"

Hank's grandfather separated them. "Carolyn," he said, "Enrique . . . was involved in the flag raising. Tomorrow, *la guardia* will look for him at my home. You must do what we discussed."

"What about you, Edgardo? Will you be all right?"

The old man didn't reply.

"Edgardo," she said, "you have to come with us."

He shook his head. "It is too late for me. I am too old to become a *gringo*. I do love you people, though."

"What's going on?" Hank said. "Where are we going tomorrow?" His mother didn't respond, and his grandfather climbed back into the car. "¡*Abuelo*!" Hank cried. "Come home with us!"

The old man leaned out the window. "The Canal Zone is closed to Panamanians until further notice."

"No!" Hank cried, clutching his grandfather's arm.

"Enrique, last night, when the boys brought back your bicycle, we talked about riding the bulls. They said . . ." The old man glanced at his daughter-in-law, and paused. Modestly switching to Spanish, so that only Hank would understand, he continued, "*Dicen que tú tienes* muchos *cojones*." Then with a wry smile he added in English, "For a *gringo*."

Hank's mother gently pulled him away from the car.

His grandfather looked at him with sad affection. "Remember, *Nieto*," the old man said, "like it or not . . . you have my blood." Then he gestured for his driver to proceed.

"Honey," Hank's mother said, entering their Houston apartment with the afternoon mail, "did you write a letter to your grandfather?"

"Yes, ma'am."

"Well, for some reason it's been returned. It's been opened, though." She lifted the unsealed flap and withdrew the contents. "Was there just one page?"

"Yes, ma'am," he said, taking it from her. He unfolded and read the letter he had composed a month earlier.

March 8, 1964

Dear Grandpa,

I hate it here in Houston. The kids are dumb. In school they are teaching stuff I learned back in 7th grade. Some of the kids here speak Spanish, but it is all jumbled up with English. They call it Texmex or something.

Mom has a job at a hospital. They won't let her be a nurse here unless she takes some classes. Now she just empties bedpans and stuff. At night I have to stay here by myself in the apartment.

There is a guy who comes over all the time to see her. I don't like him much.

I am sorry about the flag. When can we come back home?

Enrique

"Honey," his mother said, handing him the envelope, "what do these Spanish words mean?"

Hank stared at the envelope. Stamped next to his name and return address was an arrow, and the word "*Regresar*—Return to". Stamped next to his grandfather's name and address was another arrow, and the word "*Difunto*—Deceased".

1. BIENVENIDOS

Hank had a window seat on Continental Airlines flight 770, from Houston to Panama City. He was staring down at the cobalt blue Caribbean when an insistent voice interrupted him.

"Señor . . . señor . . ."

Hank turned, and an attractive Latina flight attendant leaned across the two empty seats beside him and handed him an immigration form, printed in Spanish. *"Uh . . . gracias, señorita,"* he said, experimenting with the language he had all but forgotten over the past twenty-five years.

She smiled and continued down the aisle.

Hank searched through his crammed attaché case for a pen, then began filling out the form. When he got to *"¿Compañía?"* he automatically entered "Exxon". Then, annoyed with himself, he scribbled through it.

The dull roar from the jet engines dropped to a lower pitch, as the pilot began the descent into Panama City. The flight attendant returned from the rear of the aircraft and caught Hank's eye as she passed. She gave him a quick smile as she disappeared behind the first-class curtain.

Hank turned back to the form, hesitated, then entered "Freelance writer". He guessed that's what he was now. The seat belt light went on, and he quickly completed the questionnaire. As he reopened his attaché case to replace the pen, he stared down at the raft of research material he had hastily assembled in Houston. He felt a twinge of anxiety. At age thirty-nine, Panama was a hell of a place to start over.

Inside the congested Omar Torrijos terminal building, Hank stood in line behind an elderly Indian woman. The hubbub of arriving passengers reverberated throughout the room, punctuated by the occasional roar of an airplane landing or taking off. The line crept forward, until finally the woman stepped up to the immigration desk.

"Pasaporte," said the immigration officer. His drab gray uniform looked as if it had been worn for several days; his shirt barely covered his protruding paunch. The woman opened her hemp travel bag and began fumbling about. The officer reached across the desk and pushed her aside, then gestured for Hank to step forward.

The woman located her passport and tried to give it to the officer. He waved her away with a brusque gesture, then looked up at Hank. *"¡Pasaporte!"* he said, snapping his fingers.

Hank scowled at the surly bureaucrat as he handed over his new American passport and the completed immigration form.

The officer met Hank's gaze for a moment, then glanced at the documents and said curtly, *"Abra su maleta."*

"I don't speak much Spanish," Hank said.

"¡Abra su maleta!" the officer demanded, this time pointing to Hank's attaché case.

Hank opened the case. The officer dumped the contents onto the desk, then picked up Hank's copy of *Panama: A Country Study*, published by the U.S. Department of the Army. He examined the title page, then put the book to the side. After indifferently leafing through Hank's handwritten notes and photocopies of encyclopedia entries, he stopped when he came across an eight-page pamphlet published by the U.S. Department of State, entitled "Panama: Background Notes". He also put this aside, then said, *"Cierre su maleta."*

Hank remembered 'cierre' meant 'close'; he must be done here. He reached for the book and pamphlet that had been set aside.

"¡No!" the officer barked, then picked up the two publications and walked out from behind the desk. *"Venga,"* he ordered, gesturing that Hank should follow him. The woman who had lost her

place in line plaintively asked something in Spanish. The officer ignored her. Hank gathered up the rest of the books and hurried after him, wondering what the problem was.

They stopped at a grimy office door, and Hank grew uneasy. The nameplate mounted next to it read: *Fuerza de Defensa de Panamá, Mayor Carlos Mejías*—Panama Defense Force, Major Carlos Mejías. Through a window, Hank saw the khaki-uniformed major sitting at a desk.

The immigration officer rapped on the door.

The major looked up and called out, *"¡Entre!"*

As Hank followed the immigration officer inside, the major stood up and walked out from behind the desk. His uniform was neatly pressed; although middle-aged, he moved like a conditioned athlete.

The immigration officer handed him Hank's passport and entry form. *"El dice que no habla español."*

The major thumbed through the blank pages of the passport, then said in a rasping voice, "He says, you don't speak Spanish?"

"Very little. I used to speak some when I was a kid, but I've forgotten most of it."

"Your name is Enrique Duque, and you don't speak Spanish?"

Hank shook his head.

"But Duque is a Panamanian name, no?"

"My grandfather Duque was Panamanian. My other grandparents were American."

The major studied him for a moment. "Have you been to Panama before?"

Hank felt a pang of apprehension. "I was born here . . . in the Canal Zone."

The major gazed at him for a moment, as if pondering a puzzle, then looked at the immigration form. The officer pointed to where Hank had scratched out his original entry.

"What did you write here?" the major asked.

"I made a mistake. I worked for Exxon until a few weeks ago, but now I'm a freelance writer. I'm down here to do a piece for a travel guide."

The immigration officer handed the major the two U.S. government publications. A corner of the major's mouth twitched as he leafed through them. Then he looked up and said, "Who do you work for, Sr. Duque?"

"I'm a freelance writer."

The major said something in Spanish to the immigration officer, then told Hank, "Give him your baggage ticket." Hank complied, and the immigration officer hurried out of the office.

"Deme su cartera," the major said.

Hank shook his head that he didn't understand.

"Give me your wallet!" the major demanded impatiently.

Hank handed it over, masking his rising concern.

The major checked the paper currency; the $280 more than met the requirement for entering the country. He pulled out Hank's Texas driver's license, scrutinized it, and then examined each of Hank's credit cards. Finally, he withdrew a yellowed laminated card from the back of the wallet. He shook it under Hank's nose. "And what is this?"

Hank frowned down at the Certificate of Service card he had carried for two decades.

"It says here," the major pressed, "you are a United States Marine, no?"

"No, it says I was in the Marine Corps twenty years ago."

The immigration officer returned, carrying Hank's duffel bag. Hank watched with annoyance as the major rooted through his neatly packed clothes. Finding nothing of interest, the major straightened up. "Give me your airline ticket."

Hank reluctantly handed over his round-trip ticket.

The major studied it for a moment, then looked up. "You will be here for just one week?"

Hank nodded.

"And where will you be staying?"

"Hotel Reynosa," Hank said. The major and the immigration officer exchanged glances. Hank sensed that for some reason his choice of hotels disturbed them.

"Who do you work for, Sr. Duque?" the major said.

"I told you. I'm a writer."

The major stepped closer. "Do you work for the CIA?"

"What? This is crazy. I'm an American, down here to write a travel guide."

The major gazed into Hank's eyes. "What kind of shit you feeding me, *gringo*?"

Hank shook his head. Whatever was going on here was getting out of hand.

The major gazed at him for a moment. Finally, as if having arrived at a decision, he returned Hank's wallet and the two publications. However, he kept the passport and immigration form. "You can go to the Reynosa," he said, "but do not leave the hotel until we contact you."

"Now wait a minute," Hank began. The major cut him off with an impatient gesture for him to leave.

As Hank made his way across the noisy terminal building, he shook his head at the irony of the sign over the exit: *Bienvenidos a Panamá*—Welcome to Panama.

Outside, a press of taxi drivers, friends, and families greeted arriving passengers. Hank scanned the crowd; a representative from a local tour service was supposed to meet him. He spotted "Mr. Duque" scribbled in pencil on a crude cardboard sign. Holding it was an attractive Panamanian woman. Hank walked over and said, "I'm Hank Duque."

The woman acknowledged him with an unsmiling nod. "I am Andrea Arias from Aventura Tours." Her voice was husky, her accent slight. "I will be your guide while you are here." She reached for his duffel bag. Hank started to decline, but then let her take it.

He followed her over to a battered black Pontiac sedan and they put his luggage into the car's dusty trunk. The heat and humidity were intense, and Hank was perspiring freely as he came around and climbed into the worn front passenger seat. Andrea strapped herself in. There was no seat belt on Hank's side. With a grind of gears, they jolted away from the curb.

Still unnerved at having his passport confiscated, Hank leaned back in the seat and tried to collect his thoughts. The airport drive exited onto a busy thoroughfare.

"Mr. Duque," Andrea said, "you wish to go to your hotel, no?"

"Yeah, the Reynosa."

She gave him a disapproving glance.

"Something wrong with the Reynosa?" Hank said.

She didn't respond to his question, but leaned on the horn to force a bicycle pushcart to the side of the road. This touched off a cacophony of horns from the cars around them.

They crested a hill and came to an abrupt stop. A long line of vehicles stretched out in front of them. At the foot of the hill, a Panamanian soldier leisurely waved crossing traffic through a busy intersection. Ramshackle dwellings and rundown shops lined both sides of the thoroughfare. The roadside shanties seemed so familiar, as did the pungent odor of decay wafting through the open side windows. Ragged peddlers weaved in and out of the stopped cars, hawking fruit and soft drinks.

Hank smiled, momentarily transported back to his youth. Then he forced himself out of his brief reverie and repeated, "Is there something wrong with the Hotel Reynosa?"

Andrea responded with a noncommittal shrug.

"Back at the airport, the immigration people acted strange when I told them I was staying there . . . like you just did."

"Are you in the military?"

"No, I'm down here to write a travel guide."

"Most of the Americans who stay at the Reynosa are in the military," she said guardedly, "or they . . . work for your government."

"Well, that doesn't apply to me," Hank said, wondering if by "work for your government" she meant the CIA. "I lived down here when I was a kid. I think my grandfather's home was near the Reynosa." He didn't mention that the main reason he had selected the hotel was that it was relatively inexpensive, and he was nearly broke.

The traffic finally began moving down the hill. A brightly painted bus tried to ease onto the main thoroughfare from a side street. Andrea blew her horn and forced the bus to yield. The driver leaned out the side window and angrily shouted something in Spanish. Andrea ignored him.

As they drove on, Hank studied her profile. She was an attractive woman—slender, pronounced cheekbones, a tawny complexion. Her brown hair was tinged with red and pulled into a short ponytail. She wore a starched white blouse and pressed blue jeans. Hank leaned back slightly, trying to see if she was wearing a wedding ring. She sensed his gaze and flashed her dark eyes at him. Without thinking, he asked, "Are you married?"

"Yes," she said curtly. "Are you?"

"No . . . divorced," he said, regretting having voiced his question.

They drove on in silence, until Andrea said, "Mr. Duque, when do you wish to begin your tour?"

"I'd planned to get started right away, but an army officer took my passport. He told me not to leave my hotel until he returned it."

"He took your passport?"

"Yeah."

"Why?"

"I don't know. I guess I'll just have to call your office when I get it back."

Andrea returned her attention to the traffic, and Hank returned his to the passing scene. To his right, the terrain ascended sharply, up a string of steep hills, covered with large stucco homes. To his left, it fell off abruptly, treetops hiding most of the residences. And up ahead, silhouetted against the vivid blue sky, were numerous high-rise buildings. "What street are we on?"

"*Vía España.*"

Hank nodded, remembering how as a youth he had ridden his bicycle on this busy thoroughfare, going to and from the Canal Zone. He realized they must be close to his grandfather's former neighborhood. "Is *Bella Vista* near here?"

"We are entering the banking district. *Bella Vista* is near, but closer to the ocean."

They started through what looked like a modern shopping center, several blocks long. Hank had no childhood recollection of this area. Large stores and banks lined the thoroughfare. Uniformed guards, most carrying automatic weapons, loitered conspicuously in the doorways.

Andrea forced her way into the center lane, then turned left down a side street. She pulled up in front of a tall stucco building, and it took Hank a moment to realize they had arrived at his hotel.

As they unloaded his luggage from the trunk, Andrea asked, "Will you call my office when you get your passport?"

"I'll call tomorrow morning, in any case. How early will you be there?"

"Seven o'clock," she said, then climbed back into the car. "Our tours usually begin at 8:00."

Hank nodded, and she pulled away. Too bad she's married, he thought.

After a shower, Hank stood in front of the window of his fourth floor hotel room, a damp towel around his waist and another hanging from his neck. A noisy window air-conditioner futilely tried to cool the spartan quarters.

Directly across the narrow, hillside street stood a beige apartment building, streaked with black stains from the tropical humidity. To his left, several blocks down the street, lay the placid Bay of Panama. A slow-moving freighter headed out to sea.

His gaze blurred into a vacant stare. On the flight down, his spirits had risen for the first time in weeks; he had looked forward to returning to the land of his childhood. Now, his enthusiasm had vanished. The airport run-in and the passport seizure added to a succession of recent failures. A month earlier his son had phoned from California and told him that his ex-wife was remarrying. A few days after that his boss informed him that his department was being closed down. Hank shook his head. Four months severance pay to show for seventeen years.

The jangle of the bedside telephone jarred him out of his musing. He answered it, and Major Mejías' rasping voice said, "Sr. Duque?"

"Yes."

"Come up to the restaurant on the seventh floor, immediately." The line went dead.

Hank took a deep breath; he couldn't let Mejías rattle him.

He dressed quickly—tan golf shirt, jeans, and tennis shoes. The back of his clean shirt was already damp by the time he locked his hotel room door and started down the hallway.

He found two young men waiting at the elevator. Although they wore civilian clothes, Hank guessed they were American military by their tans—faces brown to the hat line, then abruptly turning white under closely cropped hair.

"Going up?" Hank said.

"Yes, sir!" one replied, all but snapping to attention.

Hank suspected they thought he was an officer. He was older, fit, and his hair was cut short, almost like theirs.

When the elevator arrived on the seventh floor, the young men respectfully allowed Hank to precede them. They passed under a lattice arch that led to the rooftop terrace. Hank paused, looking for the major.

"Join us for a drink, sir?" one of the young men asked.

"Uh . . . no thanks, I'm meeting someone," Hank said, still scanning the open room. As they left him, heading for the bar, a man rose from his seat at a nearby table. It took Hank a moment to recognize the major, since he was now clad in civilian clothes—white guayabera shirt, gray pleated slacks, and black patent leather shoes. Hank walked over to his table.

"*Siéntese*," the major said, gesturing to a wrought-iron chair. When they were seated, he asked, "*¿Quiénes son esos hombres?*"

"I don't speak Spanish, remember?" Hank said, although he thought he understood the question.

"*¿No, Sr. Duque? Bueno*, who are those two men you brought with you?"

"Those guys at the bar? They just rode up in the elevator with me."

"I saw you talking to them."

Hank frowned; the major sounded paranoid. "They invited me to join them for a drink."

"Are they CIA?"

"CIA? How the hell would I know? I've never seen them before."

The major reached down and opened a large briefcase that was leaning against his chair. He pulled out a sheet of paper and handed it to Hank. "And this person, have you ever seen *him* before?"

Hank stared down at the photo copy of a page from his high school yearbook. The caption read "Freshmen Class". In the midst of the half-dozen photographs, circled in red, was his own smiling face. His pulse accelerated, but he kept his expression impassive. How had they identified him so quickly? He cleared his throat. "I told you people at the airport, that I'd lived down here when I was a kid."

"But you did not mention the 1964 riot, did you?"

"That was a long time ago."

"So it is not important, uh?"

A waiter came over to take their order, interrupting their exchange. The major glared up at the young man and impatiently waved him away. The waiter retreated to the bar area. "Answer me, *Sr. Duque*. Was the riot not important?"

"I was just a kid."

"It was you *gringo* 'kids', who started the riot."

Vivid memories rushed back at Hank. He blocked them out. "We didn't start the trouble," he said unconvincingly.

The major leaned forward and gazed intently into Hank's eyes. "Many *panameños* died!"

"One of them was my grandfather!"

The major leaned back. With a satisfied smile, he said, "I understand *Profesor Duque* died, protecting his *gringo* grandson, who had run away."

Hank managed to keep his inner turmoil from showing. He shifted his gaze to an isolated butte off in the distance: Ancon Hill. He wondered whose flag was up there now.

"And now you have returned," the major continued. "To make more trouble?"

Hank turned back. "I'm down here to write an article for a travel guide. If you don't believe me, just give me my passport, and I'll be on the first plane out of here tomorrow."

The major fixed him in a baleful stare for several seconds. Finally he said, "*Sr. Duque*, I am not someone to fuck with." He picked up the photo copy and returned it to his briefcase. When he straightened up, he had Hank's passport in his hand. He stood up, looked thoughtfully at the passport, then tossed it across the table. "Enjoy your stay, *Sr. Duque*."

2. LOS DOBERMANS

The next morning Hank finished breakfast in the hotel's rooftop restaurant. A waitress brought a pot of coffee to his table.

"*¿Más café, señor?*"

"*Sí, por favor.*"

The young woman refilled his cup, and Hank nodded his thanks. He hoped the caffeine would clear his thoughts. He'd spent a troubled night, waking frequently and rehashing the previous day's confrontation with Major Mejías. At dawn he'd dragged out of bed, showered and dressed, and had been the restaurant's first customer.

He needed to make a phone call shortly, either to the tour agency, or to the airline. Leaving would be the sensible thing to do; Panama was dangerous, particularly for him. He rubbed his tired eyes. What was tempting him to stay? Nostalgia? A sense of adventure after all the dull, wasted years? There seemed to be something else, but he couldn't put his finger on it.

He stood up and walked over to the wrought-iron railing that enclosed the terrace. Below, the morning traffic was already snarled on *Vía España*. A long blast on a car horn carried up seven floors, apparently a driver demanding the right-of-way.

Across the street stood the ornate Church of Carmen. Two women drew Hank's attention; they were ferrying bunches of inflated white balloons from a van into the church's side door. Hank wondered what they were celebrating.

Hank shifted his gaze to the familiar sight of Ancon Hill, a mile to the west. He wanted to see Ancon again, as well as his grandfather's old neighborhood. How much they had changed during the past twenty-five years? Then the image of Major Mejías and his veiled threat flashed into Hank's mind. He shook his head, annoyed with himself. Two tours in Nam before he was twenty, and now some tinhorn Panamanian major could shake his shit.

He turned abruptly and walked over to the cashier station. Pulling a scrap of paper from his shirt pocket, where he had jotted down the numbers of both Adventure Tours and Continental Airlines, he asked to use the phone. He dialed the Adventure number.

Later that morning, Hank waited impatiently at the hotel entrance; Andrea was twenty-five minutes late. Finally she pulled up the semicircle drive in a clean gray Chevrolet van with "Aventura Tours" stenciled on the side. Hank climbed into the front passenger seat, relieved that they wouldn't be touring the city in yesterday's old sedan. *"Buenos días, Andrea."*

"Good morning, Mr. Duque. Where would you like to go today?"

"Please, call me Hank. Let's start with the hotels in the banking district. How many are there?"

She thought for a moment. "Nine or ten, where an American tourist would want to stay."

"Okay, those are the ones I want to see. I'll be taking pictures, getting room rates, jotting down my impressions, that sort of thing. And if the managers are available, I'd like to interview them. Will you act as my interpreter?"

"Certainly, Mr. Duque, but you will find most businessmen here speak English." Then she added, "Uh . . . today, I can only work until three o'clock. I . . . have an appointment."

"That'll be fine. If we're not done by then, we can finish tomorrow. Before we start on the hotels, though, there's a place nearby I'd like to find." He opened a side pocket of his camera case and took out a city map. "My grandfather taught at the University of Panama. He lived in *Bella Vista*, near a large park." Hank pointed to a spot on the map. "I think it may be this one, here at the end of *Calle 43*."

"Parque de Urraca?"

"I think so. Is there a cattle pen across the street?"

"A cattle pen? I don't know what that is."

"You know . . . a place where they keep cows."

She shook her head. "Where you are pointing is *El Banco Exterior*. It is a bank."

"Well, let's go check it out anyway."

A few blocks from the hotel, they entered a quiet neighborhood. Well-kept tile-roofed homes lined the shady street, interspersed with an occasional two-story commercial building. Hank scanned the surroundings, hoping to see some landmark from his youth. This street seemed familiar; he looked for a small grocery that had sold chocolate candy, shaped like coins and wrapped in gold foil. No sign of it. Maybe it had been on another street, or maybe it no longer existed.

As they made their gradual descent toward the ocean, he sensed a pall over the seemingly tranquil surroundings. High walls, embedded at the top with jutting pieces of glass, encircled most of the residences; security guards, armed with automatic weapons, stood in front of many of the businesses.

They turned a corner, and Andrea said, "This is *Calle 43*."

Hank smiled, recognizing the street, lined with tall palm trees and leading down to the blue-green Pacific Ocean. "Go slowly," he said. "It's right about . . . there it is! Up ahead on the right. Pull over in front of that yellow building."

She brought the van to a stop and Hank climbed out. His grandfather's old home was as he had remembered it: two-stories, light yellow stucco, and black wrought-iron bars securing open windows. Tropical plants covered the landscaped front yard and crowded the winding concrete walkway. For an instant the scene transported him back twenty-five years. Where was Grandpa? The child's question brought a lump to the man's throat.

"Is this the place, Mr. Duque?"

Hank nodded slowly. "Yeah, this is it." He handed her his camera. "Take my picture standing over there." He jogged up the walkway and posed on the front steps, then returned and said, "Let's go around back."

As they walked along the side of the building, Hank smiled, remembering having ridden his bicycle up and down this same driveway.

The rear of the building was not as well maintained as the front. Mildew and rust stains marred the yellow stucco. He stopped and gazed up at the second floor veranda. Morning wash hung from the railing. "That was my grandfather's apartment. I used to stay with him sometimes. When it was hot, I slept out there in a hammock."

"Oh, yes?" she said indulgently.

Hank trained his camera on the balcony and snapped a picture, just as an elderly woman came out. She leaned over the railing and rattled off something in Spanish, apparently concerned by their presence.

Andrea and the woman spoke briefly. The one word Hank understood in the exchange was *gringo*. Andrea turned to him and said, "I told her you are an American visitor and that your grandfather lived here. She wants to know his name."

"Edgardo Duque," Hank shouted up.

The old woman shook her head, indicating that the name meant nothing to her. *"Bueno, señora,"* Hank said, then asked Andrea to thank the woman for letting them look around.

Andrea relayed the message and they started toward the driveway. The old woman responded with a hesitant nod, clearly relieved that the intruders were leaving.

Back on the front sidewalk, Hank gazed down the familiar street to the ocean, a block away. He took a picture, capturing on film the scene that had long been preserved in his mind. Then he started down the hill at a quick pace, motioning for Andrea to follow.

The park lay off to the left. Hank remembered it as having been shaded and manicured. He recalled the young governesses who had pushed baby carriages along the crossing brick pathways, while flirting with the local bachelors. Now the park was barren and uninviting—there were fewer trees and the grass had turned to weeds. Idle men in tattered clothes lounged about, most congregating on the remains of the old bandstand.

On the other side of the street, where the cattle pen had been, there now stood a modern bank building. Hank continued past the park and stopped at a busy intersection. "I don't remember this street being here."

"It is *Avenida Balboa*," Andrea said.

They crossed the avenue and walked over to the seawall. Leaning on the concrete rail, Hank looked back at the park and the bank. It was all so changed. Then he turned and gazed at the Pacific.

Andrea gave the ocean an indifferent glance. "Should I get the van?"

Hank didn't respond. Up the coast, the refreshment stand he had frequented as a youth was no longer there. Down the coast, the beach seemed more narrow. He mused aloud, "We road bulls here . . ."

"Bulls?"

Hank nodded. "The cattle pen used to be over there," he said, pointing to the bank. "Ships would anchor a couple of hundred yards offshore and drop cattle over the side. The cattle would swim to shore, and *vaqueros* would round them up and herd them into the pen. One time, some of the neighborhood kids and I swam out and rode the bulls."

"You had friends here?" she said with a bemused smile.

He responded with a slow shake of his head. "My friends lived in the Canal Zone. I didn't get along with the kids here." He looked her in the eye. "To them, I was just another *gringo*."

Andrea returned his gaze for a moment, then turned to the ocean.

Shortly after noon, Andrea turned off *Vía España* and pulled into the parking lot of the Riande Continental. This was the fourth hotel they'd visited. Hank climbed out of the van and took a picture of the building.

"Would you like to have lunch here at—" he began. A large army truck roared into the parking lot, interrupting him. The metal tailgate clanged down and a detachment of soldiers clambered out wearing helmets, shields, and gas masks. Some carried shotguns, others truncheons and CS gas grenades. The officer in charge shouted commands to his assembling troops. Instinctively Hank raised his camera and took pictures.

"*¡Asesinos!*" shouted Andrea.

The officer in charge turned and glared.

Hank lowered his camera. "What's going on?"

She pulled a white handkerchief from her jeans pocket and waved it defiantly over her head like a flag. "*¡Viva Endara! ¡Viva la libertad!*"

Hank grasped her free arm. "Tell me what the hell's going on!"

She yanked her arm away. "They are the Dobermans—Noriega's dogs!"

Hank frowned and looked back at the assembling troops. General Manuel Noriega had ruthlessly ruled Panama for six years. Under international pressure, he grudgingly had allowed a presidential election to be held the previous week. A committee, led by former United States President Jimmy Carter, had overseen the election and declared the opposition candidate, Guillermo Endara, the victor.

"He has lost the election," Andrea continued bitterly, "and now he wants to steal it back. *¡Viva Endara! ¡Viva la libertad!*"

The officer took a threatening step toward her. Hank grabbed Andrea's arm again and pulled her toward the hotel.

"*¡Asesinos!*" she shouted over her shoulder.

They were almost to the hotel entrance. "What are you calling them?"

"Murderers." She started to say something else, but stopped. A block away, hundreds of Panamanians marched toward them. Andrea looked back and forth between the procession and Hank.

"The hotel manager here is Fredrico Cruz," she said. "He speaks English. If it is all right with you, I will wait for you out here."

He nodded, and she hurried over to the curb to wait for the procession.

Hank hesitated in the hotel doorway, then curiosity got the better of him. He joined her at the curb and said, "Who are those people?"

She turned, surprised to see him. "Our new president, Guillermo Endara."

"Which one?"

"The big one in the middle. The men on each side are our two vice presidents."

Hank began taking pictures of the procession. As it neared, Andrea waved her handkerchief and shouted, *"¡Viva Endara! ¡Viva la libertad!"* The overweight president-elect smiled broadly and raised a chubby arm in acknowledgment.

Hank sensed movement to his left. The Dobermans from the parking lot were cordoning off the street. The procession came to a stumbling halt.

The president and his two vice presidents walked up to the soldiers, gesturing they wished to proceed. Three Dobermans leveled shotguns at the leaders' stomachs. Hank took pictures of the confrontation, then lowered his camera. "C'mon, Andrea. This is going to get ugly."

She shook her head. "I cannot leave them to the Dobermans. You go."

Hank looked back and forth between Andrea and the demonstrators. She sure as hell wasn't leaving, and he didn't feel right leaving without her.

The tense standoff lasted several minutes. Then the president said something to the people immediately behind him, and a murmur spread through the crowd, until finally it reached the perimeter, where Hank and Andrea stood. A woman said something in Spanish to Andrea.

Andrea grabbed Hank's hand. "Come," she said, then led him up *Vía España* at a fast walk.

Hank took a deep breath; apparently the confrontation had been defused. His sense of relief vanished a moment later, when he glanced over his shoulder and saw the procession had drained from the street and was now following him and Andrea down the sidewalk.

Then Hank heard a crowd roar. Ahead, in the intersection near his hotel, he saw a larger group of demonstrators: thousands of men and women, blocking the streets and waving white handkerchiefs. As he and Andrea neared the crowd, the white balloons he had seen that morning were brought out of the Church of Carmen, and moments later soared into the sky. The demonstrators let out an exultant roar.

Hank and Andrea stopped at the edge of the crowd, and climbed onto a bus-stop bench to get a better view. Andrea waved her handkerchief and joined the rhythmic chant of, *"¡Viva Endara! ¡Viva la libertad!"*

The president elect and his followers swept past them and were absorbed by his delirious supporters. Hank got Andrea's attention and pointed to the hillside across the street. Four large army trucks rolled ominously into view. They came to a stop, and a detachment of Dobermans poured out. A murmur passed through the crowd as the Dobermans lined up shoulder to shoulder. The officer in charge gave a command that carried across the intersection. The Dobermans lowered their protective visors, raised their shields, and marched toward the demonstrators.

Hank swore under his breath. He'd let Andrea get him involved in this shit. And she was married, for Christ's sake!

The crowd absorbed the first thrust of the advancing troops. Then with an angry roar, they defiantly pushed back. The Dobermans broke ranks and retreated up the hill to their trucks. *"¡Libertad! ¡Libertad!"* shouted the exuberant crowd.

Andrea moved as if to join demonstrators in the street. Hank grabbed her arm and pulled her back.

"Let me go," she said.

Hank tightened his grip.

"You are hurting me!"

"Look over there," he said, pointing again to the hillside. The

Dobermans were putting on gas masks and reforming ranks. Then they marched forward again.

Hank pulled her close, so she could hear him over the crowd noise. "Those soldiers we saw were carrying CS grenades."

"CS? What is CS?"

"It's a hell of lot worse than tear gas. It'll have you puking, not crying."

At that moment, a Doberman lobbed the first gas grenade into the crowd. A yellowish cloud rose from the feet of the demonstrators. There was a momentary delay, then people scattered in all directions. Another grenade arched through the air, then another. Two shotgun blasts put the demonstrators in full retreat.

Just moments before, this throng had roared in exaltation; now it screamed in terror. In the chaos, many fell and were trampled by others. The Dobermans clubbed the stragglers with their truncheons. A man stopped to help an injured woman to her feet, and a Doberman beat him to the ground beside her.

Hank hesitated long enough to take several pictures of the violence, then grabbed Andrea's hand and shouted, "C'mon!"

As they ran down a side street, they saw the president and his vice presidents being loaded into a sedan, then spirited away.

A short while later they made their way back to the Riande Continental. The Aventura Tours van was the only vehicle in the hotel parking lot.

"¡Aya, carajo!" Andrea wailed.

The van's windows were smashed and its body was dented. The Dobermans apparently had made it a target of their vengeance.

"Better leave it here," Hank said.

Andrea unlocked the door, brushed the shattered glass off the driver's seat, and climbed inside. She turned the key and the engine started.

"I wouldn't try to drive it, Andrea."

"I must get home. Get in. I will take you to your hotel first."

Hank went around and climbed in on the passenger's side.

The webbed cracks in the windshield obscured his view. "Can you see out?" he said.

Without answering, she pulled out of the parking lot.

"Take a cab from my hotel, Andrea."

She slammed on the brakes and brought the van to a halt in the middle of the street. "Don't tell me what to do!"

Hank raised his hands in resignation. "Okay."

Andrea put the van back in gear and they took off again.

"What's so important?" Hank said.

"What?"

"You said you had to get home."

"There is to be another demonstration this afternoon at four o'clock in *Parque de Santa Ana*. The park is between my apartment and my little boy's school. He usually walks home by himself, through the park, but because of the demonstration, I have to pick him up at the school today."

"What time does he get out of school?"

"At 3:30."

"It's almost 3:30 now," he said. They pulled into the semi-circle drive in front of his hotel. "Will your husband be at home?" he said.

She didn't respond.

"Will he?" Hank pressed.

She turned and glared. "I have no husband!"

Hank frowned. She wasn't married? "How about the son? Do you have a son?"

"Yes, *gringo*! I have a son. Now get out!"

"No, I'll go with you."

"Get out!"

"You're wasting time."

"You don't even know what any of this is about!" she said.

"Have you ever seen anybody killed?"

She frowned and shook her head.

"I have. I know what that's about."

With a grind of gears, they lurched away from the hotel.

3. BATALLON DE LA DIGNIDAD

Hank and Andrea didn't speak during the drive from the banking district to the older section of Panama City. Preoccupied, she maneuvered through the heavy afternoon traffic that clogged *Vía España*. Hank gazed out the side window at the ramshackle dwellings and rundown shops that lined the thoroughfare. A car slowed in front of them, and Andrea slammed on the brakes, then drummed her fingers on the steering wheel as the traffic crept forward.

They passed through the next intersection, and Hank caught a glimpse of Ancon, sprawled across the nearby hillside. He was anxious to see it again. "Are we getting close to *Parque de Lesseps?* I used to cut through there when I was a kid."

"I don't know a *Parque de Lesseps.*"

From her curt tone, Hank realized she was too concerned about her son's well-being to be interested in his childhood reminiscences.

They passed a sprawling plaza on the left. The jumble of shops, restaurants, and bars looked vaguely familiar, but he saw no sign of the old park. Another milestone in his life apparently now existed only in his memory. He wished he could eradicate it from there as well—the firefight in front of the Tivoli . . . the mortally wounded sergeant . . . the hail of bullets through the trees . . . Grandpa . . .

The driver of the car in front of them impatiently blew his horn, interrupting Hank's musing. The *Santa Ana* district, which dated back to Spanish colonial times, lay ahead. They started down a narrow canyon of three-story buildings. Pedestrians filled the sidewalks, all heading in the direction of *Parque de Santa Ana.*

Hank scanned the signs over the ground-level stores, looking for the bicycle shop where his grandfather had bought his English racer. He smiled at the anti-Noriega posters plastered on many store fronts. Crude caricatures, captioned *Cara de Piña*—Pineapple Face, mocked Noriega's acne scars.

The pedestrians spilled off the sidewalks and into the street, forcing Andrea to drive even slower; they were barely moving. Two young toughs swaggered past on Hank's side of the van. They wore homemade uniforms: ball caps, T-shirts, jeans, and combat boots. One carried a two-by-four, pierced with nails; the other carried a stiff rubber hose. The one closest to Hank made eye contact and yelled something. Hank only caught the word *coche*—car. He guessed the jeer had been about the condition of the van.

"*Batallón de la Dignidad*," Andrea said with contempt in her voice. "The Dignity Battalion. We call them 'Digbats'. They are garbage. Most are criminals that General Noriega has recruited from the slums."

Ahead, a wall of people blocked the street. Hank said, "We're getting close, aren't we?"

Andrea nodded. "That is *Parque de Santa Ana*."

They arrived at an intersection, and Andrea leaned on the horn again. The crowd grudgingly parted, allowing her to turn down a deserted side street.

Rundown apartment houses formed a corridor of dirty stucco. Half a block down the street, Andrea turned into a narrow alley that ran between two buildings. At the end of the alley, she pulled onto the foundation of a partially razed house. "I live over there," she said, shutting off the engine. "Please wait here." She got out and hurried into the rear entrance of a nearby building.

Hank looked around, feeling uneasy. As a boy, his grandfather had made this *Santa Ana* district off-limits to him. The local byword for the area was "*Sal si puedes*"—"Get out if you can".

The air between the moss-covered buildings was dank and still. The decaying structures were centuries old. Over time, large chunks of stucco had pulled loose from the walls, exposing rotting timber and powdering brick.

The immediate surroundings were quiet; however, off in the distance he heard the sound of cheering, like a crowd at a ball game. How long would the demonstrators be so enthusiastic? Were Dobermans already on the way?

Hank checked his camera; the exposure counter read "35". He loaded a new roll of film, then climbed out of the van and was about to take some pictures when Andrea burst from the building.

"He is not here!"

"It's almost 4:00," Hank said. "Where's his school?"

"It is on the other side of *Parque de Santa Ana*. I must go find him!"

"With that crowd out there, you'll have to go on foot."

She turned and hurried up the alley; Hank followed. They stopped at the street. Half a block away, noisy demonstrators marched down *Avenida Central* toward the park.

Hank shook his head. She wouldn't be able to locate her boy in that mob! Then he saw the anguish etched into her face, and said, "What's he look like?"

Andrea shook her head; tears welled in her eyes.

"Describe him."

"He is just a little boy."

"Tall? Short? Thin? Fat?"

"Just a little boy," she cried helplessly. The tears flowed down her cheeks. "He is only eight years old."

"How tall?"

She held her hand chest high.

"What's he wearing?"

"His school uniform . . . white shirt and dark blue pants."

"What's his name?"

"Alberto."

"C'mon, let's go find him."

They ran toward the demonstrators. At *Avenida Central*, they stopped at the edge of the boisterous procession. Hank pointed to the nearby sidewalk and shouted over the crowd noise, "Does he usually come down this side of the street?"

"I think so."

Hank shouldered his way into the mass of marchers, pulling Andrea in after him. They stumbled along the uneven sidewalk, past shops that had been boarded and locked. Andrea checked each doorway and alley, calling, "Alberto! Alberto!" Hank, taller than the press of people around him, desperately scanned the crowd, looking for a faceless eight-year-old in a parochial school uniform.

They rode the surging crowd to *Parque de Santa Ana*, with no sign of Alberto. When they reached the park entrance, Hank ducked behind a rusty section of wrought-iron fence and pulled Andrea after him. The fence shielded them from the oncoming torrent of demonstrators.

Hank shouted, "Are you all right?"

"Yes," she said, trying to catch her breath. They both were perspiring heavily. Andrea pulled herself onto a fence crosspiece, two feet above the ground. She frantically searched the crowd, screaming, "Alberto! Alberto!"

Hank climbed onto the crosspiece beside her and surveyed the chaos. Vehicle horns began to blare. A red pickup truck led a slow-moving motorcade down *Avenida Central*. As the truck approached, the demonstrators went into a frenzy. Hank recognized the three men who stood in the open bed: president-elect Endara and his two vice presidents.

Hank got Andrea's attention and pointed to the approaching motorcade. She momentarily focused on the scene. "We have never had the courage to demonstrate here before!" she cried over the clamor. "This part of the city is General Noriega's territory." Then she turned back to the park, calling for her lost child.

As the motorcade drew closer, Hank pulled out his camera. He secured the strap around his neck and captured the developing drama on film. People on the nearby balconies cheered wildly. A crescendo of voices engulfed the park, as word spread that the reform politicians were close at hand. Suddenly, over the general din, he heard Andrea emit a shrill cry. She dropped from the fence. Hank instinctively turned and jumped after her.

Andrea was down on one knee, clutching a small boy, who stared wide-eyed at the turmoil around him. Andrea kissed his face and spoke fervently to him in Spanish. Hank put his arms around them and pushed them back to the shelter of the fence.

"You found him!" Hank said excitedly.

"Yes!" Andrea said, tears streaming down her face. "He heard me, and then saw me up there."

"Is he okay?"

"Yes!" she cried gratefully. "Yes!"

Alberto gazed at Hank with a puzzled expression. Hank guessed the boy was wondering who this *gringo* was, and why he was so happy to see him.

"Stay close to the fence," Hank said. "As soon as the motorcade goes by, we'll get out of here." He climbed back onto the crosspiece and resumed taking pictures.

The president's truck was about fifty yards away, heading in their direction. Off to the right, a detachment of Dobermans in full riot gear pushed their way through the crowd. Hank scanned the park, but didn't see any place that looked safer than where they were. He turned back to the scene before him.

The Doberman's intercepted the truck and forced the politicians to climb down. The two factions stood arguing in the street for several minutes. President Endara's ample stomach pressed against one of the Doberman's shields. The crowd grew raucous, taunting the troops and cheering the politicians.

Then Hank saw fifty or more members of *Batallón de la Dignidad* approaching from the left. The sight of the paramilitary juggernaut heightened Hank's concern. Demonstrators in and around the park were in jeopardy, since both the Dobermans and the Digbats were agents of General Noriega.

Some Digbats were armed like the two he had seen earlier, with two-by-fours and rubber hoses, but most carried four-foot lengths of construction reinforcement bars. These pieces of rebar were apparently the weapons of choice.

As the Digbats bullied their way through the crowd, they chanted, *"¡Gringo no! ¡Gringo no!"* Hank frowned. Didn't they understand? It was their own countrymen holding this demonstration, not the Americans. Hank resumed taking pictures; someone needed to document what was happening here.

The Dobermans backed away, and the Digbats rushed the politicians. One attacked the president with a length of rebar, shattering his glasses and splitting his scalp. Hank grimaced, but continued to capture the violence on film. Three men, apparently bodyguards, came to the president's aid and tried to shepherd him out of the area. One of the two vice presidents disappeared under a crush of bodies; the other dived into the rear seat of a nearby car. Gunfire erupted, and the car's driver slumped over the steering wheel.

The crowd recoiled at the sound of the shots. Hank dropped from the fence, shouting, "Get down!" Andrea forced her son to the ground at the base of the fence, then lay across him, shielding him with her body. The crowd was now in full retreat.

Two Digbats ran through the park entrance, chasing a bleeding demonstrator. One wielded a length of rebar, the other a rubber hose. They broke off their pursuit when they saw Hank, and walked slowly back to him. The one with the rebar slapped it against his palm. He stopped a few feet in front of Hank and snarled, *"¡Gringo no!"* Hank's pulse pounded in his ears.

The other Digbat walked over to Andrea.

"¡Hijo de puta!" she shouted, calling him the son of a whore.

The Digbat facing Hank shifted his weapon inexpertly from one hand to the other. Hank lowered his camera to the ground as he crouched into the ready position, then waited for a telltale move. Under his breath he invoked a mantra from another time, "Battleshort," hoping it would still override his sanity.

Andrea screamed; she was being beaten. The Digbat's left shoulder twitched, and Hank quickly stepped inside. Grabbing the rebar with both hands, he pulled the Digbat forward and drove a knee into his crotch. With an agonized grunt, the Digbat released his weapon and sagged forward. Hank brought a knee up into his face, sending him sprawling backward. Hank pursued him, swinging the rebar over his head and bringing it down hard, breaking one of the man's outstretched hands and driving his nose into his face.

Hank wheeled toward Andrea. The other Digbat was almost on top of him; the rubber hose was coming down. Hank got the rebar up in time to deflect most of the blow, but the end of the hose whipped across his left ear. He shoved the Digbat away. Holding the rebar like a bayoneted rifle, he shifted it to the high-port position: forty-five-degree angle across his chest. The Digbat rushed him again, and Hank drove the extended right end of the rebar at the man's head, shattering teeth. The Digbat staggered backward against the fence, the rubber hose hanging loosely from his hand. Hank pursued him. He dipped his right shoulder and brought the end of the rebar under the man's chin, connecting solidly, ripping skin and shattering jawbone. The man's eyes rolled back in his head, and he dropped heavily to his knees. The rubber hose slipped from his grasp; he was defenseless.

"Spic motherfucker!" Hank yelled, and brought the rebar to the jab position. Targeting the man's left eye, he tensed his muscles.

"No!" Andrea shrieked.

Hank hesitated, and the helpless Digbat slumped forward into the dirt, blood pouring from his shattered mouth. Hank turned to Andrea and her son. The terror he saw etched in the child's face brought back his sanity. The battle-short cleared.

Hank brought the rebar back to high port. "Get behind me!"

They stood in the dingy hallway at the door to Andrea's second-floor apartment. Hank had to support her as she struggled to insert the key into the lock. The beating she had been given in the park, and the subsequent jostling she had received in the streets, had taken their toll. Finally, she managed to unlock the door.

Andrea stumbled as she stepped through the doorway, but Hank caught her arm. He leaned the rebar beside the door jamb and led her inside.

"Help me, please," she said, pointing to a nearby open door.

Hank assisted her into a tiny bathroom. She stopped and supported herself on the rust-stained porcelain sink. "Wait outside," she said.

"Let me see how bad you're hurt."

"Get out!" she said through clenched teeth.

"¡Mamá!" the little boy cried in alarm, rushing past Hank and throwing his arms around his mother's waist.

"Oh!" Andrea cried out in pain from his embrace. "Please, Mr. Duque . . . take Alberto . . . and wait outside."

Hank nodded. *"Ven, Alberto."*

Alberto ran from the bathroom and over to the front door. He grabbed the rebar and whirled, holding it like a baseball bat. Hank lifted his hands chest high in mock surrender. Alberto warily walked around Hank and stationed himself in front of the bathroom door.

Hank sat down on the faded living room couch and looked about the dilapidated apartment. Until this moment he had only seen Andrea's professional persona; now he realized how tenuous her existence must be.

The toilet flushed, but the bathroom door remained closed. Hank pulled out his camera and wiped off the dust from the park. The case was dented, but the film advance mechanism still worked. He'd shot a full roll during the riot; he wondered if it was of any value.

Andrea finally reemerged; her face was ashen. Hank supported her as she limped toward the apartment's single bedroom. Alberto followed and stationed himself at the foot of his mother's bed. Hank helped Andrea into a sitting position, then onto her back. "Let me see where you got hit," he said, reaching for the buttons on her blouse.

"No," she said, wincing as she tried to sit up.

Hank gently forced her to lie back down. "I need to see how bad you're hurt," he said.

"*¡No!*" cried Alberto, rushing over, waving the rebar.

Hank smiled and looked into Andrea's eyes. "Tell him it's all right."

Andrea was crying. She said something in Spanish to her son, and he lowered the rebar. She spoke to him again, and he reluctantly left the room.

Hank undid the buttons of Andrea's blouse, then loosened the top of her jeans. He eased her onto her left side and lifted her blouse. Large welts ran from her shoulder blade to her hipbone. He shook his head. What kind of savage could beat a woman this way? He gently probed his way down the row of angry bruises, asking how badly each place hurt. Finally he straightened up. "Did you urinate blood?"

"No."

"None?"

"No, not any."

"Good. I think you'll be okay. None of your ribs seem to be broken. Your worst pain is around your kidney. It may be bruised, but probably not too badly, since you're not passing blood. I suggest you just take it easy tonight, and we'll get you to a doctor in the morning." He rose to leave.

"How will you get to your hotel?"

He smiled. "We'll worry about that later. Right now, you rest, and I'll keep an eye on Alberto."

Andrea looked as if she were about to protest, but then nodded gratefully.

"Try to get some sleep," he said, covering her with a worn sheet.

Her eyelids drooped from exhaustion. "Mr. Duque . . ."

"Hank," he said with a smile.

"Mr. Duque, please have Alberto come back in. He is very frightened."

"Sure, but tell him he doesn't have to be afraid of me. I'm one of the good guys."

"*Are* you, Mr. Duque?"

A short while later, Hank flushed the toilet and stepped over to the cracked mirror. A lump had formed on and around his left ear. It was too late to put ice on it. He flipped off the bathroom light and went into the kitchen to look for something to eat.

Andrea screamed.

Hank dashed into the bedroom and found Alberto standing beside the bed, staring wide-eyed at his mother. She tried to calm him.

"What happened?" Hank said.

"Venga, mi'jo," Andrea said to Alberto, motioning for her son to come to her. She patted him reassuringly, then told Hank, "We were sleeping, and he accidentally kicked me."

"Go back to sleep, and tell Alberto to come out to the kitchen with me. I'll fix us a couple of sandwiches."

She translated what he had said, and Alberto responded with a firm, *"¡No!"*

"¡Sí!" she said sternly. With a protruding lower lip, Alberto left the room. Andrea closed her eyes.

"I'll take care of him," Hank said, and quietly shut the door behind him.

During the improvised supper, Alberto rebuffed Hank's attempts to bridge the language barrier. He followed his mother's instructions to eat, but as soon as he had emptied his plate, he slid off his chair and went into the living room. He glanced up from the couch as Hank entered the room, then buried his face in a school book.

Although night had fallen, the room was still stifling. Hank walked over to a front window and discovered a small wrought-iron balcony. A loose nail, pushed into the wooden window frame, served as a lock. He withdrew the nail, raised the window, and gingerly climbed out. He sat down on the rusty grid floor and propped his back against the dirty stucco wall. He drew his legs close to his chest and wrapped his arms around his knees.

The pungent odor of rotting produce rose from an open market across the street, and the faint strains of music drifted up from a cantina on the corner. A shudder ran down his spine, as images from the park swept over him. He closed his eyes. It had been like this in Vietnam after a firefight. It often took hours before he felt the full impact.

Hank looked over his shoulder, and he and Alberto made brief eye contact. The boy buried his face deeper in his book. Hank regretted that Alberto and his mother now feared him.

He turned back and closed his eyes again. The 1-DOG radar set he had operated in Vietnam had a sticker above a red toggle switch that read: CAUTION! BATTLE-SHORT. THIS SWITCH OVERRIDES ALL FUSES AND CIRCUIT BREAKERS. ONLY ENGAGE UNDER ENEMY FIRE. "Battle-short", the company gunnery sergeant's account of how sane men override their humanity, when fighting hand to hand. Hank opened his eyes, suddenly wishing he had a cigarette, although he hadn't smoked in more than twenty years.

He glanced over his shoulder again. Alberto was watching him. *"Venga, muchacho,"* Hank said, waving for the boy to join him.

Alberto shook his head.

"Venga," Hank repeated.

Alberto got off the couch and walked over to the window. He smiled uncertainly, then crawled outside.

Hank nodded. Alberto probably wasn't supposed to be out here. They'd catch hell if his mother caught them.

"Deme, por favor," Hank said, asking the boy for his book. Alberto reluctantly handed it over. *"Siéntese,"* Hank said, and the boy sat down beside him. Hank tilted the book so the light from the living room shone on the pages. He smiled. Although the illustrated book had Spanish captions, it reminded him of the ones he had read with his own son, a decade earlier. Many of the Spanish words were familiar—words that Hank had learned when he had been Alberto's age. *"¿Cómo se dice?"* Hank said, and pantomimed reading.

"Leer," Alberto said.

"Ah, sí, ahora recuerdo—Oh, yes, now I remember. *Lee, por favor*—Read, please."

Alberto took the book. From the way he held it, Hank knew it was a prized possession. Alberto confidently began reading the first story, which Hank gathered was about a cat that got lost.

When Alberto got to the end of the story, Hank said, *"¡Muy bien!*—Very good! *Otra vez, pero más despacio*—Again, but more slowly."

Then for the next two hours, they painstakingly taught each other the story. First, Alberto would teach Hank the words in Spanish. Then, Hank would translate the sentence into English and teach the words to Alberto. They didn't leave a sentence, until each could say it in the other's language.

Immersed in the story, they both jumped when Andrea's voice rang out, "What are you doing out there?" Alberto jumped to his feet and hung his head contritely.

Quoting from the page they were on, Hank said, *"El gato negro tiene dos pies blanco."*

"What are you saying?" Andrea said.

Alberto looked up brightly, and said in accented English, "The black cat has two white feet!"

Andrea frowned, then said to Hank, "You are teaching him English?"

"And he is teaching me Spanish."

Andrea gave a bemused shake of her head. "It is not safe for him out there, Mr. Duque."

"Vamos, muchacho," Hank said, and helped Alberto through the window and into the living room.

Inside, Andrea said something in Spanish to Alberto, and he scurried toward the bathroom. Moments later, they heard the shower running. Andrea winced in pain as she took a seat on the couch.

"That's quite a boy you've got there," Hank said, sitting down beside her.

Andrea nodded. "Thank you for watching him, Mr. Duque."

"I enjoyed it. I was surprised how quickly my Spanish started coming back. When I was a kid, I spoke enough to get by in my grandfather's neighborhood, but over the years I've forgotten most of it. Tonight, though, it was all coming back again. I think it's because Alberto and I were talking about little boy things."

Andrea smiled.

"By the way," Hank said, "your English is excellent. Where did you learn it?"

"In school, and also from . . . Alberto's father." Before Hank could reply, she said falteringly, "Mr. Duque, I appreciate what you did for us today." Hank started to protest, but she waved him off. "It was unprofessional of me to involve you in our . . . internal problems. I had responsibilities, but I should not have involved you."

"It turned out okay," Hank said.

"It turned out okay?" she exclaimed. "Mr. Duque, you were about to kill a man today, in a struggle you know nothing about."

"The struggle I saw was a man beating a woman with a rubber hose."

She gazed at him for a moment. "You told me this afternoon that you had seen killing before."

"Here . . . in 1964, and a couple of years later, in Vietnam."

"Oh." After a long silence, Andrea sighed and lowered her head into her hands.

"Are you in pain?" Hank said, placing a hand on her shoulder.

She lifted her head and pushed his hand away. "Yes," she said, "my back hurts. But that is not my main problem. I am worried about my job. I cannot afford to lose it. But I have wrecked the van and put a customer in danger."

"Just tell your boss we were at the Riande Continental, when the riot broke out—which we were. He can't blame you for the damage. I'm sure lots of cars were destroyed in that neighborhood this afternoon. As for putting me in danger, I certainly don't plan to lodge a complaint." Then he quipped, "But I *would* appreciate it if you could get us another vehicle for tomorrow."

She forced a smile. "Thank you, Mr. Duque. Tonight, I am afraid you must drive yourself back to your hotel; I am too sore. In the morning, I will call my office and arrange for someone to come and get the van. I will also have them assign another guide for you."

"I've got the guide I want."

"No," she said. "It is not possible for me to continue."

"Why not? If you're too sore to work tomorrow, I can wait a few days."

Andrea winced, having difficulty in finding a comfortable sitting position. Finally she said, "I must look after my son. I do not think General Noriega will honor the election. There will be more trouble. Alberto is in too much danger here in Panama City."

"Can his father help?"

She looked away, then turned back with a resolute expression. "His father and I were not married. He was a *gringo* soldier. He went back to the United States . . . before Alberto was born." Her eyes moistened in the pause that followed.

"Well," Hank said finally, "he must have been a dumb son of a bitch."

"What?" she said angrily.

"What I mean is, if he was dumb enough to walk out on you two, you're better off without him."

"Oh."

"How do you plan to protect Alberto?"

"Tomorrow, I will take him to Portobelo."

"Why Portobelo?"

"That is where my parents live."

"Do you plan to stay there?"

"No. I have responsibilities here. My parents will care for Alberto until it is safe for him to come back."

"Okay, then change my itinerary. Instead of touring Panama City tomorrow, I want to see Portobelo."

Before she could protest, Alberto came out of the bathroom, wearing a set of faded pajamas. He stood beside his mother, who gave him an affectionate good night kiss.

"Buenas noches, Sr. Duque," Alberto said shyly.

"*Buenas noches, Alberto,*" Hank said. Then, following the teaching pattern they had devised earlier, he said, "Good night, Albert."

"Good night, Mr. Duque," Alberto responded with a grin.

Andrea struggled to her feet and took her son into the bedroom. When she returned a few minutes later, she handed the van keys to Hank. As he rose to leave, she said, "Mr. Duque, do you have children?"

"I have a son, eighteen. He and my ex-wife moved to California. He's in his first year of college there, so I don't see much of him anymore."

She studied him for a moment, then said, "Mr. Duque, are you sure you don't mind changing your itinerary tomorrow?"

"Not at all. But I do wish you'd call me Hank."

"Mr. Duque," she said, "I am very grateful for what you have done for me today. But I must be honest with you. I do not like . . . Americans."

"*Gringos,*" he said.

She nodded. "I know that word offends you."

"It brings back unpleasant memories."

"You told me about the children in *Bella Vista,*" she said. "Mr. Duque, when they called you '*gringo*', what did you call them?"

Hank smiled sheepishly. "Spics."

"And you would fight them?"

Hank nodded.

"Like today?"

"Like today."

She looked him in the eye. "Now we understand each other, Mr. Duque."

Back at his hotel, Hank sat alone at a table in the rooftop bar, proofreading his handwritten account of the two demonstrations. The ice had melted in his second rum and Coke.

The three-piece combo in the far corner stopped playing, and Hank looked up. The tables around him were empty. Only a few customers remained at the bar—three young men, apparently

Americans, with two Panamanian women. Hank checked his watch; it was 11:20. His contact from the Associated Press was twenty minutes late.

The musicians were closing down for the night. A man and woman in their fifties began disassembling their keyboards. A younger woman, the group's singer, secured her guitar and walked over to the bar.

Hank got up from his table and went over to where she was standing. *"Me gústa su musica, señorita."*

"Thank you, sir," she said in accented English.

"My Spanish is pretty rusty," Hank said with a grin. "Did I say that right?"

"I hope so. You said you like my music."

"Can I buy you a drink?"

"No, thank you. We are leaving. I just wanted to see what the score was." She pointed to the television set behind the bar, where a soccer match was in progress.

"I haven't been following it," Hank said.

"I know. You have been very busy over there."

The bartender interrupted them. "Are you Mr. Duque?"

"Yes."

"That gentleman is looking for you, sir," the bartender said, gesturing toward a swarthy newcomer at the other end of the bar.

"Thanks," Hank said. He turned back to the singer. "Will you be playing here tomorrow?"

"We will be here all week," she said, then returned her attention to the soccer match.

Hank walked down to where the man stood. "Joe Ortega?"

The man nodded. "Are you Duque?"

"Yeah. Good, you speak English."

"I'm an American," Ortega said, "from Los Angeles."

"Sorry, it's hard to tell down here. Want a drink?"

"No, thanks. I'm working the night desk tonight."

Hank led Ortega over to his table. When they were seated, Hank reached into his attaché case and withdrew two rolls of undeveloped film. "Like I told the guy that answered the phone . . ."

"César Ruíz," Ortega interjected.

"Yeah, Ruíz. I told him I'd witnessed both of today's demonstrations, and I think I've got some good pictures—Endara and his vice presidents being attacked, the Dobermans, the Digbats, the demonstrators, and so forth. By the way, what's the latest on the condition of Endara and the others?"

"All three were hospitalized," Ortega said, "but apparently none of them is hurt too seriously. One of their bodyguards was killed, though."

"I think I've got a picture of it."

Ortega studied him for a moment. "How long have you been down here?"

"I got in yesterday."

"You got up to speed pretty fast." There was a note of skepticism in Ortega's voice. "How'd you know this shit was coming down?"

"I didn't," Hank said. "One of the locals was showing me around. Apparently the plan to hold these demonstrations was common knowledge."

"We didn't know about it," Ortega said, looking at him suspiciously.

Hank frowned. The whole damned country was paranoid.

Ortega continued, "I understand you'd like to get on as an AP stringer."

Hank nodded.

"What's your experience?"

"As a journalist, none," Hank admitted. "I've been working as a technical writer, but I got laid off a couple of weeks ago. A friend of mine is doing a travel guide on Central America, and hired me to do the section on Panama."

"We usually only work with professionals."

Hank shoved his notes and the rolls of film across the table. "Well, since you're here, why don't you go ahead and take a look at what I've got?"

The three musicians walked past the table, the singer pushing their instruments on a dolly. Hank smiled up at her, and she acknowledged him with a barely perceptible nod.

Ortega studied Hank's notes, then looked up. "You've got some details here, which we don't have. You say you've also got some good pictures?"

Hank nodded.

"If we decide to use your stuff, we'll need it tonight. Come over to the office with me, and I'll develop the film. Then we can make you an offer."

Hank shook his head. "I'm beat, man. I've been on the go for eighteen hours, and I'm probably headed for Portobelo in the morning. If you use my work, just pay me the going rate when I get back."

Ortega shrugged. "If that's okay with you, it's fine with me." As he stood up, he said, "If your pictures are good, and you've got an inside source, you may be able to sell us some more stuff in the future." The two men shook hands, and Ortega left the bar.

For several minutes, Hank sipped his watery drink and gazed out at the tropical night. Finally, he heaved himself out of the chair. The raised swimming pool was deserted as he passed, as was the hallway in front of the elevator. But just as the elevator doors started to close behind him, he caught a glimpse of the young singer coming out of the ladies room. Hank was too tired to hit the "Open" button.

4. PORTOBELO

The hotel awning shielded Hank from the midmorning sun. He glanced at his watch; Andrea was running late again. He smiled, realizing how much he looked forward to spending the day with her and Alberto. Then he spotted them coming up the hill in the old Pontiac sedan. Hank reached down and grabbed the duffel bag that lay at his feet.

Andrea pulled up the semicircular drive, and Alberto peeped over the passenger seat from the rear of the car.

"Buenos días, muchacho," Hank said as he opened the rear door. He threw his duffel bag on top of a small suitcase and an overnight bag that lay on the floor.

"Buenos días, Sr. Duque," the boy said happily.

"Good morning, Mr. Duque," Andrea said, as Hank climbed into the front passenger seat. "Did my company pick up the van?"

"Yeah, a guy came by a short while ago. How are you feeling?"

"Better, but I am very sore."

"Would you like me to drive?"

"No, Mr. Duque," she said as they pulled away from the hotel. "You have insisted that I be your guide. Now, please, let me do my job."

"Okay," Hank said with a laugh, "I'd rather not drive in this traffic anyway." He meant it. The aggressive driving and heated exchanges, routine on Panama City streets, would get a person shot in Houston. He pulled the map out of his camera case and studied it for a moment. "If you don't mind," he said, "I'd like to take the western route, through Ancon and Balboa."

Andrea nodded and changed lanes so she could turn onto *Vía España.* "Is there something in particular you wish to see?"

"I just want to take a quick look around both communities," Hank said. "Strictly nostalgia." They turned at the intersection that had been the site of the previous morning's demonstration, and Hank said, "What's the latest on the condition of Endara and the others?"

"The radio says they have been released from the hospital."

"What's going to happen next?"

"What do you mean?" she said.

"Will there be more demonstrations?"

"Yes."

"When?"

"I don't know."

"What do you think Noriega's going to do?"

"I don't know, Mr. Duque," she said impatiently.

Hank couldn't tell if she actually was uninformed, or was being evasive, so he let the matter drop. He turned to Alberto and said in Spanish, "Where is your book?"

Alberto pointed to the small suitcase.

Hank smiled and said to Andrea, "Little by little, my Spanish is coming back. Will you help me with it too?"

She shrugged.

Midmorning traffic was heavy, and it took nearly twenty minutes to reach the older section of the city. Then they turned west, and Ancon Hill loomed before them.

Hank said, "I understand Ancon and Balboa are no longer restricted areas."

"Yes," Andrea said. "The United States has returned them to Panamá."

Hank nodded. The 1977 treaty, signed by Jimmy Carter and Omar Torrijos, called for the United States to phase out of the Canal Zone by the year 2000. "There used to be an elementary school in Ancon," he said, "near Fourth of July Avenue. If it's still there, I'd like to see it."

"I know the one," she said, "but now it is a museum. And Fourth of July Avenue is now *Avenida de los Mártires*—Avenue of the Martyrs. It was renamed in honor of the Panamanians that the United States killed in 1964."

Hank looked at her, wondering if somehow she knew of his involvement in the riot. Sensing his gaze, she turned to him and frowned. Hank looked away.

They entered Ancon, turning up a familiar incline. On the left stood the old elementary school building. It brought back a rush of pleasant childhood memories. "Pull over, Andrea. I'd like to look around."

Andrea stopped the car, and Hank climbed out. Alberto looked up at him expectantly. "*Venga, muchacho,*" Hank said, opening the rear door. Alberto bounded out. "We're just going to walk around for a few minutes," Hank told Andrea. She responded with a bemused nod.

Hank glanced down the hill. The building across the street that had housed the Kool Spot was now boarded up with sheets of gray plywood. He and Alberto started up the sidewalk toward the front of the school, passing an open area where Hank had played countless games of kickball. The field was now covered with rough concrete, which years of tropical humidity had stained a mottled gray. "When I was your age," Hank said in faltering Spanish, "that was my school."

"Yes?" Alberto said.

Hank nodded. "And when my father was a boy, he went to that school too." Alberto nodded solemnly, as if showing reverence for a historic site. Hank smiled.

As they passed the side of the building, Hank slowed, remembering how he had liked to arrive at school before the doors were unlocked. A large block of ice was delivered each morning to this side entrance. When the iceman left, Hank and other early arrivals broke off small pieces and ate them. They pressed their pennies into the ice, leaving it pockmarked with impressions of Abraham Lincoln's profile. Hank regretted that his Spanish was too limited to share this recollection with Alberto.

The front of the building was shaded and quiet. Hank walked

over to a low stone retaining wall that ran alongside the sidewalk. He gazed up the familiar street, recalling how he often had waited in this exact spot for his mother to pick him up after school. The canopy of trees still covered the sidewalk, and seeds still dropped from the branches. Each seed had a long rounded fin, like a rotor blade on a helicopter. Alberto picked one up, threw it into the air, and watched it spin lazily to the ground, as Hank had done so long ago, pretending they were helicopters. How old was he then? Twelve? Not much older than Alberto here. Hank lowered his head, remembering that just six years later, a real helicopter had roared down and extracted him and three other survivors from the jungle near Khe Sanh, Vietnam.

Andrea pulled up to the curb, interrupting his musing. "Are you going inside?" she said.

Hank shook his head. "Let's go over to Balboa." He and Alberto climbed into the car.

They passed the Ancon clubhouse, which for generations had been the social gathering spot for Americans. For an instant, Hank could taste the savory hamburgers that had been served there. But the clubhouse also had undergone transformation; now it was an office building. Two khaki-uniformed Panamanian soldiers patrolled the parking lot.

Andrea turned up a tree-lined residential street. Hank smiled; the regimented rows of beige stucco duplexes were just as he re-membered them. "See that corner house there? That's where I used to live."

"Oh, yes?" Andrea said. "Do you want to stop?"

"No . . . there's not much to see. These houses all look the same, don't they?"

She nodded.

"Panamanians live here now, right?" he said.

"Yes, but there are still some Americans. Most work for the Canal Commission."

Hank remembered how when he was a boy, Ancon and Balboa had been restricted areas, generally off-limits to Panamanians. The

Panamanians seemed to be keeping it up. It hadn't gone back to jungle, yet.

They left Ancon and entered Balboa, where Hank had started high school. "I learned to swim over there at the YMCA," Hank said.

Next came the Balboa clubhouse, and Hank was disappointed to see it was closed. He had spent countless afternoons there with his friends, playing the pinball machines. Whenever the other kids were close to winning free games, they had him play their last ball. They called him the pinball wizard. Now, the Americans had abandoned the building, and Panamanian merchants had set up a flea market in front of it. Uniformed soldiers wandered between the vendors' stalls.

Andrea turned onto the Prado, a palm tree-lined esplanade. Ahead, perched high on a terraced hill, stood the Canal Commission Administration Building. Since the turn of the century, generation after generation of American school children had slid down this steep, grassy slope on flattened cardboard boxes. Hank smiled, wondering if this sledding tradition had been passed along to the Panamanian children.

Andrea turned left and they approached his old high school. In front of it, a Panamanian flag flapped in the morning breeze. Hank closed his eyes, and the guilt that had haunted him for the past twenty-five years returned. His grandfather . . . scores of others who died in the riot . . . if only he hadn't done it!

"Mr. Duque?" Andrea said.

Hank opened his eyes. The school was behind them now. He cleared his throat. "Okay, let's go see Portobelo."

They sped along the winding two-lane road known as the Transithmian Highway. The undergrowth on the hillsides thinned and there was a noticeable increase in humidity; they were nearing the Caribbean coast.

A row of dilapidated shacks lined the crest of the upcoming hill. A peasant couple strolled along one shoulder and an untended horse stood dangerously close to the other. Andrea swerved to the center of the road, leaned on the horn, and raced through the tiny community without slowing.

Hank checked the rear seat; Alberto dozed peacefully. Hank took out his map to orient himself.

Andrea said, "Do you still want to see Colón?"

"Yeah. Let's plan on spending all day tomorrow in that area. I also want to visit the Free Trade Zone and Fort San Lorenzo."

They came to a fork in the road. A faded sign indicated that Colón was to the left. Andrea veered to the right. "You will not like Colón," she said. "It is very dirty."

"Worse than Panama City?" Hank replied, and immediately wished he hadn't.

"Yes, Mr. Duque," she said sarcastically, "it is even worse than Panama City."

They followed the winding road through the coastal brush for several miles. Occasionally, they would pass a ramshackle dwelling, set back from the roadside. A mist began to fall, turning the asphalt shiny black. Hank leaned back, trying to see how fast they were going, but the speedometer wasn't working. He hoped the temperature gauge wasn't either, because it indicated the car was running hot.

They passed under a canopy of dense trees. When they emerged, they got their first glimpse of the emerald-blue Caribbean Sea, glistening in the midday sun.

"We are almost there," Andrea said.

The road abruptly cut to the right, and Hank got a breathtaking view of Portobelo Bay. Steep hills, covered with jungle, surrounded a half-moon harbor. Two small islands lay just offshore, a yacht anchored between them. Ruins of an old Spanish fortress stood silent watch over the harbor entrance.

Hank's imagination filled the wide breaches in the ancient ramparts, and he visualized Portobelo as it had been between the 16th and 18th Centuries. For 200 years, Spaniards had pillaged Central and South America. They had stored thousands of tons of plunder—gold, silver, and other riches—within these fortifications, protecting it from English buccaneers until the annual armada of galleons arrived to transport it to Spain.

"It's beautiful here," Hank said.

"Christopher Columbus thought so too. He was the one who named it Portobelo—beautiful port."

Alberto awakened. He leaned over the front seat and excitedly told Hank in Spanish, "Grandpa and Grandma live close to here!"

"Is this where you're from, Andrea?" Hank said.

"No. I have lived in Panama City all of my life. My parents had to move here three years ago."

"Had to?"

"My father was the leader of a labor union. Rich businessmen . . . made things difficult for him." She changed the subject, saying, "This is Portobelo."

She slowed as they entered the outskirts of the village. On their left lay the manicured grounds of the old fort. Rusty cannons lined the gray stone rampart. On their right stood a row of wooden shacks, typical for Panama, but unusually neat. Residents relaxed on the open porches and strolled the narrow lanes. From his research, Hank knew they were the descendants of the West Indian laborers, brought to Panama in the mid 19th Century to build the transithmian railroad.

"Do you wish to stop?" Andrea said.

"How much farther to your parents' place?"

"Less than a mile."

"Alberto's anxious to see his grandparents, so let's go there first. Then you and I can come back and see the sights. Also, we'll need to find a place for me to stay tonight."

"I will have to take you to Colón this evening," she said. "There are no hotels here in Portobelo."

"Oh," Hank said, disappointed that he wouldn't be staying in the scenic village.

Andrea turned onto a dirt road that led up a nearby hill. Impenetrable jungle walled the narrow lane and blocked the midday sun. As they labored up the steep incline, the engine began to knock.

"Sometimes the motor overheats," she said.

"Think we might be low on water?"

"No. I checked before we left. We will be all right." She seemed familiar with the problem.

As they crested the hill, Hank said, "I'd like to take some pictures from up here."

Andrea stopped the car, and he got out. Dense jungle covered the rolling hills as far as he could see. The only sounds were the sea breeze rustling the trees and the occasional shrill cries of gulls venturing inland. Hank captured the panorama on film.

"Mr. Duque," Alberto said in Spanish, "down there is my grandparents' house."

Hank looked where the boy was pointing. At the base of the hill, a tiny subsistence farm had been carved out of the jungle. Hank trained his telephoto lens on the clearing. In the center, stood a *nipa* shack, constructed from tree stalks and covered with thatched palmetto fronds. The front yard was bare, except for a hammock, slung between one corner of the shack and a nearby tree. Off to the side, lay a fenced pen for small animals and a half-acre plot for cultivating vegetables. Hank took several pictures, then climbed back into the car.

As they started their descent, Andrea shut off the engine and let the car coast. They came to a stop at a muddy path that led to the farm. Alberto bounded out of the car and ran full tilt toward his grandparents' shack. Andrea pulled the hood release.

Outside, Hank placed his hand on the hood; it was hot to the touch. He opened it and leaned over the fender. "The hoses look okay," he said. "The thermostat may be sticking. Do you have any tools?"

Andrea shook her head. "It will cool. We will be able to leave in a few minutes." She went around and unloaded her son's suitcase.

They started up the path. A man and woman, dressed in

campesino garb, came out of the shack. The man bent down and spoke to Alberto. As Hank and Andrea neared, the woman gave a hesitant wave. The man straightened, then walked over and embraced Andrea.

"Mr. Duque," Andrea said, "this is my father, José, and my mother, Mariela. This is Mr. Duque."

"Mucho gusto," Hank said.

"They speak English," Andrea said.

"Okay. Nice to meet you," Hank said, extending his hand to José.

José clasped Hank's hand in his own calloused grip. Mariela nodded impassively.

"Mr. Duque is a . . . an American tourist," Andrea said. "I will be showing him Portobelo this afternoon, and then take him to Colón tonight."

Hank sensed a lessening of tension when the couple learned the *gringo* was merely a customer and would soon be leaving.

"You will like Portobelo, Mr. Duque," José said. "But Colón is not so nice." His wife nodded her agreement.

Andrea switched to Spanish and rattled off something to her parents. Hank picked up enough of it to understand that she was telling them that there had been demonstrations in Panama City and she wanted Alberto to stay with them until the danger passed.

Mariela nodded and took Alberto's suitcase. Andrea bent down and hugged her son, then reluctantly released him. "Be good, Son" she said in Spanish, tousling his hair.

"Venga, Nieto," Mariela said.

Alberto gave Hank a shy wave and followed his grandmother into the shack.

"We will go back to Portobelo now, Mr. Duque," Andrea said.

José said something to Andrea in Spanish, spoken too rapidly for Hank to understand.

Andrea nodded at her father, then said to Hank, "If you will wait in the car, Mr. Duque, I will be there in a moment."

As Hank walked up the muddy path toward the car, he sensed

that something was disturbing this family, other than the presence of a *gringo* tourist.

Night had fallen, and Hank and Andrea were the only customers in a small outdoor restaurant that overlooked Portobelo Bay. A glass-enclosed candle flickered at their table. The mestizo proprietor sat off to one side, listening to sad Spanish music on an old radio.

Hank had just reloaded his camera. "I got a lot of good shots this afternoon," he said, setting it aside. "This is an interesting place."

"Yes," Andrea said abstractly, "it is very nice here."

The Caribbean night was clear, and the full moon illuminated the nearby stone fortress. The yacht still rode at anchor in the middle of the harbor, its running lights reflecting off the water. At the stern, someone lowered a dinghy to come ashore.

Hank turned back to Andrea. "I'm surprised how well kept everything is."

Andrea stared out to sea, preoccupied.

Hank studied her in the candlelight. She was beautiful.

She turned abruptly. "Yes, Mr. Duque?"

"Sorry," Hank said with a sheepish grin, "you caught me. Do we have time for another cup of coffee?"

"If you wish."

Hank signaled the proprietor, who pulled himself away from his radio and brought over the coffee pot. While he was at their table, Hank paid the bill.

The sound of an approaching outboard engine reverberated across the bay. Moments later, the yacht's dinghy pulled up to the restaurant dock. Four men disembarked. One, apparently a crewman, remained with the boat. The other three, dressed in slacks and sport shirts, climbed the stairs to the restaurant. They were light-skinned Latinos; all appeared to be in their forties.

The proprietor jumped up and met them as they arrived at the top of the stairway. He ushered them over to a table, close to where Hank and Andrea were seated. Hank nodded to the men as they passed, but they ignored him. One gazed boldly at Andrea as he sat down.

"We should leave," she said.

"In a minute," Hank said. The new arrivals seemed out of place, and the proprietor's deference to them made Hank curious. He tried to overhear their conversation. They spoke in hushed tones, their accents soft, almost Castilian.

One of the men passed around cigarettes, and they all lit up. The sweet pungent odor of marijuana wafted across the dining area. The man seated closest to Andrea turned in his chair and said, *"Hola, bonita*—Hello, beautiful."

"We should leave," Andrea said to Hank, this time more emphatically.

Hank took a final swallow of coffee and stood up.

The man at the other table said something else to Andrea, too fast for Hank to understand, but Hank saw the anger flash in her eyes. "What did he say?"

"It is nothing, Mr. Duque. They are just high. Please, let us go."

As they started toward the exit, the man who had been annoying them said, *"Buenas noches . . . mixta."*

Hank frowned. *Mixta?* They were in the parking lot, when he abruptly stopped and turned to Andrea. "Did he call you a half-breed?"

"It is nothing, Mr. Duque. Ignore them."

"I didn't put up with that shit twenty-five years ago—"

"But I want you to put up with it tonight," Andrea interrupted. She stepped forward and placed a hand on his arm. "Please, Mr. Duque, I am a professional guide. I cannot show you Panamá if you must fight every place I take you."

Hank smiled and shook his head. "Andrea," he said, "you may not believe this, but yesterday was the first time I've hit anybody in twenty years." She returned his smile, raising a skeptical eyebrow. Hank leaned down and pressed his lips against hers. She pushed him away and slapped him. The blow stunned him and left his ear ringing.

Andrea hurried over to the car, got inside, and slammed the door. Hank expected her to drive off, but instead she waited. He walked over and climbed into the passenger seat.

Andrea had the steering wheel clamped in both hands, her eyes riveted straight ahead. She took a deep breath. "Mr. Duque . . . I am sorry. I did not mean to hit you . . . so hard." She turned to him; tears of frustration welled in her eyes. "I cannot believe what has happened to me! I will take you back to Panama City tonight."

"No—" Hank began.

"Yes, Mr. Duque. For two days now, I have been unprofessional. There will be no charge. I am sorry for wasting your time. I will take you back to your hotel tonight, and I will arrange for another guide for you tomorrow."

Hank started to speak, but she angrily shook her head and turned the ignition key. The engine gave a grunt, but didn't start. She tried again, with the same results. And again.

"What does the temperature gauge read?" Hank said.

Andrea looked down at the gauge, then pounded the steering wheel with both hands.

Hank started to reach over to calm her, but then wisely kept his hands to himself. He looked around; the only light in the village was the one in the restaurant. One of the men from the yacht appeared in the doorway and stood watching them. Hank said, "We'll have to leave your car here for tonight."

"Leave it here?"

"We can walk back to your parents' place."

"Walk?" Then she too saw the man.

"Unless you've got a better idea."

"What about you?" she said. "I must get you back to your hotel."

"We'll have to stay at your parents' place tonight."

"But, Mr. Duque, there is no place for you to sleep."

"How about the hammock out front?"

"The hammock? You couldn't sleep there."

He opened the car door. "I've slept in hammocks before. C'mon, let's get going. We'll figure out what to do with your car in the morning."

They headed down the village's deserted main street, carrying their travel bags. The moon illuminated the otherwise dark neighborhood. The ruins of the ancient fort sprawled off to their left, and a row of small houses lined the street to their right. They passed an unpainted shack; a black couple sat on the front steps.

"Buenas noches," Hank said.

"Good night, sah," the man replied in Caribbean accented English.

They walked a bit farther, and Hank said, "Since we're here, I'd like to get a few shots of the fort at night."

Andrea frowned, but followed him as he headed across a wet grassy courtyard. They passed the ruins of a tall building, and Hank said, "What was this place?"

"*La aduana*—the customhouse. The Spaniards stored their stolen treasure there until the ships arrived to take it to Spain."

They arrived at a stone rampart that overlooked the bay. Hank set down his duffel bag and leaned against one of the ancient cannons, which had been pointed out to sea since the 16th Century. He rested a foot on the edge of the parapet and tried to imagine the excitement of the annual arrival of the Spanish armada.

"Nothing bothers you!" Andrea said exasperatedly.

Hank turned to her. "What?"

"Nothing bothers you. Yesterday, I get you in the middle of a riot, and last night you read stories to my son. Tonight I hit you, and now you want to go sightseeing."

Hank laughed. "You're certainly not a dull date."

"I am not your date! I am a professional guide."

"Take it easy," he said.

"I will not take it easy!"

"Andrea, I only kissed you. I'm sorry if I offended you. Please, don't make such a big deal out of it."

She bit her lower lip. "It *is* a big deal. Those men back there have no respect for me."

"What's that got to do with me?"

"It has to do with respect. I told you . . . Alberto's father was a *gringo*."

"Okay, I got it," Hank said. "I *do* respect you, and from now on it's strictly professional." But when she turned away, Hank risked letting his gaze rest on her for a moment. He visualized her mestizo lineage: isthmian Indians and Spanish conquistadors. What an exotic creature! He regretted that he'd never really get to know her. By this time next week, he'd be back in the States.

The two small offshore islands were silhouetted against the shimmering Caribbean. The dinghy pulled away from the restaurant and headed back to the yacht.

Hank said, "Any idea who those guys were?"

"Colombians."

Hank nodded; that would explain their precise Spanish. "Tourists?"

She shook her head. "*Drogas.*"

"Drug smugglers?"

"Not the smugglers. They are the . . . businessmen. I see men like them all the time, along the coasts and in the cities."

"The new conquistadors," Hank muttered.

Andrea nodded.

The dinghy pulled alongside and the lights went on inside the yacht. A few minutes later, the faint strains of music drifted across the bay.

"Are you sure they're not just fishermen?"

Andrea shook her head.

Hank said, "One of the books I read says the fishing's good along here. It said, in old Spanish, 'Panama' means 'abundance of fish'."

"That is one of the definitions."

"Is there another?"

"The San Blas Indians think the word comes from their language. They have a phrase that sounds like 'Panamá'."

"What does it mean?"

"A place . . . far away."

5. LA SAN BLASA

*First the pious Spaniards fell upon their knees,
then upon the aborigines.*
—*16th Century chronicler*

August 1514

"Efigenia," Ocla said softly to herself, trying the new name the Spanish captain had given her. The San Blas girl stood alone under a mango tree in her private place, a bluff that overlooked the turbulent sea from whence the fierce Spaniard had come. The sea breeze pressed the loincloth against her legs and cooled her as it blew across her bare chest and through her long black hair. "Efigenia," she said again, and her sculpted brown features crinkled in amusement as she repeated her first word in the foreign tongue.

There was a flash of lightning, and Ocla's dark eyes widened. She turned and looked toward the nearby hill. Afternoon rain clouds loomed above the impenetrable jungle that descended nearly to the sea. Then came the rumble of the thunder. This was Ocla's thirteenth rainy season; she knew the delay between sight and sound meant there was still time before she had to return to her village.

Ocla gazed back out to sea. The Spanish captain's ship rode at anchor between two nearby islands. She assumed his village on the far shore was like her own; however, their huts must be larger, since they were so tall. The captain was a giant. Ocla felt a pang of fear as she recalled his blue eyes, cold as the night rain, gazing out at her from the midst of his hair-covered face. A short while earlier, he had made one of his frequent visits to her father's hut. Her father was the *cacique*, the village leader. Ocla suspected that the two men were now discussing her. She longed to return to the more tranquil time, before the arrival of the Spaniards.

There was another flash of lightning, and this time the thunder followed more closely. Ocla reluctantly turned and started toward her village.

As Ocla arrived at her father's hut, large drops of rain began to pelt the dusty pathway that wound through the tiny village. The Spanish captain emerged and blocked her entrance. He gazed down at her with his piercing eyes, and Ocla turned away. He placed a huge hand around her throat and forced her to look at him. His mouth twisted in a strange smile, then with a snort, he pushed her aside. Ocla watched him stride up the pathway, and she trembled, sensing there would be more to come.

"Ocla!" her father beckoned from within the hut. She hurried inside. Her father sat on the edge of a woven hammock in a dimly lighted corner. Ocla positioned herself before him, hands clasped behind her back.

"You are to be the Spanish captain's woman," the cacique said. "There will be a ceremony tomorrow. Then you will share his hut."

Ocla dropped to her knees. "No, Father!"

"Yes!"

Tears flowed down Ocla's mahogany-toned cheeks. "Why must I do this?"

Her father glared at her. No one dared question the cacique's decisions, even his only surviving child. But finally his countenance softened. "The Spaniard wants you."

"Tell him no," Ocla implored.

"We must do this."

"No, Father. We can fight!" She pointed through the open entry to the assembly area outside, where four tall stakes had been erected after a recent tribal war. Impaled upon each was the skull of a warrior from a rival tribe, the Wild Boars. Although Ocla's tribe usually did not eat human flesh, these four had been taken captive, sacrificed, and then eaten in revenge for atrocities they had committed in previous wars. Ocla could still recall the unpleasant saltiness of their meat.

"We cannot fight the Spaniards," her father said. "Their weapons are too powerful . . . and their horses . . . their dogs . . ."

"But, Father—"

"They have killed all but fifteen of our warriors," the cacique said.

Ocla lowered her head. Her three older brothers had been among the warriors the Spaniards had slaughtered the day they landed.

"You must be a wife to their leader," the cacique said. "Make children with him."

Ocla shuddered.

"Learn his tongue," her father continued. "Listen, when he tells you his plans. Then tell them to me."

Ocla looked up at her father, unable to speak.

"Go, Daughter," the cacique commanded.

Ocla obediently got to her feet and walked out into the driving rain.

Now it was the dry season. Ocla and three other heavily pregnant women sat under a thatched lean-to, sewing. The other women of the village toiled in the nearby field. The woman seated next to her held up a loincloth she had finished for her husband, and Ocla responded with an unsmiling nod. Ocla's Spanish captain would wear none of the garments she knew how to make. His clothing came from his distant village across the sea. Even his mending was done by a sailor aboard the ship.

A young San Blas warrior strode down the dusty pathway. Ocla had known Tumaco all her life; he had been a close friend of her brothers. After their deaths, her father had designated Tumaco to be his eventual successor as cacique. Before the invasion of the Spaniards, Tumaco had been attentive to her. Now as he passed, he glanced down, and a look of regret momentarily broke his stoic countenance.

He stopped at her father's hut and presented himself in the entry. The cacique beckoned him.

A short while later, Tumaco stuck his head out and called Ocla's name. She struggled to her feet and followed him into the dimly lighted hut. Her father rose from the hammock and motioned for her to sit. Ocla hesitantly obeyed.

The cacique studied her for a moment, then said, "Is your husband pleased with you, Daughter?"

"Yes, Father," Ocla lied. She was embarrassed to tell him the truth in Tumaco's presence. Not only was the captain displeased with her, but so was the Spanish priest. He often visited their hut and railed at them, angry that the captain had taken her to be his wife. Ocla couldn't understand why; after all, she was the daughter of the cacique.

Her father said, "Have you learned his tongue?"

"Only a little, Father," Ocla said contritely. Early on, her husband had shown an interest in her. Although his lust had been repugnant to her, often when they had finished, he had held her gently. At these times, he had tried to speak with her, and she had felt an affection toward him. However, as her stomach had grown extended with his child, he had begun to ignore her.

"What does your husband talk about?" her father said.

Ocla thought for a moment. "He talks about gold. He likes to touch the rings in my nose and ears. In his tongue it is called *oro*."

"What does he say about it?"

Ocla thought again before replying, "Many times he asks me where our tribe gets our gold."

The cacique and Tumaco exchanged looks of concern.

"I tell him I do not know, Father," Ocla added hastily. This was the truth; only a select few men in the village knew the exact location of the tribal mine.

Her father told Tumaco, "The stories we have heard are true. The Spanish cacique, the one they call *Balboa*, is no longer satisfied with the gold his soldiers steal from the tribes to the south. Now he wants our mine."

After a long silence, a look of cunning crossed Tumaco's face. "Cacique, tell them we get our gold from the Wild Boars. And then tell them where the Wild Boars' mine is."

The cacique contemplated the scheme. Finally he said thoughtfully, "The Spaniards' weapons and horses would be of little use to them in the jungle." With a trace of a smile he added, "If the Wild Boars are victorious, we are finished with the Spaniards. If the Spaniards are victorious, we are finished with the Wild Boars."

Tumaco nodded.

The cacique turned to Ocla. "I will tell you where the Wild Boars' mine is, and you will tell the Captain."

Ocla gave an involuntary gasp. Her body was swollen with the Spaniard's child; she thought of him as her husband. Her upbringing forbade her to betray him. "I cannot, Father."

Her father glared at her, but before he could vent his anger, Tumaco interrupted, saying, "I will do it."

The cacique hesitated, but finally gave Tumaco a reluctant nod of consent. He turned back to Ocla and commanded, "Tell no one what you have heard today."

Ocla mutely lowered her head.

It was mid-afternoon, two days later, and Ocla sat on the dirt floor of her father's hut. Her hands were busy sewing, but her mind was on her husband. He had arisen early that morning and marched his soldiers into the jungle in search of the Wild Boars' mine. Tumaco and the fourteen other warriors had accompanied them. Now the cacique sat on the edge of his hammock, staring at the floor and awaiting the results of the ruse.

Ocla lifted her head and listened; someone approached. Tumaco burst into the hut, sweating heavily and covered with cuts and grime. He positioned himself in front of the cacique. "We are back. The Wild Boars drove off the Spanish."

"And our warriors?"

"When the Spaniards realized we had led them into a trap, they turned their weapons on us. Only seven of us escaped."

"And the Spaniards?" the cacique said. "How many of them escaped?"

"I don't know."

The cacique raised a hand for silence. At first there was only the sound of the afternoon breeze, whistling softly through the thatch. Then off in the distance, came the baying of the Spaniards' accursed dogs.

"Quickly!" the cacique said. "Take your warriors down the Spaniards' trail that leads south. I will tell them you have fled to the village they call *Panamá*. Find a place in the jungle where you can hide. Attack them when they pass."

Ocla's mind raced as her father ordered the next ambush. Was her husband dead? Would her child have no father?

"Go now!" the cacique commanded Tumaco, and the young warrior ran from the hut.

Ocla awkwardly got to her feet. She heard Tumaco shouting for the other six surviving warriors to join him. There was a general clamor as they quickly assembled, then dashed from the village. Their families lamented in their wake.

The Spanish priest hurried down the dusty pathway, sweating under his hooded black robe. He pushed his way past Ocla and into the hut, then railed at the cacique in his foreign tongue.

Before the cacique could respond, a Spanish soldier stormed into the hut. He rushed forward and struck the cacique in the face with a clenched fist, sending the elderly Indian sprawling across the dirt floor. The soldier drew his cutlass, but the priest stepped between them and gestured for the cacique to be taken outside. Ocla pleaded with the priest, but he pushed her aside.

The soldier grabbed the dazed Indian and shoved him through the entryway. Other soldiers herded the women, children, and old men into the assembly area in front of the cacique's hut. The young men of the village were either dead, or had followed Tumaco up the jungle trail. Ocla frantically looked about for her husband, needing him to intercede, but he was nowhere to be seen.

She turned back to where the enraged soldier was manhandling her father. The powerful cacique now seemed helpless and childlike. The soldier pushed him against one of the four stakes that held the Wild Boar skulls. The Spanish priest knelt and for a moment gazed up at the sky. Then he waved his dreaded cross at the cacique and began to babble fervently in his tongue.

Another Spanish soldier positioned himself behind the stake and slipped a length of rope around the cacique's neck. He tightened the makeshift garrote, and the cacique's bare feet clawed at the ground in agony. The priest put his demented face next to cacique's and demanded something of him.

The cacique clutched at the garrote and futilely tried to respond. Then he raised an arm and pointed down the trail that led south. The soldier behind him drew his cutlass and severed the arm just below the elbow.

Ocla screamed.

The priest said something, and the soldier sheathed his cutlass and resumed the garrotting. Ocla rushed to her father and desperately tried to get her fingers around the rope. Her father's tongue protruded from a corner of his mouth. Then his neck snapped and his head fell limply to one side.

Bedlam erupted behind her, as the other soldiers began putting terrified women and children to the sword. Frantic mothers clawed at the pitiless Spaniards, who threw San Blas infants to their pack of snarling dogs. Ocla dropped to her father's feet and hid her face to block the horror.

A thunderous roar pierced the din of torment. Dazed, Ocla looked up and saw her husband astride his horse. His leggings were torn, and his arms and breastplate were covered with dried blood. His hands held a smoking musket. He shouted commands to his soldiers, and they reluctantly withdrew from their savagery.

The surviving villagers retrieved their butchered dead and maimed, and carried them into their huts. Even after the assembly area had been cleared, the village echoed with muffled screams of pain and lament, coming from behind the thatched walls.

The captain rode over to where Ocla knelt in front of her father's hanging corpse. He gazed down at her for a moment, then with-drew his cutlass and raised it above his head. Ocla cried out and doubled forward to protect herself. The cutlass struck the stake on which her father was tied, and the cacique's body fell heavily be-side her. The captain wheeled his mount and again shouted com-mands to his soldiers, who fanned out in all directions to look for traces of the missing warriors.

Ocla dragged her father's lifeless body into his hut.

A short while later, a series of pains warned Ocla that the birth was near. She and her father's sister had sought refuge in Ocla's private place, the bluff that overlooked the sea. Now, with the old woman by her side, Ocla squatted, stoically awaiting the arrival of her child. The sea breeze soothingly rustled the tree leaves overhead.

The sound of horse hooves shattered the respite. The captain and another soldier, dressed in battle armor, rode toward them at a fast trot.

Ocla tried to stand, but a sharp pain pierced her bowels. The two men dismounted a short distance away and approached on foot. Ocla's husband shoved the old woman aside and grasped Ocla by the shoulders. She cried out, blinded by a stab of pain, as he lifted her to her feet.

"Where are the warriors?" he demanded in her tongue.

The pain passed, and Ocla could see her husband's face. Al-though terrified, she couldn't bring herself to direct him to the waiting ambush.

He slapped her hard across the face with his open hand.

Ocla cringed and tried to slump to the ground, but the en-raged Spaniard had her clasped in his powerful grip. He raised a hand to strike her again, and the girl cowered. Not remembering the words in her husband's tongue, she whimpered evasively, "*Pa na ba*", the San Blas phrase meaning "far away".

The other Spaniard put his face so close to hers that she could smell his foul breath. "Where?" he snarled.

"*Pa na ba*," she repeated entreatingly.

"¿Panamá?" her husband said. He held his huge doubled fist in front of her face. "Have the warriors gone to *Panamá?*"

The girl hesitated, then looked boldly into his eyes and said in his tongue, *"Sí . . . Panamá."*

Her husband threw her to the ground, and he and his companion ran for their horses. Ocla pressed her face to the warm damp earth and held her breath. From the corner of her eye, she saw the two men wheel their mounts toward her. She frantically lowered her arms and drew up her knees, trying to protect her unborn child. The Spaniards raced in her direction, side by side. Then at the last moment, her husband's horse whinnied in pain from a savage pull on the bridle, and it veered into the path of the other mount. The girl screamed in terror as they thundered harmlessly past her.

The sound of the hooves quieted in the distance. Soon the remaining Spanish soldiers would blunder into the trap her tribesmen had set for them on the trail. Ocla felt a warm fluid surge between her legs. She hurriedly squatted again. The birth was beginning. She was not afraid; she had seen the arrival of many babies. She hoped hers would not be cursed with its father's cold blue eyes. She would let Tumaco name it.

6. LOS MACHOS

A rooster's crow startled Hank out of a sound sleep. He snapped into a sitting position, and the cord hammock wrapped around him and rocked precariously. He disentangled his toes from the netting and swung his legs over the sides. The hammock steadied. The packed ground felt cool and damp against the soles of his bare feet.

There were no lights or movement inside the shack; Andrea and her family must still be asleep. He tilted his watch to catch the faint morning light: 4:40. Still sleepy, he considered lying back down, but the rooster crowed again. His shoes and socks lay beneath the hammock. Before putting them on, he shook them thoroughly, checking for scorpions.

Hank stood and stretched his aching muscles and joints, then stared into the dark silent jungle, trying to imagine what it would be like to live in such solitude. Panamanians called it simply *el interior*.

The rooster crowed again, and Hank started toward the rear of the shack. In the faint predawn light, he picked his way along the edge of the cultivated plot where Andrea's parents grew plantain and corn. He passed the small animal pen, and the rooster and several hens fluttered over to the wire mesh, expecting to be fed. Three muddy goats watched impassively from the far side of the enclosure.

As he turned the corner at the rear of the shack, he bumped into a water pump handle. He wanted to rinse his mouth, but decided the noise would awaken the others. A thatched outhouse stood at the edge of the clearing. Before entering, he held the door open for a moment, checking for scorpions, snakes, or other creatures that might have crawled in during the night.

A short while later, he opened the outhouse door to leave. Morning shadows still encased the yard, but the sky behind the nearby hill had turned a reddish yellow. He stepped through the doorway, and received a heavy blow to the stomach. As he dropped to his knees, it flashed through his mind that he must have walked into something. Then rough hands grabbed the back of his neck and forced his face into the stinking damp soil.

Hank gasped, trying to catch his breath. Someone held him down and clamped a filthy hand over his mouth. He heard Andrea and Mariela scream from within the shack, then Alberto cry out for his mother. Hank struggled frantically to rise, but his attackers forced him back down.

The clearing swarmed with dark figures. Hank's mind raced, trying to define the enemy. There were about a dozen—scruffy, bearded, clad in black T-shirts and camouflage fatigue trousers. Apparently this was a military unit, but it looked more like a motorcycle gang.

The men restraining Hank yanked him to a kneeling position. Two held him by his arms and a third stood in front of him, pointing an M-16 rifle at his face. On their fatigue caps they wore a primitive insignia: skull over crossed machetes. They forced Hank's arms behind his back and bound his wrists with coarse rope.

Several soldiers burst through the doorway of the shack, carrying Andrea, Mariela, and Alberto, kicking and screaming. Again Hank tried frantically to rise, but the men restraining him forced him back to his knees. The soldiers threw the two women and the boy onto the ground and bound their hands behind their backs, then secured them to a mango tree in the center of the clearing. Moments later, they dragged out Andrea's father, unconscious and bleeding from a head wound.

Hank desperately looked about for an officer. A burly black soldier standing in front of him wore corporal chevrons and seemed to be in charge.

"What do you want here?" Hank demanded.

The corporal scowled at Hank's tone. He drew back his rifle butt, as if to deliver a blow.

Hank's pulse surged. *"¡Soy Americano!"* he shouted. *"¡Gringo!"*

The corporal hesitated. Finally, he lowered his rifle and mo-tioned for Hank to stand up. *"¡Venga!"* he snarled.

The corporal herded Hank over to the mango tree, where the other soldiers had gathered around Andrea and Mariela. Those on the outer perimeter laughed and shouted, as others grabbed and fondled the two women's breasts and legs. One unzipped his pants and showed his readiness to begin the rape. Alberto screamed and strained to get to his mother.

"¡Párate!" Hank shouted, ordering the soldiers to stop. They all turned in surprise. The corporal thrust the muzzle of his M-16 under Hank's chin. But behind the cruel sneer, Hank sensed un-certainty. *"¿Donde esta su comandante?"* Hank demanded, asking the corporal where his commanding officer was, and trying to bluff him with a tone of authority.

The corporal responded too rapidly for Hank to understand.

"He says his officer is at their camp," Andrea said.

"Tell him . . . I'm with the CIA."

Andrea frowned, but quickly translated.

The corporal slowly lowered his rifle and turned to the other members of the predatory band. Before they could confer, Hank said, "Tell them to untie me and get the hell out of here!"

Andrea again quickly translated.

Several soldiers, including the corporal, exchanged uncertain glances.

Hank shouted, "Tell 'em they're about to have the whole U.S. Southern Command down on their ass!"

At Andrea's translation, the corporal barked an order to the other soldiers. They reluctantly sidled away from their captives. Hank felt his bonds being loosened. The soldier standing over the women with his member extended was the last to concede. Fi-nally, he turned to José, still lying unconscious on the ground, and urinated in his face. His comrades laughed with bravado. Then the band vanished into the nearby jungle.

Hank untied the others. Andrea hugged Alberto and tried to

quell his hysteria. Hank dragged José over to the water pump and, with Mariela's help, washed the blood and urine from his head.

Hank, Andrea, and Andrea's family trudged down the hill toward Portobelo. The birds, hidden in the dense forest that lined the muddy road, quieted as they passed. Hank and Andrea carried their travel bags, and Mariela had a hemp sack slung over one shoulder. They had to go slowly; José was still unsteady on his feet. Alberto held his grandfather's hand.

"Andrea," Hank said, "do you know who those guys were back there?"

"Los Machos del Monte—The Mountain Men. They are very bad."

"Are they part of the PDF?"

She nodded. "They are Noriega's favorites. They are very loyal to him." Then she frowned. "Mr. Duque . . . you told them you were with the CIA?"

Hank gave a quick laugh; obviously, he had raised doubts in her mind too. "I was just bluffing. This country's so paranoid about the CIA, they fell for it."

"Mmmm," she said, as if not entirely convinced.

The sound of an approaching vehicle carried up the hill, interrupting their exchange. As they moved to the edge of the road, a PDF Jeep rounded the nearby curve. It was upon them before they could conceal themselves in the underbrush.

"La guardia," Andrea's mother said with a mix of fear and loathing.

The Jeep slid to a stop in front of them. The driver climbed out, holding a rifle at high-port. He was stocky, bearded, and wore a black T-shirt. A tall, light-skinned lieutenant stepped down from the passenger side. He was clean shaven and dressed in standard military fatigues. As he sauntered over to Hank, he unsnapped his holster flap, exposing the butt of a 45-caliber pistol. "Are you the *gringo* who attacked my soldiers?" he said in accented English.

"*I* attacked *them?*" Hank exclaimed.

"They gave me a complete report."

"That's bullshit!"

The driver stiffened. The lieutenant glared at Hank. "Maybe in your country, it is . . . 'bullshit', *señor*. But we are not in your country." Hank stifled a retort, and the lieutenant gave a tight nod of approval. "Give me your passport," he ordered.

As Hank reached into his duffel bag, the driver brought his rifle into the firing position. Hank froze. He looked at the officer, who nodded again. Hank slowly withdrew his passport and handed it over. The lieutenant thumbed through it, then handed it back.

"Who are you Mr. Duque?" the lieutenant said. "What are you doing here?"

"I'm a writer. I'm down here to write a travel piece."

"You told my men, you worked for the CIA."

"I lied."

"So, Mr. Duque, you admit you are a liar. But how am I to know if you were lying then . . . or if you are lying now." Turning to Andrea, he said in Spanish, "And you, señorita, who are you?"

"I am Andrea Arias," she responded in Spanish. "I work for Aventura Tours. I am Mr. Duque's guide."

"Is he a writer, as he says?"

Hank held his breath, awaiting her reply.

"Of course," Andrea said. "Mr. Duque has hired me to show him our country."

"On foot?" the lieutenant said sarcastically.

"My car is at La Paloma Restaurant," Andrea said. "It broke down yesterday."

The lieutenant studied her for a moment, then said, "I saw a car there this morning." He secured the flap on his holster. Turning to José and Mariela, he said brusquely, "I know who you are. Go back to your farm." Switching to English, he said to Hank, "You and your guide, get in the Jeep."

Alberto released his grandfather's hand and started toward his mother, but Andrea stopped him with a firm, "*¡Véte!*—Go!" The boy looked at Hank, who nodded. Reluctantly, Alberto rejoined his grandparents.

Hank and Andrea climbed into the rear of the Jeep, and the lieutenant and his driver got into the front. Moments later, they careened down the hill toward Portobelo.

No one spoke again until they roared into the village. As they approached the La Paloma Restaurant, the lieutenant ordered his driver to pull in beside Andrea's car, then turned and said, "What is the problem?"

"It's overheating," Hank said. "I think it may be the thermostat."

"There are no repair shops here in Portobelo," the lieutenant said.

They climbed out of the Jeep and walked over to the car. Andrea opened the hood, and Hank leaned over the radiator. "Do you have any tools?" Hank asked the lieutenant.

The lieutenant relayed the question to his driver, who went to the rear of the Jeep and opened a utility panel. He returned and handed Hank an adjustable wrench and a large screwdriver.

The bolts that connected the thermostat housing to the engine block were rusted in place, but Hank finally managed to break them loose. He pried out the thermostat and found it clogged with rust and dirt. He bolted the housing back in place, then straightened up and told Andrea, "Give it a try."

The engine started, and within a few seconds idled smoothly. Hank closed the hood and came around to Andrea's side of the car. "I'm pretty sure this was the problem," he said, showing her the thermostat. "We can leave it disconnected. The car will run okay without it."

The driver took back his tools, and the lieutenant said, "Mr. Duque, let us agree that this morning was . . . just a misunderstanding. We will not make charges against you."

Hank suppressed a response.

The officer continued, "Your friends will not be bothered again. You have my word."

Hank looked at Andrea; she gave a reluctant nod. He turned back to the officer. "Okay."

The two soldiers climbed into their Jeep and roared off down the road. Hank and Andrea got into the car, and sat in silence for a moment. The midmorning breeze blew small whitecaps across the bay. The Colombian yacht was gone. Finally, Hank said, "Let's go back to the farm."

Andrea nodded. "If everything is all right there, then I will take you to Colón."

"You're not going to leave your family here, are you?"

She sighed. "Mr. Duque, everywhere in Panamá is dangerous. I do not trust the PDF, but my family will be safer here than in Panama City. They can come back when . . ." Her voice trailed off.

When what? Hank wondered. Was there a movement to get rid of Noriega? Now, however, wasn't the time to press for information.

"There is an Aventura office in Colón," Andrea said. "They will assign another guide for you."

"I told you before, Andrea, I've got the guide I want."

She shook her head. "When you are done in Colón, your new guide will take you back to Panama City."

"Why change now?"

"After all that has happened," she said, "it will be better if you have another guide."

"Andrea, I'd really like you to be the one to show me around Colón." She appeared to waver, and he added with a smile, "After all, what *else* could happen?"

Finally, with a resigned shake of her head, she said, "Okay, Mr. Duque. One more day."

7. COLON

Hank entered the coffee shop of Colón's venerable Hotel Washington. He felt refreshed, having showered and put on clean clothes. Andrea sat at a window booth; her hair was damp, and she too had changed clothes.

Hank dropped into the seat across from her. "You must be hungry. You even beat me down here."

"I am starving," she said with a laugh. "We didn't eat this morning, you know."

"Is your room okay?"

"Everything is fine. I called the local Aventura Tours office and explained about the car problem. I told them we would be staying here another day. When we are done with lunch, I need to go by the office and get some expense money."

A waiter came over and handed Hank a menu. Hank asked Andrea, "What looks good to you?"

"I'm having the *sancocho*. It is a chicken soup."

"Mmmm . . . I'm hungrier than that." He looked up at the waiter and took the opportunity to practice his Spanish. "*Arroz con pollo, por favor*—rice with chicken, please."

The waiter left with their orders, and Hank gazed out the window. A low concrete wall enclosed the hotel grounds. Beyond the wall, a line of freighters and cruise ships waited to enter the canal.

"My grandfather brought me here once," Hank said.

"Oh, yes?"

He turned back to her. "One night Grandpa and I ate in the dining room next door. It was just before . . . he died. He wanted to show me what life was like in the early days, when he and my grandmother were young. They used to take the train across the isthmus and spend the night here at the Washington."

"What was the Canal Zone like back then?"

"What do you mean?"

"We Panamanians always imagine it was very . . ." She struggled for the appropriate word in English. "Very organized."

"It *was* organized. Discipline was strict. The Canal Commission ran everything—not only the canal project, but people's personal lives as well. The Commission dictated where people lived and how they behaved."

"I could not live like that," Andrea said.

Hank nodded slowly. "One of the books I recently read dismissed it as having been a vast experiment in social engineering. But you know, after I left here, I missed it."

"You missed people telling you what to do?"

Hank smiled. "Zonians did forfeit some individual rights, but what they got in return was a strong sense of common purpose. Everybody, from engineers to commissary clerks, felt they played a significant role, first in building the canal, then in keeping it operating."

"Even so . . ."

"The only time people in the States have had that sense of common purpose was when NASA won the race to land on the moon."

Andrea raised a skeptical eyebrow. "I would still prefer Panamá, over the Canal Zone . . . or the moon."

Hank laughed. "My grandfather must have agreed with you. My grandmother was an American, but after they got married, they settled in *Casco Viejo*. Matter of fact, just a few blocks from where you live."

Andrea studied him for a moment. "How many children did they have?"

"Just my father."

She frowned. "If your father grew up in *Casco Viejo*, I am surprised you don't speak more Spanish."

"My father didn't live long enough to have much of an influence on me. He died from tuberculosis when I was seven. He'd attended school in the Canal Zone, then gone to the States for college. When he came back, I guess he decided he wanted to be an American. He married my mother and they settled in the Canal Zone. That's where I grew up. Spanish was never spoken at home. What little I picked up, I learned from my grandfather, after my father died."

"So your mother was American."

Hank nodded. "From Texas. She came down here right after nursing school. She was looking for adventure, and signed a one-year contract. Then she met my father. After he died, Mom and I stayed on for several years, then . . . we moved to Houston."

"And you became a Texan too."

Hank gave a short laugh. "I've lived in Houston for over twenty years, but still don't feel like a 'Texan'."

A plaintive blast from a ship's horn drew their attention. A rusty freighter got underway, heading toward the canal entrance.

Hank turned back. "Grandpa told me the canal construction years were the most exciting of his life. He liked Americans; they worked hard and played hard. He and my grandmother went to a dance every Saturday night. The Canal Zone Women's Club put them on. One week, the dance would be here at the Washington; the next week, at the Tivoli Hotel on the Pacific side. That reminds me, I want to see the old Tivoli when we get back to Panama City."

"It was torn down."

"Torn down?" he said, disappointed. "When?"

"I'm not sure . . . maybe twenty years ago. I was a little girl."

Hank looked back out to sea. The vivid recollection of the 1964 riot rushed back at him: the whiz-smack of the incoming Panamanian sniper fire, and the roar of the American response.

The waiter arrived with their orders, returning Hank to the present.

A half-hour later, Hank and Andrea drove through Colón's ramshackle business district. Built by the French at the end of 19th

Century, the city had been styled after the *Vieux Carré* in New Orleans—two-story structures, with overhanging verandas. But now the stylish colonial architecture was faded, cracked, and crumbling. The brassy din of automobile horns and radios reverberated off the wooden buildings. Tattered descendants of the Africans and West Indians, who had slashed the jungle passages, loitered on the dirty city sidewalks.

Andrea turned off *Avenida Bolívar* and drove two short blocks to *Avenida del Frente*. The shops along this avenue looked less dilapidated, and the pedestrians moved with more purpose.

Andrea parked in front of a small storefront. Flaking black letters on a dirty window identified it as the Aventura Tours office. As they climbed out of the car, Hank said, "I'll wait for you out here."

Andrea nodded and entered the office.

Hank reached back into the car and retrieved his camera. He slipped the strap around his neck and took a picture of an old railway station across the street. Then he turned and took several more pictures of the activity up and down the avenue. A ship horn sounded from the nearby bay.

He crossed the street and walked down to the end of the railway station. On the other side of the tracks lay the community of Cristobal. The contrast struck him: the regimentation of the Canal Zone in front of him, and the desperate spontaneity of Panama at his back.

He focused his camera on the Canal Zone scene. Suddenly he felt a hand grab at his wallet and heard a male voice with a Caribbean lilt say, "What you got for me, mon?" Hank spun around, knocking the hand away.

The mugger raised his fists to chest level. His ebony countenance contorted with hatred. He had the face of a fighter: scarred eyebrows, flattened nose, distended lips. Hank dropped into a defensive crouch. He heard Andrea cry out from across the street, but kept his gaze fixed on the mugger, who stared back with yellowish, bloodshot eyes.

Another man's voice rang out, "You there! Get along with you!" The mugger looked to his right, then lowered his hands uncertainly. Hank risked glancing to his left, and saw Andrea and a large black man hurrying across the street. The mugger snarled something unintelligible, then turned and shuffled off.

"Are you all right, sah?" the man with Andrea asked, arriving short of breath.

Hank kept a wary eye on the retreating figure. "I'm okay. What the hell was that about?"

"He wanted to steal from you, sah. You should not be out on the street alone. And you should never carry a camera where people can see it."

"I'm sorry, Mr. Duque," Andrea said. "I should have warned you. I thought you were going to stay by the car."

The mugger disappeared into an alley. Hank turned and said, "It wasn't your fault."

As they started across the street, Andrea said, "Mr. Duque, this is Mr. Lowe. He is the manager of the Aventura office here."

The two men shook hands as they walked, and Lowe said, "I am sorry about the automobile problems you had yesterday, sah, and about this incident just now. Hopefully, the rest of your visit to our beautiful country will be peaceful and enjoyable."

"I'm sure it will be," Hank said. He glanced at Andrea, who just shook her head.

They arrived at Andrea's car, and Lowe said, "I understand you wish to spend the night here and do more sightseeing tomorrow."

Hank nodded. "I'd like to see the Free Trade Zone this afternoon and the ruins of San Lorenzo in the morning. Then we'll probably head back to Panama City."

"Very good, sah."

The two men shook hands again, and Lowe returned to his office.

A few minutes later, Hank and Andrea drove down *Calle 13*. Ahead, a long massive wall separated the Free Zone from the rest of Colón.

"Must be quite an operation in there," Hank said.

"*Zona Libre* is the second largest free trade zone in the world," Andrea said. "Only Hong Kong is larger."

"As I understand it, companies operate out of free trade zones because they don't have to pay duties, or even have licenses."

She nodded. "There is little government interference. More than six hundred companies have outlets here. Their annual sales exceed four billion dollars."

"Four *billion*," Hank repeated, wondering how much of that figure was laundered drug money.

They pulled up to a modern gated entrance. A uniformed security officer stepped out of the guard building, checked Hank's passport, and waved them through.

As they entered the compound, Hank was surprised by the neat rows of glass and chrome storefronts that lined the well-maintained streets, contrasting sharply with the abject poverty outside the walls. Andrea found a parking spot along the curb, and they climbed out of the car.

"The stores are in this area," Andrea said, "and the warehouses are in the back. Most transactions are done in wholesale lots, but visitors like yourself can also make smaller, duty-free purchases."

They strolled down the bustling sidewalk. The Free Zone reminded Hank of a modern U.S. shopping center, featuring everything from antiques to sporting goods. He paused in front of a jewelry store. "Let's take a look inside."

They entered the brightly lighted shop. The carpeting was plush and the display cases were crammed. A neatly dressed clerk approached them. "Can I help you, sir?"

"We're just looking," Hank said.

The clerk nodded and left them to browse.

As they walked around the store admiring the jewelry, Hank was again struck by the sharp contrast to the poverty outside the compound. He shook his head. He'd hate to be in here when the locals came over the wall.

"Is something wrong?" Andrea said.

"No, I was just thinking. Remember the old customhouse we saw in Portobelo, where the Spaniards stored their loot?"

"Yes?"

"This Free Trade Zone reminds me of it."

Andrea smiled.

They walked a bit farther, and she stopped at an earring display. Hank looked over her shoulder and said, "I'd like to pick up something for a friend. Which one of these do *you* like?"

"Mmmm . . . I think those." She pointed to a pair of gold filigree dangles.

The tag indicated they were only fifty dollars. Hank called the clerk over and made the purchase. The clerk wrapped the earrings in tissue and slipped them into a small tan envelope. Hank dropped it into his shirt pocket, and he and Andrea left the store.

Out on the sidewalk, Hank saw a lunch stand across the street. "I could use some coffee. How about you?"

"Yes," she said gratefully. "I am suddenly very tired."

They got their coffee and took a sidewalk table under a red and blue Cinzano umbrella. For a while, they sat in silence, watching the shoppers file up and down the street. Finally, Hank said, "Four billion dollars, huh?" repeating the figure Andrea had mentioned earlier.

"Yes," Andrea said. Her eyelids drooped. She shook her head and took a sip of her coffee.

"Do you think those Colombians we saw in Portobelo were heading for here?"

"Probably," she said, "or coming *from* here. There are no trade restrictions in the Free Zone. Much of the business is done in cash. Panamanian banks are not particular whose money they take . . . or where it comes from."

"Money laundering," Hank mused. Andrea had confirmed his earlier suspicions. "Think Noriega's involved in it?"

She nodded. "Anyone who wants to do business in Panama must pay the General."

"Even the drug traffickers?"

"Especially them," she said. Then, apparently feeling she was confiding too much to an outsider, she grew quiet again.

Hank let the matter drop. "Well, I've seen enough of the Free Trade Zone. Let me take a few pictures, then we can head back to the hotel."

Andrea took a final swallow of coffee.

That evening, Hank and Andrea sat in the main dining room of the Hotel Washington. They had finished dinner and were relaxing over rum and Cokes. Most of the tables were occupied, and a combo played softly in the far corner.

Hank looked up at the turn-of-the-century high ceiling, decorated with sculpted crown molding and a crystal chandelier. Saturday night at the Washington. The thought pleased him, and he looked at Andrea and smiled.

She responded with a quizzical frown.

"I was thinking about my grandfather," Hank said. "How he and my grandmother used to come here."

Andrea smiled.

Hank reached into his shirt pocket and withdrew the small tan envelope. "I'd like you to have these," he said, carefully unfolding the tissue around the delicate earrings.

"No, Mr. Duque. I cannot accept those."

"I bought them for you. I was going to give them to you when we got back to Panama City tomorrow, but now seems like a better time."

"I'm sorry, Mr. Duque. It would not be proper."

"Please. I know this trip hasn't gone the way you wanted, but I really appreciate your sticking with it."

Andrea shook her head no.

Hank nodded yes.

Reluctantly, she accepted the gift. She admired the earrings for a moment, then replaced the pearl studs she had been wearing.

"Perfecto," Hank said.

Andrea self-consciously shifted her gaze to two elderly couples out on the polished dance floor.

"Would you like to dance?" Hank said.

She smiled. "Yes, but . . ."

"But what?"

"Well, everyone is dressed up, and we . . ." Hank and Andrea still wore the clothes from their afternoon excursion.

Hank stood up and extended his hand.

She politely shook her head.

Hank said, "I think my grandfather would want me to dance here."

Andrea hesitated, then rose and followed him onto the dance floor. She pressed her body to his, and he stumbled slightly. "Tennis shoes," he whispered in her ear.

She gave a quick laugh, then cupped her hand around the back of his neck.

They stood in the hallway outside her room. Andrea unlocked the door, then turned to him. "Thank you again for the earrings, Mr. Duque."

Hank nodded. She looked lovely, and he hoped she was going to invite him in.

"Mr. Duque," she said, hesitantly, "again, I am sorry about the problems we—"

"Please, don't apologize," Hank interrupted, smiling. "I wanted to see the real Panama, and you've certainly shown it to me."

She returned his smile. Then she entered the room, and closed the door behind her.

The next morning, they drove through Cristobal, the Canal Zone community adjacent to Colón.

"Do you know this place?" Andrea said.

"It feels familiar," Hank said as they passed the neat rows of residential quadruplexes, "but it's probably because all these Canal Zone towns look pretty much the same. I don't think Grandpa ever brought me here."

"The Canal Zone all looks the same to me, too," Andrea said.

They left Cristobal, and a few minutes later arrived at the Gatun Locks. The bridge over the canal had been swung aside to allow a tanker to enter. Andrea parked the car, and Hank got out. He took pictures, as the locks slowly raised the huge ship 85 feet, from sea level to the level of Gatun Lake. The sights and sounds of the operation brought back childhood memories of the Miraflores Locks. Tomorrow, Miraflores would lower this ship back to sea level on the Pacific side of the isthmus.

"Hard to believe," Hank mused, as he climbed into the car, "that something built seventy-five years ago is still functioning, and is still so important."

"Mmmm," Andrea said.

"And Panamanians are operating it now?"

"There are still some American specialists," Andrea said, "but we will take over completely in ten years, when—"

She was cut off by the sounding of a shrill bell, indicating they could proceed.

They drove across the steel bridge, and moments later sped along a rough asphalt road, following the Caribbean coastline. Their destination was the ruins of Fort San Lorenzo. Off to the right, through dense roadside brush, Hank occasionally got a glimpse of the sea. To his left, rose a wall of jungle.

A six-ton army truck suddenly came into view. Andrea slowed and steered onto the right shoulder. As the truck rumbled by, Hank saw a U.S. Army white star stenciled on the door. The rear of the truck was filled with soldiers wearing camouflage fatigues, apparently on maneuvers. Andrea accelerated again, and Hank gazed out at the passing jungle. He wondered if he could still survive in terrain like that.

As if reading his mind, Andrea said, "You said you were in the Army?"

"Marine Corps."

"And you were in Vietnam?"

He nodded.

"It must have been very bad there."

Hank didn't respond for a moment, then said, "It was for me. When I got there, I was only seventeen."

She shook her head. "So young."

"Too young. After my mother and I left here, I had trouble adjusting to life in the States. I wound up dropping out of high school and enlisting. I celebrated my eighteenth birthday in a place called Khe Sanh." He fell silent for a moment. Then, rubbing the tender area beneath his rib cage, he said, "Panama reminds me a little of Nam. Particularly yesterday morning."

Andrea responded with a wry smile.

Hank sensed an opportunity to probe for information. "Andrea, explain what's going on down here?"

"What do you mean?"

"General Noriega, the PDF . . . and all the other stuff."

Andrea tightened her grip on the steering wheel. "Noriega is the problem. He is a . . . criminal. He runs everything. The military, the government, guns, drugs . . . everything."

"Is he worse than General Torrijos?"

"Yes. Omar Torrijos was a dictator also, but not so bad as Noriega. Torrijos was just a . . . playboy. He was very popular with the people, particularly after he negotiated the treaty with your President Carter. When Torrijos died in a plane crash, Noriega took his place. Many people suspect that Noriega was responsible for the crash."

"Those soldiers who attacked your parents' farm yesterday, are they typical?"

"The PDF is everywhere," she said, "but *Los Machos* are the worst."

Hank broached the question he had been waiting to ask. "Where's the resistance to Noriega coming from?"

"From many people," she said. "Political parties, independent newspapers, students . . . and now even the *rabiblancos*."

"*Rabiblancos?*"

"The rich people, who own the big businesses."

Hank smiled. Literally, a *rabiblanco* was a timid, white-tailed bird. Most of Panama's wealthy citizens were light-skinned. "How about you?" he said. "Are you involved in the resistance?"

"I am a member of the *Federación de Estudiantes Revolucionarios*—the Federation of Revolutionary Students."

"You're a student?"

She relaxed her grip on the steering wheel. "Yes. I attend the University of Panama at night. We are between semesters now."

"What are you studying?"

"Business. I am in my last year."

"That's great," Hank said, surprised and impressed. "Must be tough for you—raising Alberto by yourself, working as a tour guide, and going to school."

"I am used to it," she said with a shrug.

"Andrea, getting back to Noriega, how does he stay in power? Through his military force?"

"And yours."

"Mine? What do you mean?"

"Your government, Mr. Duque," she said tolerantly. "He works for the U.S. government."

"What are you talking about?"

"I am talking about the CIA."

"CIA? Do you have proof Noriega's working for the CIA?"

"Proof?" she said with an angry glance. "Why must I prove this to you?"

Hank realized he was pressing too hard and decided it was time to change the subject. "Tell me about this fort we're about to see."

"Fort San Lorenzo," she began, lapsing into a tourist lecture, "was built by the Spanish in the Sixteenth Century. They selected this location because it was at the mouth of the *Río Chagres*. The fort withstood many attacks by the English, until the pirate, Henry Morgan, captured it in 1671. Then he crossed the isthmus to attack *Panamá Viejo*—Old Panamá."

As if on cue, they rounded a bend and the ruins of the stone fortress lay before them. Andrea parked the car under a tree, and they got out. An old blue Volkswagen van was the only other vehicle in sight.

They paused, taking in the remote site. Shrill cries from soaring gulls pierced the buffeting wind coming from the sea. Hank withdrew his camera and took several pictures. Then they walked toward the mottled stone ruins. The saw grass along the edge of the pathway was knee-high, and Hank kept an eye out for snakes or other creatures.

They approached the outer perimeter of the ruins, and Andrea pointed to an arched doorway. Hank followed her into a dank chamber. Moss clung to the walls, and moisture covered the floor. "This was—" Andrea began, but was interrupted by the sudden commencement of loud music.

"What the hell's that?" Hank said.

They hurried through the chamber and emerged in a grassy clearing. On the level above, they saw five musicians, apparently playing for their own enjoyment. Hank and Andrea continued across the clearing to a stone rampart that overlooked the sea. They leaned against the parapet and listened to the joyful rhythm of the drums, gourds, and guitar.

"Reminds me of Carnival," Hank said.

Andrea nodded. "Congo music."

"Did you go to the parades when you were a kid?"

She turned to him with a companionable smile. "I still do." The breeze blew her hair away from her face.

Hank returned her smile. How lovely she looked. Then, remembering the slap in Portobelo, he pushed the perilous thought from his mind. He gazed out to sea and tried to imagine what it would have been like to have been a Spanish sentry, scanning the horizon for British pirates. He looked over his left shoulder, to where the *Rio Chagres* flowed down from Gatun Lake. He tried to envision the buccaneer captain, Henry Morgan, after capturing Fort San Lorenzo, striking out across the uncharted isthmus to attack Panama City.

Hank turned and looked down at Andrea. She was silently

studying him. Instinctively, he leaned down and pressed his lips against hers. She parted her mouth slightly, not pulling away. Finally, they separated. She looked up at him with a winsome smile and gave a slow shake of her head, as if amused with herself. Hank leaned down again, but this time she stepped back. "Come, Mr. Duque, there is much to see here."

8. EL CIMARRON

I come not hither to hear lamentations and cries,
but to see gold!
—English pirate, Henry Morgan

January 1671

"Diego, wake up," the elderly San Blas woman said in her tongue, as she shook his muscled black shoulder.

Diego lay naked on his side. He had slept but a short time since arriving back in the village, after several wakeful days of hunting in the jungle. Now he reluctantly allowed consciousness to return. He rolled over on the woven mat and pulled his tall frame into a sitting position. The rays of first light penetrated the walls of the thatched hut.

The wrinkled woman kneeling next to him was the mother of his deceased wife. She started to speak again, but Diego put two fingers across her mouth to silence her. In the distance, he heard the sound of unusual thunder. The diminutive woman, her dark eyes open wide, nodded.

Diego stood up and walked unsteadily across the packed dirt floor. He stopped at the open doorway and listened again to the irregular thumps. It had been several years since he had heard cannon fire coming from the fort the Spaniards called San Lorenzo.

Although it would take him half a day to reach the site of the conflict, Diego knew he must go there. He didn't know who was attacking the fort, but if anyone was killing Spaniards, he wanted to be a part of it.

It was late afternoon, and Diego perched high on the bough of a giant mahogany tree, clad in a loincloth and armed with a spear and a machete. The river the Spanish called *Río Chagres* passed sluggishly beneath him. Dense jungle pressed down to the water's edge, and mangroves then extended out to snare the unwary.

In the distance, smoke rose from the stone towers of Fort San Lorenzo, but the cannons were now silent. Below, five large boats and thirty canoes struggled upriver, carrying more than a thousand white invaders.

Diego stayed out of sight and watched, as the ragtag armada noisily negotiated the stream and as the waterside inhabitants—the alligators, the herons, and the monkeys—retreated from the clamor. Could it be, Diego wondered, that these invaders now planned to cross the isthmus and sack the Spanish city of Panamá?

The lead canoe, carrying four men, veered from the irregular line of boats and headed toward the tree where Diego was perched. For a moment Diego thought he had been seen, but then he spied a large, slow-moving monkey that apparently had drawn the invaders' interest. The canoe rammed into the waiting mangroves, which opened momentarily, then closed behind them, swallowing them like a hungry boa. A large branch struck a man seated at the bow, and the small boat rocked erratically. A man at the stern stood, and the canoe capsized.

A roar of laughter went up from the hundreds of invaders who watched from midstream. Then an anguished wail silenced them. One of the men in the mangroves had waded onto an enormous submerged alligator. The creature had the flailing man's midsection clamped between its powerful jaws. The ancient reptile threw back its head and lifted its prey, as if displaying it, then plunged into the water, abruptly cutting off the man's tortured scream.

A second canoe raced toward the mangroves. Its crew fired their muskets at the area where the alligator had last been seen. An errant shot hit a man in the water. He thrashed about, and another alligator attacked him. This creature didn't dive, but raced through the mangroves and into the jungle, with its prey screaming in agony.

The two terrified survivors made their way to the relief canoe. They were pulled on board, and the small boat retreated from the mangroves and rejoined the others in midstream. An eerie quiet settled over the river, as the invaders gazed over the gunwales at the enigmatic jungle, discerning for the first time the green hell into which they had entered. Then they turned away, and the procession resumed its dogged trek upriver.

Like the Spaniards, Diego surmised, these invaders also must be in search of gold. The stupidity of whites appalled him. Why, he wondered, are they driven to steal beautiful ornaments, only to melt them into ugly bars? Then he gave a tight smile, remembering an incident when a small contingent of Spaniards had tried to loot his village. After the battle, the Indians had held down the sole Spanish survivor and had poured molten gold down his throat. At least one Spaniard's thirst for gold had been quenched.

Diego's hatred for Spaniards had been forged during his father's lifetime, and tempered during his own. His father and mother had been *Africanos*, kidnaped and brought to this forbidding land by Spaniards. Diego had been born a slave in Panamá; he had been named by his Spanish master. When he was twelve, his mother had died in captivity. Shortly after her death, his father had awakened him one night, and the two had escaped into the jungle.

They had begun the long trek across the isthmus, hoping somehow to return to his father's native land. After several days, they had happened upon a remote Indian village. The night of their arrival, Diego's father had fallen victim to the jungle's mysterious vapors. Three days later he had died in a sweat-soaked delirium. Diego also had become deathly ill; but he had survived, and now was immune. That had been nearly ten years ago. The Indians had accepted the black youth into their community. He had learned to speak their tongue, but he still formed his thoughts in the pidgin Spanish he had been taught as a child. These Indians were the remnants of a jungle tribe the Spaniards had decimated for generations. They had once been known as the Wild Boars.

Diego stood on a forested knoll, hidden by dense underbrush and late afternoon shadows. He had stalked the invaders for days, using the skills he had learned tracking jungle prey, moving stealthily along the dense river shoreline and remaining just out of sight.

Even from a distance, Diego could tell that the white men were nearly spent. It was the dry season; two days earlier they had been forced to abandon their boats and proceed on foot. As they trudged along the dry river bed, they glanced fearfully at the nearby jungle. The only supplies they carried with them were their weapons and ammunition. When the wind shifted, Diego could smell the powder and wadding they used in their muskets. They had been without food since leaving their boats, yet apparently were afraid to enter the jungle to hunt. And now as they approached, they shouted orders and curses at each other, unwittingly driving off the nearby game that would have fed them.

Behind Diego lay the smoldering ruins of a village. Its Spanish inhabitants had evidently learned of the invaders' approach and had fled after setting fire to their wooden houses. Only a large stone building remained intact.

One invader pointed toward the village, apparently having seen the faint wisps of smoke. The entire contingent broke from their irregular ranks and charged up the creek bed.

Diego looked about. Near the stone building stood a wall of dense jungle, unscathed by fire. He ran over and concealed himself in the undergrowth. Moments later, the men flooded through the razed village and began a frantic search for food. Their curses grew loud when they realized the fleeing inhabitants had destroyed everything they couldn't carry off.

Five scavengers captured a stray dog that had taken refuge in the stone building. While one slit the wretched animal's throat and hacked it into pieces, his companions fanned a smoldering fire. Then they devoured the charred pieces of dog meat.

Shouts of rage and disappointment reverberated throughout the village, as hundreds of starving men continued their futile search for food. Thirty or more burst from the stone building, carrying empty leather provision bags. Diego watched as they cut the tough leather into small strips, then boiled and roasted the pieces over an open fire. They ate ravenously, washing down their feast with large gulps of water.

As night fell, the group that had devoured the provision bags came across two jars of wine that the villagers had left behind. For a short while, they carried on with drunken hilarity, but soon the fermented drink mixed with the undigested leather, and their laughter was replaced by moaning and vomiting.

Finally the village quieted, and Diego moved deeper into the jungle. He climbed onto a low hanging bough and allowed himself a nap.

Agitated voices awakened him. He cautiously moved back to the edge of the clearing and peered through the branches and vines. Someone had rekindled a fire; shadows flickered eerily off the stone building. Four older men were tormenting a younger member of the invading party. The youth cowered and pleaded. Diego understood the young man's terror; it was not the first time Diego had seen the countenance of cannibals.

Then another man stalked into the flickering light, shouting at the four predators. They drew back from their prey. Diego surmised that the new arrival was their leader. They spoke to him in their foreign tongue with a tone of respect, addressing him with a word that sounded similar to the Spanish title, *capitán*. Finally the leader withdrew, taking the youth with him. Diego returned to his tree bough.

An agonized scream awoke Diego at dawn. He lowered himself

from the tree and crept back to the edge of the clearing. The captain had returned. With arms crossed, he stood watching, as three of his men drove long thorns under the fingernails of another.

The victim pleaded hysterically with his torturers in their tongue. Then in desperation, he begged in Spanish for God to help him. *"¡Dios, ayúdame! ¡Por favor, ayúdame!"*

The captain demanded something of him.

"¡No sé, Capitán! ¡No sé dónde est la ciudad!" the man continued in Spanish, indicating that he didn't know where the city was. The captain slapped him across the face, and the man resumed his pleading in the foreign tongue.

Diego shook his head. Apparently these fools had taken a Spaniard as their guide, who didn't know the way to Panamá. The captain gestured for the torture to resume, and again the victim cried out in agony. Diego pushed aside the branches and vines. *"¡Párate!"* he shouted.

The startled inquisitors and their victim all turned at the sound of Diego's voice. He saw their fear of the jungle in their expressions. And he was part of the jungle.

Diego took one step into the clearing, allowing the invaders to see him. He flexed his knees slightly, ready to leap back at the first threatening movement. *"¿Hablas español?"* he said, asking if anyone spoke Spanish.

"Only I," the victim whimpered in Spanish.

"Who are these men?" Diego demanded.

"They are English pirates. They took me prisoner at Fort San Lorenzo, because I could speak their tongue. Now they are making me lead them to Panamá. But the Río Chagres has turned . . . and I am lost."

The captain said something to the Spaniard, who quickly translated. "Captain Morgan wants to know who you are and what you want."

"Tell him my name is Diego . . . and what I want is . . . to see dead Spaniards. Tell him!"

The Spaniard hesitated, then translated Diego's words into

English.

A look of amusement crossed the English captain's face. He said something to the Spaniard, who translated, "He wants to know if you are a '*cimarrón*'."

"Yes," Diego said. The word meant 'wild'; it was what the Spaniards called runaway slaves.

Captain Morgan spoke again, and the Spaniard translated. "Can you lead them to Panamá?"

"Yes."

"How far is it?" the captain asked through the interpreter.

"Two days."

"Which direction?"

"You must follow me," Diego said, "or you will get lost."

The captain hesitated, then said, "All right, you will be our guide. Now, join us here. No harm will come to you."

"No," Diego said. He pointed to the grassy summit of an isolated hill, off in the distance. "Remain here in the village, until you see smoke come from there. Then follow me. If you get too close, I will hide in the jungle and leave you to die."

After receiving the translation, Captain Morgan gazed thoughtfully at Diego, then nodded in agreement.

Diego turned and started into the jungle.

"Wait!" the captain called after him.

Diego stopped and returned to the edge of the clearing.

"We need food!" the captain said.

"There will be food for you in Panamá," Diego replied, then vanished into the jungle. Behind him, he heard an abbreviated scream, as the Englishmen slit the wretched Spaniard's throat.

Two days later, Diego clambered up the backside of a wooded knoll. He knew he was close to the end of the journey; the air smelled of salt, and sea gulls circled lazily overhead.

When he reached the crest, he stopped and gazed out at the panorama before him. Immediately in the foreground lay a broad savanna, its tall grass undulating in the morning ocean breeze. A herd of cattle grazed on the peaceful grassland, and several black herdsmen lounged under a tree near the ocean. On the other side of the savanna, lay the city of Panamá.

Diego felt an unfamiliar pressure in his throat, as he recognized the familiar square tower of the great cathedral, looming over the spires and tiled roofs of the vast city. A childhood memory came back to him. A side door of the cathedral had once been left ajar, and he and another slave child had sneaked a look inside. Diego vividly recalled the magnificent interior, lighted with countless candles. Huge paintings had hung on the side wall, and at one end had stood a dazzling altar, made of what he now knew to be gold. And above the altar had been a statue of a white man being tortured on a cross. Diego had hoped the man was a Spaniard.

Diego thought of his mother. It bothered him that he could no longer remember her face. He wondered what his life would have been like, had she not died. His father would probably still be alive, but they would all be slaves. Diego brusquely drove these thoughts from his mind. It mattered not; he had returned as a cimarrón, and one thousand starving Englishmen followed close behind.

The snap of a twig broke his reverie. He whirled, spear at the ready. Three mulattoes approached: an elderly dark man, who walked with a pronounced limp, flanked by two lighter-skinned youths. The three wore tattered clothes and apparently were herdsmen. Diego feinted with his spear, signaling them to stop. However, the old man gave a tired smile and continued forward, and the boys followed.

"*¿Hablas español?*" the old man said as he approached, inquiring if Diego spoke Spanish.

"*Sí,*" Diego said, his spear still poised.

"We mean you no harm," the old man continued in Spanish, stopping in front of him.

Diego snorted at the notion that these mulattoes might harm him. He moved his free hand, so it rested on the handle of the machete that hung from his loincloth.

"Are you a cimarrón?" the old man said.

Diego nodded, and the two youths tensed, as if preparing to

run.

"Have you been to our city before?" the old man said.

"I was born there. My father took me away when I was a boy."

"Come with us then. We are going home now. You can spend the night with us."

Diego lowered his spear, but shook his head. He had no intention of mingling with these mixed breeds. And yet, something about them, perhaps their meekness, again made him think of his mother.

The old man shrugged, and the three passed by Diego and started down the knoll in the direction of the city. Diego momentarily was concerned that they would alert others to his presence, but then decided it was of no consequence. The Englishmen would be here shortly.

At the bottom of the knoll, the three herdsmen rounded up five fat cows, then started across the savanna. For the first time, Diego had doubts about having led the invaders to the city. He had not considered the fate of the dark-skinned people, who also lived within the city.

"*¡Abuelo!*" he called down the knoll, respectfully addressing the elderly mulatto as "grandfather".

The old man stopped and looked back.

"Stay outside the city tomorrow!" Diego shouted.

The old man gazed at Diego for a moment, then nodded and limped off after the others.

It was midday before the English invaders caught up with Diego. They trudged up the back of the knoll, starved and footsore, having lost even the strength to curse and argue with one another.

Captain Morgan spied Diego and angrily strode through his plodding troops to get to him. Then the captain saw the panorama before him. As his starving band crested the knoll, they noticed not Diego, the city, nor the ocean, but only the cattle. With raucous whoops, they ran full tilt down the knoll toward the

docile beasts. The herdsmen lounging by the ocean saw the swarming invaders and fled toward the city, leaving their animals behind.

A slaughter followed, as the pirates rounded up frightened
animals and hacked them into gobbets. Some built fires and attempted to cook the fresh meat, but most impatiently ate it raw.
Cattle gore soaked the pirates' filthy beards. Diego remained in
the grove at the top of the knoll, watching the nauseating feast
defile the pastoral savanna.

When they had filled their gullets, the cutthroats lolled about
the hillside, singing and shouting with great hilarity. One satiated
lout stood up and shouted something, and three loud cheers went
up, as if the battle for Panama were already over.

Diego was awake at dawn the next morning. On the long grassy
slope in front of him, the English officers mustered their troops.
The pirates were in good spirits, as they gnawed the cold remains
of the previous day's slaughter and boisterously shouted back and
forth to each other.

Until this moment, Diego had assumed the English would
prevail, since the Spaniards usually fled when challenged. However, having seen the pirates' stupidity and lack of discipline, he
now reconsidered. And there was another factor: the pirates would
merely be fighting for gold, while the Spaniards would be defend-
ing their families and homes. That should inspire even the most
cowardly Spaniard.

Diego tried to reassure himself that it made no difference who
prevailed, since white men would be killing white men. Again,
however, he felt a pang of concern for the nonwhites in the city.

Captain Morgan appeared at the top of the knoll. The English
rabble quieted. He shouted a command that carried down the
hillside, and the invaders eagerly formed into four companies.

Diego gazed across the savanna and saw an approximately equal
number of Spanish infantry, forming ranks in front of the city.
They spread out across the savanna. Then four squadrons of horse-

men trotted out of the city and took positions on either flank. For the first time, a murmur of concern passed among the invaders on the hillside.

Occasionally, the sun glinted off a Spaniard's helmet or breast-plate. However, many of the defenders wore no armor; those without protection appeared to be men of color. The city of Panamá had neither walls nor cannons. The Spaniards would have to defend their city from the savanna.

Captain Morgan gave a command that was echoed by his four lieutenants, and the invaders began their advance. The Spanish defenders responded by sending forth their horsemen, followed closely by their infantry. The English vanguard company wheeled to the left and vanished into a stand of trees. For a moment, it appeared they had turned tail. When they reemerged, however, they were positioned so that the morning sun and wind were in the defenders' eyes.

Across the savanna, a shrill horn sounded and the Spanish horsemen broke into a full gallop. Their exultant shouts of *"¡Viva el Rey!"* carried to the hillside. When the horsemen reached the middle of the savanna, they slowed, as if bogged down in the marshy loam. Then came the roar of the English vanguard's muskets, and more than a hundred Spanish horsemen went down. The terrified survivors wheeled and fled to the city, leaving their infantry unprotected.

As the horsemen retreated, black herdsmen stampeded hundreds of bulls and oxen toward the invaders' main body. The pirates opened fire; their first volley killed or wounded at least half the animals and scattered the remainder across the savanna and into the nearby hills.

The Spanish infantry halted in the middle of the savanna. They were close enough that Diego could see that only the white defenders had muskets; the mestizos, blacks, and Indians were armed with halberds, lances, and bows. The Spanish commander ordered his men into their firing positions. Diego saw smoke pour from their muskets, and a moment later heard the roar. There was a pause, then raucous laughter swelled across the hillside; the shots from the Spaniards' antique arquebuses had fallen far short of their targets.

Then at Captain Morgan's command, all four English companies opened fire on the helpless Spanish contingent. One long volley was enough; most of the Spaniards who survived threw down their arms and ran. The Spanish commanders tried to stop their flight by shooting at the deserters, but moments later, the commanders also turned and fled.

The pirates raced headlong after the fleeing Spaniards, slashing the laggards with their cutlasses. They overtook several slow-running monks and showed them no more mercy than they had shown the docile cattle the previous day.

Suddenly there was an earthshaking explosion, and dark smoke billowed into the air near the great cathedral. Fires sprang up nearby. The Spaniards were destroying their city, rather than relinquish it to the English.

Standing alone on the hillside, Diego watched as the crazed invaders raced headlong into the burning city. On the savanna before him, hundreds of defenders lay dead and dying. The agonies of wounded animals drowned out the agonies of dying men.

Early the following morning, Diego threaded his way through the hundreds of corpses that still littered the savanna. The English had not allowed the families of the slain defenders to collect the remains. Vultures fluttered from corpse to corpse, indiscriminately devouring both man and animal.

As Diego approached the outskirts of the city, he noted that the wooden shacks in the mulatto and mestizo areas were still standing. Toward the center of the city, however, the stately homes of the pure-blooded Spaniards had been destroyed; all that remained were the smoldering remnants of walls. Off to the right, where Diego remembered the Spanish militia had been quartered, the area was leveled. The explosion the previous day had apparently been caused by the retreating Spaniards igniting their gunpowder supply.

Diego started down one of the dusty paths that wound through the ramshackle outskirts. There were no invaders in sight, yet the mulatto and mestizo men of the neighborhood had a beaten look. They stole curious glances at him, and at his weapons, but immediately turned away when he fixed them in his resolute gaze. He heard respectful whispers of *"cimarrón"*.

Then he heard the word shouted aloud. The old herdsman he had encountered the day before stood in the doorway of a dilapidated shack.

Diego stopped. *"Hola, Abuelo."*

"Hola, Nieto," the old man replied, as if greeting a grandson. "Come here," he continued in Spanish.

Diego walked over to the shack, then followed the old man inside. Morning sun streamed through an open window, lighting the single room. A lovely mulatto sat on a mat in the far corner, her legs drawn up under her. She was light-skinned, like the two boys who had accompanied the old man the previous day. Her cheerful red and yellow frock contrasted with the sullen expression on her face.

"What is your name, cimarrón?" the old man said.

"I am Diego."

"I am called Pepe," the old man said. "And this is my granddaughter, Mariposa."

Diego nodded to the young woman. Her name meant "butterfly"; however, scowling up at her grandfather, she reminded Diego more of a coiled scorpion.

The old man said, "Mariposa, fix Diego something to eat."

She gave her grandfather a sullen look, but got to her feet.

"I have already eaten," Diego said.

"Ah, yes," the old man replied, "the cattle on the hillside."

Diego shook his head. "I do not eat with white men."

The old man smiled, then turned serious. "Why have you returned to Panamá, Diego?"

"To see dead Spaniards."

"Well," the old man said with a sigh, "there are plenty of those here."

Diego turned back to the young woman, who now seemed to include him in her hostility. He was unaccustomed to such insolence from women. "What is the matter with you?" he demanded.

The old man quickly interceded. "I have told her she must remain here, hiding, until the Englishmen leave. They are now in the Spanish part of the city, robbing and raping. Although Mariposa is not white, she is comely and they will want her."

"They cannot be worse than the Spaniards!" she said.

"These Englishmen are worse than animals," Diego said.

"You are all cowards," the young woman retorted. "You call yourselves men, yet now you hide here from the English . . . like you hid from the Spanish." With that, she bolted through the open door, before her lame grandfather could stop her.

The old man looked at Diego with profound sorrow and tried to explain. "The Spaniards . . . mistreated her . . . and her mother before her." He was unable to continue.

"She should not be out there," Diego said.

The old man nodded and limped toward the door. Diego intercepted him, placing a hand on his shoulder. "Stay here, don Pepe. I will bring her back."

The old man responded with a look of gratitude.

Diego stepped outside the shack and was confronted by the two youths from the hillside. He asked them, "Do you know Mariposa?"

"She is our sister," the older answered.

"Which way did she go?"

Neither boy replied.

The old man limped through the doorway. "Tell him where she has gone. He is going to bring her back."

The older boy pointed in the general direction of the great cathedral, and the younger boy said, "We will go with you, cimarrón."

"No," Diego said. "Wait here with your grandfather." He turned and strode down the dusty pathway.

When he neared the center of town, he heard the exuberant shouts of the tormentors and the piteous wails of the tormented. He came upon the charred ruins of what had been a lavish Spanish home. Two pirates held a kneeling Spaniard, and two others pried out stones from the floor immediately in front of him. Blood covered the victim's head, and one arm hung awkwardly, as if it had just been broken. With a shout of glee, one of the digging pirates reached down and pulled out a leather sack. He turned it upside down, and gold pieces-of-eight showered across the floor.

As one of the pirates scurried after a rolling coin, he looked up, saw Diego, and drew his cutlass. Diego brought his spear to the ready. Two of the other pirates shouted something in English, and their comrade lowered his cutlass. The others apparently had recognized Diego from the trail.

The pirate retrieved the loose coin and gave Diego a grudging nod. Then he walked back to where the victim still knelt and placed the tip of his cutlass against the man's throat. In Spanish, the terrified homeowner tried to divulge the location of his neighbor's hidden valuables. But the pirate couldn't understand him, and killed the pleading man with a slow thrust through the neck. As Diego walked on, the four pirates excitedly divided their spoils.

Barbaric turmoil reverberated throughout the center of the city, as drunken pirates marauded unimpeded. Spanish men were being tortured to make them divulge the whereabouts of their valuables. Diego saw pirates tearing apart the remains of floors and walls, and even climbing down water wells, looking for plunder. And from secluded corners came the piteous pleas of Spanish women.

Apparently, the fighting men of the city had been slain or subjugated; the cowards had fled the previous day. Amid this chaos, Diego wondered if he would be able to find the willful Mariposa.

He continued on toward the great cathedral. Its massive stone walls had withstood the explosion and fire. As he approached, he saw Captain Morgan emerge from the front door, followed by an aide, who led a pale Spanish woman by the arm. The captain stopped short at the sight of Diego. He gazed at him for a moment, then reaching back, he grasped the young woman's arm and pulled her forward, as if offering her to Diego. The woman fixed her blank stare on the ground in front of her. Diego shook his head, and the captain responded with an amused look. He said something to his aide, who turned and walked away. Captain Morgan gave Diego a curt nod, then led the woman down the street.

Diego strode up the stone stairs and into the stately cathedral, which had been closed to him as a boy. This time, however, there were no lighted candles, and the paintings and the statue of the tortured white man had been removed. The priests also were missing; the only person in the room was an old nun, kneeling at the front of the church. Diego surmised that the rest of the clergy must have fled with their riches when they heard the invaders were coming.

Diego walked up the center aisle and stopped near the altar. The old nun's eyes were closed and she mumbled incantations, as her bony white fingers fluttered over a string of shiny black beads. She reminded Diego of the vultures on the savanna.

Diego looked up and frowned. The dazzling golden altar he remembered from his childhood was gone. The existing one was formed from a primitive, dark material. Then Diego smiled. Apparently the golden altar had been too heavy to move, and the clergy had camouflaged it with a dark coating, perhaps mud from the savanna. He extended the tip of his spear to scratch the surface. The nun gasped. Diego looked back; the old woman's face was drawn in anguish. He thought of the Spaniards in the city, who would willingly divulge the locations of their neighbors' valuables, but would not reveal the existence of this religious relic, which might completely satisfy the invaders. Diego was unable to comprehend the values of whites; nevertheless, he turned and walked from the cathedral, leaving the old nun with her secret.

He descended the cathedral stairway. Down the street, lay the compound that had previously housed the Spanish militia. In front of it, he saw several young dark-skinned women, mingling with a group of pirates. He wondered if that had been Mariposa's destination.

As he approached the compound, he continued to draw stares. However, most pirates recognized him, and no one challenged him. He heard a man cry out in anguish from within a stone building. When Diego had been a boy, he had been told about a torture device kept there, known as the rack. The Spaniards had used it to subjugate slaves and other men of color. Now, the English were using it on the Spaniards.

Diego entered a large courtyard. He remembered how slaves had always kept it green and trimmed. Now fire had burned it black, and two mutilated Spanish corpses hung from a tree.

Diego heard muffled voices coming from the ruins of a nearby stone building. He crossed the courtyard and stepped through a breach in the wall. In the far corner, he saw three men grappling with a woman; two held her down, the third was astride her. Diego recognized the red and yellow frock that had been pulled up and used to muffle the woman's screams.

He crossed the room in three strides. Only the pirate holding Mariposa's left arm saw him coming. As the man started to rise, Diego drove his spear into the center of his chest, lodging it deep in his spine. The rapist withdrew from Mariposa and tried to stand, his pantaloons about his ankles. Diego struck him across the eyes with his machete, splitting the man's skull. The third pirate bolted from the room.

Mariposa leaped to her feet, her face livid with rage and humiliation. Diego grabbed her arm and pulled her toward a breach in the rear wall. Mariposa broke away and ran back to the impaled corpse. She struggled with the spear, then finally dislodged it from the pirate's spine.

Diego hurried back to her. "Come, Mariposa!"

She turned toward the other end of the building, where the third pirate had escaped.

Diego blocked her path. "Come!" he demanded, but warily kept an eye on the spear in her hand.

Voices rose in the nearby courtyard. Finally, Mariposa turned, and they raced headlong for the safety of the nearby jungle.

Diego had been gone from their campsite all morning. He returned to find Mariposa lying naked on a woven mat. She was drying off in the sun, after bathing in the stream that ran beside their lean-to. She drowsily opened her eyes and gave him a trace of a smile, then closed her eyes again.

Diego stood watching her for some time, putting off the inevitable. Finally he said, "The English are leaving." The occupation of Panamá, which had lasted twenty-six days, at last was over.

Mariposa sat up. "They are leaving?"

Diego nodded.

She jumped up, grabbed her still-damp clothes off a nearby bush, and hurriedly began to dress. "Will you come back with me?" she said.

"Back to being a slave?" he said contemptuously.

"The days of slavery are over, Diego. The Spanish have been beaten down. Never again will they be able to rule as they have."

"Come live with me in my village," Diego said.

"I have told you, no. I am not an Indian."

"Then let us stay here. I will build a hut for us."

"We have spoken about this, Diego. I am not a cimarrón either. I cannot live in the bush."

"You are probably carrying my child," he said morosely.

She looked at him with a tender expression he had never seen before. "No doubt," she said. Then the tenderness was gone. "If you are not coming with me, at least show me the way back to the city."

Diego nodded mutely, and Mariposa collected her meager possessions.

A short while later, Diego and Mariposa stood under a shade tree near the grassy summit of an isolated hill. Above them, a scarlet flag flapped in the breeze. The British had left it, like pumas, shitting to mark their territory. Their caravan passed below: one thousand cutthroats, six hundred Spanish hostages, and two hundred mules, heavily laden with plunder. The faint tinkle of mule bells drifted up the hill.

"Will you go back with them?" Mariposa said.

"No," Diego said. "You and I will go directly to my village."

She shook her head. "I must return home." She shifted her gaze to the expanse of jungle that lay between her and her ravaged city. "Will you give me your machete for protection?" When he didn't respond, she turned and withdrew it from his loincloth.

He grasped her free wrist. "Come with me to my village!" he demanded, pulling her to him.

She pressed the sharp point of the machete against his taut stomach, then gazed into his eyes, poised, ready to rip into his organs with his next move.

Such insolence from a woman! Diego thought. But aloud he said, "All right then, we will go this way." And he led her down the hill, toward the city of Panamá.

9. NORIEGA

Hank sat in the hotel's rooftop bar, gazing out at the grassy summit of Ancon Hill. The sounds from the early afternoon traffic drifted up from the street. He glanced to his left and saw Joe Ortega, the Associated Press journalist, approaching from the elevator. The two men shook hands, and Ortega took the stool beside him. The bartender came over.

Hank said, "Can I buy you a drink?"

Ortega checked his watch. "Yeah, I've got time for one." He glanced at Hank's bottle of Balboa, but ordered a Budweiser. "How'd you like our use of your pictures and description?"

"I haven't seen it. I've been over on the Caribbean side the past couple of days. Just got back about an hour ago."

Ortega handed Hank a white envelope. "You got the byline. I translated your report into Spanish, and we ran it in both languages in the States. *La Prensa* picked it up locally."

"*La Prensa?*"

"It's the only independent press in the country. I don't know how they keep going. Noriega's busted up their office and thrown their reporters in jail a couple of times, but they won't back down."

Hank opened the envelope. $1,200!

"That okay?" Ortega said.

"Yeah, that's fine," Hank replied, masking his elation. He slipped the windfall into his wallet.

The bartender returned with Ortega's beer. Ortega took a long swallow, then said, "César Ruíz is out of the country, otherwise he'd have met with you himself. He says, if you can provide us with this quality of material in the future, we'll take you on as an AP stringer."

Hank's casual nod belied his excitement. The $1,200 for one day's work was nearly half what his friend in Houston was paying him to write a 10,000-word travel piece.

"Do you have anything new?" Ortega said.

Hank picked up a folded packet of paper off the counter. "Yesterday in Portobelo, I had a run-in with some thugs called *Los Machos del Monte.* Have you heard of them?"

Ortega nodded. "They're an elite force that spends most of its time in the interior, intimidating the *campesinos.* I saw a T.V. clip a few months ago that showed them drinking blood in their initiation ceremony. They're crazy sons of bitches."

Hank handed Ortega the packet. "They terrorized my guide's family, day before yesterday." "This is an account of what happened. No chance for pictures this time."

"Okay, we'll take a look at it. Anything else?"

"I'm trying to come up with something on Noriega."

"Noriega?"

"Yeah. Apparently, he's in the middle of everything of interest down here."

Ortega nodded.

Hank said, "Do you think he's on the U.S. payroll?"

Ortega took another long swallow from his beer. "There's never been any concrete evidence. The closest anyone's come was the Iran-Contra scandal a couple of years ago. The congressional hearings proved Noriega worked for Oliver North, funneling arms into Nicaragua."

"Yeah," Hank said, "but Reagan and Bush stonewalled. They claimed North was a loose cannon, who dreamed up the scheme on his own."

Ortega nodded.

"How about the CIA?" Hank said. "Do you think Noriega's been in bed with them . . . maybe even now?"

"Have you heard something?"

"Just an offhand comment by one of the locals."

Ortega gave a short laugh. "Panamanians suspect *everybody* of working for the CIA."

"So I've discovered. A PDF officer named Mejías harassed me the day I landed. He accused me of being with the CIA, even confiscated my passport for a few hours."

"Major Carlos Mejías?"

"Yeah. Know him?"

"I know enough to stay away from him. He's Noriega's protégé. Works in the PDF's G-2 section. That's where Noriega got his start—doing intelligence work for Omar Torrijos."

"Suppose it's true," Hank pressed, "that Noriega's on the CIA payroll."

"If you could prove it," Ortega said, "you'd definitely have a story. We'd certainly pay a lot for it. Linking Noriega directly to the CIA would be tough, though. The locals, those who could actually verify it, are scared shitless of him."

"He's that dangerous?"

"He's that dangerous," Ortega said. "I interviewed him recently. They'd just opened the Atlapa Convention Center, and he was interested in promoting tourism." Ortega drained the last of his beer, then stood up to leave. "Noriega's one scary son of a bitch. I wouldn't want him pissed off at me."

Back in his room, Hank placed a telephone call to Houston. There was the hollow echo of switches being thrown on the international line, then a familiar voice said, "Bob Westlake."

"Bob, this is Hank."

"Hey, man. When did you get in?"

"I'm not back yet. I'm calling from Panama. I wanted to let you know that I'll be down here a little longer than I'd planned."

"Having some problems?"

"No, the piece is going fine," Hank lied. Although he had several photographs he could use, he hadn't even started the narrative.

"Good," Westlake said. "I just got back from Belize, yesterday, and I'll be going to Guatemala the week after next."

"How was Belize?"

"Interesting, but primitive. The country's so small that I was even able to get an interview with the prime minister, George Price."

Westlake talked on about Belize, but Hank's mind was elsewhere. The comment about interviewing the Belizean prime minister had given him an idea.

Finally, Westlake said, "Okay, Hank, give me a call when you get back in town."

"Will do, Bob," Hank said, then hung up.

He sat on the edge of the bed for a moment. The window air-conditioner struggled against the afternoon heat. The bearings sounded loose. He looked up at the mildew-stained ceiling. Twelve hundred dollars and only a possibility of selling other articles. Did it make sense staying on in Panama for that? Probably not. Then he smiled, remembering Andrea's response to his kiss that morning at the Fort San Lorenzo ruins. He picked the telephone book and looked up the number of the American Embassy.

Later that afternoon, Andrea pulled up in front of the hotel, driving the van that had been vandalized by the Dobermans. The shattered windshield had been replaced, but the dents remained.

"You look very happy," she said as Hank climbed into the passenger seat.

"I am. After we tour the *Panama Viejo* ruins, can I take you to dinner to celebrate?"

"Celebrate what?" she said as they pulled away from the hotel.

"The start of a new career, hopefully."

"Oh, yes?"

"I'll give you the details at dinner. Can you make it?"

"You are being very mysterious," she said with an amused smile. "I can make it, if we eat early. The new semester begins tonight, and I have a class at eight o'clock."

"We'll eat early."

A few minutes later, they turned onto *Avenida Porras*, and Andrea said, "Have you been to *Panama Viejo* before, Mr. Duque?"

"I rode my bike out there a few times when I was a kid," he said. Then he added, "Andrea, would you please call me Hank?"

She suppressed a smile.

"Just try it," he coaxed, "one time."

"You are a customer."

"We're friends," he said. *"Amigos."*

She smiled, but didn't reply.

"We're comrades," he said. "Together, we've now fought the PDF on both coasts."

Andrea laughed. *"Bueno* . . . Hank," she said at last.

Hank thought how pretty she looked. Damn, what a good day!

"Yes?" she said, sensing his gaze and raising her eyebrows inquiringly.

Hank just smiled and shifted his attention to the passing scene. "I remember that golf course. Grandpa took me there once."

"You and your grandfather did a lot together."

"Yes, we did. My grandfather and I were close. He was more like a father to me, after mine died." Hank pulled the map out of his camera case. "This area's known as *San Francisco*, isn't it?"

"Yes."

"Where the rich folks live?"

"Some of them. Many prefer penthouses in the banking district."

"I understand General Noriega lives out here."

"He has a house for his wife and daughter, right over there," she said, pointing toward a fashionable residential neighborhood.

Down the shaded side street, high walls and wrought-iron gates secured large estates. Hank circled *Calle 78* on his map.

Andrea continued, "He also has an apartment in the city where his mistress lives."

"Busy man," Hank mused.

They turned onto a winding oceanfront street, and the estates gave way to smaller stucco homes. Then a few blocks farther, they entered a jumble of shanties, thrown together from scrap wood and rusty corrugated iron.

"I don't remember this neighborhood," Hank said.

"It is dangerous here," Andrea said.

Where wasn't it? Hank thought. Ahead stood the familiar square tower of the great cathedral, looming over the three-hundred-year-old ruins of the once vast city. "Give me the spiel you give the tourists."

"*Panama Viejo* originally was an Indian fishing village," Andrea began. "Then in the early 16th Century, the Spanish settled here. They named it *Panamá* which, as you know, meant 'many fish'. For 150 years it was the center of the New World in Central America. Then in 1671, the English pirate, Henry Morgan, crossed the isthmus and destroyed the city. All that remains now are the ruins of the stone buildings."

They pulled up in front of the cathedral tower and climbed out of the van. "Stand over there in the doorway, while I take some pictures."

"No, Mr. Duque . . . Hank," she protested.

"C'mon. I need people in my pictures."

Reluctantly, she complied.

Hank took several shots of the cathedral and the remnants of the stone structures around it. Then they went into the tower. Hank stopped and stared at the remains of a spiral stone staircase.

"Do you see something?" Andrea said.

"A flashback. You know how sometimes you have sharp recollections of the past? This is one of mine. I clearly remember these stairs, from when I was a kid."

She smiled.

They left the tower and entered an enclosed area. Andrea said, "This was the main part of the church." The afternoon sun was setting, and Hank snapped some final pictures. "Do you know the story of the Golden Altar?" she said.

"No. Or if I ever did, I've forgotten it."

"When the Spaniards learned that Captain Morgan was coming to attack the city, they hid their riches. This cathedral had a golden altar. It was too heavy to move, so the nuns hid it by covering it with mud."

Hank raised a skeptical eyebrow. "And the English didn't see it?"

"No," Andrea replied solemnly. "They never discovered it."

"Sounds like a legend to me," Hank said.

Hank had left the choice of restaurant to Andrea, saying only that he preferred an ocean view. She had chosen the Belvedere, on the eighteenth floor of the circular Plaza Paitilla Inn. High-rise buildings sprawled around the sides, and the Bay of Panama lay placidly in front. Since it was early evening, only two other tables were occupied.

When the waiter had left with their order, Andrea smiled and said, "Now, tell me what we are celebrating."

"The official start of a new career."

"Oh, yes?".

"This afternoon, I got paid for my first freelance piece."

Andrea frowned. "You haven't always been a writer?"

"Not a freelancer. I was a technical writer for Exxon for seventeen years. Then, last month, they closed down my department and laid us all off. They called it downsizing."

"Oh," she said. "So today you got paid for the travel guide?"

"Not the travel guide. For pictures and accounts of the political demonstrations the other day. I sold them to the Associated Press. *La Prensa* carried it locally."

"You had a story in *La Prensa*?" she said, surprised.

"Yeah. It's the first thing I've ever sold. And I've submitted another article, about the incident yesterday at your parents' farm."

"My parents farm? Mr. Duque, what did you say in these articles?"

Back to 'Mr. Duque' again, Hank noted. "My main thrust is the public's dissatisfaction with Noriega. I've got an interview set up for tomorrow that should also turn into something."

"With who?"

"Noriega himself," Hank said, trying not to look smug.

Her eyes widened.

"I called the American Embassy this afternoon," Hank said, "and they put me in contact with one of Noriega's aides. I told him my partner had recently done an interview with the prime minister of Belize, and that I'd like to do one with the general. Turns out that Noriega had seen my write-up in *La Prensa* and wanted to talk to me about it."

"Noriega wants to see you?" she said, concern in her voice.

"Yeah," Hank said. "I've managed to get thirty minutes with him, tomorrow morning."

"Mr. Duque, you do not understand what is happening here in Panamá."

Hank shrugged. "But I'm learning."

She shook her head. "You should not be meeting with the general."

"Why not?"

She hesitated, then said, "If you mention names . . . or anger him . . . it could cause trouble."

"I understand."

"No! You cannot understand. You don't live here!"

"Andrea, I'll watch what I say tomorrow."

The waiter interrupted them, arriving with their order. After he left, Andrea was still uneasy. She checked her watch.

"What time did you say your class was?" Hank said.

"Eight o'clock."

"We can make it," he said, and began to eat. He regretted their evening was ending so awkwardly, but now he was anxious to get back to the hotel. He needed to prepare for the interview.

Midmorning the following day, Hank walked up to a bus stop, a half-block from his hotel. As he joined the half-dozen people standing at the curb, he felt out of place, and it annoyed him. As a youth, he had confidently ridden *chivas* all over the city.

He shifted his weight and felt someone touch his camera case. He whirled in the direction of the contact. An elderly woman scowled up at him defensively.

"*Perdóneme, señora,*" Hank said.

Her lined face broke into a snaggletoothed smile. "*De nada,*" she said, accepting his apology.

Hank looked down the thoroughfare and spotted the bus he needed to catch. In its previous life, it may have carried school children. Now, it was airbrushed in vivid pink, white, and blue. Paintings of brilliant macaws and other jungle birds decorated the side, and the names of women adorned the windows. The sign above the windshield read "*San Francisco*". The interview that morning was to be conducted at General Noriega's family home.

Hank followed the old woman onto the bus and dropped into an empty seat immediately behind the driver. The passengers close-by turned and looked at him. Several smiled, and two young boys laughed outright. The driver scowled back at him in the rearview mirror. The old woman, who had taken a seat across the aisle, smiled. Finally, she said in Spanish, "Drivers reserve that seat for pretty girls."

Hank smiled; he had forgotten the custom. "*Gracias, señora,*" he said, and obligingly got up and moved to the back of the bus. He dropped into a window seat, beneath the name *Alicia*. As the bus lumbered down *Vía España*, the passing sights and sounds brought back childhood memories. He wondered what his life would have been like here, had he been allowed to stay. No Vietnam. No marriage and divorce from Carole. His son, now eighteen, would never have been born. No layoff at age thirty-nine. Who would he have married had he stayed here? What would he have done for a living?

The sight of the golf course brought him out of his musing. Ahead, lay *Calle 78*. He stood up and walked toward the front of the bus, calling out, "*¡Parada!*". The driver steered toward the curb, slowed, and opened the side door. Hank stepped down before the bus came to a complete stop, as he had seen the locals do and as he had done as a youth. With a grind of gears, the bus pulled away.

Hank entered the affluent residential neighborhood. As he strolled down the shaded lane, he admired the lavish haciendas, nestled behind high walls and wrought-iron gates. Most were white or salmon pink stucco, with terra-cotta roofs. He came to a particularly imposing stone entrance. Emblazoned on blue and white ceramic, imbedded in the stone, was the name "Noriega".

A PDF soldier met him at the gate. Hank showed his passport, as Noriega's aide had instructed. The guard apparently expected him. He opened the gate and escorted Hank across the landscaped yard and up the tiled front steps. The guard rang the bell, and a moment later a woman servant opened the ornate steel front door.

"I'm Hank Duque. I have an appointment with the general."

"Si, Sr. Duque. Venga." She ushered Hank through the polished tiled foyer and down a narrow hall. As they passed an open doorway, Hank caught a glimpse of a small chapel. A life-size statue of the Virgin Mary stood with open arms; a large icon of Christ on the cross hung from the wall.

The servant ushered Hank into the general's office and gestured to the guest chair in front of a large mahogany desk. When he was seated, she left the room. Hank looked about the office, surprised that he had been left alone in the general's private quarters. The room reflected order, yet was crammed with plaques, mementos, and other bric-a-brac.

Several minutes passed, and no one came for him. Finally, Hank stood up and listened. The hallway was quiet. He pulled out his camera and snapped several pictures of the room. A door slammed somewhere else in the house, and he quickly put away the camera.

Hank waited expectantly, but no one appeared. He walked over to the polished book shelves that covered one wall. A section had been reserved for conquests of power, with an entire shelf dedicated to Nazism. Figurines of Adolf Hitler and other dictators adorned a table top.

Hank crossed the room. A half-dozen teddy bears, dressed in military uniforms, lolled on an ornamental bench. Nearby, a hundred or more brightly-painted ceramic toads squatted on two glass-shelved cabinets.

Hank was peering down at the toads, when a voice startled him. "You like my *sapos*?" General Noriega entered the room.

Hank's first impression was that the general was much shorter than he had expected. He was dressed in casual civilian clothes—a yellow guayabera shirt, white cotton trousers, and white running shoes with the bold Puma logo. Hank extended his hand. "Uh, interesting collection, General."

Noriega hesitated, then responded with a limp, moist clasp. He walked over to his desk. "Do you speak Spanish?" he said in heavily accented English.

"A little," Hank said.

"I speak a little English," the general said, gesturing for Hank to be seated. "My interpreter will be here in a moment."

There was an awkward silence. Through the window blinds behind the desk, Hank saw tree tops swaying against the bright blue tropic sky. From somewhere close-by, came the sounds of children playing. The general leaned against one arm of a seemingly oversized chair. The acne scars in the political caricatures had not been exaggerated. His manner seemed diffident, almost feminine; yet his glassy reptilian stare filled Hank with foreboding. Hank sensed that to be near the general was to be near death.

Noriega finally broke the silence. "You are a writer, no?"

"Yes, I'm down here to do a piece for a travel guide."

The general frowned. "I thought you write for the newspaper."

"I sold a piece to the Associated Press a few days ago. It was my first."

The general gazed at him distrustfully. "What you say in the newspaper . . . is not true."

"What part wasn't true?"

The general lifted his head pugnaciously. "You say the Panamanian people do not like me. That is not true."

"The demonstrations seemed to indicate . . . they're ready for a change, General."

"No!" the general retorted. "They respect me. They respect me because I am *strong!*"

Hank didn't reply. The interview was getting off to a bad start.

"You think you know what the Panamanian people want?" the general demanded.

"It seemed pretty clear to me the other day."

Noriega gazed at him intently. "You *gringos* always know what is best for Panamá, no?"

"I just reported what I saw," Hank said uncomfortably. The general leaned back in his chair in stony silence. The interview so far was a disaster, but Hank had no choice but to press on. "General, do you plan to step down?"

Noriega leaned forward. "Step down?"

"Will you let Endara become president?"

The general peered at him shrewdly. "I will 'step down' . . . at the correct time."

Movement in the doorway interrupted their exchange. Hank turned, anticipating the arrival of the interpreter. Instead, a sturdy middle-aged woman strode into the room. Ignoring Hank, she berated Noriega in Spanish. The general respectfully listened to her tirade, occasionally nodding and muttering, *"Bueno, muñeca,"* the Spanish word for doll. Hank followed enough of the conversation to surmise that Noriega was late for some sort of activity, involving his daughter. The woman gave Hank a scathing glance, then stamped out of the room.

"Mi esposa—my wife," the general said with a resigned shrug, and stood up. "I must go with her. But I want to talk more with you, *Sr. Duque.* You will come to my office at *La Comandancia* tonight?"

"Sure, General. What time?"

"Check with my aide," Noriega said. He came out from behind his desk and escorted Hank to the doorway. Again, Hank was conscious of the difference in their heights. The general gestured the way to the front door. Then, without a handshake, he went off in the other direction.

Hank headed down the hallway and noticed a door ajar. He stopped. Through the narrow opening, he saw what looked like a primitive altar. Hank looked around; the hallway was deserted. He eased the door open. It wasn't the chapel he had seen earlier, but rather a small alcove.

Several religious figurines lay on a polished wooden table. Surrounding the figurines was an array of dried flowers, husks, grain, and bottles of unlabeled dark fluids. In the middle of the makeshift altar stood a large earthen bowl, filled with burned paper. A recollection of a trip to the interior with his grandfather flashed into Hank's mind. *Santería?* Was the general a member of the Afro-Caribbean cult that worshiped the saints?

Behind the bowl Hank saw what looked like a piece of spoiled meat, folded over, with a large nail driven through it. Hank's jaw dropped. Jesus! A tongue? Too large to be a human's . . . maybe a cow's. A scrap of paper, the size of his thumb, protruded from the fold. He saw writing, and reluctantly took the paper between his fingers and pulled it loose from the rotting tongue. Not *Santería. Magia Negra*—Black Magic!

He pocketed the scrap and took a picture of the display. The clatter of heels rang out from the tiled hallway. Hank's pulse accelerated. He quickly secured his camera and stepped from the alcove.

"¡Senor!" cried an alarmed voice. The servant who had escorted him to the general's office hurried toward him.

"I was looking for the front door," Hank said.

"But, sir, it is this way," she said, gesturing over her shoulder.

"Perdóneme, señora," Hank apologized.

Obviously troubled, she led him up the hallway. As they entered the foyer, the bell rang. She opened the front door. Major Carlos Mejías stood on the stoop.

Mejías stepped inside, blocking Hank's exit. "I learned you were here. What do you want?"

"I had an interview with the general."

"You?" Mejías said scornfully. "Why are you talking to the general?"

"I'm interviewing him for the travel piece I'm writing."

Mejías turned to the servant and demanded in Spanish, "Where is the general?"

"He is not here, sir. He went with his wife."

Mejías turned back to Hank. "Get out!" he ordered, then strode down the hallway.

Outside, Hank paused at the foot of the stairs and pulled out his camera. He was more than ready to leave, but wanted to get a picture of the hacienda's exterior.

"*¡No fotos!*" shouted an agitated voice. The gate guard jogged up the driveway toward him. "The general does not permit photos of his home," he said in Spanish.

"Okay, I didn't take any," Hank lied. The guard took him at his word and escorted him to the gate.

Hank felt a surge of relief as he started up the shaded sidewalk, distancing himself from the general's ominous enclave. By the time he reached his bus stop, however, relief had turned to disappointment over how poorly the interview had gone. He needed to do a lot better tonight.

10. LA PREVENTIVA

The dilapidated taxi rumbled through the *Santa Ana* district, taking Hank to his seven o'clock meeting with General Noriega. Hank had decided against going by bus; PDF headquarters were located in the middle of Panama City's worst slum. The driver repeatedly tapped his horn; *Avenida Central* was congested as usual.

They entered Andrea's neighborhood, and Hank smiled at the thought of her. However, the smile faded as he looked down the shabby side street where she lived. What an existence she had. He needed to be careful; she didn't need another gringo screwing her around.

They passed *Parque de Santa Ana*, the site of the anti-Noriega riot. This evening, however, the park was peaceful. Neighborhood residents clustered around the wooden benches and strolled the cobblestone paths.

They turned right at *Avenida A*. Hundred-year-old wooden tenement houses lined the littered street. Tattered figures huddled in the filthy doorways and shuffled between the dilapidated buildings.

The driver had rebuffed Hank's earlier attempts to converse in English, so now Hank tried his broken Spanish. *"¿Éste es El Chorrillo?—*Is this El Chorrillo?"

"Sí, señor," the driver said, glancing into the rearview mirror.

"¿'Manos de Piedra' es de aquí, verdad?" Hank said.

The driver looked back again, now showing interest. *"Sí, señor,* he said, verifying that world champion boxer Roberto Durán, known as "Hands of Stone", had risen from these slums."

"¿Y Manuel Noriega también?" Hank said.

"Sí, señor, y 'Cara de Piña' también," the driver said, confirming

that General Noriega had also been spawned in this filth and destitution.

Hank returned his gaze out the window. In a few minutes, he would be meeting with the man the driver contemptuously referred to as 'Pineapple Face'.

They drove a few more blocks, then turned left. Ahead, rising from the tinderbox tenements, loomed a stark four-story structure that covered most of the block: *La Comandancia*—headquarters of the PDF. Hank grew uneasy at the sight of the forbidding fortress. The driver stopped in front, and Hank got out and paid his fare. With a grudging nod, the driver pulled away.

Hank climbed the short flight of concrete stairs, pushed open the steel front door, and entered the bleak anteroom. Dust and debris covered the bare concrete floor; booted footfalls and angry shouts echoed up an adjacent corridor.

Hank presented himself to a sergeant seated behind a counter. The sergeant asked to see Hank's passport, then recorded his name and brusquely motioned to row of chairs lined against the far wall. Hank took a seat amid a half-dozen doleful men and women already waiting there.

A quarter-hour passed. Finally, the sergeant's phone rang. He spoke in hushed tones for a moment, then stood up and motioned to Hank. *"Venga."*

Hank followed the sergeant down the noisy cinder block corridor, into the bowels of the complex. They made several turns. At one point, they left one building, entered another, and went up a flight of stairs. Hank lost all sense of direction.

Finally they stopped in front of an unmarked door. Hank frowned; clearly, this wasn't the general's office. The sergeant opened the door and gestured for Hank to enter. The small, dingy room was furnished with only a battered metal table and two mismatched chairs. *"Espere aquí*—wait here," the sergeant said, then left the room, closing the door behind him.

Hank leaned against the edge of the table. His instincts told him to get out, but he knew he wouldn't be able to retrace the tortuous route from the anteroom. The doorknob turned. Major Carlos Mejías entered the room.

"What's going on?" Hank said, pushing away from the table.

"Sit," Mejías ordered in a rasping voice.

Hank sat down in one of the chairs.

"Give me your passport and wallet," Mejías said.

Hank complied, and the major pocketed both. Hank's apprehension grew.

"And give me that," Mejías said, pointing to Hank's camera case.

Hank felt a stab of fear. The pictures from Noriega's house were still in the camera! With affected indifference, he shoved the case across the table to the major.

Mejías withdrew the camera and set it aside, then emptied the other contents of the case onto the table. He thumbed through the map and inspected each of the camera attachments. Finally, he picked up the camera again. He looked at the frame counter. "You have been taking pictures, *Sr. Duque.*"

Damn it! Hank thought. "Tourist stuff, for the travel piece I'm writing."

"*¡Sargento!*" the major shouted. The door flew open, and Mejías handed the camera to the sergeant. "Process the photos," he ordered in Spanish.

Mejías closed the door again, then took a seat across the table from Hank. "Why are you in Panamá?" he demanded.

Hank took a deep breath, trying to quell his apprehension. "We've had this conversation before. How many times do I have to tell you? I'm down here to write a travel guide."

"Watch how you talk to me, *gringo!*"

Hank didn't risk a reply.

"Three days ago," Mejías said, "one of our *sapos* saw you passing information at your hotel."

"*Sapos?*" Hank said. The word meant "toads".

"Informers," Mejías translated.

The image of the toad figurine collection in Noriega's home

flashed into Hank's mind. The general's private joke? Flaunting his network of informers? Hank cleared his throat. "I haven't passed any information to anyone. I told you—"

"Film and notes," Mejías snapped. "At your hotel restaurant."

Hank kept his expression impassive. The lounge singer must have been the *sapo*. "I sold an article to the Associated Press about the recent political demonstrations. Maybe that's what your '*sapo*' saw."

Mejías studied him for a moment. "*Sr. Duque,* it will go much easier for you, if you cooperate."

"Cooperate with what?"

"With me, *Sr. Duque.* Tell me what I want to know."

Hank squirmed. He couldn't let this interrogation go on too long; he needed to be clear of *La Comandancia* before they developed his film. "I'm just here to complete my interview with General Noriega."

Mejías shook his head in annoyance.

"What do you *think* I'm doing here?" Hank said.

"I think you have returned to Panam to undermine our government."

"That's bullshit!"

"Oh, yes?" Mejías said with a malevolent smile. "Well, before you leave here, we will know the truth."

"I want to call the American Embassy."

"This is not one of your American jails, *Sr. Duque.* You get no phone calls here . . . unless, of course, you wish to contact your superiors."

"What superiors?"

Mejías shrugged. "The CIA perhaps."

"You're nuts. I don't have anything to do with the CIA."

"*Bueno, Sr. Duque,*" Mejías said, rising from his chair. "We will talk again, later."

Mejías left the room, and the sergeant entered. "*¡Venga!*" he said. He led Hank down the stark corridor. Nothing looked familiar; Hank realized they weren't headed back to the anteroom. They descended a flight of stairs and arrived at a guard station. Several soldiers lounged in front of a barred security door. A corporal made a derisive comment that Hank didn't understand. The others laughed.

"Lock him up," the sergeant ordered in Spanish.

"I want to see General Noriega!" Hank shouted. The soldiers laughed again. The corporal grabbed Hank's arm and pulled him through the security door into a large holding cell. Hank gagged at the stench of human waste. A hundred or more men were crammed into the room. Shadowy figures approached, silhouetted by a single overhead light bulb.

"Take off your shoes," the corporal ordered.

Hank reluctantly removed and handed over his shoes. The guards left the cell, slamming and locking the door behind them.

The inmates surrounded Hank. A savage looking mestizo stood in front of him. "Give me your money," he demanded in Spanish.

"I don't have any. They took my wallet."

The mestizo reached toward Hank's pocket, and Hank pushed his hand away. Several inmates grabbed Hank, turned him around, and shoved him against the wall. They pressed his face against a small window that overlooked the corridor. On the other side, the guards laughed, giving their tacit approval of the assault.

The mestizo showed Hank a homemade knife, then pressed the blade under his jawbone. Hank stood motionless while several hands rummaged through his pockets. His heart pounded. Someone behind him swore in disappointment and delivered a savage kidney punch. Hank felt the sharp edge of the knife against his throat, and struggled to remain standing.

Finally the mestizo lowered the knife. Hank turned and faced him, pressing his back against the wall. The mestizo gestured with the knife that he wanted Hank's watch. Hank gave it to him. The mestizo glanced at it, then slid it through a slot beneath the window. One of the guards in the corridor received it.

A short black inmate in tattered rags moved forward, licking his lips. "Make him 'give the favor'," he said with a lewd grin. He reached forward and unzipped the mestizo's fly. The mestizo smiled; his eyelids drooped.

"Bring him here to me," a voice called out in Spanish from the rear of the cell.

The mestizo turned toward the voice, obviously annoyed by the interruption. He grabbed Hank's arm, and the other inmates cleared a pathway.

Hank walked on weak knees toward the rear of the cell. In the far corner, an old man sat on a strip of dirty cardboard. His clothes were tattered and filthy, yet his bearing and light skin suggested he was a *rabiblanco*—a Panamanian aristocrat.

"Sit," he told Hank.

Hank sat down on the bare concrete.

The old man motioned for the other inmates to back off. Only the mestizo and his black companion remained within earshot, squatting just a few feet away. The old man said to Hank in accented English, "Who are you?"

"Hank Duque. I'm an American. I'm a writer."

"Why have they brought you here?"

Hank shook his head. "I don't know. I didn't do anything. What is this place?"

"*La Preventiva*. It is the PDF jail. What have you been accused of?"

Hank hesitated, not knowing who he was talking to. Finally he decided he had little to lose. "They claim I'm trying to undermine Noriega."

The old man smiled. "Are you?"

Hank shook his head. "I'm working on a travel guide, and picking up some extra money as an AP stringer."

The old man studied him for a moment, then said, "You are the first American I have met, with the name Duque."

"My grandfather was Panamanian."

"Oh, yes? What was his full name?"

"Edgardo Duque."

The old man responded with a bemused smile. "Was he a university professor?"

"Yes."

"When did he die?"

"In . . . 1964."

The old man chuckled. As if thinking aloud, he said, "So *this* is the grandson . . ."

"You knew my grandfather?" Hank said hopefully. The other inmates obviously deferred to the old man; Hank needed his friendship.

"I did not know him personally," the old man said. "I am Luis Fuentes. Your grandfather and I were *Arnulfistas* back then. We opposed the military regime. He was a leader, and I was just a young follower."

"An *Arnulfista*?" Hank said, surprised. "I didn't know Grandpa was an activist."

Fuentes nodded.

"*Sr. Fuentes*, how long have you been locked up here?"

"I am not sure. What day is today?"

"May thirteenth."

"Then I have been here . . . almost two months . . . this time."

"Because of your politics?"

"Yes," Fuentes said, "but I will not be here much longer."

"They're letting you go?"

Fuentes shook his head. "They are moving me to *Isla de Coiba*. It is an island prison." His gaze went vacant for a moment, then he added softly, "No one returns from *la isla*."

Hank felt a pang of concern, both for the old man and for himself. "When do you think they'll move you?"

"The guards say in the morning."

A commotion at the front of the cell interrupted their exchange. The mestizo squatting nearby rose from his haunches and pushed his way through the other inmates. His black companion followed. Moments later, the mestizo returned, dragging a woman with him.

He presented her to Fuentes. The old man dispatched her with a disgusted wave of his hand.

"What's a woman doing in here?" Hank said, concerned for her safety. He started to rise.

Fuentes placed a hand on his arm, restraining him. "That is not a woman. It is a man, dressed as a woman. He comes here for his own pleasure." Out of sight, but within hearing, the homosexual assault began. Those waiting their turn with the transvestite noisily encouraged those coupling with him. "Fools," the old man said. "They know he has the disease."

"AIDS?" Hank said.

Fuentes nodded. "Now they will have it, and give it to each other. And those who get out will take it to the rest of the city."

"Jesus!" Hank said, turning away in disgust.

"Tomorrow night," Fuentes said grimly, "you may be taking his place."

Hank looked around apprehensively. "Is everybody in here queer?"

"It has little to do with sex," Fuentes said. "It has to do with hate. These people feel they have been violated, and now they violate back. In Spanish, our word for 'violate' and 'rape' is the same: *violar.*"

The transvestite's lust apparently had been quickly satiated. Now he begged for a respite. His pleas seemed to fan the excitement of those still wanting him, and they slapped and kicked him until he resumed giving the favor.

"How can I get out of here?" Hank said urgently.

"Who put you here?" Fuentes said.

"A PDF major—Carlos Mejías."

Fuentes gazed at Hank for a moment, then said, "Major Mejías was in charge of *La Preventiva* in 1964. Your grandfather died in his custody."

Hank stared at the old man, stunned. Grandpa died . . . in here . . . like this! He fought to gain control over his revulsion, and his fear. He needed to make the most of Fuentes' counsel, before the old man was moved. "How can I get out of here?" Hank said again.

"If Major Mejías put you here, only he or General Noriega can release you."

"What does he want?"

"He wants you dead," Fuentes said, "or at least broken. Mejías is a coward. This is the way of cowards." The old man lapsed into a fit of coughing. When it subsided, he said, "I must rest." He raised up and pulled one of the scraps of cardboard from under him. He handed it to Hank. "The concrete floor is unhealthy." Then he eased onto his side, assuming a sleeping position.

Hank sat down on the strip of cardboard, his back against the wall. He began to shake; in Vietnam what he had feared most was being taken captive. Somehow, it was as if he always knew it would happen. He drew his legs close to his chest and wrapped his arms around his knees. He rested his head on his forearms and desperately tried to devise a way out. Nearby, the sexual assault continued.

Hours passed; Hank lost track of time. There was no way out. He could only wait for, and dread, the arrival of morning.

Three times during the night, guards had come to the window to harass the inmates, ordering them to stand, to sit, and to kneel. The inmates had submissively obeyed the guards' commands, and Hank had followed their lead. After each of these lengthy sessions, there had been laughter from the corridor and muted grumbling from within the cell.

Now, most of the inmates were asleep again. The room echoed with the low rumble of restless snoring, punctuated by occasional cries from tortured sleep. The transvestite's spent body lay close to the cell door. Hank stood up, and picked his way across the sleeping figures to a makeshift latrine. The primitive bowl had no plumbing and overflowed with human waste. The stench was overpowering. As Hank relieved himself, he held his breath to keep from gagging.

He started back toward his corner, and suddenly the cell door swung open. *"¡Enrique Duque!"* shouted a threatening voice. *"¡Enrique Duque! ¡Venga!"*

Fear rose in Hank's throat. The other inmates awoke and struggled to their feet. Hank threaded his way over to the cell door. He stepped over the inert body of the transvestite, and two guards grabbed him and pulled him through the doorway.

They led him down the corridor to a smaller cell. Inside, a dozen or more men slept on the floor. One of the guards rousted them, then herded them down the hallway. The other guard pushed Hank into the cell. "Take off your clothes!" he ordered in Spanish.

Hank shook his head. Two more guards entered the cell; one reached for him. Hank swung wildly and missed. All three descended on him. They forced his arms behind his back and secured his wrists with handcuffs. Hank kicked the guard in front of him, and received a blow to the back of his head. He dropped to his knees. Someone pulled a coarse burlap hood over his head and pulled a cord tight around his neck. Terrified, Hank tried to stand. The guards kicked and beat him until he toppled to the floor. They held him down, while they ripped off his shirt; then they forced him onto his back and yanked off his trousers and undershorts. They shackled his ankles, then forced him to stand, blind and naked. The shackles bit into his flesh, as they secured his arms and legs to the cell bars. Someone tightened the cord around his neck. "I can't breathe!" Hank cried. The cord was pulled tighter. His own screams from within the burlap hood blocked all other sounds.

Suddenly the cord went slack. Hank gratefully inhaled the stench from the squalid cell. "Now, we talk again, *Sr. Duque*," said a rasping voice.

Out the bottom of the hood, Hank saw the toes of the major's patent leather shoes. "What do you want from me, Mejías?" Hank gasped.

"Nothing, *Sr. Duque*," Mejías said with a laugh. "We are going to take you back to the others now."

"No!" Hank screamed. He tried to move away from the sound of Mejías' voice, but the shackles restrained him.

Mejías laughed again as he struggled. "Perhaps you would rather stay here and talk with me?"

"Don't put me in there like this!" Hank begged.

"*Sr. Duque*—" Mejías began, then stopped.

Hank was aware that someone else was standing close to him. Out the bottom of the hood, he saw a pair of running shoes, with a Puma logo. "What do you want from me?" Hank cried.

"What do you think?" Mejías purred.

Hank felt something rough being pushed between his buttocks. "No!" he screamed.

"Would you prefer to talk," Mejías said, "or enjoy this broom handle?"

"I'll tell you anything!" Hank cried.

"Why did you take pictures of General Noriega's house?"

"For the guide book," Hank lied. "I would have cleared them with the general before I used them."

"Oh, yes?" Mejías said sarcastically.

More pressure was applied, and Hank yelled, "I swear it!"

"Who do you work for, Sr. Duque? Why have you returned to Panamá?"

"I told you," Hank pleaded, "I'm down here to write a guide book."

Mejías started to speak again, but stopped. Hank heard whispering. Finally, Mejías said, "What will you do if we release you?"

"I'll go home," Hank said.

"Home?" Mejías said.

"I'll leave Panama. I'll go back to the States."

There was another exchange of whispers. Then the Puma running shoes moved out of sight. Mejías' voice was close to Hank's ear. "You *gringo* pussy. Your grandfather was an old man, but he lasted for three days!"

Hank held his breath. Finally, he heard Mejías order, "Release him." Then the patent leather shoes moved out of sight.

The guards removed the hood. Mejías was gone. They unshackled Hank, and laughed and jeered as he pulled on his shorts and trousers. His shirt was in shreds, but he draped the remains over his shoulders. One of the guards threw him a filthy pair of shoes, not his own and at least two sizes too small. He forced his feet into them.

A few minutes later, two guards herded him across a dusty courtyard. They stopped at a barred opening in the high wall that surrounded the compound. The gate sentry looked at Hank and laughed with contempt.

On the other side of the bars lay the squalor of *El Chorrillo*. Hank waited, holding his breath, but the sentry didn't open the gate. Instead, he gestured toward the headquarters building. Hank turned and saw Major Mejías strolling across the courtyard. They were going to shoot him! Death, however, was preferable to returning to *La Preventiva*.

"*Sr. Duque,*" Mejías said mockingly as he approached, "you are still here?" The three soldiers laughed at their commander's wit.

The backs of Hank's legs trembled as the major stopped in front of him. Mejías smiled and handed Hank his wallet.

Hank automatically checked the contents.

"We have deducted your lodging expenses for the night," Mejías said.

The soldiers laughed again.

"We have rescheduled your departure from Panamá," Mejías said. "You leave this afternoon, at 5:40. Be at the airport two hours early. Your passport will be at the immigration office." He nodded at the sentry, who opened the gate.

Hank passed through, awkwardly stepping across an overflowing gutter.

"*¡Parate!*" Mejías shouted, ordering Hank to halt.

There was no place to dive for cover. Hank braced himself for the impact of bullets. No one fired, and he slowly turned.

Mejías walked through the gate. He handed Hank a one-dollar bill. "Your bus fare, *Sr. Duque*," he said with a grin. Then he reentered the compound, slammed the gate behind him, and shared the joke with his soldiers.

Hank limped into the destitution known as *El Chorrillo*.

11. LA VISION

Hank staggered down the littered hallway to Andrea's apartment. He hammered on the door, and a moment later heard her muffled voice ask, *"¿Quién es?"*

"It's me, Andrea. Hank."

The bolt slid, then the door opened. Andrea's face registered shock.

"Please . . . can I come in?"

She grabbed his arm and ushered him inside.

He limped through the living room and into the kitchen. "I need some water."

Andrea got a bottle from the refrigerator and poured a glass. Hank drained it. "Mr. Duque," she said, pouring another, "what has happened to you?"

He dropped into a chair at the table. "Yesterday, you warned me to stay away from Noriega. You said I didn't understand what was going on down here. You were right."

"But what happened? You look terrible."

"They put me in *La Preventiva.*"

"*La Preventiva!* What did you do? Why did they put you there?"

Abject fatigue swept over him; he rubbed his eyes. "I . . . got into some trouble down here . . . back when I was a kid. The army killed my grandfather because of it."

She frowned. "I don't understand."

"A major named Mejías . . . thinks I've come back to undermine Noriega."

"Carlos Mejías?"

Hank nodded.

"He is very dangerous."

Hank closed his eyes and said softly, "Yes, he is."

"How did you get out of *La Preventiva*?"

"By agreeing to leave the country." He reopened his eyes. "They're deporting me this afternoon."

"Hank, how can I help you?"

"Can I sleep here this morning?"

"Certainly."

He struggled to his feet. "I don't want to be at the hotel, if Mejías decides he wants to screw around with me some more." He started in the direction of the bedroom.

"Uh . . . Hank," she said, "if you can manage it . . . you need a shower first."

Hank nodded and veered toward the bathroom. He could only imagine how bad he must smell.

"I have a tour this morning," Andrea called after him, "but my afternoon is free. Would you like for me to stop by your hotel and get clean clothes for you?"

He stopped at the bathroom door and turned back to her. "I'd appreciate that."

"I could pick up all your things if you wish. Then you could go directly to the airport from here this afternoon. I could drive you."

He thought for a moment. "Yeah, that's even better. The hotel took my credit card imprint when I arrived. You shouldn't have any problem checking me out."

A few minutes later, as the unheated water trickled over his head, he heard Andrea call out that she was leaving. His shoulders sagged, and he surrendered to the need to cry.

Hank stretched out in Andrea's bed. The sounds from the street below drifted through the open window. The faint scent of her perfume and her person still clung to the sheets. His thoughts blurred. He should take her back to the States with him . . . they'd need to get her son . . . but Hank had nothing in Houston . . . Sleep overtook him.

He was imprisoned in the Bella Vista cattle pen, mired in mud and shit. Through the gray horizontal bars, he saw his grandfather approaching. The old man was looking for him. A bull was loose! Hank tried to shout a warning, but found himself mute. He tried to move, but the foul muck clung to his legs. It pulled him down, onto his back, until he was unable to see. Then he could see again. His grandfather drew nearer. The muck transformed to a shimmering bed of snakes. He was lying on them! They were striking him! Paralyzing him. He was dying. Still he tried to warn his grandfather. But the approaching figure was no longer his grandfather. Now it was Andrea. "Andrea!"

He awoke in her bed and sat bolt upright, sweat pouring, heart racing. He wondered if he had actually screamed her name aloud. He waited for someone to respond, but heard only the muted sounds from the street below. Still sweating, he lay back down and pulled the threadbare sheet over his head.

Hank was sitting shirtless on the tiny balcony, when he heard Andrea's key in the lock. He rose and stepped through the open window.

"Did you sleep?" she said, wrestling his duffel bag and attaché case through the door.

"Yeah, I got a couple of hours," he said. He crossed the room and took the duffel bag from her. "Thanks for getting this stuff for me. Did you have any trouble checking me out?"

"No. The clerks know me."

He knelt down and opened the bag. "What time is it?"

"One-thirty. What time is your flight?"

Hank didn't answer. The contents of the bag were in disarray. He rummaged around, found a T-shirt, and pulled it on.

"Someone had searched your room," Andrea said. "Your clothes were all over the floor."

"They must have broken in last night." Hank found his shaving kit and dumped the contents onto the floor. He ran his finger along a surreptitious cut in the bottom lining. "Damn it."

"What's the matter?" Andrea said.

"I had the rest of my cash hidden in here. They found it." He opened his attaché case and pulled out one of his reference books, *The Path Between the Seas.* He spread open the front and back covers, and inserted a finger along the spine. "But they missed this," he said with grim satisfaction, as he pushed out a folded cashier's check. "It's the $1,200 the Associated Press paid me for my article on the demonstrations."

"So much . . ." Andrea said, raising her eyebrows.

Hank pushed his finger deeper into the spine and withdrew the blood-stained scrap of paper he had taken from the general's home. He reread the scribbling, then said, "Does *Familia Spadafora* mean anything to you?"

"The Spadaforas are a well-known Panamanian family, who are seeking justice for the murder of Hugo Spadafora. Hugo was a freedom fighter, a hero of the common people."

"What happened to him?"

"The PDF captured him near the Costa Rica border and took him from village to village, torturing him. They did horrible things . . . between his legs. The doctor who examined the body said he was still alive when they cut off his head. His head still has not been found."

Hank showed her the piece of paper. "I found this in Noriega's house, nailed inside what looked like a cow's tongue."

"*Magia Negra,*" she said. "Black Magic. Noriega was putting a curse on the family."

Hank stood up and walked over to the open window. He gazed down at the littered street below.

"What time is your flight?" Andrea said again.

"Five-forty . . . but I'm not leaving."

"Not leaving? Why not?"

He turned, walked back, and sat down on the couch. She joined him.

"They scared the shit out of me last night, Andrea."

"I have heard it is very bad there."

"They were going to rape me with a broom handle. I would have said anything, or done anything they asked. Mejías told me he tortured my grandfather to death . . . and I just begged him to let me go."

"He tortured your grandfather . . . in *La Preventiva?*"

Hank nodded.

Tears welled in Andrea's eyes. "Tyrants have used rape against women throughout our history. Now, the PDF also uses it to break men."

"They broke me," Hank said grimly.

"My father . . ." she began, but didn't finish.

"During my whole tour in Vietnam," Hank said, "I was afraid I'd be taken prisoner. When I went out on patrol, I always kept one round in my pocket . . . to use on myself, if necessary."

"You must go back to the States, Hank. *Sal si puedes*—Get out if you can."

He shook his head. "The past twenty-four hours have brought my whole wasted life into focus. I realize I'm afraid of captivity and torture, but not of death. I'm not afraid of death, because I've given up on life."

She frowned, but let him continue.

"I've lived in the States for the past twenty-five years. I've got nothing to show for it, because I shouldn't have been there in the first place."

"Hank—" she began.

"I'm staying. There's nothing in the States for me to go back to."

"But Major Mejías . . ."

"Mejías is the main reason I'm staying, but Noriega's another."

Andrea looked at him with a sad smile. Then she slid across the couch, put her arms around his neck, and pulled him to her. "Now, you understand," she whispered.

They embraced for a time; finally, they kissed. "Do you have to go back to work this afternoon?" Hank said huskily.

Andrea gave him a winsome smile, then stood up. She reached down and took his hand.

Hank awoke amid afternoon shadows. Andrea's hip pressed against his stomach He squeezed it through the crumpled sheet. She pushed his hand away, and he raised up on one elbow. Andrea rolled onto her back and stared at the ceiling. Her eyes were dry, yet haunted.

"What's the matter, Andrea?"

"Nothing."

"Tell me."

"Nothing!"

He rolled her toward him. She resisted, pushing her hand against his bare chest, but he pulled her into his arms. She acquiesced. He slid his hand under her hair and gently massaged the prominent bones behind her ears.

After he had held her for some time, she slowly drew back from him.

"Andrea, are you feeling guilty about this?"

She winced.

"Because I'm a gringo?"

"*Another* gringo."

"Don't feel that way."

"Do not tell me how to feel!" she retorted. But a moment later she turned to him. "It is not your fault. You are a man. I know this means nothing to you."

"Not true," Hank said with a chuckle. She glared at him, and he quickly explained. "Today's the first time I've made love in almost a year."

She frowned. "Oh, yes? Why?"

Hank shrugged, embarrassed.

"Do you have a disease?"

"No, I don't have a disease!"

She waited, eyes narrowed with suspicion.

"I just . . . haven't . . . been close to anyone."

"Oh," she said. The haunted look left, replaced by one of

amused affection. "A year!" she said in mock alarm. "Hank, are you *sure* you have Latino blood?"

"I'm sure," he laughed. He pulled her close to him again and made her grasp him.

"*Sí, Enrique,*" she sighed, "I guess you do."

When they awoke again, night had fallen. Andrea gave him an affectionate kiss, then climbed out of bed. She walked across the room, naked. At the doorway, she paused, looking back over her shoulder. Seeing him admiring her, she gave him a saucy smile and disappeared into the next room.

A few minutes later she returned, carrying two glasses of cold water. She climbed back into bed, and they sat shoulder to shoulder, sipping their drinks and listening to the muffled noises from the street below.

"You have missed your plane," she said.

Hank nodded. "And the PDF knows it. Somebody's still got my passport."

"What do you plan to do?"

"First, I need to get some money. Can you help me get my check cashed?"

She thought for a moment. "I can pass it through Aventura Tours."

"Money launderer," he said with a smile.

She poked him in the ribs.

"Next, I need to find a place to stay."

"Stay here with me."

He shook his head. "The PDF's going to be looking for me, and you've got enough problems of your own."

"They won't look for a *gringo* here in *Santa Ana.*"

Hank wavered.

With a ring of finality she said, "You will stay here."

He leaned over and kissed her.

"Hank, I still do not understand what you hope to do here in Panamá."

"I'm not sure myself. Mejías murdered my grandfather. Somehow, he's got to pay."

"What happened between him and your grandfather?"

Hank closed his eyes. In a husky monotone he confided the details of the 1964 riot. He concluded, "Because of me, Grandpa, the Marine sergeant, and God knows how many Panamanians died."

"Oh, Hank, you were just a boy."

He shook his head. "I'm responsible."

"Hank, the hatred between Americans and Panamanians existed long before you were born. Your grandfather forgave you. Forgive yourself."

"I can't."

"What do you intend to do?"

"I don't know, but Mejías has got to pay. Helping to bring down Noriega is a good place to start."

"Would your grandfather want you to risk your life to avenge his death?"

"No, he wouldn't."

"Then forget about Major Mejías."

"Grandpa was a gentle man, Andrea, but he also was strong. He did what he thought was right, in his way. I have to do this, in my way."

"Hank—" she began.

He shook his head. "I have his blood."

They sat in silence for some time. Finally Andrea pulled the sheet over her shoulders and rested her head on his chest. "Hank," she said, "you never mention your grandmother."

He heaved a sigh. "I don't know much about her, except that she was an American. She died before I was born."

"How did they meet?"

Hank thought for a moment. "I'm not sure. It was in the early 1900s, while the canal was being built. I think Grandpa was an interpreter or something. I don't remember what my grandmother was doing down here, or how they got together."

12. LA GRINGA

Send forth the best ye breed.
—Kipling

November 1906

Gladys Johnson sat in the living room of her father's home in Ancon, Canal Zone, when she heard the expected knock. She daubed again at the perspiration on her face, annoyed at being unable to control her body's response to the tropical heat. She slipped the moist handkerchief into her skirt pocket, then rose and went out onto the screened front porch.

A young Panamanian stood at the top of the wooden stairs, looking through the screen door with an eager-to-please expression on his delicately handsome face. His youthfulness surprised her; she had expected the Panama Canal Commission to nominate a much older man to teach Spanish to the American ladies of Ancon.

"Good afternoon," he said formally, with a noticeable accent. "I am Edgardo Duque. I have come for the interview."

The young man's dark eyes fixed on hers, and Gladys flushed. "And you are Mrs. Johnson?"

"*Miss* Johnson," Gladys replied, more brusquely than she had intended. "Please come in," she amended quickly. There was a moment of awkwardness when he stumbled, backing down the stairs to allow the screen door to swing open. He recovered and followed her into the house.

"Please have a seat, Mr. Duque," Gladys said, motioning to a polished mahogany armchair. She sat down on the couch across the coffee table from him.

Edgardo looked about the spacious room and said, "Your house is very nice."

Gladys acknowledged the compliment with a smile and a nod. She surmised that, like most Panamanians, he had never been in a Canal Zone home, all of which were drearily similar. Only small items, such as personal pictures, distinguished one Zonian's home from another. The Commission selected all major furnishings and issued them in varying amounts, based on the employee's professional status. Zonian passersby could tell that her father was a Commission superintendent and that his salary was $5,000 per year, simply by noting the wicker furniture and the net hammock on his front porch.

Gladys now perspired freely. She retrieved the handkerchief from her pocket, wishing she had a dryer one. The young man seemed immune to the humidity, despite his starched white collar and tightly fitting plaid suit.

"Edgardo," Gladys said, "please tell me what experience you have."

"I teach English in Panama City, at the San José primary school . . ." he began.

Gladys only partially listened. She had scanned his résumé, and in any case, she considered this preliminary job interview to be just a formality. She suspected that Mrs. Stevens, the energetic president of the Canal Zone Women's Club, had just given her the assignment to make her feel useful. Mrs. Stevens undoubtedly would make the final decision herself.

Gladys studied Edgardo as he earnestly recited his qualifications. He appeared to be in his late twenties, at least five years younger than she. His skin shade was light, probably denoting Spanish ancestry; however, there was a smoky undertone, suggesting a Panamanian blending of Indian and Negro. His black hair was slicked back, and his thin mustache was neatly trimmed. As he spoke, he accentuated his words with his hands. He looked refined, almost European.

As Gladys sat nodding to the words of the handsome young man, she felt plain and unattractive, and a familiar feeling of melancholy came over her. It was the sadness of a woman who, at thirty-two, had already resigned herself to a life of spinsterhood.

Near dusk that evening, Gladys sat on the front porch awaiting the arrival of her father. She checked her watch and frowned. He was already an hour and forty-five minutes late. It was unusual for him to vary from his daily schedule; he disciplined himself as relentlessly as he disciplined his Quartermaster Corps subordinates.

The neighborhood was quiet; it was supper time in the regimented, far-flung American territory. Gladys settled back in her wicker chair and looked down the street, smiling tolerantly at the perfect symmetry with which the Commission engineers had laid out the community. The two-story wood-frame duplexes were evenly spaced, and each was painted the same drab battleship gray.

The trees and shrubbery that surrounded the houses also had been dictated by the Commission. Tall palms lined both sides of the street, like soldiers on parade. Residents were allowed only one small measure of creativity: selecting plants for their porches. Gladys looked about the screened enclosure, pleased with her recent arrangement of lush ferns and delicate orchids.

The sound of an unmuffled exhaust interrupted her musing. She rose and went over to the screen door. A moment later, a muddy lorry rolled into view, its open bed filled with American canal workers. It pulled up noisily in front of the house, pausing just long enough for her father to climb down from the cab. Gladys had never seen him so disheveled. His six-gallon hat was askew, and his white shirt and khaki trousers were saturated with sweat and grime. He trudged up the walkway, preoccupied and exhausted.

"Papa, are you all right?" Gladys called out as she opened the screen door.

He looked up and gave a halfhearted wave. "Sorry I'm late, honey," he said, then sat down on the bottom step and unlaced his mud-caked brogans.

"I was getting worried about you," she said, joining him at the foot of the stairs.

"We had another mud slide at the Culebra Cut. I had to see for myself how bad it was."

Gladys nodded understandingly. She had been in Panama for four months, and she had developed an appreciation of her father's commitment to the canal project. He had been sent to the Isthmus in 1903, immediately after the United States had sponsored Panama's secession from Colombia. Gladys' mother had followed shortly thereafter. Tragically, her mother had been among the thousands in the early contingents who had contracted yellow fever. Her father had buried her mother in the Ancon cemetery. Clearly, he had no intention of ever returning to Minnesota.

Then three years later, newspapers had carried the triumphant announcement that the United States Medical Corps had eradicated yellow fever from Panama. And a short while after that, in the midst of a bleak winter in St. Paul, Gladys had resigned her elementary school teaching position and had sailed to join her father in the Tropics.

Now her father looked up and said, "It's so darn frustrating. Our engineers were sure they'd finally got the banks cut back to the right slope . . . and then this morning, we have another slide. We lost two weeks' work. And to make matters worse, Teddy Roosevelt's due down here in ten days."

"The president's coming to Panama?" Gladys said in surprise.

"We got the news this morning."

"President Roosevelt . . . coming to Panama," Gladys mused aloud. "It's hard to believe."

Her father slowly got to his feet, brogans in hand. "It'll be the first time a sitting president has ever left the United States. The canal project obviously is quite important to him."

"Stay out here," Gladys said. "I'll bring you a drink."

"Let me clean up first," he said, as he started up the steps. "I don't want the neighbors to think me a drunkard."

A short while later, after a quick supper, Gladys and her father were again seated on the darkened porch. He had been preoccupied throughout the meal, and Gladys hadn't pressed him for conversation. Now, with a scotch and water clasped in his hand and the hint of a breeze penetrating the wire-mesh screen, he finally seemed to relax. "The day was already hectic," he began, "and then this afternoon we got the news about Culebra."

Gladys listened as her father gave the details of the latest setback. From their past discussions, she knew the Culebra Cut was the most difficult and dangerous section of the fifty-mile canal. Even its name rang ominous; in Spanish, "culebra" meant "snake". It was here that American engineers were attempting to sever the string of rugged mountains at the continental divide. Repeatedly, weeks of dredging had been lost, as tons of porous volcanic material slid back into the channel.

Her father sighed. "There's so much to do . . . and now we've got Roosevelt coming down. His aides say he'll only be here for three days, but he wants to see *everything*."

"In three days?"

Her father nodded ruefully. "And this morning, John Stevens made me responsible for developing his itinerary."

"Papa!" Gladys said, concerned that the chief engineer already had her father overloaded.

"I've put together a tentative schedule," her father continued. "Roosevelt's due in Colón on the fourteenth. I plan to have a welcoming ceremony there the next morning, and then bring him across the Isthmus by train. He'll spend the afternoon at Commission headquarters. Then, that night, we'll have the formal reception at the Tivoli Hotel."

"That sounds like too much activity for one day."

"The other two days are going to be just as hectic. He wants a meeting with *Presidente* Amador, a sightseeing trip through Panama City, and an inspection tour of the Canal Zone. He particularly wants to see the Culebra Cut." With a discouraged tone her father concluded, "And then today, we had to have that darned slide."

"Surely he'll understand."

"The man doesn't want excuses. He orchestrated the Panamanian revolution to get this franchise. Now he wants results."

"But things like landslides can't be avoided."

"I might have avoided this one," her father said with regret, "or at least postponed it until after his visit. At this morning's meeting, I almost proposed that we freeze work at Culebra until after he left. But to do so didn't seem quite right somehow, so I kept quiet. And now the cut is filled with muck and mire."

"Is there anything I can do to help?"

Her father shook his head. For a while he was lost in thought; then he said, "Planning that darned reception at the Tivoli is probably going to be the most troublesome part for me. It's the kind of thing your mother was so good at . . . and I don't even know how to get started."

"Let me handle it, Papa."

"You?" he protested. "What do you know about planning receptions?"

"More than you do," she said with a smile.

"Well, I don't know . . ." He studied her for a moment. "All right, see if you can handle it." Then he struggled to his feet and went inside.

Gladys suddenly felt charged with her existence. Just that morning, she had been moping about her father's spartan quarters, feeling of little use. Now she was responsible for a presidential gala!

Sometime later, she lay in bed, making mental notes on how to get started and who to see for help. Finally she rolled onto her side, assuming her sleeping position. Then for some reason, the young Panamanian tutor came to mind. She wondered if he was married.

The following day, Gladys hiked up a winding residential street on the side of Ancon Hill. A seagull shrieked overhead. She looked up and for the first time noticed the flagpole that had been erected on its grassy summit. The forty-five-star American flag flapped in the afternoon breeze.

She stopped under a large shade tree to wipe her brow. Her

favorite frock, suitable for St. Paul summers, was much too heavy for the Tropics. She had brought along three handkerchiefs for her trek; one was already saturated.

Gladys glanced at her watch. It was 1:35; she was twenty-five minutes early for her appointment with Mrs. Stevens, wife of the chief engineer and president of the Canal Zone Women's Club. Gladys decided to take this opportunity to pause and compose herself, since she wanted to arrive precisely at 2:00. When she had telephoned that morning, Mrs. Stevens had sounded harried. Finally, however, she agreed to work Gladys into her already busy schedule.

Now, as Gladys stood fanning herself, she gazed down the hill. Less than a mile away, the Panama City peninsula jutted into the Pacific Ocean. She wondered what life was like within that cramped jumble of buildings. During the four months she had been on the Isthmus, she had left the confines of the Canal Zone only once. On that occasion, her father had taken her on an excursion to see the ruins of Old Panama. Gladys had gotten a fleeting look at the teeming city—the bustle of the dark urban masses, the cries of the sidewalk vendors, the dust billowing up from the streets, and the smell of overripe fruit. Panama City had contrasted sharply with the sterile Canal Zone, and Gladys had been excited by its seemingly exotic charm.

The clop-clop of horse hooves interrupted her musing. An open hackney labored up the hill; in the rear passenger seat sat the Panamanian tutor, Edgardo Duque. He shouted something to the hackman in Spanish, and the young Negro reined in the horses.

"¡Hola, Señorita Johnson!" the young man cried, as he bounded down from the carriage. "You should not be out walking in our midday heat."

Gladys flushed as he walked over to her. "I'm going up to the Stevens' house," she said, pointing to the stately residence, less than a hundred yards farther up the hill.

"That's where I am going too," he said happily. "Please, share my carriage."

Gladys automatically checked her watch; she was still twenty minutes early. But before she could decline, the enthusiastic young man took her by the elbow and guided her toward the old hackney. As she lowered herself onto the cracked leather seat, she hoped it wouldn't discolor the back of her beige frock.

The hackney jolted forward, and Edgardo said, "I am meeting with Señora Stevens at 1:30."

"It's almost 1:40, Edgardo."

"Then I am right on time." When Gladys frowned, he explained with a laugh, "*Tiempo panameño*—Panamanian time."

A few minutes later, the hackney entered the winding drive that led to the chief engineer's recently-built residence. Gladys noted that the grounds had been landscaped since her last visit. They stopped in front of the spacious two-story home, and Edgardo climbed down from the carriage. The driver gave the building an indifferent glance, then reached for his fare. Edgardo gave the man an American dime. The driver kept his hand extended, apparently wanting more, and the two men began arguing in Spanish.

"Edgardo," Gladys interrupted, "you're going to be late."

Edgardo looked up at her and said exasperatedly, "He wants a second fare, because we stopped for you." Gladys opened her purse, but Edgardo said quickly, "No, please, allow me." He grudgingly gave the hackman a second dime, then helped Gladys down from the carriage.

"*¡Carajo!*" cursed the hackman. With an angry snap of the reins, he pulled away from the house.

"How are you going to get back to Panama City, Edgardo?"

"I didn't think of that," he said, frowning as the hackney pulled out of the driveway and headed down the hill. Then he brightened and said, "In any case, we are here now. Let us go inside."

Edgardo rattled the porch screen door, and a moment later a Panamanian servant appeared. Edgardo addressed her in Spanish. She looked at him disdainfully, but then she recognized Gladys and ushered them into the home. "Please wait here," she said to Gladys in accented English.

A few moments later, Mrs. Stevens appeared. "Oh, hello, Gladys," she said distractedly. "And you must be . . . Señor Duque. Have you come together?"

"Mr. Duque just gave me a ride up the hill," Gladys said, then was annoyed with herself, realizing her comment sounded as if she wished to separate herself from the handsome Panamanian, which she did not.

"It is my pleasure, Mrs. Stevens," Edgardo said, stepping forward and bowing slightly.

"Please, join me in the breakfast room," Mrs. Stevens said. "I'm waiting for John to come home for lunch, and I've been working back there."

The breakfast area was a cozy corner room. A magnificent view of the Pacific harbor filled the front window, and a steep jungled hill pressed against the side.

"Please sit down, and do excuse the mess," Mrs. Stevens said, gesturing to the papers that covered the table. "I've got so many things going on right now." Addressing Edgardo, she said, "Our president will be visiting here next month, you know."

Edgardo raised his eyebrows, indicating pleased surprise.

"All right," Mrs. Stevens began, "first let's discuss the Spanish program, so we don't detain Mr. Duque."

She was interrupted by heavy footfalls approaching from the living room. A moment later, a powerfully built figure filled the doorway and scowled down at the unexpected visitors.

"Darling," Mrs. Stevens said, "you remember Avery Johnson's daughter, Gladys, don't you?"

Chief Engineer John Stevens, gave Gladys a curt nod. As he did so, smoke billowed from the cigar butt that was clamped in the middle of his handsome, weather-beaten face. Gladys struggled to suppress a smile, remembering the canal workers' nickname for the chief engineer: "Big Smoke".

Mrs. Stevens continued, "Avery has asked Gladys to organize the president's reception at the Tivoli."

Stevens frowned, apparently having been unaware that Gladys

had been given this responsibility. Gladys hoped this premature disclosure wouldn't prove awkward for her father.

"And this is Mr. Duque," Mrs. Stevens said. "He's applying for the job to teach Spanish at the Women's Club."

Edgardo rose and extended his hand.

With a grunt, the chief engineer leaned across the table and grasped it. "You're a translator, are you?"

"Uh . . . I am a teacher, sir."

"Let me clear a space here, dear," Mrs. Stevens interjected. "Lunch will be ready in a few minutes."

Stevens dropped into the unoccupied chair at the table, and Mrs. Stevens handed him a copy of the weekly newspaper, *The Canal Record*. The chief engineer immediately turned to the second page. He read for a moment, then closed the paper and announced with a satisfied grunt, "Shovel number 274 is still way out in front. They'll never catch her."

Gladys smiled; that morning at breakfast, her father had made the same comment. The *Record* kept weekly tallies of the tonnage produced by individual steam shovels and dredges. Canal Zonians followed the fierce machine rivalries, as avidly as their countrymen to the north followed the baseball team standings.

The chief engineer set the paper aside and turned his attention back to Gladys. "So you're the one who'll be handling the reception?"

"Uh . . . yes . . ." she responded, again feeling uneasy. "Hopefully, with the help of the Women's Club."

"Good," Stevens said. "Glad to hear you women are taking charge. Avery's no better at organizing that type of thing than I am." With that matter apparently settled to his satisfaction, he turned to Edgardo. "How good's your English, young man?"

"Ah . . . I have been told that it is quite good, sir."

Stevens asked Gladys, "What do you think?"

"About his English?" Gladys said uncertainly. "It seems . . . very good."

Turning back to Edgardo, Stevens said, "President Roosevelt's coming down here next month, and I need a Panamanian guide. Would you be interested?"

"Certainly, sir!"

Stevens continued, "We're already making plans for Roosevelt to meet with *Presidente* Amador on your side of the border. I'm sure there will be an American translator with him for these meetings. But while he's over there, he also wants to do some sightseeing. For this part of his visit, I want a local—someone who knows what he's talking about, and can say it in English. Still interested?"

"But of course, sir," Edgardo said. Then he added, "However, you will need to notify my government that I will be working for you."

Stevens turned to Gladys. "You've reviewed his qualifications?"

"Uh . . . yes," Gladys said, wishing she had spent more time actually studying Edgardo's résumé.

"Done then," Stevens said. "You work out the details."

Gladys nodded uncertainly.

A few days later, Gladys stood on the Ancon side of Fourth of July Avenue. The Corps of Engineers had graded the thoroughfare to designate the border between the U.S. Canal Zone and the Republic of Panama. Across the avenue lay *Parque de Lesseps.*

Gladys opened her purse and rechecked to be sure she had the penned map and notes Edgardo had prepared for her. He had been eager to show her the primary school where he taught, and she had agreed to meet him there. Afterward, they were to review his tour plans.

Gladys took a deep breath, then crossed over into Panama. She descended the wide concrete stairway that led down to the park. Enormous shade trees formed a dense canopy, blocking the sun and preventing grass from growing in the packed dark soil.

She followed a gravel footpath. Although it was early afternoon, the benches were occupied. Idle men flirted with young women, most of whom were governesses, tending small children. Under a far tree, a couple reclined in a passionate embrace.

Gladys felt conspicuous as she picked her way along the uneven walkway. She neared the middle of the park and heard someone off to her right emit a "ssst" sound. Male laughter followed. She tried to keep her eyes straight ahead as she continued on, but stumbled on a large stone. Her bonnet slid forward, momentarily blocking her vision and prompting more laughter.

Up ahead, to her left, two young men were playing a game she hadn't seen before. They had a small leather bag, the size of an egg, which they kicked back and forth, without letting it touch the ground. As she passed, one of the men received the bag and juggled it on the side of his foot, while he boldly gazed at her. The other man drew her attention by making the "ssst" sound between his teeth.

Gladys finally arrived at the far side of the park, and six hackmen descended upon her. She pointed to an elderly mulatto, who seemed less aggressive than the rest. The others grudgingly accepted her decision; however, as they walked away, they exchanged comments among themselves that evoked raucous laughter.

The driver led her over to his hackney. It was clearly the least travel worthy of the six. One of the wheels had several broken spokes, and filthy padding protruded through large splits in the leather seats. A stunted wiry nag, harnessed in a frayed rope, flicked at flies with a dung-encrusted tail. Reluctantly, Gladys climbed into the old carriage.

The hackman got into the driver's seat and asked her something in Spanish. Gladys opened her purse and took out Edgardo's notes. She read, *"Yo . . . quiero . . . ir . . . a la escuela . . . de San José."*

The hackman frowned and shook his head. Gladys held out the sheet of paper. He accepted it, but from his vacant expression, Gladys suspected the old man was illiterate. Finally he handed back the paper with a noncommittal shrug.

Gladys tried again. *"La . . . escuela . . . de San José."*

The hackman's face brightened. *"¿La Escuela de San José, señorita?"*

"Uh . . . *sí.*"

"*Muy bien, señorita.*" He slapped the reins, and the carriage lurched forward.

They pulled from under the park trees, and the tropical sun radiated down on them. The hackman turned and said something in Spanish. Gladys smiled and shook her head, trying to convey that she didn't understand. The driver nodded, then turned away, just in time to avoid hitting a woman who had pushed a perambulator into the street.

Gladys settled back, hoping she hadn't inadvertently agreed to something disastrous. On the left stood the city railway station. A five-car train was being loaded with passengers and freight for a trip across the Isthmus. She checked Edgardo's map and verified they were headed in the right direction, south on *Avenida Central.*

A block farther, they entered the commercial district. Brightly-colored three-story buildings pressed against the narrow street. Exotic shops crammed the lower level, and private residences towered overhead. Wash hung from many of the wrought-iron balconies. Dark-skinned pedestrians swarmed up and down the narrow sidewalks, preoccupied with their own lives and ignoring the street traffic.

The carriage paused in front of an open market. Gladys recoiled at the odor of overripe fruit and spoiling meat. A large man, standing behind a fly-covered butcher block, saw her and held up a horned iguana, nearly five feet long. Its short legs had been twisted behind its back, and the reptile writhed helplessly in the man's grasp. The butcher smiled, then laid the iguana on the block and cut off the last two feet of its tapered tail. Mercifully for Gladys, the hackman drove on.

They entered *Casco Viejo*, the section of the city that dated back to Spanish colonial times. Gladys smiled with excitement. What a story she'd have to tell Papa! Two days earlier, he had accepted her expanded role in the Roosevelt visit with surprisingly good humor, saying, "Perhaps we should also let you handle the Culebra Cut." He might not have been so sportive, had she told him she would be traversing Panama City on her own.

They neared an intersection, and Gladys checked her map to be sure they were still on the correct route. However, before she could orient herself, the driver abruptly made a right turn. Her bonnet again slipped over her eyes. As she grabbed for the side of the carriage to steady herself, the map flew out of her hand. "Driver!" she cried out, but the clatter of the horse hooves and metal-rimmed wheels on the rough cobblestones drowned out her voice. She looked over the rear of the carriage in disbelief. Her map blew about the street, then disappeared.

They descended through a corridor of stucco tenements that pinched down to the emerald-blue ocean, two blocks away. The third-floor balconies on either side of the narrow street almost seemed to touch. Suddenly the carriage jolted to a stop in front of an old church.

The hackman turned to her. *"Aquí es la Iglesia de San José, señorita,"* he said, then reached back for the fare.

"I don't understand," Gladys said. "I'm looking for a school."

"Diez centavos," the hackman said, gesturing with the fingers of his extended hand that he wished to be paid.

Gladys sat immobile, trying to remember the Spanish word for "school".

"¡Diez, centavos!" the hackman demanded.

She rummaged through her purse and found a U.S. dime. She gave it to him, then hesitantly climbed down to survey the scene. She was barely clear of the carriage, when the hackman slapped the reins and noisily pulled away.

Gladys climbed onto the nearby sidewalk, which was two feet higher than the street. This was a church, not a school. Tears of frustration burned her eyes. How could she have been so clumsy!

Then from behind the church, she heard the faint sound of singing. Even in a foreign language, she recognized the familiar voices of school children. She hurried down the side street. At the rear of the church lay a walkway that led to a secluded courtyard. A weathered wooden sign hanging over a stone arch read: ESCUELA DE SAN JOSE.

'Escuela', that was the word! With a sigh of relief, she started down the walkway. Voices of children repeating rote lessons now harmonized with those who were singing. She entered a modest courtyard and found it enclosed on all sides by an aging two-story school building. Through an open window, she saw Edgardo leading children in song. As she approached, Edgardo saw her too, and gestured for her to come in.

As Gladys entered the classroom, the children abruptly stopped singing. Edgardo introduced her in Spanish, and they cried happily in unison, *"¡Buenas tardes, Señorita Johnson!"*

Gladys smiled and walked to the front of the room. She had taught school for eleven years, and the expectant young faces turned up to her seemed so familiar. Yet here she couldn't speak to them. She turned to Edgardo for help.

"La señorita no habla español," he told the class. Then he said to Gladys, "I explained that you don't speak Spanish."

"Then you must teach me," she said. "Is *buenos días* correct?"

"Very close. In this case, *buenas tardes* is more correct, since it is afternoon. And 'children' is *'niños.'"*

Gladys turned to the class. *"Niños . . . buenas tardes,"* she said, having trouble rolling the "r". The children laughed, but clapped at her willingness to try.

Edgardo pointed to writing on the dusty blackboard. "We are learning this song for Carnival. Will you join us?"

"Certainly," she said with a smile.

"'Certainly' is *'claro',"* he said, continuing her first Spanish lesson.

"Claro," she repeated, faring better with the "r". Then for the next twenty minutes, she joined in the singing.

Too quickly for Gladys, the school day came to a close. After the last child had shyly told her goodbye, Gladys said to Edgardo, "Now, tell me what we were singing."

"This song is most popular during our Carnival . . . the days before Lent. It is about happiness—*alegría*. We Panamanians are a happy and carefree people. There is a rhythm to our lives. We like

to laugh . . . to dance . . . to love. And this song tells about it."
Then he softly sang the first two lines from the board.

"*Panameño, panameño,*
Panameño vida mía,
This says, 'Panamanian, you are my life—my love,'
Yo quiero que tú me lleves,
Al tambor de la alegría.
This means, 'I want you to take me, to the rhythm of happiness'."

Gladys and Edgardo exchanged smiles. Then he said, "Now, shall I show you our city?"

She stole a final glance at the blackboard, then rep*lied*, *"Yo quiero . . . que tú me lleves . . . al tambor de la alegría."*

Several days later, on a Sunday afternoon, Gladys and Edgardo sat on a wooden bench in *Parque de Santa Ana.* The ancient church, for which the park was named, loomed behind them. An orchestra entertained the well-dressed crowd, many of whom promenaded about the central pavilion—an inner circle of young men, three abreast, walking clockwise; and an outer circle of young women, also three abreast, walking in the opposite direction. Occasionally a man and woman would linger to talk, then move to one of the benches.

As Gladys watched the courting ritual, she took a sip from the *sangría* Edgardo had purchased from a street vendor.

"Drink it slowly," he cautioned. "We take our drinks strong on Sundays, and you are not a Panamanian, yet."

She smiled and leaned back, having become increasingly comfortable in this now not so strange culture. There was a lull in the music, and she heard a faint reverberation, like distant cannon, reminding her of her countrymen's ongoing dynamite attack on the Culebra Cut.

President Roosevelt was due to arrive in two days. For the first time, Gladys felt completely comfortable with the preparations. As it had turned out, the reception at the Tivoli had required relatively little of her time. Mrs. Stevens had called a meeting of the Women's Club, and the members had enthusiastically assumed responsibility for making the arrangements. The sightseeing trip through Panama City had been another matter. Chief Engineer John Stevens had questioned each aspect of the tour in considerable detail, but eventually had accepted the proposed itinerary. The cathedral behind them was to be the last stop.

Gladys' musing was interrupted by someone making the "ssst" sound. A young olive-skinned Panamanian woman sauntered by, gazing boldly at Edgardo. He gave her an amused smile, then returned his attention to Gladys.

"I hear that sound all the time," Gladys said. "Does it mean, what I think it means?"

Edgardo chuckled. "It is the . . . 'Panamanian love call'. But it is not to be taken seriously. It is meant in good fun, and is just used to get someone's attention."

"Mmmm," she said, not entirely convinced. She took another sip from her drink. "It's lovely here, Edgardo."

He smiled.

They had been meeting daily, and Gladys had the rare feeling of being completely happy—not wanting to be anywhere else, other than where she was now. Or with anyone else. "I can't tell you how much I've enjoyed this past week," she said. "It's been . . . wonderful."

"I too have enjoyed it very much."

Their exchange was interrupted by a flash of lightning, followed closely by a clap of thunder. Startled, Gladys looked up at the clear sky over the pavilion.

"We must go," Edgardo said, rising and extending his hand. "It is our rainy season, and showers come up quickly."

A few minutes later, they hurried up *Avenida Central*. Ahead of them, the high narrow sidewalk was dry; yet twenty feet behind them, rain poured, and seemingly chased them.

"Hurry, Gladys," Edgardo exhorted. Taking her hand, he turned down *Calle 8* and picked up the pace to a near trot.

Ahead she saw *La Iglesia de San José.* They jumped down from the sidewalk, cut across the intersection, and ducked into the vestibule of the venerable church.

"I don't believe it!" Gladys laughed, looking through the open doorway at the torrent pounding on the street. "Being chased by rain like that."

Edgardo put a finger against his lips, indicating they shouldn't disturb any late-afternoon worshipers who might be inside. "It happens like this during the rainy season," he whispered. "Small, heavy clouds, blown by the wind. When I was a boy, we used to run in the streets like that . . . pretending we were in Spain . . . running before the bulls."

Gladys smiled. Gazing into his dark eyes, she wished to know more of his life.

"Come," he said. "I have been showing you all the cathedrals in Panama City, but you have not seen our own famous church." He quietly opened the inner door, and Gladys looked inside. People were scattered throughout the room, worshiping privately. The church interior was modest, but at the far end stood a spectacular altar. "That is *El Altar de Oro*—The Altar of Gold. It was made for the Cathedral of St. Augustine in *Panama Viejo*—Old Panama. Remember, we visited the old cathedral's ruins yesterday?"

Gladys nodded.

"The legend is," Edgardo continued, "that when the English pirates destroyed *Panama Viejo* two centuries ago, the Spanish nuns hid the altar by covering it with mud. Then after the pirates left, they brought it here."

Two elderly women, draped in black shawls, entered the church and looked at them inquiringly. Gladys felt she might be intruding. "Perhaps we can come back and see it later, when we won't disturb anyone."

Edgardo led Gladys through the vestibule. The rain had let up, but as they stepped from the church thunder rumbled nearby.

"I don't think you should try to go home just yet," Edgardo said. "My apartment is on the next street. Would you like to wait there?"

"Yes," she said, "that would probably be best."

A few minutes later, however, she had reservations. Edgardo ushered her through an uninviting gateway and up two flights of dirty stairs. Then he led her down a gloomy passageway to a grime-covered door. He unlocked it and held it open for her.

Gladys hesitantly stepped inside. She jumped when a rasping voice cried out, *"¡Hola, Edgardo! ¡Hola, Edgardo!"* Across the room, a caged red and blue macaw excitedly flapped its wings.

Gladys looked about and was surprised to find the apartment spacious and immaculate. Polished dark wood furniture filled the living room; embroidered doilies decorated the side tables. In the dining room, porcelain figurines and delicate pieces of china covered the hutch shelves and a floral spray adorned the table. Disturbingly, these furnishings indicated a woman's presence.

Edgardo walked over to the far side of the room and opened the tall French windows and a door that overlooked a long veranda. Then he removed the bird from the cage and quieted it by stroking its head. He fastened a chain to its leg and took it onto the veranda.

Gladys followed him outside. A comfortable breeze circulated across the third floor balcony. She leaned over the iron railing and gazed down at the glistening street. "Edgardo," she said, "are you . . . do you live here alone?"

"Oh, no," he said, as he fastened the macaw's chain to an open perch. Then he joined her at the railing. Their arms touched lightly. "My mother and sister live here with me. They are in Chepo, visiting my aunt."

"Oh," Gladys said, relieved.

"I will introduce you to them when they return next week," he said. Then he added with a knowing smile, "Did you think I was married?"

His directness caused her to flush. She felt his hand touch her shoulder. She turned and found his face close to hers. He took her in his arms. Could this be? His lips pressed against hers, and she fervently returned his kiss.

After several moments, Edgardo placed his hand on her waist and gently turned her toward the open doorway. "Come with me to be alone," he whispered.

She smiled at the charming figure of speech, then allowed him to lead her through the living room and down the dimly lighted hallway to a rear bedroom. She took a deep breath. It was going to happen . . . with this handsome young man.

He led her to the bed, and they sat down. "I'm not . . . experienced," she confessed.

Edgardo kissed her again and said softly, "*Relájate*—relax."

Gladys had the curious feeling that she had turned herself over to a physician in a foreign land, uncertain of his skills, yet urgently in need of them. The sounds from the street were muffled now. He unfastened the clasps that ran down the back of her frock, then turned his attention to her corset. She interrupted him just long enough to slip under the sheet. Moments later, their union was painless, his touch as gentle as her own.

Gunfire awakened them. Edgardo threw back the sheet, leaped from the bed, and raced through the bedroom doorway. Gladys scrambled to the foot of the bed. She retrieved the sheet and clutched it about her neck. Several more shots rang out, followed by a staccato of angry shouts. The clamor came from the street below.

Edgardo ran back into the room, naked. "Get dressed!" he shouted, then frantically rummaged through the clothing piled on the floor.

Gladys sat transfixed; she had never seen a naked man before. Then another shot rang out, and she jumped from the bed. "What is it Edgardo?" she said as she hastily began to dress.

"*Gringo* soldiers."

They edged up the dark hallway to the living room. The gunfire ceased, but an ominous chorus of angry Panamanian voices replaced it.

"Wait here," Edgardo said. In a crouch, he moved through the French door and onto the veranda.

"Spiggoty bastards!" a man below yelled in English. It was followed by a scream of pain.

"Ed, are you—" shouted another voice, before it was abruptly silenced.

Gladys rushed onto the veranda. Scores of Panamanian policemen were manhandling a dozen or so uniformed U.S. Marines. Three of the Marines lay in the street, arms and legs twisted grotesquely. A policeman kicked one of the inert forms.

"Stop it!" Gladys shrieked. "Leave him alone!"

The policeman paused and looked up at her. *"¡Puta gringa!"* he shouted, then gave the prostrate Marine another savage kick to the rib cage.

Gladys turned wild-eyed to Edgardo. "Stop them!"

Edgardo looked back and forth between her and the violence below. Finally, he started toward the living room.

"No, wait!" she cried. She threw her arms around him. "Don't go down there. They'll kill you."

"The *gringos*," he said uncertainly, "they must have done something."

Gladys and Edgardo looked back over the railing. Hundreds of spectators now filled the street. They jeered at the Marines as the police herded them in the direction of the ocean. The three unconscious Marines were dragged by their arms, and the spectators kicked and spat on them as they passed. Belligerent cries of *"¡Gringo no!"* echoed up the street long after the barbaric procession had disappeared around a corner.

"Where are they taking them?" Gladys said.

"Probably to *Chiriquí* Prison . . . it will be bad for them there."

"Edgardo, we have to do something."

He stared at her for a moment, then said, "I must get you to the Canal Zone. You can notify your authorities when you get there."

He started to move toward the door again, but Gladys grabbed his arm. "Edgardo, what's going on here?"

He gazed at her, as if contemplating an abyss. Finally he said, "There are deep problems . . . between our peoples."

Her father's words at breakfast that morning rushed back to her. He had cautioned her to keep her direct contact with Panamanians to a minimum. "They're a sullen lot," he had said, "ready to explode, given the slightest excuse. They foster a hatred for us that we can't fathom."

Now Gladys plaintively asked Edgardo, "Why do you dislike us so?"

He stared past her, not responding.

"Why, Edgardo?" she pressed. "Everyone has seemed so happy . . . so friendly toward me this week. You and me. What's happening?"

He fixed his gaze on her, his countenance grim. "You *gringos* have no respect for us."

"Respect?"

"Yes, respect!"

His vehemence startled her. "Edgardo . . . I don't know what you're talking about."

"You think we are ignorant . . . mongrels. You scorn us because of our mixed blood . . . like the Colombians before you . . . and the Spaniards before them."

"Edgardo—"

"No!" he said with an angry shake of his head. "No more! Come. I will return you to the Canal Zone . . . to your little piece of America."

Gladys stood beside her father in the Tivoli Hotel ballroom, awaiting the arrival of Theodore Roosevelt. A ten-piece orchestra was playing, but no one was dancing. Instead, the invited guests clustered in small groups, eagerly anticipating the unprecedented presidential appearance.

"You *did* remember to invite Mr. Duque, didn't you?" her father said. "I'd like the president to meet him before the tour tomorrow."

"Yes, Papa," Gladys said. However, she hadn't heard from Edgardo since the hostilities two days earlier. Twenty-four hours after the incident, Panamanian authorities had released nine brutalized Marine survivors, and the bodies of their three comrades. Americans in the Canal Zone were still incensed that their government had not retaliated militarily.

Gladys dejectedly scanned the ballroom, fearing that Edgardo's general resentment of Americans was stronger than any personal allegiance he had for her. How could she explain his absence? What would she do about the tour in the morning? She'd had little sleep the past two nights, anguishing over what had transpired and having no one in whom she could confide. What if she was pregnant!

Then, entering the front door, she saw him. Clad in a new dark suit, he stood out from the Americans in their light-colored tropical garb. He paused, looking uncertainly about the room. Gladys waved and got his attention. He threaded his way over to her. She had to fight back tears of relief when he respectfully acknowledged her with a smile and a nod, then formally presented himself to her father.

"You're late, Mr. Duque," her father said as they shook hands. "We were getting worried about you."

"Tiempo panameño," Edgardo replied, then prompted Gladys with an inquiring look.

She smiled and translated for her father. "That means 'Panamanian time'."

"Ah . . . yes," her father said, studying the two of them for a moment. "Well, please be on American time tomorrow morning, Mr. Duque. And, by the way, your tour plans are excellent."

"Your daughter was most helpful, sir."

Gladys heaved a sigh of relief. She wanted to hug her enigmatic Panamanian.

The orchestra struck up a fanfare, interrupting their exchange. A side door opened, and President Roosevelt strode into the ballroom. His entourage, led by Chief Engineer John Stevens, streamed in after him. The assemblage broke into spontaneous applause.

Edgardo moved next to Gladys; their shoulders touched. He inclined his head toward hers and whispered, *"Lo siento."*

Again tears welled in Gladys' eyes. The Spanish phrase meant "I'm sorry". She discreetly found his hand and gave it a squeeze, then tried to focus on the proceedings.

An unofficial reception line formed at the edge of the dance floor. As the president worked his way along the row of well-wishers, Gladys noted he was shorter than he appeared in photographs; still, he dominated the room. He was clad in a white suit, and his face shone with the ruddy glow of a man who had spent too much of his first day in the Panamanian sun. She made a mental note to get him a proper hat for tomorrow.

The reviewing party stopped in front of Gladys' father. "Mr. President," John Stevens said, "may I present Avery Johnson, supervisor of our Quartermaster Corps."

"Pleased to meet you, Johnson," the president said, peering through his pince-nez glasses at Gladys' father. "Head of the Quartermaster Corps, eh? What kind of problems are you having? What can I do to help?"

The directness of the president's questions obviously caught Gladys' father off guard. "Ah . . . well, sir . . . I . . . uh . . . don't know."

The president gazed at him intently, indicating he expected a better response.

"Our biggest problem . . . is the Culebra Cut," Gladys' father said, apparently rallying with the first thing that came to mind. Then he quipped, "Perhaps you could help us dig while you're down here, sir."

The president seemed momentarily taken aback, but then flashed his well-known toothy smile and said, "I understand we'll be out at Culebra tomorrow afternoon, Johnson. Have a shovel ready for me."

"Mr. President," John Stevens interjected, "May I present Avery's daughter, Gladys, who organized this reception. She'll also be responsible for your tour of Panama City in the morning."

"Hello, my dear," the president said, directing his attention to Gladys. "It sounds like I've been taking up too much of your time."

"Oh, no, Mr. President. I've enjoyed it. And may I present Señor Edgardo Duque, who will be your guide tomorrow."

Edgardo respectfully came to attention and extended his hand. The president, however, didn't take it. Instead, he narrowed his eyes and said, "Duque, eh? Related to the traitor, Gabriel Duque?"

To her horror, Gladys saw Edgardo's countenance darken, as it had the night of the street disturbance. She instinctively grasped the back of his elbow.

"I *believe* he is my father, sir," Edgardo said.

"You believe?" Roosevelt exclaimed. "You don't know who your father is?"

Edgardo's dark eyes locked on the president's.

"You know, John," Roosevelt said, addressing the chief engineer, "Gabriel Duque damn near cost Panama its independence. While we were negotiating our support for the revolution, and drawing up the canal treaty, Duque disclosed the entire proceedings to the Colombians." Roosevelt kept Edgardo fixed in his gaze, as if challenging him to respond.

John Stevens cleared his throat, clearly uncomfortable with the situation unfolding before him.

Edgardo said levelly, "Sir, once the revolution started, Gabriel Duque supported it fully. He led his fire brigade into the streets. I was in the brigade."

Roosevelt appeared unmoved.

"The treaty you speak of," Edgardo continued, "was negotiated and signed by a Frenchman, Philippe Bunau-Varilla. Not one Panamanian signature is on the document!"

"The Hay/Bunau-Varilla Treaty," Roosevelt snarled, "married our two countries in the greatest project of all time!"

"Do not begin a marriage with a rape!" Edgardo retorted.

Gladys gasped at Edgardo's impertinence and squeezed his elbow as hard as she could.

A grim smile formed on Roosevelt's face. "I believe you're quoting another Frenchman—Balzac—are you not?"

Edgardo responded with a grudging nod.

"I'd forget what you learned from the French while they were here," Roosevelt said. "They quit . . . and we're not going to. We're going to dig that damned ditch!" With that, he turned to continue down the reception line. But then he swung back to Edgardo, as if to take his measure one last time. He looked down at Gladys' hand, still clutching Edgardo's elbow. Suddenly the president thrust out a meaty hand. "I enjoyed our chat . . . *Señor Duque*," he said. "And I look forward to continuing it tomorrow morning."

"I too, sir," Edgardo said tersely, and accepted the extended hand.

The following afternoon, Gladys and Edgardo stood on a wooden observation platform in the midst of the presidential party. Below lay the infamous Culebra Cut.

A dozen steam shovels gouged out ten-ton scoops of loosened rock and dumped them into a seemingly endless line of railroad cars. A half-mile away, five monster dredges cleared the channel of the soft volcanic rock from the recent slide. And throughout the site, mighty cranes swung huge buckets of concrete, cauterizing the vast wound man was making in the continental divide.

Gladys felt slightly faint from the heat and the heavy meal they had eaten an hour earlier. Her itinerary had called for a light luncheon at the Tivoli Hotel. However, the president had insisted on eating with canal employees in a mess hall, which had featured a workman's meal of beef, boiled potatoes, beets, and a greasy concoction called *chile con carne*. Gladys reached into her bag, withdrew a fan, and tried to stir the humid air in front of her face. Edgardo moved solicitously closer.

President Roosevelt stood at the forward railing, flanked by Chief Engineer John Stevens and Gladys' father. The din from the massive construction site was too loud for Gladys to hear what the men were saying, but the president was gesturing with a clenched hand, clearly enthusiastic about what he was seeing.

Roosevelt's meeting with *Presidente* Amador that morning had gone well, as had the informal tour through the city that had followed. While on the tour, Roosevelt had bombarded Edgardo with pointed questions, political as well as historical. Edgardo's answers had been direct; however, there had been no recurrence of the previous night's rancor. At the end of the tour, Roosevelt had insisted that Edgardo accompany them on his inspection of the Canal Zone.

Now at Culebra, a light mist began to fall, and several members of the presidential party popped open their parasols. An aide offered one to Roosevelt, but the president shook his head. He looked back at Gladys and smiled. He tapped the wide brim of the hat she had given him that morning, and shouted over the din below, "How did you know it was going to rain this afternoon?"

"It's our rainy season, sir," she shouted back.

"'Our'?" the president mouthed with a bemused grin.

Gladys looked up at Edgardo, who also smiled. A klaxon's shrill wail split the air. Gladys flinched and grabbed Edgardo's hand. Below, the clamor subsided, as engineers shifted scores of mighty machines into idle. Most of the manual laborers also stopped in place. The chief engineer pointed to an area on the opposite side of the cut, where five workers scurried away from a large drill rig. "Stand by, sir!" the chief engineer shouted to the president.

A moment later, a long ominous tremor shook the earth, then gradually dampened. The president looked inquiringly at the chief engineer.

"That was a 40,000-pound charge, sir!" Stevens shouted. As he spoke, an earthen glacier on the opposite hill sheared loose, then slid slowly to the bottom of the manmade ravine.

"Damn!" Roosevelt said.

The heavy equipment below remained idle, and a hundred or so khaki-clad American engineers clambered up the muddy hillside to the observation platform. The Americans were followed by an equal number of tattered, black West Indian laborers. Roosevelt peered down at the throng with a friendly snarl. When they were assembled in front of the platform, he shouted down oratorically, "This is one . . . of the great works of the world! I go back a better

American . . . a prouder American . . . because of what I have seen the pick of American manhood . . . doing here on the Isthmus!"

The American engineers roared their appreciation. The West Indian laborers looked on in silent amusement.

The president pointed down the hillside to a ninety-five-ton Bucyrus steam shovel. "Johnson," he shouted, "is that the shovel you promised me yesterday?"

"Yes, sir!" Gladys' father said with a laugh. "If you want it, sir. Everything here is yours."

"Well then," the president said, "I want to see it!" He clambered down the muddy hillside, mindless of the damage to his white suit. His entourage of officials, guests, photographers, and now engineers comically slid down the hill after him. Only Gladys, her father, and Edgardo stayed behind on the platform.

A man who ran the giant steam shovel helped the president onto the operating platform and showed him the levers that controlled it. The photographers went into a frenzy, taking pictures of the man who three years earlier had promised to "make the dirt fly". He had now personally taken the controls of a gigantic Bucyrus.

The klaxon sounded, and the massive effort around him was again put into gear.

Gladys looked across the platform to her father. He was smiling at the scene below in unmistakable pride. Then she turned to Edgardo. He was looking grimly up the hill. High on a gravel road above, stood a band of *campesinos*, silently watching the foreigners destroying their homeland.

"Edgardo?" Gladys said.

Without turning, he said bitterly, "Americans engineer it . . . West Indians dig it . . . and we Panamanians only watch."

Gladys grasped his arm and pulled him close. Her father turned toward them at that moment. A look of profound regret crossed his face. Then he turned his back and gazed down the cut, to the dense jungle beyond.

Gladys released Edgardo's arm. Tears welled in her eyes. She took a deep breath, then crossed the platform to her father. "Papa, please—"

"No," her father interrupted, turning to her with a sad smile. "I'm glad you've found someone, honey. It's just that for a moment there . . . all I could think of was your mother. God, how I wish she could be here with us. Clearly, you and I have come to stay."

Gladys turned and waved for Edgardo to join them.

13. LOS ESTUDIANTES

Hank sat alone in the Aventura Tours van, parked on a deserted dark street at the edge of the University of Panama. The only illumination of the surrounding area came from the second floor of the nearby building, where Andrea was attending class.

The van windows were open and the radio volume was turned low. A song ended, and the announcer gave the time as 9:40. Hank stretched; he had twenty minutes more to wait. The sound of footfalls echoed in the night. They grew louder, and Hank switched off the radio. A moment later, a young man jogged into the illuminated area, glancing furtively over his shoulder. As he passed the van, he spotted Hank and broke into a sprint. He disappeared into the darkness behind the van.

A truck careened around the corner, then slowed, as someone played a searchlight across both sides of the street. Hank ducked behind the van's dashboard. The truck stopped nearby, and angry shouts filled the night air. Looking up through the windshield, Hank saw the silhouettes of students gathering at the lighted second-floor windows.

Someone in the truck shouted up to the students, challenging them to come out. The students responded with jeers and catcalls. From the students' taunts, Hank could tell the men in the truck were PDF soldiers, probably Dobermans. He shook his head. Damn it!

The exchanges between the soldiers and students grew more heated. Hank took a deep breath and placed his hand on the door handle. He hesitated; the soldiers would see the interior light if he opened the door. Movement at one of the classroom windows caught his attention. One of the students climbed above the others and appeared to remove something from the ceiling. Then another hurled a spear-like object toward the street. There was a pop, followed by angry shouts and the sounds of the soldiers scurrying for cover.

In the confusion, Hank threw open the van door and dived for the nearby curb, landing on his right shoulder. Ignoring the stab of pain, he kicked the door closed. Then he waited, wedged between the van and the curb. The side door of the school building was about twenty-five feet away. More objects rained down from the classroom. One exploded nearby, and Hank realized the students were throwing fluorescent light tubes.

Gunfire erupted from the street. Andrea! Hank thought. He leaped to his feet and raced for the building entrance. The doorknob was loose, but he managed to yank open the door, then threw himself headfirst onto the hallway floor. Outside, he heard someone shout an order, and the firing ceased.

Hank scrambled to his feet and ran down the hallway, then up a rickety flight of stairs to the second floor. Terrified students poured from the classroom. *"¿Dónde está Andrea?"* Hank shouted. The students fled past without responding.

He pushed his way into the classroom and saw her kneeling beneath a shattered window. "Andrea!" he cried. He rushed over and dropped down beside her. She turned to him with a look of anguish. A young man with a severe head wound stared sightlessly from her lap.

Hank placed his hand against the young man's throat, feeling for carotid pressure. There was none. Hank gazed down at the ashen countenance, so like those who had died in the jungle near Khe Sanh. Yet there, those young men had been soldiers in war; death had been a logical consequence of the minutes, days, and weeks immediately preceding. While here, this young man had had no portent of death; minutes before, he simply had been listening to the drone of a university professor.

"He's dead, Andrea."

"No!"

Hank moved the bloody youth from Andrea's lap, then put an arm around her and helped her to her feet. She stared down at her classmate, unwilling to leave him.

"Andrea," Hank said, "we've got to go."

He guided her out of the classroom and down the stairway. On the first floor, he took her hand and pulled her toward a set of double glass doors that opened onto the school grounds, away from the street. She stopped at the doorway, still dazed. "But the PDF is not allowed on the campus . . ." she said.

"What?"

"Panamanian law forbids the PDF to enter the university."

"Panamanian law! You've got to be kidding." He led her out of the building and into the night.

They ran between the structures of the dimly lighted campus. Occasionally they caught glimpses of other fleeing figures. After several hundred yards, Andrea pulled up. "Wait!" she said, gasping for breath.

Hank pushed her into the shadows of a nearby concrete stairway. He gave her a moment to recover, then whispered, "C'mon. They may be right behind us."

"Un momento," she said. She looked about, orienting herself, then pointed into the darkness. *"La Cresta* is on the other side of that hill. My aunt lives there."

Hank couldn't see where she was pointing, but when she tugged at his hand, he raced blindly after her.

Hank was awakened by the sound of a toilet flushing on the other side of the bedroom wall. Morning light filtered through gauzy curtains. His right shoulder ached from his dive from the van the previous night. He sat up and swung his legs over the side of the narrow bed. The ceramic tile felt cold against the bottoms of his bare feet. He looked about the neatly furnished guest room. Apparently, Andrea's aunt had married well.

Hank rose and walked over to the window. Down the steep hill, the traffic was already heavy on *Vía España*. On the other side of the thoroughfare stood the Hotel Reynosa, where he had stayed the night he arrived in Panama. Two weeks ago? Was that possible? So much had happened.

A faint smile formed. In the distance, the rising sun illuminated Ancon Hill. The scene triggered a flashback to his grandfather's apartment, and Hank recalled the last time he stayed overnight there. Twenty-five years later, here he was back, taking up where he'd left off—violence and all. The smile faded.

A short while later, he found his way to the spacious kitchen. A San Blas cook was busy at the stove. She saw him and said, *"Buenos días, señor."*

"Buenos días, señora."

A middle-aged *rabiblanco*, clad in a conservative dark-gray business suit, sat at the breakfast table. He looked up from his newspaper with an inquiring expression.

Hank walked over, extended his hand, and said in Spanish, "I'm Hank Duque. I'm a friend of Andrea's."

"My wife told me about you," the man said in accented English as they shook hands. He gestured for Hank to join him at the table. "I was sleeping when you arrived last night. I am Humberto Castillero."

"I appreciate your hospitality, Sr. Castillero."

Castillero nodded. "I understand you were caught in a disturbance at the university last night."

"Yeah. Some soldiers fired on Andrea's class. One of the students was killed."

"Those students," Castillero muttered, shaking his head.

"The students didn't start it," Hank said. "They were unarmed."

"Well," Castillero said, "they must have done *something*."

Hank let the matter drop. The cook brought him a steaming plate of scrambled eggs, bacon, and toast. *"Gracias, señora,"* he said. She smiled and returned to the cooking area.

"So you are a Duque, eh?" Castillero said.

Hank nodded. "My grandfather was Edgardo Duque."

Castillero looked at him appraisingly. "Edgardo Duque . . . the university professor?"

"Yeah. Have you heard of him?"

"Yes," Castillero said with a short laugh, "I was a student of his. Officially, he taught me economics. Unofficially, he tried to teach me the doctrine of the *Arnulfistas*."

Hank smiled; his grandfather had touched many lives.

"So you are the grandson . . ." Castillero began. Apparently, he too knew the circumstances of Edgardo Duque's death, but decided not to voice them. Instead he said, "The Duque family is well known. As a matter of fact, there is a statue of . . . one of your relatives, just down the street."

"Really? Who's that?"

"Gabriel Duque," Castillero said. "Do you know who he is?"

"I think so. My grandfather told me about a Gabriel Duque. I think he may have been my great-grandfather."

Castillero smiled. "Here in Panamá, it is not unusual for men of prominence to have . . . more than one family." He shrugged, indicating it was of little importance that Hank's grandfather had been born out of wedlock.

"Grandpa told me Gabriel Duque was involved in the 1903 revolution."

"Yes," Castillero said. "He also became very wealthy. He founded the lottery, a newspaper, and various other businesses."

"I'd like to see that statue," Hank said.

Andrea and her aunt entered the kitchen, interrupting their exchange. "*Buenos días, Enrique*," the aunt said with a smile.

"*Buenos días, Tía Celia*," Hank said, addressing the older woman as Aunt Celia, as she had requested the previous night.

The aunt stayed in the cooking area. Andrea put two pieces of toast on a plate and joined the men at the table. "I see you have met *Tío Humberto*."

Hank nodded. "How are you feeling this morning?"

"I had trouble sleeping," Andrea said. "I did not know the boy who was shot last night, but he seemed so young . . ."

Aunt Celia came over and patted Andrea reassuringly on the shoulder. She glanced at her husband with the deference that many Latin women show their men. Then she returned to the cooking area.

Castillero took a final swallow of coffee, collected his newspaper, and stood up. "I regret we could not talk more, Sr. Duque," he said, "but I have a jewelry store I must open. Come again sometime." He gave Andrea and her aunt curt nods, then strode from the kitchen.

Andrea's aunt joined them at the table, carrying a mug of coffee.

"You are not eating, *Tía?*" Andrea said.

"I ate earlier, with the cook," her aunt said with a smile. "What are you two going to do now?"

"We must go back to the school and get my van," Andrea said. Turning to Hank, she added, "And there are some student leaders I want you to meet."

Her aunt frowned. "Andrea, you must stay away from those people. They make trouble."

"*Tía,*" Andrea said impatiently, "it is not the students who cause the problems, it is *la quardia.*"

"But Humberto says . . ." her aunt began, but her voice trailed off.

Later that morning, Hank and Andrea walked through the affluent hillside neighborhood. A security guard, with a rifle slung over one shoulder, stoically observed them from the shade of a carport. Off in the distance lay the blue-green Pacific.

"Andrea," Hank said, "*Tía* Celia is your father's sister, right?"

"Yes."

"But their lives are so . . . different. Your parents are struggling on a small farm, and your aunt and uncle are living here in *La Cresta.*"

"We were a close family when I was a girl. But then my father became a member of the People's Party and a leader in the National Workers labor union."

"Communist organizations?"

"Both had ties to Moscow."

"And your family split up over this?"

"Yes. My uncle refused to speak to my father. Then, three years ago, the government sent my father to *La Preventiva*. When he got out, he was broken. My mother took him to Portobelo, and they have been there ever since."

"And you got caught in the middle."

She nodded. "*Tío* and *Tía* worry because I live in *Santa Ana*. They would like me to live with them, but I cannot do so without showing disrespect for my parents."

They rounded a bend, and Andrea pointed to the end of the street. A small circular park had been fashioned in the cul-de-sac. In the middle, perched atop a six-foot marble base, was the life-size bust of a man. Hank walked up the weathered concrete sidewalk and read the inscription:

En Memoria
Del Ilustre Filantropo
Jose Gabriel Duque
1849-1918

Hank smiled. In Houston, the name "Duque" was uncommon; he often had to spell it for people. Here in Panama, it was chiseled in marble. He took a step back, gazed up at the polished dark countenance.

Andrea moved beside him; their shoulders touched. She raised her eyebrows inquiringly. "So, that 'Illustrious Philanthropist' is your great-grandfather, eh?"

Hank nodded, still smiling.

"Well," she said, "to me, you are still just another *gringo*." Hank frowned at her, and she gave him a playful poke in the ribs. "*Venga, gringo*," she said, "let's go see if I have a van."

This time the van was intact. The Doberman's lust for vengeance apparently had been satiated by the killing of the student. The school building was deserted; its shattered windows gave mute testimony of the previous night's violence.

As Hank and Andrea drove away from the campus, she said, "I have a tour in an hour. I can leave you with some friends, and then pick you up when I am finished."

"Sounds good. Will these be the student leaders you mentioned at breakfast?"

She nodded.

They entered a ramshackle neighborhood—unkempt one-story houses, interspersed with an occasional small business. Andrea pulled up in front of a shabby restaurant. A rusty Coca Cola sign hung crookedly over the front door and read simply: Restaurante y Bar.

They got out of the car, and Hank followed her through the rusty screen door. Only one of the half-dozen mismatched tables was occupied. An old man, apparently the proprietor, sat reading a newspaper. He glanced up as they walked by and grudgingly returned Hank's nod. They passed through the filthy kitchen and by a fetid rest room.

A makeshift patio lay behind the restaurant, enclosed by a rotted fence, held up by debris and uncut foliage. Three warped cable spools served as tables. Two young men and a woman sat at a table beneath a shade tree.

"Andrea, ¿como estas?" the young woman said in greeting. She looked with interest at Hank.

"Bien, Silvia," Andrea said. Turning to Hank, she said, "Hank, this is Silvia, Tico, and Pablo."

All three wore T-shirts and jeans. Silvia was perhaps twenty, slightly heavy, but attractive. Tico was thin, smiling, and looked the part of a young scholar. Pablo was older, perhaps Andrea's age, muscular, with the demeanor of a mean-street mestizo.

"Mucho gusto," Hank said.

"And this is Hank," Andrea said, completing the introductions. "His Spanish is getting better, but we should speak in English."

Silvia and Tico smiled; Pablo stared impassively.

The proprietor appeared, carrying two rusty folding chairs. "*¿Cerveza, señor?*"

Although it was still morning, a beer sounded good. But Hank saw the students were having soft drinks, and instead said, "*Una Coca Cola, por favor.*" Andrea said she'd have the same.

The proprietor went inside, and Hank and Andrea joined the others at the table. Andrea told them about the incident at the school the previous night. When she had finished, Silvia said to Hank in accented English, "You are in Andrea's class?"

"No, I was just waiting for her when the trouble broke out."

"He is the writer," Andrea interjected. "I showed you his story in *La Prensa*—the one about the demonstrations."

"It was very good," Silvia said, and Tico nodded. Pablo gave them a cutting glance. He obviously was the leader of this group and didn't want any competition for their respect.

Trying to bring Pablo into the conversation, Hank asked him, "What's been your experience with Noriega and the PDF?"

"Why do you want to know?"

"I'm looking for another story."

"Why?" Pablo said. "Panamá means nothing to you *gringos*."

"It means something to *him*," Andrea said. "He is one-quarter Panamanian. The PDF put him in *La Preventiva* for writing his last story." The students, even Pablo, seemed to regard Hank with new respect. "His grandfather—"

Hank interrupted, "Have there been any recent student protests?" He wanted to steer the conversation away from the personal nature of his involvement.

"Yes," Silvia said. "We took part in those demonstrations you wrote about. We are members of the *Federación de Estudiantes Revolucionarios*—the Federation of Revolutionary Students."

"And your federation opposes Noriega?" Hank said.

Tico spoke up. "We oppose both the military and the *rabiblancos*."

"The *rabiblancos*?" Hank said, thinking not only of his grandfather, but also of Humberto Castillero, who had given him shelter the night before, and of Luis Fuentes, now imprisoned on *Isla de Coiba* for resisting Noriega. "What do you have against the *rabiblancos?*"

"Power must be returned to the people," Pablo said. "The *rabiblancos* oppress the working class."

Rather than get sidetracked with socialist dogma, Hank tried to focus the exchange on Noriega. "But don't the *rabiblancos* oppose Noriega?"

"They just want to return power to themselves," Pablo retorted. Then he added, "Would you rather be fucked by a puma, or a jaguar?"

The memory of the broom handle in *La Preventiva* flashed through Hank's mind. "I think I understand what you mean."

Andrea stood up and said to Hank, "I have to go to work. Will you be okay here?"

"Sure," Hank said. As Andrea passed, she reached down and touched Hank's shoulder, and he briefly covered her hand with his own. He saw Pablo scowl at the exchange.

"*Prefieres leche que café, eh, Andrea?*" Pablo said sullenly.

Andrea glared at him. Then with an annoyed shake of her head, she left the patio.

Hank tried to translate Pablo's comment. Andrea prefers milk to coffee? At first it didn't make sense; then he understood. It was a reference to his white skin. Her son's father also had been white. Hank remembered the taunts of the Panamanian kids in his grandfather's neighborhood. He said to Pablo, "You don't like whites?"

"I do not like *gringos*," Pablo said, returning Hank's gaze.

Tico interjected, "We oppose the United States. We want our canal. It is our country. Why should the United States own our canal?"

"Well," Hank said, "without the United States, there wouldn't be a canal. There wouldn't even be a Republic of Panama. You'd still just be the northern province of Colombia."

"See!" Pablo said vehemently. "All *gringos* talk the same shit!"

Realizing he was alienating the three students, Hank said, "In any case, the Carter-Torrijos treaty calls for the U.S. to pull out of Panama entirely in only ten years. So what's the problem?"

"Treaty!" Pablo scoffed. "Treaties mean nothing to *gringos* when they want something."

Silvia joined the exchange, asking Hank, "You don't think the United States army will actually leave, do you?"

"You could be right," Hank acknowledged. "The U.S. seldom gives up military bases. But, on the other hand, the bases are here to protect Panama."

"From who?" Pablo demanded. "No one wants to invade Panamá."

"See how good the system works," Hank joked, still hoping to ease the tension.

Pablo remained unsmiling. "The United States army is here to suppress the Panamanian people."

Hank weighed the charge. To some extent, Pablo was right. Historically, U.S. military interventions in Panama had been to control local uprisings, not to repel external aggression. The canal had always been, and would continue to be, vulnerable to sabotage, regardless of whether or not U.S. troops were stationed on Panamanian soil. That was the reason the United States had two navies: an Atlantic fleet and a Pacific fleet.

Pablo continued, "Also, your army created our army. We have no need for an army. But you forced one on us. Now it rapes the people."

"There's truth in what you say," Hank conceded, as again the night in *La Preventiva* flashed through his mind. Then he said, "Do you think you students can bring about political change?"

"We have in the past," Pablo said. "The Panamanian flag flies in the Canal Zone because of the 1964 student riot."

As Hank gave a grudging nod, he suppressed saying, "And if you were ten years older, my friend, we'd have been on opposite sides of Fourth of July Avenue."

Tico chimed in, "The 1964 riot was the reason your President Carter negotiated the treaty."

Hank had to nod again. Their views on United States-Panamanian relations were simplistic, but not without merit. "What do you students plan to do next?"

Tico started to respond, but Pablo silenced him with an emphatic shake of his head. Hank understood their need for discretion. He was someone they scarcely knew.

Silvia picked up a canvas knapsack off the ground, then stood up and said with a smile, "I have a class. I hope to see you again."

The other two also rose and collected their things. Tico said, "I enjoyed our discussion. I will watch for your next story." Pablo simply gave Hank a curt nod.

They filed into the restaurant, and a moment later, the proprietor appeared.

Hank said, "*Señor, déme una Balboa, por favor.*"

The proprietor ducked inside to get the beer, and Hank leaned back in his chair, discouraged. In years past, idealistic students had been effective in changing Panama's political landscape. Jimmy Carter had been moved by their passion. But these students lacked clear direction. And Manuel Noriega bore no resemblance to Jimmy Carter.

14. LOS RABIBLANCOS

Hank descended the steps from Andrea's century-old apartment building. The mix of pungent smells from the open market and the nearby ocean was now familiar. He started up the littered side street, unhurried; he had more than an hour before his first appointment. The afternoon air was hot and humid, but his loose-fitting *guayabera* shirt felt comfortable, unlike the tight-meshed golf shirts he had worn on his arrival.

He came to the intersection and paused in front of a dilapidated cantina. He pretended to look inside, but behind his sun glasses he actually was checking his reflection in the window. His mustache was a week old; his hair, which he had always worn short and dry, was now slicked back. Deciding he could pass for *panameño*, he turned and strolled up *Avenida B.*

Pedestrians swarmed along the sidewalks of the busy thoroughfare. Occasionally, one would step into the street, showing a matador's disdain for the onrushing vehicles.

A PDF soldier directed traffic at the next intersection. Hank drifted closer to the storefronts that lined the sidewalk. Having no passport, he needed to remain inconspicuous. As he arrived at the corner, a car sped up the side street. Hank tried to stop at the curb, but the pedestrians behind him pushed forward. The car had to slam on its brakes to avoid hitting him. The soldier glared at Hank, then waved the car through. Hank was swept across the street by the wave of people behind him.

A half-block farther, he spotted a bus stop on the other side of the street. He waited until a young woman next to him stepped boldly into the street, then followed, letting her run interference.

Safely on the other side, he joined a group of people waiting for an oncoming bus. No one seemed to take notice of him.

An hour later, Hank had found his way to the small restaurant near the university campus. This time, there were no customers. The proprietor gave him a nod of recognition as he entered. Hank took a table next to the front window. "*Déme una Balboa, por favor.*"

The old man brought over the beer and said in Spanish, "Where are your friends today?"

"In school, I guess," Hank replied in Spanish.

A green Land Rover pulled up outside, and Joe Ortega, Hank's Associated Press contact, climbed out. The swarthy Californian entered the restaurant and spotted Hank.

"You're early," Hank said as the two men shook hands.

"Thought I might have some trouble finding this no-name restaurant of yours." The proprietor came over, and Ortega said, "*Déme una Budweiser.*"

"*No tengo Budweiser,*" the proprietor said.

Ortega glanced at Hank's beer. "*Bueno, déme una Balboa.*" After he had received his beer and taken a swallow, Ortega told Hank, "Looks like you've gone native."

Hank removed his sun glasses. "I had some problems with the Noriega interview."

"So I gathered. I warned you to stay away from that son of a bitch."

"Yes, you did."

"A couple of days ago," Ortega said, "Major Carlos Mejías came by our office, looking for you. He'd seen your articles, and knew you were working for us as a stringer. He told us he'd pulled your passport and you were in violation of a deportation order."

Hank nodded.

"Why'd he pull your passport?"

"The anti-Noriega piece, I guess." Hank didn't know Ortega well enough to go into the personal aspect of the vendetta between him and Mejías.

L

"I'd never met the major before," Ortega said, "but the stories I've heard seem to be true. He strikes me as being another Noriega."

Hank nodded.

"Your account of conditions in *La Preventiva* went out this morning," Ortega said. "Other than pissing off Mejías, it probably won't cause much of a stir down here. It might be a revelation for people in the States, though." Ortega withdrew an envelope from his shirt pocket and handed it to Hank. "Cash, as requested. Four hundred for the *Los Machos del Monte* story, and four hundred for *La Preventiva*. If you'd been able to get pictures, it would have paid more."

"I need to buy another camera," Hank said. "The PDF confiscated mine." He withdrew a folded packet of paper from his trousers pocket and handed it to Ortega. "This is a piece I did on the student that the PDF killed at the University of Panama the other night."

"Who's your source?"

"Me. I was there when it happened."

"You seem to have a knack for being where the action is," Ortega said, with a hint of suspicion in his tone.

Hank didn't respond.

Ortega unfolded the packet and read through the piece. When he finished, he looked up and said, "We can use this, but I'm not sure I agree with the conclusions you draw at the end. Why do you think the student protests are ineffective?"

"Youthful idealism. The students aren't focused. They're expending as much energy opposing the *rabiblancos* and the *gringos*, as they are Noriega."

"But historically," Ortega countered, "Panamanian students have been successful in getting what they wanted."

"Against the United States, yes," Hank said. "But Noriega's different. I don't see him backing down. I think he sent them a firm message the other night."

Ortega studied him for a moment, then nodded in agreement. He pulled out a pen, jotted a few notes, then looked up. "What do you plan to do next?"

"I'm going to try to get a better understanding of the *rabiblancos'* position."

"How do you plan to do that?"

"I've made a contact that I think will be helpful."

"Who with?"

"A business leader. I can't give you his name."

Ortega gave a grudging nod, then said, "When we spoke with Mejías, we told him we had no knowledge of your whereabouts, which was true. It's probably in your best interest, as well as ours, that we keep it that way."

Hank nodded.

Ortega said. "Will the young lady who dropped off your last article be our go-between?"

"Probably. And you can give her any future payments."

Ortega nodded, then rose to leave. "Hank," he said, "we can use your work. But personally, I recommend you get the hell out of Panama."

"I appreciate your concern, Joe," Hank said, rising and shaking the correspondent's hand, "but I'm staying."

A short while later, Hank strolled past the row of shops that lined *Vía España* in the fashionable banking district. Pedestrians crowded the sidewalk, but most were simply loitering. Andrea had forewarned him that street demonstrations were planned for that afternoon.

Ahead he saw the sign he was looking for: *Joyería Castillero*—Castillero's Jewelry Store. The front of the shop was imposing—white marble laminate, with an etched glass door. A private security guard stood near the entrance, an automatic rifle slung over one shoulder. He stepped forward as Hank approached.

"I am here to see Sr. Castillero," Hank said in Spanish. "My name is Enrique Duque."

"*Espérate*," the guard said, gesturing for Hank to wait outside. Then he entered the store and spoke briefly with another guard. A few moments later, Castillero appeared.

"Hank, good to see you," the jeweler said as they shook hands. "Andrea told me you would come by today." He ushered Hank through the plush display room, and back to his office at the rear of the store. When they were seated, the jeweler said with a smile, "Is this a social call, or can I sell you something?"

"Neither, Sr. Castillero. I'd like to interview you."

"Interview *me*?"

"I'd like to get an understanding of the business community's attitude toward General Noriega. From what I've seen—" He was interrupted by a crescendo of car horns and what sounded like people beating on pots and pans. He and Castillero jumped up and hurried into the display room. A mob of demonstrators surged in front of the glass door, waving white handkerchiefs. Both security guards were now inside the store, their weapons pointed toward the doorway.

The crowd suddenly parted, and Hank saw a blue-gray van pull up, with the silhouette of a dog's head stenciled on its side. Four Dobermans, in full riot gear, climbed out and approached the doorway. They angrily gestured for the security guards to unlock the door. When neither responded, a Dobermans pointed his shotgun at the door and fired. Hank instinctively ducked, as bird shot and glass fragments exploded across the room. The two security guards threw down their weapons and raised their hands. The clerks and the half-dozen customers fled to the rear of the store and huddled against the wall.

The Dobermans stalked into the store. Two stationed themselves just inside the doorway. Castillero hurried over and demanded in Spanish, "What do you want here?" One of the Dobermans whipped a rubber hose across the jeweler's face, driving him to the floor. Hank took a step forward, but froze as the other Doberman walked toward him, pointing a shotgun at his stomach.

A young clerk rushed to Castillero's aide. She pulled a white scarf from around her neck and tried to stem the blood flowing from his forehead. The Doberman who had hit the jeweler grabbed the young woman by her hair and pulled her to her feet. He yanked the bloody scarf from her hand and scrubbed it over her face. She tried to fight him off, her cries muffled by the cloth.

Hank took another step forward, but the Doberman standing next to him pressed the shotgun muzzle against his ribs. The Doberman raised his chin, as if steeling himself to pull the trigger. Hank froze. The tense moment passed. The Doberman finally took a deep breath.

Castillero, still prostrate, groaned. The Doberman who was holding the clerk kicked the jeweler in the ribs. Castillero gasped, then quieted. The Doberman leaned against a display counter and pulled the clerk to him. He yanked her head back and ran his hand between her legs. Then he grasped her wrist and forced her hand against his crotch. "You will give the favor here," he murmured, "or you will give it to everyone in *La Preventiva*." He pulled the young woman in the direction of Castillero's office.

Hank tensed. No way to win, but he couldn't just stand there.

Suddenly a cry rang out, *"¡Fuego!"* The demonstrators in the street had set fire to the Dobermans' van.

The lead Doberman threw the young woman to the floor, and all four ran outside. They opened fire on the demonstrators, their shotgun blasts igniting screams of pain and terror.

Hank rushed over to Castillero. He was conscious, but still stunned. "Is there a back way out?" Hank shouted.

"¡Señor!" the clerk said. "It is this way. I have the key."

"Get these people out of here!" Hank said.

The young woman jumped up and herded the others toward an emergency exit at the rear of the store. The two private security guards were first out the door.

Castillero sat up and groggily shook his head. "Are the Dobermans gone?"

"For now," Hank said, helping the jeweler to his feet. "C'mon, we've got to get out of here."

"I can't leave my store."

"Fuck the store!"

Castillero pulled out a set of keys and staggered over to a nearby display case. He began stacking trays of rings on top of each other.

Hank glanced through the shattered doorway. The sidewalk had cleared, and the gunfire had moved down the street.

"You go," Castillero said. "I must lock up my merchandise." He gestured toward the massive door of a walk-in vault.

Hank looked distractedly toward the sidewalk. Then with a shake of his head, he rushed over and helped the jeweler secure his merchandise.

It took several anxious minutes to empty the display cases. Spilled jewelry littered the steel vault floor by the time Castillero finally closed the door and turned the tumbler. Moments later, they hurried up a *La Cresta* side street, away from the continuing demonstration.

Hank paced about Sr. Castillero's luxurious living room. The jeweler lay on the couch, holding the dressing that covered the laceration over his right eye. Sra. Castillero peered anxiously through the front window.

The telephone rang and all three jumped. Sra. Castillero answered it. With a look of relief, she covered the mouthpiece and said, "It is Andrea. She is all right." To Andrea she said, "Just a minute. There is someone here who has been worried about you." She handed the phone to Hank.

"Andrea?" Hank said.

"What are you doing at *Tía* Celia's?" Andrea said.

"Are you okay?"

"Of course."

"Where are you?"

"I'm at work. I just called to talk to *Tía* Celia."

"You didn't get caught in the rioting?"

"No, I was in the demonstration on *Vía Argentina*, near the university. It was peaceful. But I heard on the radio that there was shooting on *Vía España*."

"No shit. Most of it took place at your uncle's jewelry shop."

"Oh, no! Was anyone hurt?"

"Your uncle got a bad rap on the head, but he's okay. One of his clerks got roughed up, but she'll be all right. The store's a mess, though."

"Do I need to come over there?"

"Are there any more demonstrations planned for today?"

"Not that I know of."

"Then you might as well stay where you are. Now that we know you're okay, your uncle will probably want to go back to his store and see what needs to be done." Hank looked at Sr. Castillero, who nodded. Hank covered the mouthpiece. "Can I go along with you?" Castillero nodded again. Hank asked Andrea, "Do you have a class tonight?"

"Yes, at 8:00."

"Pick me up here then, after class."

"Okay, Hank. I have to go now. I have a tour in a few minutes."

"Show 'em the city while you can," he said. "The way things are going, it may not be here for long."

Sr. Castillero parked his Cadillac in front of the jewelry store. As he and Hank climbed out, the jeweler swore, *"¡Aya, carajo!"* He stood for a moment, shaking his head in dismay at the damage that had been inflicted on his and the other stores on the block.

They entered the shop, shattered glass crunching under their feet. Looters had smashed the empty display cases, broken a mahogany desk, and taken everything that could be carried away—chairs, mirrors, and merchandise racks. Even the telephones were gone. The steel vault was marred, but still secured.

"Do you have insurance that will cover this?" Hank said.

The jeweler shook his head.

A pickup truck pulled up outside, and two workers climbed out. They entered the store and surveyed the wreckage around them, barely concealing their amusement. Castillero irritably told them to get a larger truck and clean up the mess, then to board up the entryway. He checked his watch, and said to Hank, "We will come back later. Come, there is someone I must see."

They drove two blocks to the *El Panamá*, the city's premier hotel. Castillero pulled into a reserved parking spot at the rear of the sprawling twelve-story building. He led Hank through a side door and across the spacious hotel lobby, toward a neon sign that read "Club Coco".

They paused just inside the doorway, letting their eyes adjust to the dim lighting. It was early evening, and happy-hour patrons crammed the horseshoe bar and secluded booths. Several couples occupied the dance floor.

A young man, apparently the club manager, came over. "*Buenas tardes, Sr. Castillero.*"

"Good afternoon, Paco," Castillero replied in Spanish. "Is Alejandro Remos here?"

"This way, sirs," the manager said, and led them through a labyrinth of booths, lighted only by flickering table candles. In the far corner, a heavyset man sat in a circular booth, studying some papers. A young woman, seated beside him, watched as they approached. The man looked up, squinting over the top of his reading glasses. "Humberto," he said in surprise. "What happened to your head?" He stood up and the two men embraced in the Latin *abrazo*.

"The Dobermans attacked my store this afternoon, *don* Alejandro," Castillero said. He placed a hand on Hank's shoulder. "I would like you to meet Hank Duque."

The two men shook hands, and Remos sat back down. He said something in the young woman's ear, and she stood up. She gave Hank and Castillero a deferential nod and left the booth. Remos gestured for them to be seated, then said to Castillero, "Tell me, Humberto, what happened?"

As the jeweler recounted the destruction of his shop, Remos listened with interest. When Castillero had finished, Remos turned to Hank. "And you, Mr. Duque, are you a visitor in our country?"

"He is a reporter for the Associated Press," Castillero interjected.

Remos drew back.

"He is also the grandson of *Profesor* Edgardo Duque," Castillero added.

Remos leaned forward again. "Oh, yes?"

Hank sensed the opportunity to again draw on the store of good will that his grandfather had left behind. "I've been living in the States for the past twenty-five years," he said. "Now I'm a stringer for the AP."

Remos said, "Are you the grandson that had to leave the country during the 1964 riot?"

"Yes," Hank said, then waited to see what impact the disclosure would have.

"Your grandfather and I often did not agree," Remos said. "He was a teacher—an idealist. I am, how you say . . . a pragmatist?"

Hank nodded.

"I do business," Remos said, "regardless of who is in power."

"Can you really do business with a man like Noriega?"

Remos smiled. "The stories about Tony are usually . . . exaggerations."

Hank frowned. So, Noriega was "Tony" to Sr. Remos. "From what I hear, he's pretty ruthless."

"Americans always like to have a villain," Remos said. "It justifies whatever they do."

"You don't believe the stories about Noriega?"

"Exaggerations," Remos said again, "harmful to the business climate."

"What about Sr. Castillero's store today?"

"Probably a misunderstanding." Remos turned to Castillero. "I will look into the matter."

Castillero nodded gratefully.

Hank realized both men were under the delusion that "Tony" could be controlled. Since Remos apparently was an influential figure in Panama, Hank tried a different tack. "I'd like to present the business viewpoint in an article. Would you let me interview you?"

Remos studied the request for a moment; finally he nodded.

"Humberto and I are flying out to *Isla Contadora* for a meeting tomorrow. If you would like to come with us, I could arrange for you to speak with me and several other businessmen."

Hank's mind raced. It would be a unique opportunity, but he couldn't risk the airport—no passport.

"We are leaving tomorrow morning at 7:00," Remos continued, "from Paitilla Airport."

Hank remembered the small municipal landing strip from his youth. A passport shouldn't be necessary for a local flight. "I appreciate your offer, Sr. Remos. I'll take you up on it."

"Bueno," Remos said. "I will see you tomorrow morning at 7:00." Then turning to Castillero. "I would like for you to stay. We have some business to discuss."

Hank shook hands with the two men, then left.

"Hank," Andrea said, "I still don't think this is a good idea." It was 6:45 the following morning, and they were driving down *Avenida Balboa* in the Aventura Tours van.

"I'll be okay, as long as no one asks to see my passport."

"It is not only that. You don't know these men you will be meeting with."

"Your uncle will be there."

"Hank, Humberto is my uncle, but . . ."

"But what?"

"He is a *rabiblanco*. Like many rich people, *Tío* doesn't care what Noriega does, as long as it doesn't affect him or his business."

"Is your uncle's attitude typical among the *rabiblancos*?"

"Some have spoken out against Noriega and have taken part in demonstrations, but most have not."

"I'll put that slant on my article then."

Andrea gave a resigned shake of her head. She pointed up ahead. "We are coming to the airport."

They drove along a chain-link fence that enclosed one end of the airstrip. Hangars and small aircraft lined the single runway. Since it was early, there was little activity.

Hank smiled at the familiar scene. "I used to ride my bike over here from Grandpa's and watch the planes take off and land. It looks the same . . . except there weren't any jets back then."

Andrea pulled into a pot-holed parking lot. "This is the *Camino Real* hangar." She parked next to the steel building and turned to him with a worried frown.

Hank leaned over and kissed her. "I'll call you when I get back."

"Hank," she said, grasping his hand, "I don't think this is a good idea."

"I'll be okay. I'm just meeting with some businessmen."

She shook her head. "The PDF hangar is next to this one."

"I'll keep an eye out for them." He patted her hand.

She shook her head again. "Having a hangar next to the PDF is a sign of . . . respect. It means the *Camino Real* group has close ties to Noriega."

Hank frowned. Whenever he felt he had developed an understanding of life in Panama, a subtlety, such as a hangar location, proved he had not. The roles of Noriega and the PDF were particularly perplexing.

"I'll be okay," he said again, as much to himself as to her. He kissed her again and climbed out of the van. She gave another resigned shake of her head, then pulled away.

Hank walked over to the hangar entrance and found the door locked. He went over to the nearby chain-link fence and looked out at the familiar airstrip. Twenty-five years had passed . . . hard to believe. The sound of an approaching vehicle drew his attention. A Jeep with PDF markings crossed the parking lot and pulled up in front of him. With the fence at his back and the Jeep between him and the street, there was no place to run.

A khaki-clad figure climbed out of the passenger side. He reached into the Jeep and withdrew a travel valise. Then he casually returned a salute from the driver and walked over to where Hank was standing. "Are you going to *Contadora* this morning?" he said in Spanish as the Jeep pulled away.

"Yes, I'm a guest of Sr. Remos," Hank replied in Spanish, hoping the name he was dropping would mean something to the officer.

"I am Captain Cortés," the officer said, extending his hand.

"Nice to meet you," Hank said, as the two men shook hands. "And you are?"

Hank reluctantly replied, "Enrique Duque."

The captain looked at him with increased interest. "Who do you represent, Sr. Duque?"

Hank took a deep breath. "I'm a . . . freelance writer."

Captain Cortés gazed at him intently for a moment, then switched to English, "I have seen your articles in *La Prensa.*"

Shit! Hank thought.

A van pulled into the parking lot, interrupting their exchange. It stopped near the hangar entrance, and two men got out, one wearing a pilot uniform and the other wearing overalls. The pilot unlocked the hangar door.

A white limousine entered the lot and pulled up beside the van. The chauffeur jumped out and opened the rear door. Remos emerged. He walked over and shook hands with Hank and the captain. "Well," he said, "we are all here."

"What about Sr. Castillero?" Hank said as they started toward the hangar.

"He is not coming," Remos said.

As Hank stepped through the hanger doorway, he looked around for a means of escape. The pilot was removing the wooden chocks from around the wheels of a sleek twin-engine Aero Commander, and the mechanic was raising the main hangar door. The pilot went around to the side of the aircraft, opened the cockpit door, and invited his passengers to board.

"*¡Un momento!*" someone shouted. Hank turned toward the voice, and his pulse accelerated. A PDF sergeant walked through the hangar doorway. The sergeant saluted the captain, then said respectfully, "*Buenos días, Sr. Remos.*" The businessman responded with a curt nod. Turning to Hank, the sergeant said, "*¿Pasaporte, señor?*"

"I . . . left it at home."

The sergeant frowned. "But you must have it to travel, señor."

Remos looked on impassively.

Hank cursed himself for having taken this risk.

"It is all right, sergeant," Captain Cortés interrupted in Spanish. "He is traveling with me."

"Bueno, Capitán," the sergeant said, saluting. He turned and left the hangar.

Hank followed the others onto the plane, wondering why Cortés had intervened on his behalf.

The flight across the Bay of Panama to *Isla Contadora* took less than twenty minutes. Now they circled at 1,200 feet, waiting for another private plane to take off from the airstrip that bisected the small island.

The turquoise water and white beach shimmered in the morning sun. Hotel buildings and a golf course sprawled across the lower third of the island. Private vacation homes, nestled into scrub foliage, dotted the perimeter. The Aero Commander's engines changed pitch, and the pilot lowered the aircraft's nose.

Awfully short runway, Hank thought.

A few minutes later, they were safely on the ground. Hotel golf carts lined the edge of the tarmac. Remos and his pilot climbed into one; Captain Cortés got behind the wheel of another. "Come, Mr. Duque," he said, "you can ride with me."

As they started down a sandy road, Cortés said, "You have been ordered to leave Panamá, no?"

Cortés' directness caught Hank off guard. "If you knew that," Hank said warily, "why didn't you do something back in the city?"

"There was no hurry. You cannot escape from this island . . . unless you can swim fifty miles."

Hank waited, sensing the taciturn officer wanted something.

"Why have you come to *Contadora?*" Cortés said. "What is your connection with Sr. Remos?"

"I'm here to get some background for my next article. Remos

is letting me interview him and some other businessmen."

"What will be the subject of this article?"

Hank hesitated, aware he was talking to a Noriega subordinate. "It'll be about the political situation here."

"And what is your opinion of our . . . 'political situation'?"

Hank hesitated again, still wondering what Cortés was after. They entered the hotel grounds. Two and three-story buildings lay scattered along a winding cobblestone drive. The French-colonial architecture brought to mind the early Canal Zone structures. They pulled up in front of the hotel's main building. Cortés shut off the motor and turned to Hank, waiting for his reply.

"I'm trying to understand conditions down here," Hank said. "I've come to *Contadora* to get the business perspective."

Cortés gazed at Hank for a moment, seemingly unconvinced. Finally he said, "Go do your interview. But before I will let you leave the island, you and I must talk."

Hank climbed out of the golf cart, and Cortés drove off.

Remos stood at the hotel entrance, watching them. As Hank walked over, he said, "How long have you known Captain Cortés?"

"I just met him this morning."

"You seemed very friendly," Remos said, eyeing him suspiciously as they entered the hotel. Across the lobby, a man signaled that he would hold the elevator. "My meeting is about to begin," Remos told Hank. "I will try to make time for you after lunch." He left Hank and headed for the waiting elevator.

Hank automatically checked his bare left wrist. Somewhere, there was a *La Preventiva* jail guard who knew what time it was. He spotted a clock over the lobby desk and saw he had at least four hours to kill.

He walked past the dining room and exited through a side door to the pool area. The only guests were three children, playing noisily at the shallow end. Hank sat down at a poolside table. A waiter came out of the hotel to take his order. *"Café, por favor,"* Hank said.

As he waited for his coffee, he tried to collect his thoughts. The behavior of both Cortés and Remos was puzzling. The captain was in no hurry to arrest him, and the *rabiblanco* was no longer cordial. And each seemed concerned about his relationship with the other. Hank shook his head. The whole damned country was paranoid.

A young woman came out of the hotel, carrying a serving tray. Her thick dark hair bounced as if it had just been freed from rollers, and her rich tan was set off by white shorts and a bright yellow halter. She stopped at his table. Looking down at Hank, she said in accented English, "How would you like it?"

"My coffee?"

"Yes, your coffee," she said with an impish smile. She sat down in the chair beside him and moved it a little closer. "What did you think I meant?"

Hank smiled, and felt himself flush. "I take my coffee black." Her features had the softness of youth; he couldn't tell if she was twenty-five, or fifteen.

"My name is Sofía," she said, handing him his cup. She diluted hers with sugar and cream. As she took a sip, she gazed boldly at him. Then lowering her cup, she said, "You looked lonely out here."

Hank wondered what the hell was going on now. "I'm just . . . killing a few hours."

"We could go to your room," she said, "and kill them there."

"I don't have a room. I'm only out here for the day."

"They provide us with rooms," she said.

Hank wondered who "they" were. "I think you may have me mixed up with somebody else."

She frowned. "Aren't you a guest of Sr. Remos?"

"Yeah, I'm with Remos," Hank said guardedly, concerned she might be setting him up for something. Or was he getting paranoid like everyone else in Panama?

She smiled. "If you are with Sr. Remos, then I am not mixed up. What is your name?"

"Hank . . . Hank Duque. Uh, Sofía, are we talking about, what I think we're talking about?"

The impish smile formed again. "What do you think we are talking about, Hank?"

"Where I come from, sometimes people get set up in situations like this."

"Oh, yes? Who sets them up?"

"Could be anybody. Sometimes, it's the police."

She laughed in genuine amusement. "You think I am a policeman?"

He shrugged. Whatever her motive, he found himself enjoying the flirtation.

"Well," she said, smiling, "then I must prove to you that I am not a policeman."

"And how are you going to do that?"

"We will go to the room, and we will continue this talk . . . after I take off all my clothes. Would a policeman do that?"

Hank laughed and shook his head. "I appreciate the offer, but I've got to pass."

She settled back into her chair. "Are you a *maricón*? Don't you like women?"

"I *love* women," he said with a laugh. "But I've got a girlfriend, who wouldn't understand our . . . proving you're not a policeman."

"This girlfriend, is she *gringa*?"

"No, *Panameña*."

"Is she here on *Contadora*?"

"She's in Panama City."

"Panama City is very far away," she said, leaning forward and resting the palm of her hand on the back of his.

"Still, she's . . . very close to me," he said.

She leaned back and said with a playful pout, "Most *gringos* do not say no to me." Then her lips relaxed into a faint smile. "Your girlfriend is very lucky. And I am glad she is *Panameña*." She slid back her chair, preparing to leave.

Hank said, "A PDF captain flew out with me this morning. His name was Cortés. Do you know him?"

"Yes."

"I'd like to get together with him this morning. Do you know where I can find him?"

"The PDF has a . . . holiday house on the other side of the island. He is probably there."

"How do I get there?"

"Take the road in front of the hotel, until you come to the water. The PDF house will have a soldier in front of it." She stood up, straightening her shorts. "Are you sure you prefer to spend the morning with the captain?"

Hank smiled, and reluctantly nodded.

Hank trudged up a sand-covered road, a quarter-mile from the hotel. Ahead, a sentry slouched against the trunk of a palm tree. Behind him stood a squarish two-story, concrete dwelling. Rust from heavy security bars streaked the stark gray walls beneath the windows.

Hank turned onto the driveway, and the sentry straightened. "Is Captain Cortés here?" Hank said in Spanish.

"In the rear," the sentry responded in Spanish, gesturing toward a path that wound around the side of the building.

Some security, Hank thought. He walked up the path, picking his way through scrub foliage that had been allowed to grow wild. At the rear of the building, he found a small private beach. Low rollers washed between two gray rock formations and across coarse white sand. A man and a young woman in swim suits lay on their stomachs, taking in the sun.

"Captain Cortés!" Hank called out as he approached.

Cortés' head jerked and he rose, all in a single motion.

"Let's have that talk," Hank said.

The young woman also got up. Like Sofía, her age was questionable, but her function was not.

"Get us something to drink," Cortés told her in Spanish. The woman obediently disappeared into the building. Hank followed Cortés onto the wide concrete veranda that overlooked the ocean. He started to speak, but Cortés gestured for him to remain silent. The young woman reappeared with their drinks: Coca Cola in tall glasses, poured over ice. Cortés waved her back to the beach, then turned to Hank.

"What do you want from me?" Hank said.

Cortés gazed at him intently, not responding.

"You obviously want something," Hank pressed. "What is it?"

"Why were you put in *La Preventiva*, and why was your passport taken?"

Hank's mind raced. What the hell was this guy after? "I guess General Noriega doesn't like my articles."

Cortés studied him for a moment, then said, "But many of us do."

Hank gazed at Cortés. Was this guy anti-Noriega? That would explain his behavior. Hank decided to take the risk. "Noriega's a gangster. I'm trying to expose what he's been doing. It might get the U.S. to intervene, so Endara can take office."

Somewhere within the building a door slammed. Cortés rose and motioned for Hank to follow him. The young woman still lay face down on the beach, apparently dozing. Cortés ushered Hank around to the side of the building, where they were hidden by the scrub foliage. Someone opened a second floor window, and a woman's lilting laughter drifted down.

Cortés whispered, "Other officers are spending the day here. They must not see you. I will contact you in Panama City, tomorrow. Where are you staying?"

"I'll have to contact you," Hank said, not wanting to put Andrea at greater risk.

"*Bueno,*" Cortés said. "Call me tomorrow morning, at 555-4530. My office is in *La Comandancia*, so do not identify yourself, or talk to anyone but me. Call at nine o'clock, *en punto*. I will be waiting."

Hank repeated the phone number.

Cortés nodded, then said, "Stay away from the *rabiblancos* who are meeting here. They are close to General Noriega."

"Okay, but then how do I get back to the city?"

"The airplane these officers arrived on will be going back in about twenty minutes. The pilot should be Lieutenant José Errigo. Verify it is Errigo, and then tell him I want you to go on this flight. If he asks for proof, tell him 'Panamá-5'."

"Panama-5?"

Cortés nodded. "I am putting my trust in you, Sr. Duque." The two men shook hands.

Moments later, hurrying up the sandy road in the direction of the airstrip, Hank reflected on the events of the past forty-eight hours. The students had the passion and the *rabibilancos* had the resources; however, differences within and between these factions made them ineffective. Tomorrow he would find out if the military was also marked by differences. If so, perhaps it could be turned against itself.

15. EL CUARTELAZO

Hank was dozing on the couch, when the rattle of a key in the front door awakened him.

Andrea entered the apartment and said in surprise, "Back from *Isla Contadora* already?"

"My trip got cut short," he said, sitting up. She crossed the room to him and he pulled her onto his lap. They shared a long kiss. Finally she drew back with a bemused smile. He leaned toward her again, but she pressed a palm against his chest.

"Later," she said, moving from his lap to the seat beside him. "Now, tell me what happened."

"Your uncle didn't show up at the airport this morning. Any idea why?"

"No," she said with a frown.

"Well, he didn't make it. But a PDF captain did."

"A PDF captain?" Andrea said, concern in her voice. "Did he know who you were?"

"Yeah, he recognized me from my *La Prensa* articles. But he seemed to approve of what I've been writing. He hinted he was part of a PDF faction that's opposed to Noriega."

Andrea smiled tolerantly. "And did he tell you there was going to be a *cuartelazo*?"

"What's that?"

"A . . . barracks revolt."

"Not in so many words."

"I am surprised. PDF officers whisper about *cuartelazos* all the time. But it is always just smoke—no fire."

"Mmmm," Hank responded, disappointed. Then he remembered the captain's demeanor. "This one might be worth following up on, though."

"Hank," she said, pulling him to her, "you must stay away from those people."

Her lips were at his ear; he could feel her breath. He decided to put off telling her that he had agreed to contact the captain in the morning. They kissed, first tenderly, then passionately. She drew back and gazed at him for a moment. An intimate smile played on her lips. Hank pulled her to him again.

"I need to shower," she whispered.

"Me too," he murmured. "We'll do that later."

The next morning, Hank and Andrea sat at the kitchen table finishing their coffee. Hank glanced at the old windup alarm clock ticking on the sink counter; he was supposed to call Captain Cortés in ten minutes. "What time's your tour this morning?"

Andrea stood up. "I have to leave in a few minutes." She walked over to the sink and rinsed her coffee cup. "Hank, I miss Alberto. I need to see him."

Hank smiled. "Shall we go get him?"

"I can't bring him home yet, but I want to visit him."

"When?"

"Saturday morning, and come back Sunday night."

"Sounds good."

Andrea went into the living room and placed a call to her parents' farm. Hank checked the clock again; he had about eight minutes. He heard Andrea first speak with her mother, then say, *"¡Hola, Hijo!"* and excitedly tell her son they would come to see him that weekend.

Hank joined her in the living room. When she hung up the phone, she was smiling. "My father is feeling much better, and Alberto is doing very well. My father put him in charge of the goats and chickens. I can't wait to see him!" She checked her watch. "I have to go."

"What time will you be back?" Hank said, walking her to the door.

"About 10:30 tonight. I have class." She gave him an affectionate peck, then left.

Moments later, Hank heard a voice on the other end of the telephone line say, "Cortés."

"This is your nine o'clock call," Hank said.

"*Teatro Lux.* Two o'clock." The line went dead.

As the brightly painted bus rumbled down *Vía España*, Hank positioned himself on the bottom step of the open doorway.

"*Calle 34,*" the driver called out.

"*Gracias,*" Hank said. "*Parada.*"

The driver steered closer to the curb and slowed, and Hank jumped. He stumbled when he landed and had to take several running steps to regain his balance. Then he started down the tree-lined sidewalk in the direction of the ocean.

The neighborhood, a mix of modest shops and restaurants, was familiar, even after twenty-five years. He savored the momentary return to his youth.

Teatro Lux stood on the next corner. The marquee indicated the feature movie was Rambo II. Hank walked up to the window and purchased a ticket.

Inside, he crossed the littered lobby. The familiar smell of popcorn again momentarily transported him back in time. He pulled open one of the metal doors and stepped into the darkened theater.

He hesitated in the aisle, letting his eyes adjust. Only seven other people occupied the theater: a couple seated in the center, and five others scattered across the front rows. Hank took the aisle seat at the rear. The feature apparently had been on for some time; Sylvester Stallone was on the offensive, slaughtering caricature Vietnamese. Where'd they film this shit? Hank wondered.

The door to his left opened, then closed. Hank recognized Cortés, although the captain wore civilian clothes. Hank moved over a seat and Cortés sat down beside him.

"Did you have any trouble finding the theater?" Cortés whispered.

"I knew where it was. I used to come here when I was a kid."

"Sr. Duque, you are looking for a story, no?"

"Yeah."

"Suppose I told you, there was going to be *cuartelazo* against General Noriega?"

Hank remembered Andrea's skepticism the previous day. "If it were true, it would make quite a story."

Cortés hesitated, then said, "Some of us are considering such a move."

"Why are you telling me this?"

"We need your help. We cannot trust your government, particularly now. General Noriega is too close to your president."

Noriega's connection to the United States government was the story Hank was looking for. "How can I help you?"

"We need the support of the American people," Cortés said. "Your position with the Associated Press will give us access to them."

"You're looking to me for press coverage?"

Cortés nodded.

"Okay," Hank said, "give me the details, and I'll tell you if it's something the AP would be interested in."

"Knowing our plans will put you in danger."

"I'm already in danger."

"That is why I chose you. I know about your . . . situation with Major Mejías . . . and about your grandfather."

"How do you know about that?"

"I am in the G-2 section," Cortés said with a tight smile. "I work for Major Mejías."

Hank's mind raced, trying to fathom the machinations within the PDF.

"If you betray us," Cortés continued, "we will kill you . . . and your girlfriend . . . and her family."

Damn it! Hank thought. How had they found out about Andrea? It was too late to back out now, though.

"We cannot talk here," Cortés said. "You must come to a meeting tonight."

"Where and what time?"

"Do you know where Curundú is?"

"Which one? The one in the Canal Zone, or the one in Panama City?"

"Canal Zone."

"Yeah, I know where it is. I played tennis there when I was a kid."

"Good. My house is directly across the street from the tennis courts—number 47. Come at ten o'clock."

"Number 47, ten o'clock. I'll be there."

Cortés rose and slipped out of the theater.

Deep in thought, Hank stared at the movie screen, where the celluloid slaughter raged on.

That night, Hank walked up a quiet Curundú residential street. He'd had the cab driver drop him off a block away. Four tennis courts lay off to his left; an orderly row of squarish white homes lined the street to his right.

When he had last been here, Curundú had been an Americans-only community. The Canal Commission had dictated the environment, including all landscape and building adornments. Now the homes were privately owned, most by Panamanians. Personalized arrangements of bushes, ferns, and flowers covered the yards and brightly colored drapes hung from the lighted windows. Hank shook his head. The old commissioners would've had a fit.

As he passed the tennis courts, he vaguely recalled that the week of the riot he had won a tournament of some sort here. What would he have thought then, if someone had told him that he wouldn't be back for twenty-five years? And that when he did return, it would be under these circumstances?

He arrived at number 47. The two-story stucco building looked like the other houses on the block, except the stoop was dimly lighted and the front windows were dark. There was no doorbell. Hank decided against knocking—the neighbors might get curious. He stepped off the walkway and started across the lawn.

At the side of the house, the terrain declined. Past the back-yard, illuminated by the lights of a major thoroughfare, Hank recognized the 500-yard no man's land that had been cleared by the United States, a half-century earlier. A chain-link fence, topped with barbed wire, still divided the two communities with the common name: Curundú. Although Panama now had sovereignty over both, the affluence of the former Canal Zone still contrasted sharply with the destitution on the other side. Against the night sky, concrete tenement buildings rose surreally from the tinderbox squalor surrounding them. Windows without panes seemed to stare across the fence, like empty sockets in ravaged skulls.

Hank paused at the rear of the house. The window blinds were closed, but light escaped from around the edges. A bed sheet on a nearby clothesline flapped in the night breeze. He continued over to the back door, and heard hushed voices coming from inside. He knocked softly; the voices quieted. Then the door flew open, and light from the interior momentarily blinded him.

"*Venga,*" someone said in a hoarse whisper.

Hank stepped through the doorway and onto the worn linoleum of a small kitchen. Captain Cortés, dressed in civilian clothes, gave a curt nod and closed the door behind him.

"*Siéntese,*" Cortés said, gesturing to a cheap chrome and Formica table, where two other men were seated. Although they also wore civilian clothes, Hank surmised they too were officers. One of the strangers was mestizo, like Cortés; the other was black. Both gazed intently at Hank as he took a seat. Apparently there would be no introductions.

"We will not keep you long, Sr. Duque," Cortés said.

Hank waited.

"Sometime, within the next few days," Cortés said, "General Noriega will . . . retire."

"Retire?"

"We are going to . . . require the general to meet with us. After we talk with him, he will realize it is time for him to retire."

Not likely, Hank thought. "Okay, what's my role in this 're-tirement'?"

"Our meeting with the general will be held at *La Comandancia*. We will want you there to accurately report what happens."

Hank nodded, masking the stab of fear he felt at the mere mention of the military headquarters where he had been jailed.

"We are confident we can take over *La Comandancia* without help from the United States. But to hold it in the days that follow, we will need the support of the American people."

Hank realized these men were serious. If they could pull off the coup, he'd have a hell of a story.

"We will contact you just before we act," Cortés said. "You will be the only foreign reporter allowed inside the compound." He unsnapped a telephone pager from his belt. "Carry this with you at all times. The first three numbers will tell you where to go; the last four numbers tell you when to be there. Do you know military time?"

Hank nodded.

Cortés continued, "A '111-0800' means go to *Teatro Lux* at eight o'clock. A '222-1400' means come here to my home at two o'clock. A '333-2100' means go to *La Comandancia* at nine o'clock. If you receive a '444-0000', you are to call my *La Comandancia* office number *immediately*. Say '444' and talk to no one but me."

Hank repeated the instructions as he secured the pager onto his belt, then said, "Don't you expect the general to resist your . . . retirement program?"

"We have the support of most of the junior officers. The general will understand that he has no choice. He must retire."

"What about Major Mejías?"

"He will retire also."

"Are you getting any U.S. backing?"

The other two men had watched the exchange without comment, but now the black officer said, "*Todas las carreteras—*"

Cortés silenced him with an angry glance.

The other mestizo gave Cortés a barely perceptible nod.

Cortés cleared his throat. "I can tell you that we have received . . . encouragement from your government."

"Are they backing you with troops?" Hank pressed. The black officer had started to say something about "all the roads".

"This is to be a *Panamanian* revolution," Cortés said emphatically. "Our people will not accept the outcome if they feel the *gringos* forced it on them."

"I understand," Hank said, "but is the U.S. government actually supporting you?"

Cortés looked at the other mestizo, who gave another quick nod. Cortés said, "Our American contacts have arranged for the Southern Command to conduct military maneuvers at strategic locations during the *cuartelazo*. They will have troops near both airports and on the major roads leading to *La Comandancia*."

"To keep Noriega from getting reinforcements?"

Cortés nodded.

Hank smiled at the irony. "So history repeats itself."

Cortés frowned.

Hank said, "It's the same tactic Teddy Roosevelt used during the 1903 revolution. He stationed U.S. warships in Panama's ports to intimidate the Colombians."

The officers smiled.

"The American contacts you mentioned," Hank said, "are they people you can count on?"

"They are agents of the CIA," Cortés said. "Our plan is part of a covert action they call 'Panamá-5'."

CIA! Hank thought. If the rumors about Noriega were true, then the CIA was backing a coup against one of their chief operatives.

Cortés said, "You are to speak to no one about what you have heard tonight. No one!"

"I understand."

"Do you? Sr. Duque, these men know you now. And they know about your girlfriend."

"Threats aren't necessary, Captain."

Cortés stood up without responding. The meeting was over.

Early the following morning, Hank tried in vain to work a persistent buzzing sound into his dream, but it slowing dragged him into consciousness. Suddenly he was awake. It sounded like an electrical short! He snapped into a sitting position and looked around the semi-dark room. Andrea, sleeping beside him, grunted at the disturbance.

The noise came from the far wall. Hank threw aside the sheet, jumped out of bed, and hurried across the room. The pager that Captain Cortés had given him was vibrating on the dresser top. Hank picked it up and turned off the alert. The display read "444-0000".

He hurried into the kitchen. As he picked up the phone, he glanced at the clock on the counter; it was 5:45. He dialed Cortés' office number.

Someone answered on the first ring. *"¡Cortés!"*

"Four, four, four," Hank said.

"Duque?"

"Yeah, it's me."

"Do you have any contacts in the Southern Command?"

"Contacts in the Southern Command?" Hank said, confused. "No. What's going on?"

"The *cuartelazo* will be this morning."

"This morning?"

"Yes. We plan to take General Noriega into custody when he arrives here at *La Comandancia*. He has a meeting scheduled at 8:30."

They were really going to do it!

"But we have a problem," Cortés continued. "Our observers report there are no U.S. troops at Omar Torrijos Airport and there is no sign of them along *Vía España*."

"How important is this to the operation?"

"*Very* important. Most PDF units will support us. Even Battalion 2000, a creation of your government, has promised to remain neutral. But there is one infantry company, *Los Machos del Monte*, that is fanatically loyal to General Noriega. We must be sure they do not intervene."

"*Los Machos*," Hank said.

"You know about them?"

"Yeah," Hank said, remembering their attack on Andrea's parents' farm.

"They are our main concern. Their base camp is at *Río Hato*, eighty miles from here. We must be sure they cannot arrive by either road or air."

"Have you notified your CIA contacts that there seems to be a problem?"

"I have been paging them for an hour. They do not answer."

"Do you know anybody in Southern Command you can call?"

"We have been dealing only with two CIA agents. They gave me an emergency number at Southern Command, but there is no answer there either."

"Doesn't anyone else in your group have a contact?"

"No," Cortés said dejectedly. "It was my responsibility to secure the airports and roads."

Hank had a thought. "There's a guy in the AP office who might be able to help us. He usually covers the night desk, and may still be there."

"No one else is to know about the *cuartelazo!*" Cortés snapped.

"In that case, Captain, I don't know how I can help you."

There was a long silence. Finally Cortés said, "Can you trust this man?"

"I think so. Do you want me to try and get hold of him?"

"Yes . . . please."

"Will you be at this number?"

"For at least another hour."

"Okay, I'll call you back—same code." Hank hung up and pulled the phone book out of the kitchen drawer. He was scanning the pages for the Associated Press number, when Andrea padded into the kitchen.

"Hank, what is happening?"

"The *cuartelazo* is this morning," he said grimly. He found the phone number he was looking for.

"But last night, you said we had a few days."

"That's what they told me. Apparently, they wanted to keep me in the dark until the last minute. Now, their plan's going sour. The Southern Command troops that were supposed to block Omar Torrijos Airport and *Vía España* haven't shown up."

"*¡Gringos!*" Andrea spat.

Hank gave a grudging nod, then said, "Get packed. You need to get on the road right away."

"Hank," she said, grasping his forearm, "you must come too."

"We went over this last night, Andrea. I've put us in the middle of this shit, and I've got to stick it out. But you need to look after your family."

She gazed at him, not moving.

"You have to go," he said. "The PDF knows about you, and your family." He gave her a gentle push toward the bedroom. "Get ready. I've got to make a phone call."

Reluctantly, she left the kitchen. Hank dialed the AP number. The phone rang six times before it was finally picked up and a voice said, "Associated Press. Ortega."

"Ortega, this is Hank Duque. Thank God you were working tonight."

"Actually, I just got here," Ortega said. "I'm covering General Thurman's first news conference this afternoon, and I came in to pick up some background information."

"Who's General Thurman?"

"General Maxwell Thurman—new chief of the Southern Command. He took over, day before yesterday."

"Damn!" Hank exploded. "What a time to change command. No wonder things are screwed up over there."

"What's your problem, Duque?"

"Ortega, would you be able to get in contact with General Thurman this morning?"

"This morning?"

"Right now!"

"I don't know . . ." Ortega said. "Why would I want to?"

"Ortega, you've got to trust me on this. Something big's about to come down."

"What are you talking about?"

Hank hesitated, then said, "We need to get together right away. Can you pick me up at . . . *Parque de Santa Ana . . .* in fifteen minutes?"

"You've got to give me some idea what's going on," Ortega said.

"Do you know what *cuartelazo* means?"

"Of course," Ortega said. "You don't mean today?"

"This morning."

"Jesus! What—"

"Pick me up. I'll fill you in on the details on the way over to Southern Command. And, Ortega, don't mention this to anybody, before I see you. If you do, you could get a lot of people killed."

"I'll pick you up in fifteen minutes at *Parque de Santa Ana.*" The line went dead.

Hank called Cortés. "I got hold of my man at the AP. He's coming over right away. We're going to try to get into Southern Command headquarters."

"How long will it take you?"

"I have no idea. At least a couple of hours."

There was a long silence. Finally Cortés said, "We will go forward with our plan then."

"Wait a minute!" Hank said. "There's no guarantee I can get into Southern Command. Stay by the phone, and I'll call you if I'm successful."

"I cannot stay here in my office. I must be downstairs, waiting at the door when General Noriega arrives at 8:30."

Damn it! Hank thought.

"Do your best for us, Sr. Duque. We are counting on you."

"Wait a minute!"

"Vaya con Dios." The line went dead.

Hank hurried from the kitchen into the bedroom. Andrea had dressed, and now stood at the side of the bed, stuffing clothes into a suitcase. She looked up, tears of frustration in her eyes. "I feel like I am running away!"

"You're doing what you have to do," he said, then hurriedly dressed.

"Hank, I heard what you said on the phone."

"It's looking bad, but hopefully Ortega can get me in to see the new Southern Command general."

"I heard what you said . . . about people getting killed."

Hank walked over and took her in his arms. Her fingers dug into his back, communicating unspoken desperation. Finally they separated and he said, "I'll call you at the Hotel Washington as soon as I can."

She looked up at him, her face etched with concern. She lost her battle to control her tears.

"I'll be okay," he said. "You just look after your family, and yourself."

She wiped her eyes with the palms of her hands. Hank grabbed her suitcase off the bed, and they hurried from the room.

Hank stood on the sidewalk at the edge of *Parque de Santa Ana*, impatiently looking up *Avenida Central*. The usually filthy streets had been washed clean by an early morning rain. Hank hoped that was an omen. Then, heading in his direction, he recognized Joe Ortega's green Land Rover.

Ortega slid to a stop at the curb, and Hank climbed in. "Thanks for getting over here so fast," Hank said as the two men shook hands.

Ortega pulled away from the curb. He turned right at the first corner and had to swerve to avoid an oncoming pushcart vendor. They headed in the direction of the Canal Zone. "Fill me in, Duque. What the hell's going on?"

"A group of PDF officers are going to attempt a coup at *La Comandancia* around 8:30."

"Eight-thirty!" Ortega glanced at his watch. "It's 6:15 now."

"According to them," Hank said, "Southern Command has promised to conduct some phony maneuvers around Omar Torrijos

Airport and on *Vía España*, to keep Noriega from getting reinforcements from the interior."

"Southern Command's in on it?"

"They're supposed to be. But their troops aren't in place."

Ortega sped up. The damp cobblestone street wound through the narrow canyon of tenement buildings. At the next intersection, he leaned on the horn to claim the right-of-way. "How'd you find out about all this?"

"One of the leaders approached me. He'd seen my articles in *La Prensa*." Hank noticed they had entered the destitute *El Chorrillo* district. "Are U.S. military headquarters still in Quarry Heights?"

Ortega nodded. "Duque, what's your role in this? Are you covering this story, or are you helping to stir things up?"

"I guess I'm part of it now," Hank said. "Ortega, the story's yours. Just help me get some backup for these poor devils."

"Who's the leader?"

Hank didn't answer. His pulse quickened. The high walls of *La Comandancia* loomed up ahead on the left. What the hell! He instinctively flattened his left hand and moved it across his chest, beneath his right armpit. He braced his feet on the floorboard, ready to deliver a blow across Ortega's Adam's apple.

Ortega looked out the driver-side window as they started past the forbidding fortress. "Looks quiet enough," he said, then glanced at Hank. "You okay?"

They were past the building now. Hank nodded and looked away. He slowly lowered his left hand to his side. Jesus! He'd been about to kill this guy.

"Who's the leader of the coup?" Ortega said, repeating his question.

Hank took a deep breath. "The person I've been dealing with is a Captain Cortés. Yesterday, I met with him and two others. I wasn't given their names."

They came to a stop. Several vehicles were lined up in front of them, trying to merge onto *Avenida de los Mártires*.

"I haven't heard of Cortés," Ortega said. "What rank were the other two?"

"I don't know. They were wearing civilian clothes."

"Describe them."

"Cortés and one of the other guys were mestizo; the third guy was black. I don't think Cortés is the leader. He's apparently responsible for seeing that the airports and road are blocked, and for getting favorable U.S. news coverage. But a couple of times he deferred to the other mestizo."

"What did this mestizo look like?"

"Good-looking guy. About my age—late thirties. Dark complexion—about like yours. Physically fit. Looked like a soldier."

"Does the name Giroldi ring a bell? Major Moisés Giroldi?"

"I don't recognize it."

The vehicles ahead of them crept forward.

"For the past two weeks," Ortega said, "I've received leaks about a possible coup attempt. Yesterday, my source gave me Giroldi's name."

"Know anything about him?"

"Yeah. For one thing, he fits the description you just gave me. For another, it would be possible for him to get close enough to Noriega to pull this thing off. Giroldi was a hero in putting down the last coup against the general. Now, he's one of the few officers Noriega trusts."

"Giroldi put down the last coup, and now you think he's organized this one?"

Ortega nodded.

Hank shook his head, wondering if he'd ever figure out what was going on within the PDF. "How reliable's your source?"

"He's a junior officer."

They finally reached the corner. "Do you think the CIA's changed their mind?" Hank said. "Have they decided to back their man, Noriega, and let these poor devils twist in the wind?"

"We'll find out in a few minutes," Ortega said as he intimidated a Volkswagen sedan and merged into the heavy traffic.

Ahead, Hank recognized the road to Quarry Heights, which wound up the side of Ancon Hill. Ortega turned off the thoroughfare and headed up the manicured drive. They followed the twisting road until they arrived at the front gate, where U.S. Army military police were stopping vehicles and checking credentials. There were two cars ahead of them. An M.P. corporal was talking with the driver of the lead car.

"Will you have any problem getting me in?" Hank asked Ortega.

"Uh-oh. I forgot that you don't have a passport."

The corporal waved the lead car through, then leaned down and spoke to the driver of the next one. A sergeant came out of the small sentry building at the side of the road. He glanced at Hank and Ortega, then walked over. He leaned down at the driver side window. "Morning," he said with a smile. "What are you doing up so early?"

"Uh . . . good morning, Sarge," Ortega said. They apparently knew each other from Ortega's previous visits. "I've . . . got an interview today with your new C.O., General Thurman."

The sergeant nodded and looked across the car to Hank. "And you, sir?"

"I'm with him," Hank said. The sergeant's smile faded, and Hank added, "I'm also with the AP."

The car ahead of them had been denied access, and made a U-turn. The corporal came back and joined the sergeant at the Land Rover window.

"I'll need to see both your passports, please," the sergeant said. Now he was all business.

Ortega pulled his passport out of his shirt pocket and handed it over. The corporal checked it against a sheet on his clipboard, then returned it. "He's on the list for today," he told the sergeant.

"Sarge," Hank said, "I'm afraid I left my passport at home."

"Then you'll have to go back and get it, sir."

"Please make a U-turn, sir," the corporal told Ortega. "You're blocking traffic."

Ortega put the vehicle in gear.

"Wait!" Hank told Ortega. "You go on inside and . . . do what needs to be done—Omar Torrijos Airport and *Vía España*. I'll wait for you out here." He opened the door and climbed out.

The sergeant frowned and walked around to the passenger side.

"Sarge," Hank said, "we're on kind of a tight schedule. Will it be okay if I wait over there?" He pointed at the gravel parking area just outside the gate.

The sergeant shrugged. "Sure, if that's what you want to do."

"Ortega," Hank said, "what time do you have?"

"Six twenty-five."

"We've got two hours, maybe less. Come back within an hour and let me know what's going on."

"Move it!" the corporal said.

"I'll let you know," Ortega said as he pulled away.

Hank crunched across the gravel to the shade of a scraggly tree. A battered sedan pulled into the parking area. It paused long enough for a stocky Panamanian woman to get out, then pulled away. The woman showed her credentials to the corporal. He waved her through.

Hank shook his head. Panamanian domestics were allowed in; he wasn't. He watched the woman walk up the winding tree-lined lane. Although Hank had grown up in Ancon, less than a mile away, he had never been inside this secure military post.

He turned and looked down the hill, across *Avenida de los Mártires*. *La Comandancia* was less than a quarter-mile away. From this high vantage point, Hank could see inside the forbidding compound. The main building and several smaller structures surrounded a dusty courtyard.

He leaned against the tree trunk, thinking of the young officers down there, preparing for the *cuartelazo*. Soon they would be putting their lives on the line, not knowing whether or not *Tío Sam* was waffling on yet another promise. Captain Cortés' words haunted him: "We are counting on you." Yet here he stood, waiting helplessly.

Time passed slowly. He would check up the hill for Ortega,

then down the hill for any sign of activity at PDF headquarters. Occasionally, cars passed through the gate, or dropped off Panamanian workers in the parking area. *La Comandancia* was quiet.

He checked his bare left wrist, then shouted over to the gate sentry, "Hey, Corporal, what time do you have?"

"Almost 7:30."

A tan Suburban pulled up to the gate. Three Panamanian women were squeezed into the front seat and five children were crammed into the seat behind them. The rear of the vehicle was piled high with suitcases. Hank couldn't make out the driver's words, but he heard the strain in her voice as she argued with the sentry. Finally, the corporal ordered her to make a U-turn and clear the entrance. As the car passed, heading down the hill, Hank saw fear and confusion etched into the women's faces.

"What was that about?" Hank shouted over.

The corporal shook his head in disgust. "Claimed their husbands are PDF officers. Said they'd made some kind of arrangements for them to come on the post this morning."

"And you turned them away?"

The corporal tapped his clipboard. "They're not on my list."

"What were their names?"

"I don't remember."

"Was one of them Cortés?"

"Could have been," the corporal said, then turned his attention to the next car coming up the hill.

Damn it! Hank thought. Cortés must have made arrangements with the CIA to protect his family. Now the Army was reneging on that too.

A cacophony of horns from the street below drew his attention. A military Jeep, followed by two dark blue Mercedeses and another Jeep, forced its way through the snarled morning traffic. Hank guessed it was General Thurman. If it was, he was pissing off the locals. Hank expected the four-vehicle motorcade to turn up the hill, but instead they cut across the thoroughfare and headed into El Chorrillo.

Hank's eyes widened. What the hell? They were heading toward *La Comandancia*! He sprinted across the gravel parking area to the sentry building. "Sarge," he said, startling the sergeant, who was seated at a desk, making a log entry. "Do you have a pair of field glasses?"

"Well, yeah," the sergeant said uncertainly.

"Let me borrow 'em for a minute."

The sergeant frowned and didn't move.

"I'll give 'em right back. There's something down the hill I want to check out."

The sergeant opened the drawer and withdrew a pair of military field glasses. "Be careful with 'em."

Hank stepped outside and trained the glasses on *La Comandancia*. The motorcade filed into the compound. Hank recognized the gate he had passed through the morning of his release from *La Preventiva*. The two Jeeps pulled into what apparently was the motor pool. The two Mercedeses stopped at the main building's side entrance.

The doors of the lead Mercedes opened, and four men wearing PDF uniforms climbed out. They looked about the compound; apparently they were bodyguards. The driver of the second car got out and opened the rear door. General Noriega emerged—an hour early!

The main building's side door flew open, and Captain Cortés stepped out, holding a pistol aimed at the general. The bodyguards drew their sidearms, but Noriega waved for them to hold their fire. Noriega appeared calm as he spoke at length to Cortés, occasionally flashing a menacing smile. Finally, Cortés lowered his pistol, and one of the bodyguards hurried over and disarmed him. Another bodyguard positioned himself back to back with Noriega and ushered him up the steps and into the building. Hank watched the scene in disbelief.

A volley of gunfire erupted inside the building Noriega had just entered. As if on cue, hidden figures began firing from the windows of several smaller buildings. The two bodyguards who had remained with the general's car managed to get one door open, before they were cut down.

"What's happening?" demanded a voice to Hank's left. The sergeant stood beside him, peering through another set of field glasses. More gunfire erupted from the compound. "Crazy spics," the sergeant muttered.

"I need to get hold of Ortega," Hank said, "the guy I came here with."

Without responding, the sergeant reentered the sentry building, and Hank followed. The sergeant placed a phone call, apparently to a superior.

Hank waited impatiently, as the sergeant reported the gunfire and its points of origin. "No, sir," the sergeant concluded, "I've got no idea what they're shooting at."

"Let me talk to him," Hank said, reaching for the phone.

"Get the hell out of here!" the sergeant said.

"I know what's going on down there. Gimme the fuckin' phone!"

"It's some civilian, sir," the sergeant said into the mouthpiece. "He doesn't have a passport. I don't even know if he's an American." The sergeant listened for a moment, then said, "Yes, sir." He handed the receiver to Hank.

"Hello. This is Hank Duque."

"This is the Officer of the Day," a curt voice said. "What do you want?"

"Listen," Hank said, "there's an attempted coup against Manuel Noriega underway, right now, at *La Comandancia.* Has Joe Ortega gotten through to General Thurman?"

There was a long pause before the officer said, "Who did you say you are?"

"Damn it! It doesn't matter who I am! Has Joe Ortega gotten in to see General Thurman?"

"I don't know who you are, and I don't know any damned Joe Ortega. Put the Sergeant of the Guard back on."

A vehicle horn blew outside. Through the window, Hank saw

the green Land Rover speeding toward the gate. Ortega circled behind the sentry building and slide to a halt in the parking area. Hank slammed down the receiver and ran out of the building.

"Did you see the general?" Hank said as Ortega climbed out of the vehicle.

"No, but I spoke to one of his aides. They know what's happening down there."

"What about blocking the airport and road?"

"I told the aide. He promised he'd pass along your concern."

"Concern?" Hank exclaimed. "The lives of those men—"

"Hank," Ortega interrupted, "I did all I could."

"Sorry, Joe. I'm sure you did. But they've got to understand—"

"Hank, they fully understand what's going on. I'm just not sure . . . they're going to do anything about it."

Hank looked at Ortega in disbelief.

The Sergeant of the Guard came over. "The Officer of the Day is on his way."

Hank trained his field glasses down the hill. There was no movement within the compound.

A polished Jeep whipped into the parking area, showering gravel. A young U.S. Army captain climbed out and hurried over. As he returned the sergeant's salute, he said to Hank and Ortega, "I'm the Officer of the Day, Captain John Hennelly. Who are you people?"

Ortega pulled out his credentials. "I'm with the Associated Press. This is Hank Duque. He's with me."

The captain looked suspiciously at Hank, but didn't ask for identification. He took the field glasses from the sergeant and scanned the compound. Then he lowered the glasses and turned to Hank and Ortega. "How much do you people know about what's going on down there?"

Hank said, "Some junior officers are trying to overthrow General Noriega."

The captain nodded. "According to their last report, they've got him in custody."

"You've heard from them?" Hank said, surprised. Maybe the plan was working after all.

"I talked to a PDF officer named Cortés about twenty minutes ago," the captain said. "He'd been trying to get through to our command center all morning, but they weren't answering the number he'd been given. So he tried the Officer of the Day number."

"What did Cortés say?" Hank said pressed.

"He was in a panic . . . something about needing a road blocked. I told him I couldn't help him, but I transferred the call into the command center."

"Are they going to block the road?"

"I have no idea."

A six-ton Army truck roared into the parking area, and a detachment of military police poured out the back. They fanned out and set up a perimeter defense on both sides of the gate.

Once they were in place, a staff sergeant came over, saluted the Officer of the Day, and handed him a two-way field radio. "Sir," the staff sergeant said, "H.Q. wants us to secure and hold this position. They'll keep you apprised of the situation."

The Officer of the Day radioed in and notified his superiors that the front gate was secure. Then he listened for a few moments. Finally, he signed off, and turned to Hank. "The coup leaders are getting the help they asked for."

"Are you sure?" Hank exclaimed.

The captain nodded. "H.Q. says Army troops have neutralized the PDF's Fifth Rifle company at Fort Amador, and the Marines are in position to block *Los Machos del Monte.*"

"Well, I'll be damned," Hank said, smiling for the first time that morning.

Gunfire erupted again in the compound, as rebel soldiers attacked a building. The black officer from the previous night's meeting in Curundú directed the operation. Then there was a lull in the shooting, and a door opened. The building occupants docilely filed out, hands folded on top of their heads. The rebel forces moved to another building and repeated the process. One by one, the buildings emptied. The troops supposedly loyal to Noriega surrendered with little resistance.

"Sir!" called out the sergeant from inside the sentry building. "Civilian radio has an announcement."

"Turn it up," the captain said.

Ortega translated, "He says he's Major Moisés Giroldi . . . that he has taken control of *La Comandancia* . . . General Noriega is in custody . . . Noriega and all other senior officers are being retired immediately . . . OAS supervised elections will be held soon." The radio went silent for several seconds, then returned to a music program.

"They did it!" Hank shouted, then turned to Ortega. "I need to get down there right away. Cortés promised me an exclusive story."

"Let me check in with the office first," Ortega said, "then I'll drive you."

"Don't tie up the phone too long," the sergeant told Ortega.

Hank gazed down at the now quiet compound and smiled. They'd pulled it off! But then he remembered Major Mejías, and his smile faded. They couldn't just let that son of a bitch retire.

Ortega hurried out of the building. "*Los Machos del Monte* are heading this way."

"What?" Hank exclaimed.

"I just talked to César Ruíz," Ortega said. "He told me *Los Machos* rolled by the AP office about five minutes ago."

"Captain!" Hank said, turning to the Officer of the Day. "You said the Marines had blocked *Los Machos*."

The captain frowned. "H.Q. told me they'd blocked off the highway at the Bridge of the Americas."

"Bridge of the Americas! What about Omar Torrijos Airport? What about *Vía España*?"

"They didn't say anything about the airport or . . ." The captain's voice trailed off as he too realized that the U.S. military support apparently had been only halfhearted.

"Damn it!" Hank exploded. He turned to Ortega. "Joe, I've got to get down there and warn them."

"Too late," Ortega said, nodding toward the thoroughfare below.

Avenida de los Mártires had been all but deserted since the initial gunfire that morning. Now a convoy of tanks, trucks, and armored personnel carriers rumbled into view.

The captain radioed the command center. As Hank watched the scene unfold through his field glasses, he heard the captain report to his superior: "Sir, a PDF convoy is coming down *Avenida de los Mártires*. A reporter here at the main gate suspects *Los Machos* have landed at Omar Torrijos Airport and—"

The captain stopped in mid-sentence. Hank turned and saw the captain shake his head in disbelief. Looking at Hank, he said into the mouthpiece, "Oh, you already knew that?"

"Son of a bitch!" Hank exploded.

"The vehicles have Battalion 2000 markings, sir," the captain continued into the two-way radio.

"That's the other group Cortés was worried about," Hank said.

"*Los Machos* may have linked up with Battalion 2000, sir," the captain relayed to his superior.

Hank turned to the scene below. The convoy swerved off *Avenida de los Mártires* and filed down a side street. Moments later, the vehicles encircled *La Comandancia*. Scores of loyalist troops poured out of the trucks and armored personnel carriers, then ran into the tenements that overlooked the compound. The detachment that was deployed near the main gate sported the beards and black T-shirts of Los Machos.

The captain continued his report to the command center. "They're setting up all around the *Comandancia*, sir. I see some antitank weapons . . . grenade launchers . . . 50-calibers . . ."

Hank whirled and grabbed the radio away from the captain. "Get some God-damned troops down there!" he shouted.

The captain snatched the radio back. Covering the mouthpiece, he said to Hank, "We're not going in. H.Q. says, for the past ten minutes, the rebels have been begging us to come take Noriega off their hands. But orders have been passed down for us to stay out of it."

Before Hank could reply, there was an explosion. He turned in time to see a cloud of smoke and dust forming near the *Comandancia* motor pool. Rebels ran for the cover of a nearby building; a 50-caliber machine gun sprayed dust at their feet. Loyalist riflemen opened fire from the windows and balconies of the surrounding tenements. Then there was another explosion as an antitank shell disintegrated the compound's main gate.

The loyalist fusillade lasted several minutes, with no discernible response from the rebels inside the compound. Finally, the firing ceased. The main building's side door opened and a distraught rebel officer stepped onto the stoop, waving a white piece of cloth. The *Machos* detachment poured into the compound and fanned out across the courtyard. Two rushed up and grabbed the surrendering officer. They dragged him down the concrete stairs and forced him to kneel.

"That's the guy I've been working with," Hank said grimly. "That's Cortés."

The Battalion 2000 troops now streamed into the compound. Building by building, they flushed out the rebels, who surrendered without a fight. The rebels were herded into the courtyard, where they were forced to kneel, hands clasped behind their heads.

Major Mejías stepped through the side doorway. A few moments later, General Noriega joined him. The two men embraced in the Latin *abrazo*, then stood side by side, acknowledging the cheers from the loyalist troops.

Four grinning *Machos* brought out two more rebel officers, heads bleeding as if they had been beaten. The *Machos* dragged them down the steps and forced them to kneel beside Cortés.

"That's Major Giroldi on the left," Ortega said, "the coup leader."

"He's one of the guys who was at Cortés' home last night," Hank said. "The black guy beside him is the other."

Noriega stood smiling on the stoop above them. He raised his

arms in triumph, and another loud cheer went up from the loyalist troops. Noriega turned and said something to Mejías, who smiled
and saluted. Then Mejías descended the stairs and walked over to
where the three rebel officers knelt. He withdrew his pistol and
placed the muzzle against Cortés' temple.

"Oh, no, man . . ." Hank said.

Cortés' body jerked, and a moment later the sound of the shot
reached the Americans on the hill.

"Christ," Ortega said softly.

In a dull monotone, the Officer of the Day reported the ex-
ecution to his superiors in the U.S. command center.

The black officer pleaded. The grinning Mejías shot him in
the face, and the officer's body slumped on top of Cortés'. Major
Giroldi defiantly struggled to his feet. Mejías took careful aim,
but Noriega shouted something, and Mejías lowered his pistol.
Two *Machos* grabbed Giroldi and dragged him up the stairs and
into the building. Noriega and Mejías followed, eager expressions
on their faces.

The loyalist troops cheered one last time, some firing their
weapons into the air. Suddenly a U.S. Apache assault helicopter
appeared from behind Ancon Hill. In panic, the loyalists scattered
for cover. The helicopter hovered over the compound for several
minutes, unchallenged. Finally, it withdrew, returning to its base
behind the hill.

"Just observers," the Officer of the Day said apologetically.

Tears of frustration burned Hank's eyes. "*Gringo*
motherfuckers!"

Hank and Ortega sat at a table in the cantina, just down the street
from Andrea's apartment. Through the grimy front window, the
afternoon traffic moved slowly up *Avenida B*. Several laborers stood
at the bar, their voices loud and their laughter frequent. Three
prostitutes gossiped at a nearby table and occasionally smiled at
Hank and Ortega.

"As far as these people are concerned," Hank said with a resigned shake of his head, "it's like nothing happened this morning."

Ortega looked up from the notepad on which he had outlined his report of the failed coup attempt. "That's Panama," he said with a shrug.

"If just one more road had been blocked," Hank said, "their lives would have been so different."

"Think so?" Ortega said, closing the pad and putting his pen in his shirt pocket.

"Don't you?"

"Panamanians are a mystery to me."

Hank sighed. "I'm part Panamanian . . . and part American . . . and I don't understand either one."

Ortega smiled.

"Joe, why the hell didn't the Southern Command support those people?"

"May have been a chain-of-command problem," Ortega said. "Not only was General Thurman new, but so was his boss—an Army general named Colin Powell. Powell just took over as chairman of the Joint Chiefs of Staff three days ago."

"You think, because they were new, they didn't have the guts to pull the trigger?"

"Could be. Or maybe their boss tied their hands."

"President Bush?"

The veteran reporter leaned forward. "CIA spooks use the term 'blowback'. It's when you hire people to do your dirty work, but instead they turn on you. This fiasco reeks of it." Ortega paused.

"Go on," Hank said.

"When Bush was head of the CIA, Noriega was a CIA operative. And remember Iran-Contra? Bush was vice president. Ever since Noriega took over Panama, he's been bragging he's got Bush by the balls."

"Wouldn't Bush have wanted to see him taken down?"

"Taken down," Ortega said with a tight smile, "but not taken alive. My guess is, if Noriega were to spill what he knows, Bush would be caught in the blowback."

"So Bush only wins, if Noriega is killed in the coup," Hank said. "He loses if Noriega retires, or if he's taken prisoner."

Ortega nodded. "U.S. law prohibits the CIA from assassinating foreign leaders. So they may have tried to put Giroldi in a position where he had to do it."

Hank frowned.

Ortega continued, "All Giroldi had to do was kill Noriega, and the coup would have been successful. With him dead, even *Los Machos* would have conceded. But the U.S. picked the wrong guy to do their dirty work. Giroldi's a fierce nationalist."

"What do you think Noriega's going to do with him?"

"Noriega's going to want the names of everyone who was involved in the coup. If Giroldi's not already dead, he's probably begging for them to kill him."

Hank stared through the cantina front window for a moment, masking the fear and revulsion he felt at the memory of *La Preventiva's* interrogation cell. Finally, he looked back at Ortega. "Are you going to include your blowback conjecture in today's release?"

"No, I'll just report what we saw."

"How do we get the real story out, Joe?"

"We don't know the 'real story'. But if you want to put forth what we *think*, why don't you write an editorial?"

"I might try that," Hank said. "Anything else you need from me this afternoon?"

"Nope. I'll go over to the office and file what we've got. Joint byline okay?"

Hank nodded.

"Will your girlfriend pick up your money?"

"I'm not sure," Hank said. "She's out of town." Then he stood up. "I need to go call her and let her know I'm okay."

The two men walked through the cantina and out the front door. Pedestrians filled the sidewalk, going about their afternoon affairs, seemingly oblivious to the drama that had taken place just that morning.

Hank and Ortega walked around the corner and down the side street to where the Land Rover was parked. Ortega climbed inside and extended his hand through the window. "Stay alive, *amigo*," he said as they shook hands. "I'm looking forward to working with you again."

"Maybe one day we'll be able to tell the *whole* story," Hank said.

"I doubt it."

"We've got to, Joe. The only way to get rid of Noriega and his thugs is to put a light on whatever they, and possibly the U.S. government, are trying to hide."

"Hank, why are you taking this so personally?"

As Hank stepped away from the vehicle so Ortega could leave, he said, "Today's not the first time I've gotten in the middle of something I didn't completely understand . . . and then stood by helplessly on the side of that God-damned hill."

16. EL NECROCOMIO

Hank and Ortega's postmortem of the failed coup had broken up a few minutes earlier, and Hank was preoccupied when he arrived at Andrea's apartment. He fumbled with the lock for a moment, then opened the door. As he stepped inside, Andrea jumped up from the couch and rushed into his arms.

"How'd you get back so soon?" he said in surprise.

Andrea didn't respond, just tightened her embrace.

"Are Alberto and your parents okay?" he said, concerned. He craned his head back, trying to see her face.

"Everyone is all right," she said, still clutching him. "They are still at the hotel."

Finally she sighed, and Hank felt her relax. He led her back to the couch. They sat facing each other; Hank took her hands in his. She had been crying.

"Why didn't you call me, Hank?" she said reproachfully.

"I just got home. The coup—"

"I didn't know what had happened to you! I thought you might have been in *La Comandancia* during the *cuartelazo*."

Hank gazed at her, moved by her concern. She had become so much a part of his being. He took her in his arms. "I'm sorry."

They held each other for some time. Finally Andrea leaned back and pulled a handkerchief from her jeans pocket. She wiped her eyes and gave him a faint smile.

"Tell me about your family," Hank said.

"Everyone is fine. Alberto asked about you. He wants to come home. My parents want to return to their farm, but they agreed to stay at the hotel until I found out what happened here."

"Did reports of the coup reach Colón?"

"It was very confusing. At one time, the radio said that it had been successful. Then Noriega came on the air, laughing, like it was all a big joke."

Hank nodded ruefully, then told her what had transpired during the day, including a recap of the discussion in the cantina and Joe Ortega's "blowback" conjecture.

"What now?" she said when he had finished.

"To get to Mejías, I wanted to help bring down Noriega. But now I realize, Noriega's not coming down unless his connection with prominent people in the U.S. government is exposed. As long as this connection is hidden, they'll keep protecting the son of a bitch."

"How can you prove this . . . 'connection'?"

"I don't know. I saw Noriega and his thugs execute two of the three officers who could've helped me. The only one left is Giroldi, and his chance of survival is pretty slim."

They sat in silence for a while. Finally Hank said, "I haven't eaten today. Let's go get something."

Andrea was still lost in thought. "Hank," she said, "what about the officers' families?"

Hank looked at her with a half-smile; her question triggered a recollection. "Three women got turned away from Quarry Heights, just before the shooting started. My guess is, they were the coup leaders' wives."

"Maybe they could help."

"They must know something about the coup," Hank said slowly, "or they wouldn't have been seeking sanctuary this morning."

"You should talk to them."

Hank got to his feet. "I know where Cortés' house is. I need to get to his wife before anybody else does. Can I borrow your van?"

"I will go with you."

"No, I've already put you in enough danger."

"I am not asking you," she said. "I am telling you that I am going with you."

Hank looked at her for a moment, then smiled. "Haven't you heard? Latinas are supposed to defer to their men."

She glared at him.

"That was a joke, Andrea."

"I am not laughing."

"C'mon," he said, "let's go to Curundú."

Hank's knock was answered by one of the women who had been turned away from Quarry Heights. Her matronly face was gaunt, her eyes bloodshot, her hair unkempt. The black suit she wore looked as if it had been hastily pulled on; a midriff button was undone.

"Mrs. Cortés?" Hank said.

"Yes," she said resentfully. "Are you agent Salinas?"

"No, I'm Hank Duque, and this is Andrea Arias." The woman moved as if to close the door, but Hank held it open. "Mrs. Cortés, I'm sorry about your loss. I was here last night. I met with your husband and the two other officers."

Mrs. Cortés allowed Hank and Andrea to enter. They had to step around several pieces of luggage that lay near the entryway, probably some of the suitcases Hank had seen in the Suburban that morning.

She led them into the living room, then slumped onto the couch and buried her face in her hands. Andrea sat down beside her and placed a comforting arm across her shoulders. Hank took the chair across from them. Two children, kindergarten age, stood in the hallway, peeping shyly around the corner. Hank forced a smile and waved, and they ducked out of sight.

"Mrs. Cortés," Hank said, "are you going someplace?"

She looked up and said bitterly, "They are taking us to Miami."

"Who is?"

She didn't reply.

Hank said, "You thought I was an agent when you answered the door. Is the CIA taking you to Miami?"

She still didn't reply.

"I know this is a terrible time for you," Hank said, "but we need to talk. Particularly if you're about to leave the country."

"My husband is dead! My children have no father!" She buried her face in her hands again and began to cry.

Hank had to press on. "Please, tell me why you're going to Miami."

She raised her head and took a deep breath, trying to regain her composure. "An American army officer came by a short while ago. He told me we are in danger and must leave immediately. He said an agent Salinas would pick us up in a few minutes."

"Mrs. Cortés, I'm a correspondent for the Associated Press."

"I know who you are. My husband told me about you this morning. You were supposed to help him!" She began to cry again.

"I tried," Hank said lamely.

"You *gringos* never do what you say," she said with a sob.

"Mrs. Cortés, someone, either in the CIA or the Southern Command, let your husband down. Did he tell you anything, or leave anything behind, that would help me understand what happened? Major Giroldi is still in Noriega's custody. Maybe I can help him."

She glanced toward the luggage.

There was a loud knock on the door. Before Mrs. Cortés could get to her feet, the door flew open. Two men in business suits entered the room. They seemed to be Americans, although one was Latino in appearance. He strode into the house as if he owned it. The other was younger, with a light complexion and hair so blond it was almost white. He diffidently stayed close to the entryway.

"Who are you people?" the swarthy one demanded of Hank and Andrea.

Before they could answer, Mrs. Cortés said, "They are neighbors. They came to console me."

"Weren't you told not to talk to anybody?" the man snapped, then turned to his companion. "Take the luggage out to the van." The younger man grabbed two suitcases and hurried outside.

The two children rushed into the room. Wide-eyed, they took positions on the couch on either side of their mother.

"Let's go, Mrs. Cortés," the man said curtly. "Your plane leaves in half an hour."

Mrs. Cortés stood up and looked distractedly about her home. Her eyes locked on the luggage. "I must attend to something," she said, then hurried over and picked up an overnight case.

"We gotta go *now*, lady!" the man said.

"Just a moment, please. I must go to the bathroom."

"Hurry up," the man said.

Mrs. Cortés, looking flustered, disappeared into the bathroom. Her children waited anxiously in the hallway.

The man glared at Hank and Andrea, tapping his foot. "You two," he said finally, "get out of here."

At that moment, Mrs. Cortés reappeared. The toilet flushed in the background. She walked over and handed a set of keys to Andrea. "Please look after things for me," she said. "And check the windows to be sure they are locked."

"Let's go," the man said. He grabbed the overnight case and ushered Mrs. Cortés and her children out the front door.

Hank and Andrea stood in the doorway, watching as the grieving family was loaded into a gray military van parked at the curb. Two other women and several children made room for them. As the van pulled away, Mrs. Cortés' distraught face was framed in a passenger-side rear window.

Hank and Andrea hurried back into the house and headed straight for the bathroom.

"She said to check the windows," Andrea said. She pushed aside a brightly-patterned curtain and pulled out a sealed, business-size envelope.

"C'mon," Hank said, "let's get out of here."

They hurried outside and climbed into Andrea's van. She made a U-turn, and Hank said, "Take that side street, just past the tennis courts."

She turned onto a mottled asphalt lane. "Do you know where this goes?"

"I know where it went twenty-five years ago," he said. "We'd better stay off the main road. Those guys saw your van and may call for backup to find out who we are."

Hank's circuitous childhood route eventually took them out of Curundú and onto *Avenida de los Mártires*. As they headed up the thoroughfare, he turned his attention to the envelope. The outside was blank. He unsealed the flap and pulled out a single sheet of lined paper. Scrawled in blue ink were:

Raúl Salinas y James Broderick 555-1471
Banco del Mar 555-8142 A094876 'Panamá-5'

"What did you find?" Andrea said.

"There's a phone number here for a Raúl Salinas and a James Broderick. They must have been the two guys back there at the house. I've got a hunch they were also the CIA contacts Cortés told me he was working with. Now they're probably trying to cover their asses, and their agency's, by hustling the wives up to Miami."

They drove down a familiar stretch of the thoroughfare. Up the hill on the right stood the old Ancon elementary school.

"Pull in there at the Roosevelt Hotel," Hank said.

Andrea changed lanes and made a left turn into the small hotel parking lot.

"I'll just be a minute," Hank said, opening the door. "There ought to be a public phone in here. I'll try these numbers, in case there's something I can do to help Giroldi."

He returned a few minutes later and climbed back into the van. "No luck. The number beside the two names just gave me a pager tone. The other number gave me a recording—said the bank would open again at nine o'clock tomorrow morning."

They sat in silence. Finally, Hank looked at Andrea. She obviously was as exhausted as he was. "There's nothing else we can do this evening," he said. "Do you know a quiet place where we can eat?"

"Of course," she said, forcing a smile. "I am a guide, remember?"

They pulled out of the parking lot and merged into the *Avenida de los Mártires* traffic. They were on the stretch of the thoroughfare that separated Quarry Heights from *El Chorrillo*. They both looked at the ominous, now-quiet *La Comandancia* compound, but neither spoke.

They drove in silence for several blocks. Finally, Hank said, "So, where are we going?"

"The Amador Officers' Club."

"Officers' Club?"

She nodded. "It is close to here, and should be quiet this early in the evening. I haven't been there myself, but the other guides tell me the food is good and the view is nice."

"Are civilians allowed in?"

"I think you just have to be an American."

"When I was a kid," Hank said, "Fort Amador was a secured army post, closed to the public." As he spoke, he recognized what had been Fort Amador's main gate. Now, it stood unguarded. High chain-link fences on both sides of the boulevard formed a corridor that allowed motorists to pass through the middle of the fort, without actually entering the premises. On the other side of the fences lay regimented rows of tan quadruplexes, just as he remembered them. He looked in vain for the old post movie theater.

They continued past a long row of barracks and administrative buildings. Hank studied the military unit emblems on and around the structures. Some had Spanish inscriptions. "Does the PDF use this fort too?"

Andrea nodded. "Both countries have soldiers assigned here."

They passed the golf course. Ahead, near the entrance to the causeway, stood an impressive white building. Hank saw a familiar emblem over the front door: eagle, globe, and fouled anchor. "Marines live pretty good here," he said wryly.

Andrea pointed farther up the causeway. "That is the Officers' Club."

Hank nodded. "I remember it. We used to sneak into the fort and swim over there on that first island."

"Oh, yes?" she said, turning into the nearly empty parking lot. She parked close to the front door.

"Somehow, I still feel like I'm sneaking in," Hank said as he climbed out of the van.

An energetic young American woman met them at the front door. Her straw-colored hair was feathered back in a severe pageboy cut, and her blue eyes were bright and alert. "Afternoon, folks," she said. "Can I help you?"

"We would like to eat," Andrea said, assuming her role as guide.

"Uh . . . we aren't ready to serve evening chow . . . I mean . . . dinner," the young woman said. "We're still getting things squared away."

"Sandwiches will be fine," Andrea said.

"Uh . . ." the young woman said uncomfortably, "this club is reserved for United States officers."

"I am a guide for Aventura Tours," Andrea said, "and this gentleman is an American tourist."

The young woman turned to Hank and said with obvious discomfort, "I'm sorry, sir, but unless you have some military identification . . ."

Hank didn't respond right away, and she started to turn away. Then Hank said, "You say you're getting squared away for evening chow?"

"Yes, sir," the young woman said, turning with renewed interest.

Hank pulled out his wallet, withdrew his yellowed Certificate of Service card, and handed it to her.

She studied it for a moment. Then she looked up with a half-smile. "Former Marine lance corporal, huh?"

Hank nodded.

"That's good enough for me," she said briskly, returning his card. "Please follow me."

As they crossed the deserted dining room, Andrea frowned at Hank. He smiled back.

The young woman seated them at a pleasant window table, overlooking the Bay of Panama. She handed them their menus and said, "I recommend the hamburgers. The cook this afternoon is from our Marine billet down the street."

"Hamburgers okay with you?" Hank asked Andrea.

She nodded.

"I'll place your order, and they'll be out in a minute," the young woman said. "And if anybody gives you any crap while you're here, tell 'em to come see me—Lance Corporal Davis." With a smile, she left them.

Andrea raised her eyebrows inquiringly at Hank. "Do you have some sort of code you use when you talk to *gringas*?"

"Only if they're *gringa* Marines."

"Oh, I see," she said with a laugh.

Hank reached across the table and took her hand. They smiled at each other for a moment, then turned their attention to the scene outside the window. A luxury cruise ship headed toward the Pacific. Farther up the coast, the steel-arched Bridge of the Americas spanned the Canal, reconnecting the continent man had severed at the turn of the 20th Century.

"Let me see what was in the envelope," Andrea said.

"Tomorrow," Hank said.

"Now," she said, holding out her hand.

He gave her the envelope.

A young Panamanian waiter arrived with their order. Hank was ravenous. "Good burger," he said with his mouth full.

Andrea nodded abstractly. She nibbled at her own sandwich and studied the sheet of paper. Finally, she looked up and handed it back to him. "Do you think this will lead to anything?"

He looked again at the scrawled notes:

Raúl Salinas y James Broderick 555-1471
Banco del Mar 555-8142 A094876 'Panamá-5'

"I don't know. I'll just have to try these numbers again tomorrow morning."

She nodded. "Hank, let's go home now. I need to call my parents and let them know everything is all right."

He signaled the waiter for the check, then said, "Maybe one day, things won't be so hectic for us."

"I hope so."

The following morning, Hank was drinking coffee at the kitchen table when Andrea padded in, wearing one of his T-shirts. She was about to take the chair beside him, but he pulled her onto his lap. "What time is your first tour?" he murmured, nuzzling her soft neck.

"Ten o'clock," she said, playfully pushing him away. She got up and poured herself a cup of coffee, then came back and handed Hank the phone. "Make your calls."

Hank dialed the first number.

Someone picked up the phone on the fifth ring, and a woman's voice said in Spanish, "Banco del Mar. Account number, please."

"Uh . . . A094876," Hank said, reading from Cortés' notes.

There was a pause, then the voice said, "What service would you like?"

"Uh . . . account balance, please."

"Password, please."

"Panamá-5," Hank replied, again reading.

"Account balance is $73,475. Would you like to transfer funds?"

"Uh . . . not at this time," Hank said. "Thank you." He hung up and turned to Andrea, who had watched with interest. "It's a numbered bank account. There's over $73,000 in it. Apparently, I could have transferred the funds someplace else, simply by having the right password: Panama-5."

"An emergency account for Mrs. Cortés?"

"Maybe, but I don't think Mrs. Cortés knew what was in the envelope. I doubt she would have knowingly turned over $73,000 to us."

Andrea nodded.

"Also," Hank continued, "Cortés didn't strike me as being a devoted family man—he had a young girlfriend out on *Isla Contadora*. No, I suspect the envelope was an insurance policy for Cortés himself, in case the coup failed. He probably just left it with his wife for safekeeping."

"Are you going to try the other phone number again?"

Hank shook his head. "It's just a pager number. And I don't know who I'm paging."

Andrea stood up. "I have to get ready for work. What are you going to do today?"

"Ortega suggested I write an editorial, exposing the United States bungling the opportunity to get rid of Noriega. I think I'll give it a try."

"Good," she said, bending down and giving him an affectionate peck on the lips. "That should keep you out of trouble for a change."

Hank sat at the kitchen table, perspiring in the early afternoon heat. Except for a quick lunch break, he had worked steadily on his editorial. Now, as he read over it, he was satisfied with the wording, but uncomfortable with the content. He alluded to treachery and asked questions, but could supply few answers.

He dialed the Associated Press office number and asked for Ortega. After a long wait, the veteran reporter picked up the phone, saying, "Ortega."

"This is Hank, Joe. I wrote that editorial this morning. I'd like to get together with you and see what you think."

"Okay . . ." Ortega said. He sounded preoccupied. "Listen, Hank, something's come up . . . may affect what you've written. I got a call a few minutes ago from a source at *Hospital Santo Tomás*. He said the PDF just delivered eleven bodies to the morgue there."

"Coup members?"

"Yeah. My source works in the hospital administrative office. He says he can get me inside around 5:00. You want in on it?"

Hank glanced up at the clock on the counter; it was 2:25. "Yeah. Should I meet you there at the hospital?"

"Do you know where it is?"

"Yeah, the big one on *Avenida Balboa*."

"Right, but meet me around back, on the *Calle 34* side. You'll see my Land Rover."

"See you at 5:00," Hank said, then hung up.

He sat for a long time, lost in thought, his hand still resting on the phone. The sheet with Cortés' notes lay on the table in front of him, and his eyes settled on the 'Panama-5' password. In the back of his mind was a thought that wouldn't quite surface. Then he had it. Cortés had tended to reuse codes, possibly so he wouldn't forget them. He had used 'Panama-5', the CIA code name for the coup, as passwords for both the *Contadora* pilot and the bank. Had he done the same thing with pager codes? Hank picked up the receiver and dialed the pager number. When he got the pulsating tone, he entered 111-1600. Now he'd see who showed up at *Teatro Lux* at four o'clock.

At 3:45, Hank was already stationed at a window table in a small restaurant, diagonally across from Teatro Lux. The only other customers were four Panamanian businessmen at the far end of the room, immersed in a discussion. The elderly proprietress had just replenished Hank's coffee, and now sat near the cash register, watching a Spanish soap opera on a portable black and white T.V. set.

A ragged young boy in short pants banged through the screen door. "*¿La Prensa, señor?*" he asked Hank.

"*Sí,*" Hank said, and purchased a newspaper.

The businessmen waved off the boy, and he banged back out the door. Hank adjusted his position so he could see the theater over the top of the newspaper. The marquee still advertised *Rambo II*. He glanced down at the paper. The article Ortega had submitted under their joint byline was on page one. Hank was scanning it, when the restaurant door banged open again. He looked up and found himself gazing into the washed-out blue eyes of the pale agent from Curundú.

The agent looked at him in surprise, then turned to leave.

"Broderick!" Hank called out. The agent froze. Hank was confident that he now knew names of both of Cortés' CIA contacts.

Broderick approached the table. "Who are you?"

"I'm the person who paged you. Sit down."

Broderick hesitated, then removed his suit coat and took a seat.

The proprietress stood up, and Hank called over, *"Otro café, por favor, señora."*

After the woman had brought the coffee and returned to her T.V. show, Broderick said again, "Who are you?"

Hank studied the young man for a moment. His face was drawn and tired, as if he were operating on little sleep. Hank turned the newspaper so Broderick could read it, and put his forefinger under his name in the byline.

"Are you Panamanian?" Broderick said.

"American."

"Shit," Broderick muttered. "How'd you get the pager code?"

"Cortés gave it to me."

"And he told you my name?"

"Yeah," Hank said, bluffing. "He told me quite a bit about you . . . and Panama-5."

Broderick winced. "What do you want?"

"Your account of why the coup failed."

"The rebels just blew it."

"They didn't just blow it," Hank said levelly. "You, your buddy Salinas, and the Southern Command bugged out on them."

The agent nervously pushed his blond-white hair away from his forehead.

"Where's Salinas?" Hank said.

"Miami," Broderick said with a trace of rancor.

"Was Panama-5 your operation, or his?"

"I can't discuss this with you any further," Broderick said. He shifted his weight as if to leave.

Hank reached across the table and grasped him by the forearm. "How well did you know Cortés and Giroldi?"

Broderick grimaced at the mention of the names, but didn't answer.

"Do you know what happened to them?" Hank pressed.

Broderick took a deep breath. "I understand Cortés . . . died. But I haven't learned what happened to Moisés Giroldi."

"They blew Cortés' brains out," Hank said in a hoarse whisper. "I saw it!"

"Have you heard anything about Moisés?" Broderick said.

"Did you know him well?"

"I considered him . . . a friend," the young agent said.

Hank released Broderick's arm. "I've been invited to a secret news conference in about thirty minutes. Do you want to come with me?"

"Whose news conference?" Broderick said suspiciously.

"The coup participants."

"The coup participants? Where?"

"Within walking distance of here."

"I'll have to notify my office."

"No way."

"Will Moisés be there?"

"They'll all be there. Are you coming?"

Broderick pressed his lips together in a thin line. Finally he said, "Yeah, I need to . . . talk to Moisés."

A few minutes later, they walked in silence down *Calle 34.* Two blocks away, the green Pacific glistened in the late afternoon sun. *Hospital Santo Tomás* loomed over the palm trees to their left.

Broderick looked from side to side. Finally, he said, "Are we going to the Embassy?"

"No," Hank said. The American Embassy was three blocks away, on the other side of the hospital. They arrived at an intersection, and Hank pointed down the side street. "We're meeting the guy sitting over there in that green Land Rover."

Ortega was out on the sidewalk by the time they arrived. "Who the hell's this?" he demanded.

"This is CIA agent Broderick," Hank said. "I invited him to attend the news conference with the coup participants."

"Attend the news conference?" Ortega said, frowning.

"Major Giroldi was a friend of his," Hank said quickly. "I think he feels some responsibility for whatever has happened to him."

Ortega stood expressionless for a moment. Finally, he said, "C'mon."

They crossed the street and walked up to the hospital loading dock. A private security guard, seated in the doorway, gave them a barely perceptible nod. As they headed down the tiled hallway, Hank asked Ortega, "Is your source going to meet us?"

"I don't know. I know where to go, though."

A hospital orderly passed, pushing a canvas cart piled high with dirty linen. They made a turn and arrived at a heavy set of double doors. A sign read *"Necrocomio"*.

"What are we doing at the morgue?" Broderick protested. Apparently he spoke Spanish.

Hank grasped him by the back of the arm and pulled him through the swinging doors. Unattended, eleven naked corpses had been laid out side by side on gurneys. All showed signs of severe trauma; most had portions of their heads blown away.

"Oh, God, no," Broderick moaned, looking down at the closest gurney. The agent's normally pale face was now completely white. He turned away in revulsion. Major Giroldi's corpse was riddled with bullet holes. Huge purplish blotches covered his entire body. A strand of barbed wire was embedded into one wrist. Although his body had been laid straight on the gurney, it was apparent that most of the major bones had been broken.

Hank, still holding Broderick by the arm, coldly turned him around and forced him to look again at the gurney. "Is that your friend?" he demanded.

Broderick lowered his head and vomited onto the stark concrete floor. Sweat poured down his face.

Hank grabbed Broderick's hair with his other hand and forced the agent's face up. "Is that your friend?" he demanded again.

"Please!" Broderick begged.

"Get him out of here," Ortega hissed.

Hank pulled Broderick through the swinging doors and down the empty hallway. The security guard looked up and smiled at the deathly pale *gringo*, with vomitus spilled down his suit front. Apparently the guard knew what lay inside the *necrocomio*.

Hank pushed Broderick into the rear seat of the Land Rover and climbed in after him. Not wanting to give the agent a chance to recover, he said, "You'll be a confidential source—no name. And nothing will be used that can specifically be tied to you."

Broderick closed his eyes and leaned his head against the back of the seat. "I can't tell you anything."

"I know about the Banco del Mar account," Hank said. "I have the password."

Broderick's eyes opened wide. He looked at Hank, making no effort to mask his concern.

"If I have to do it the hard way," Hank said, "I'll backtrack the electronic fund transfers, and blow the whistle on everyone I find. If we do it the easy way, you'll tell what I need to know, and you'll remain a confidential source."

Broderick leaned forward, trying to get the blood to flow to his head. Hank pulled him upright. "Tell me what happened yesterday morning."

"We had Noriega in custody," Broderick said bitterly. "Panama-5 was working, just the way we laid it out."

"Why was the plan changed?"

"They wanted Noriega dead. When he surrendered and agreed to step down, they went to a contingency plan that I didn't know about. They let the *Machos* in. They wanted the rebels to kill Noriega in the firefight."

"Who made the decision to let the *Machos* in?"

"I don't k*now*," Broderick said. "Until a couple of weeks ago, I'd been in charge of the operation. Moisés and I had set the thing up. Then Salinas came down from Washington and took over."

"Where did the funding for Panama-5 come from?" Hank said, still trying to hone in on responsibility.

"We had the money left over from an earlier operation, Panama-4."

"What was that?" Hank said.

"A propaganda blitz against Noriega. The Senate Intelligence Committee gave us $10,000,000 to influence the May elections. We didn't handle it well. We wound up embarrassing the reform candidates."

"Did the Intelligence Committee also approve Panama-5?"

Broderick shook his head. "I don't think it was ever presented to them. Moisés moved too fast."

The young agent's color and composure returned. He squirmed out of his fouled suit jacket and folded it across his lap so that the vomitus was on the inside.

Hank saw a snub-nose pistol, snuggled into a holster under his left arm.

"You can't quote me on any of this," Broderick said.

"Like I told you, you'll be a confidential source—"

They were interrupted by Ortega opening the door and climbing into the driver seat. He started the engine and pulled away from the hospital.

"Problems back there?" Hank said.

"Just the ones you generated," Ortega said tersely.

"Let me out at the next intersection," Broderick said.

Hank shook his head. "I've got some more questions."

"I've told you enough. Now let me out of here!"

"We'll take you to your car," Hank said. "Is it back at the restaurant?"

Broderick's hand went to his shoulder holster. "Let me out now, God damn it!"

"Pull over, Joe," Hank said.

Broderick jumped out before the vehicle came to a complete stop, and took off down the sidewalk.

Hank got into the front passenger seat. "If his car's at the restaurant, he's headed in the wrong direction."

"Probably doesn't care," Ortega said as he pulled away from the curb. "Just wants to get away from you. You're a cold-blooded son of a bitch, Duque."

Hank shook his head. "I almost puked back there myself. I've seen corpses lined up like that before, but it's been twenty years—Vietnam."

Ortega gave him an appraising glance, then a nod.

Hank said, "What happened in there after I took Broderick outside?"

"Well, for one thing, I had to pay an orderly twenty bucks to clean up the puke. Told him I did it."

"You're okay, Joe," Hank said with a short laugh.

"Otherwise, nothing happened. My source met me in the hallway as I was leaving. He verified that I hadn't taken any pictures—I'd agreed not to."

"Seems like getting in there was too easy, Joe."

Ortega smiled. "You're learning, Hank. Noriega rules by fear. He wants people to know the fate of those who oppose him—but no pictures. He maximizes his cruelty by encouraging the fear, while denying the proof."

"Are you saying that you think Noriega approved your seeing the bodies?"

"It's not the first time. There's probably some other newsmen in there right now."

They turned onto *Vía España* and headed toward the older section of the city. Hank stared out the window, momentarily lost in thought. Turning back, he said, "Noriega did the same thing to me a few weeks ago, when I interviewed him. He gave me plenty of opportunity to browse all the sinister stuff in his home, but he didn't want any pictures taken."

Ortega nodded.

Hank said, "Sorry I put you on the spot today, springing Broderick on you."

"Well, I picked up on what you were doing and figured it was worth the risk. By the way, how'd you get hooked up with that guy, and why didn't you let me in on it?"

Hank explained the Curundú encounter, the phone numbers, and meeting Broderick in the restaurant. Then he said, "As soon as I started talking to him, I sensed he felt guilty about his role in yesterday's fiasco. I thought he might talk, if I showed him what actually happened to those poor bastards. He's also worried about Cortés' private bank account. I've got a hunch, he's personally been involved in the transfer of funds."

They entered the old *Santa Ana* district. As Ortega weaved cautiously through the *Avenida Central* traffic, he said, "Did Broderick actually admit to CIA involvement?"

"Yeah. Apparently, yesterday's coup was the fifth of a series of covert operations." Hank gave Ortega the details.

"Looks like you got a story, *amigo*," Ortega said, as they turned down the narrow side street that ran in front of Andrea's apartment building.

"How much of this can we include?" Hank said.

They came to a stop. "Write it the way you see it," Ortega said. "Ruíz is a good editor; he'll delete anything he doesn't want to use."

Hank nodded, then said, "I think someone ought to go up to Miami and interview the widows of the coup leaders."

"Ruíz and I discussed that possibility this morning."

"Since I don't have a passport," Hank said, "it can't be me."

"I wouldn't mind making the trip," Ortega said, "but after what those women have been through, I doubt they'll be interested in talking to reporters."

"Mrs. Cortés might. Her husband's numbered account has over $73,000 in it. As far as I know, I'm the only person who can access it. I suggest you go up there, have her open up a Miami account, and I'll transfer the funds into it. After that, she may be willing to talk to you. She might even encourage the other two women to do the same."

"Sounds like a bribe."

"Whose money is it?" Hank said as he climbed out of the Land Rover. "Sure as hell isn't mine."

Ortega gave a wry shake of his head. "I'll call you from Miami," he said, "probably tomorrow."

"Work it as a joint byline?"

"No, we'll work it together, but you take the byline," Ortega said. "I want to stay on Noriega's guest list."

17. VENGANZA

Hank and Andrea climbed out of the van in front of her uncle and aunt's home in the exclusive *La Cresta* district. An hour earlier, *Tía* Celia had telephoned and invited them to lunch. The front door opened as they started up the walkway, and Sr. Castillero appeared. His stern expression confirmed Hank's suspicion that the hastily called luncheon was to be more than just a family get-together. Castillero had a folded newspaper tucked under one arm.

"*Hola, Tío,*" Andrea said, and kissed her uncle on the cheek.

Castillero perfunctorily shook Hank's hand and ushered them inside. Andrea's aunt waited in the tiled foyer; she appeared apprehensive.

In the living room, Hank and Andrea sat down on the couch. Sr. Castillero pulled up a straight-backed chair across the coffee table from them, and Sra. Castillero took a cushioned seat off to the side.

Sr. Castillero looked at Hank and slapped the newspaper with the back of his hand. "I have read your latest editorial."

"I take it, you didn't like it."

"You attack General Noriega, and you call your own president a coward. You slander everyone."

"It's not slander; it's the truth."

Castillero shook his head and said resentfully, "You don't understand things here in *Panamá*."

"I keep hearing that. Why don't you explain them to me?"

"This continual uproar—editorials, demonstrations, riots, *cuartelazos*—must cease. It is bad for business!"

"It was Noriega's Dobermans who destroyed your store. Explain how that was good for business."

"That was a mistake," Castillero muttered. "They made restitution."

Hank guessed Remos had interceded with Noriega, in Castillero's behalf. Although Castillero was Andrea's uncle, clearly he couldn't be trusted. "Why didn't you show up for that *Isla Contadora* trip?"

Castillero studied him for a moment, then said, "After Sr. Remos invited you, he and I discussed the situation further. Because of your newspaper stories, we decided it was best for me to . . . distance myself from you."

"Then why have you invited me here today?"

"To warn you. For Andrea's sake, you must stop making these accusations."

"What I've written is the truth," Hank said confidently. He couldn't disclose that his sources were the CIA agent who set up the failed coup and the widows of the three lead conspirators.

"You are badly misinformed," Castillero said.

"I'm not 'misinformed'. Noriega's nothing but a gangster. It's common knowledge he hired out to the CIA and smuggled arms to the Contras. But my sources also told me about another operation he ran at the same time, funneling Colombian drugs into the United States."

Castillero leaned forward, eyes narrowed. "*¡Estúpido!* It was the same operation."

Hank frowned. "What?"

"They used the *same planes*. The CIA sent down arms; the Colombians sent drugs back. In the same planes!"

Hank stared at Castillero, now fully understanding the significance of the Paitilla Airport hangar locations.

Castillero turned to Andrea and said in Spanish, "Your association with this fool is dangerous for you . . . and for your family."

Andrea angrily rose from the couch. "Are you threatening me, *Tío*?"

Her aunt jumped up and hurried over. "Please," she said, clutching Andrea's arm, "you must not argue. Lunch will be ready in a few minutes."

Andrea glared at her uncle. "You drove my father from the city. Now must I leave too?"

Castillero pointed to Hank. "*He* is the one who should leave. He is in the country illegally and does not belong here."

Hank got to his feet.

"You are not a *panameño*!" Castillero railed. "You dress like one now, and your name is Duque, but you are still a *gringo*!"

Hank followed Andrea through the foyer and out the front door.

"You must be stopped!" Castillero shouted after them. "You *will* be stopped!"

Hank awoke with a start. It sounded like someone running in the hallway. Pushing aside the sheet, he eased out of bed. He paused in the bedroom doorway, listening intently, while reaching behind the dresser for the length of rebar. It slipped from his fingers and clattered onto the floor.

Andrea sat up in bed. "What is it?"

Hank picked up the rebar and signaled her to stay where she was. He edged through the doorway, crossed the living room, and threw open the front door. The hallway was empty. The only sounds came from the street below. Somewhere close by, probably the open market, he heard a rooster crow.

He closed and locked the door, then turned to find Andrea standing in the bedroom doorway. "It's okay," he said.

She came over and put her arms around his waist. "What was it?"

"I don't know. I thought I heard somebody in the hall."

"Hank, we can't go on living like this."

"We've got to stay alert," he said. Several days had passed since her uncle's threat. Since then, Hank had written another scathing article, this one concerning the PDF harassment of an American Navy officer and his wife. Hank's piece had been picked up by most major U.S. newspapers and carried locally in *La Prensa*.

They entered the kitchen, and Hank checked the clock. "It's almost ten. Do you have to go to work this morning?"

"I don't have to go in at all today," she said with a smile. "They gave me the day off because I worked on Sunday. Do you want some breakfast?"

"Day off, huh?" he said, taking her into his arms.

"You are not hungry?" she teased.

"I've got an idea. Let's go someplace nice for an early lunch. How about that *Las Bóvedas* place you told me about?"

She frowned. "It is too expensive."

"A romantic brunch . . . then a quiet afternoon at home?"

"I love you," she said.

"I love you too."

Hank and Andrea decided to drive the short distance from *Santa Ana* to *Casco Viejo*. Manuel Noriega had proclaimed the day to be "Loyalty Day", and both neighborhoods were unusually quiet. Apparently, most Panamanians felt neither loyal to the general, nor willing to be out on the streets with those who were.

Andrea turned the van down a cobblestone street and they passed along a row of rundown shops and open markets. "Casablanca of the Americas," Hank mused.

They entered a tidy plaza that contrasted sharply with the surrounding neighborhood, and Andrea said, "This area is known as *Paseo de las Bóvedas*—The Dungeon Promenade. Over there is the French Embassy."

The two-story embassy building was painted a pastel blue with white trim. Wrought-iron bars enclosed the window air-conditioners, apparently to prevent their being stolen.

Andrea pulled in an area reserved for tour vehicles. They got out and started down a stone walkway that ran along the top of the seawall.

"Give me your tour lecture," Hank said.

Andrea smiled. "After the English pirate Henry Morgan burned *Panamá Viejo* in the 17th Century, the Spaniards rebuilt the city here. This peninsula was chosen because it would be easier to defend against future attacks."

They arrived at the plaza, and Andrea continued, "Here we have *Plaza de Francia*, dedicated to the Frenchmen who tried to dig the canal. They began work in 1881, and finally gave up in 1898."

Hank and Andrea slowly traversed the semicircular walkway, viewing busts of twelve Frenchmen who had engineered the failed project.

They stopped in front of a marker, and Hank read the inscription. "Twenty-two thousand canal workers died during the French attempt," he said reflectively, "and they only dug a couple of miles."

Andrea nodded. "Tourists like this plaza, but it always seems very sad to me."

A few minutes later, they walked along a row of caverns beneath the wall of the old city. "These are the dungeons," Andrea said. "Sometimes, high tides filled the cells, and prisoners were left to drown."

They passed a cavern that had been turned into an art gallery, then came to the one that had been converted into a trendy restaurant and bar. The room's elegant decor clashed with its barbaric history.

The hostess came up and showed them to a window table overlooking the Bay of Panama. Two American couples sat nearby; the men wore starched Army fatigues. Something about the Americans seemed unusual to Hank, but he couldn't put his finger on what it was.

The waiter arrived. Hank scanned the menu, then said to Andrea, "I'm not familiar with most of this stuff. How about ordering for me?"

"Good idea," she said with a smile. "I don't think they have hamburgers here. Would you like to start with a cup of *sancocho*?"

"Yeah. I know what that is: chicken soup."

She nodded. "Chicken soup, with yucca, potatoes, plantain, and other things. And for the main course, I think, *ropa vieja*."

"Old clothes?" Hank said in mock alarm.

"Literally, yes, 'old clothes'. It is shredded beef with tomatoes, onions, and peppers, cooked in red wine. And we'll want some rice. Then for desert, *sopa borracha*."

"Drunk soup?"

"It is a sponge cake, made with rum."

The waiter left with their order. For a while they sat admiring the view, lost in private thoughts. Finally Andrea said, "What are you thinking about?"

"Panamanian history. Five hundred years of . . . dreams . . . cruelty . . . treachery . . . and cowardice."

She responded with a resigned nod. "What are you going to do next?"

Hank returned to the situation at hand. "I need to get the straight story on what's driving U.S. policy in regard to Noriega. Ortega tells me, even his usual sources have dried up the past few days."

"Oh, yes?"

"It's like there's something in the wind, but nobody's able, or willing, to say what it is."

"Noriega is more arrogant than before," Andrea said.

Hank nodded. "Watching him on T.V. last night, he acted like he's got a photograph of George Bush fucking a goat."

Andrea laughed at his figure of speech, then turned serious again and said, "The PDF has been going out of their way to antagonize Americans. Yesterday morning, I saw them detain a bus full of American school children. There was no reason for it."

"The U.S. military is behaving strangely too," Hank said. "The crap they're putting out. Secretary of Defense Cheney is claiming that Giroldi orchestrated the coup by himself."

"That the *gringos* weren't involved?"

"Cheney claims they offered Giroldi help, but he refused it," Hank said in disgust. "In reality, Giroldi was tortured to death, because the U.S. reneged on the help they'd promised." Hank was getting worked up, just talking about it.

Andrea reached over and patted his arm.

Hank glanced at the nearby table. The four Americans were chatting amiably among themselves. Suddenly he knew what had bothered him about the scene. He leaned closer to Andrea. "When I was in the service, we only wore fatigues off base if we were on some sort of an alert. Andrea, there's something going on."

At that moment, the waiter arrived with their *sancocho*. When he left, Andrea said, "Hank, let's put this aside for now and enjoy our lunch."

Hank glanced at the Americans again, then reached over and squeezed her hand. "You're right. Let's enjoy lunch . . . and the rest of the afternoon."

Hank and Andrea stood transfixed in front of her apartment door. At their feet lay a rooster head, which apparently had been ripped, not severed, from the bird's body.

"*Venganza,*" Andrea whispered. "It is a sign of vengeance."

Hank unlocked the door and swung it open in a single motion. The living room appeared undisturbed. He stepped across the rooster head, into the room. Gesturing for Andrea to stay behind him, he glanced into the kitchen-dining area; it too was undisturbed. He could see into the bathroom; no one there.

They entered the bedroom and saw the gore. Andrea gasped, covering her mouth with her hand. The carcass of the dead rooster lay in a pool of blood in the middle of their bed. All four walls were splattered with blood, as if the beheaded bird had been swung by its feet. Hank took Andrea into the living room.

"They came into my home!" she cried.

Hank went over to the window and checked the balcony. "Come here, quick!"

Andrea hurried over.

A Jeep pulled up across the street, and a PDF officer and three armed enlisted men climbed out and strode toward the apartment building.

Hank grabbed Andrea's hand and pulled her toward the front

door. In the hallway, they froze, hearing heavy footfalls start up the stairway to their left. Andrea pulled Hank in the other direction. Apartment doors lined both sides of the dingy hall; a barred window blocked the end. They ducked into a doorless utility alcove, then pressed up against the stone sink, hiding behind the door jamb. Andrea's door opened and closed.

Hank checked the hallway. Empty. "C'mon," he whispered, grabbing her hand. They moved stealthily past her doorway, then hurried down the stairs and out the rear of the building. They jumped into the van, and moments later sped down the walled alley. The tires broke traction as they swerved into the street. Hank looked up at the apartment. The window over the wrought-iron balcony opened, and one of the soldiers leaned out. He saw them.

At Hank's urging, Andrea had driven out of the turmoil that was Panama City and into the relative quietude of the former Canal Zone. They came to a stop under a shade tree near Balboa High School. Andrea was still visibly shaken, and Hank reached over and took her hand.

"Just give me a minute," she said, pulling her hand away. She closed her eyes and leaned her head against the seat.

Hank studied his old school for a moment, then turned his attention to the *Prado*, the wide esplanade that led up to the Canal Commission Administration Building. The familiar surroundings transported him back twenty-five years, and he recalled the Panamanian university students who had proudly carried their national flag into the Canal Zone.

The school building door opened, returning him to the present. A custodian emerged, lit a cigarette, then sat down on the front steps.

Hank said to Andrea, "I'm going to see if I can use a phone in there."

"Who are you going to call?"

"I want to check in with Ortega at the AP office and find out if there's anything else going on that we ought to know about."

She placed a hand on his arm. "Hank, I am concerned for my family."

He opened the van door. "C'mon. We'll see if we can call them too."

Hank told the custodian they had car trouble and asked to use a phone to call a friend. The custodian told him there was one they could use, just inside the door. He stayed outside, finishing his cigarette.

The phone was on a counter in the outer office. As Hank dialed Ortega's number, he smiled at the familiar surroundings.

Then a voice on the other end of the line snapped, "What?"

"Ortega?" Hank said.

"Yeah. Who the hell's this?"

"It's Hank Duque. What's the matter?"

"Man, you wouldn't believe this shit. I got a phone call about a half-hour ago from a reporter at *La Prensa*. He said the Dobermans had busted up their office, so I rushed over here. Our computers and communication equipment have been destroyed, our furniture's smashed, and our files have been dumped all over the floor. It looks like a bomb went off in here."

Hank said, "Somebody broke into my girlfriend's apartment and made a mess in there too."

"Apparently, General Noriega's decided that he's had enough bad press," Ortega said.

"Joe . . ." Hank said uneasily, "I feel like I'm responsible for a lot of this."

"Don't blame yourself, Hank. You've just been doing your job. But now, something big's coming down. I don't know what it is yet, but I've got a feeling the shit's about to hit the fan."

"What can we do?"

"You and your girlfriend better stay out of sight for a while. Call me at home tonight. I've got to go." The line went dead.

Hank handed the receiver to Andrea. "Call your parents. Tell them we'll be there in an hour. They need to be packed and ready to leave."

"Why? What is happening?"

"I'll tell you on the way. Call them."

As Andrea dialed the number, the custodian came into the building.

"Un momento," Hank said.

The custodian nodded, but remained nearby, apparently to ensure the visitors left the building before he returned to his chores.

"¿Papá?" Andrea said into the mouthpiece. Suddenly her eyes widened in horror, and she demanded in Spanish, "Who is this?"

Hank reached for the receiver, but Andrea kept it clenched in her grasp. He put his ear close to her's and heard a din of terrified animals, punctuated by raucous shouts and cruel laughter. And in the background, they heard Alberto's plaintive voice, begging someone to please stop killing his animals.

"What are you doing to my son?" Andrea screamed.

"¡Puta de los gringos!" a man's voice snarled. Then the line went dead.

Andrea frantically dialed the number again, but no one answered.

Hank's mind raced. "Who can we call?"

"There is no one," Andrea said with a groan. "It is the authorities who are *doing* this." Dropping the phone, she hurried past the custodian and through the front door. Hank ran after her.

Minutes later they careened up the Transithmian Highway. Traffic on the two-lane road was light, and Andrea had the accelerator pressed to the floorboard. She swerved out to pass a slow-moving car, then had to brake and duck back in at the last second to avoid hitting an oncoming bus. Hank automatically jammed the nonexistent brake pedal on the passenger side. She looked at him defiantly, and he said, "Go!" She swerved into the oncoming lane, flew by the slow-moving car, and raced toward the Caribbean.

For thirty tense miles, neither Hank nor Andrea spoke. There was nothing to say. Nothing to plan. They both had heard Alberto's final scream. Hank's mind focused on a single thought: Kill the motherfuckers!

They finally arrived at the Portobelo turnoff. Andrea swerved onto the asphalt road that cut back toward the east. For another quarter-hour, they raced along the winding road, through the coastal brush and past the ramshackle dwellings.

"How much farther?" Hank said.

"We are close," she said grimly. "Hank, it is *Tío* Humberto who is responsible for this."

"Are you sure?"

"I know him. When he threatened you, he meant it."

They passed under a canopy of dense trees and saw the emerald-blue Caribbean. Andrea slowed only slightly, and leaned on the horn as they entered the outskirts of Portobelo. The black inhabitants along the roadside shouted and gestured for her to slow down.

On the other side of the village, they bounced onto the dirt road that led up the steep hill. Moments later, they crested the hill and roared down the other side. In the clearing below, they could see the farm. There were no signs of movement around the *nipa* shack. The animal pen was empty.

They slid to a stop in front of the farm, jumped out, and ran up the dusty path. The front door stood open. In the shadows, something lay heaped on the floor.

Hank and Andrea stopped in the doorway. Hank gagged. Andrea emitted a long mournful cry. A vulture, sitting atop a shapeless form in the corner, leaped into ungainly flight. It flew toward them, and they threw up their arms to ward it off. It flapped through the doorway and out into the bright sunlight.

Apprehensively, they entered the shadowy one-room shack and picked their way through the carnage. The marauders had brought the goats and chickens inside for the slaughter. The heat was intense, and the room was already alive with flies and other insects, swarming over the remains of the family livestock. However, there were no signs of Alberto or his grandparents.

Hank led Andrea outside. As they stood blinking in the late afternoon sun, several *Machos* emerged from the nearby tree line, training assault rifles on them.

Hank whispered to Andrea, "Don't move."

Other *Machos* now edged around the side of the shack. They surrounded Hank and Andrea. Blood and grim covered their beards and black T-shirts.

"Where is my son?" Andrea cried.

The *Machos* laughed. Several grabbed Hank and pushed him facedown onto the ground. They ran their hands over his body, checking for weapons.

Then they searched Andrea. "Please!" she pleaded, ignoring their violation of her person. "Where is my son?"

"*¡Mamá!*" came an anguished cry.

Hank was able to turn his head, and saw the terrified youngster running from the tree line toward his mother. Behind him, came his grandparents, herded forward by *Machos*. Andrea dropped to her knees and caught her son as he raced headlong into her arms.

The *Machos* dragged Hank to his feet. They appeared to be the same savages who had attacked the farm the last time. "Let me talk to your officer!" Hank said in Spanish.

"*I* am in charge here," snarled a voice behind him. Hank turned and saw the burly black corporal from the first encounter. Now, however, master sergeant chevrons adorned his sweat-lined fatigue cap.

"Let me talk to the lieutenant!" Hank demanded. "He promised to leave these people alone."

The sergeant barked an order, and the troops restraining Hank pulled his arms behind him and tied his wrists together with rope. The sergeant shouted another order, and his troops withdrew toward the tree line. Someone pushed Hank forward. As he stumbled across the clearing, he was relieved to see that all the troops were withdrawing. Andrea and her family were being left behind.

"No!" Andrea screamed. She rose from her knees, as if to follow.

"Andrea!" Hank shouted. "Stay there! Protect your family! I'll be okay!"

She hesitated, torn between loved ones.

"Go back to the city! Contact Ortega!" Hank shouted over his shoulder, as he and the *Machos* disappeared into the jungle.

The sergeant led the patrol up a narrow trail in single file. Hank was in the middle of the column, his hands still tied behind him. Occasionally he would stumble, and the soldier behind him would prod him with his rifle muzzle.

This jungle was denser than anything Hank had encountered in Vietnam. An impenetrable green wall rose on either side of the trail—serpentine roots, dense underbrush, towering trees. The chest-high tangle of thorned bushes and knife-edged ferns ripped his clothes and cut his flesh. This was reptilian jungle; man was the only mammal foolish enough to trespass.

As the patrol followed the labyrinth of twisting trails along the base of the hills, Hank occasionally got a glimpse of the sun. They seemed to be heading east.

Finally, they emerged into an area where the underbrush had been cleared, but where towering trees still blocked the sun. Two-man tents occupied most of the clearing. A command tent, perhaps ten-by-ten, stood off to one side, close to a stream. Hank was surprised to see a Jeep behind the tent. He had assumed the trek from the farm had taken them to a more remote area.

"*¡Parate!*" the sergeant snarled, ordering Hank to halt. Then he forced him to kneel.

The tent flap opened, and the lieutenant from the earlier encounter stepped out, carrying a duffel bag. "Get up," he told Hank.

"You gave your word," Hank said, struggling to his feet.

"The situation changed. I was given a direct order to capture and detain you."

"What about the others, back at the farm?"

"They were just . . . bait. You were the one *El General* wanted."

"What are you going to do with me?"

"I don't know," the lieutenant said with an air of resignation. "I have been ordered to return to Panama City. The sergeant is in charge here now."

Hank turned to the sergeant, who gazed back with a look of eager anticipation.

The lieutenant seemed to want to say something else, but then shook his head and walked away. He threw his duffel bag into the rear of the Jeep, and he and his driver drove out of the compound. Hank felt a stab of fear, realizing that he had lost his last contact with humanity.

The beatings began immediately.

Unwanted consciousness returned. Hank knew it was not the first time. He had no recollection of what had been done to him, only that he was in excruciating pain. His arms and shoulders felt as if he were being pulled apart. Mosquitos and sandflies swarmed over his face, seeking his mouth, nose, and eyes. However, he remained absolutely still, so as not to alert his torturers. He kept his eyes narrowed to unnoticeable slits.

He realized it was night; a Coleman lantern hissed nearby. He heard a voice, not talking to him, but to someone else. There was movement in front of him, and he opened his eyes a bit more. The frightened faces of several Indians came into his view. He was looking down at them. He must be hanging by his arms. Would the Indians free him? The sergeant's boots came into view, and Hank closed his eyes. Too late.

"Ah, you are awake again, my friend," the sergeant said. He delivered a savage punch just below Hank's rib cage. Hank felt neither pain from the blow, nor shame over his body's release of waste.

"You made a fool of me when you came here last time," the sergeant hissed, "but you are not so smart now, are you?"

Hank saw the bloody black fist coming up at him, and again lost consciousness.

Hank inhaled water. Good, he thought, trying to suppress the contractions of his throat. He told himself, don't fight it . . . breathe deeply . . .

Someone pulled him up into a sitting position, and he choked.

Pain shot through his torso, as if he were being beaten again. Reluctantly, he opened his eyes. He was in the shallow stream that ran through the encampment. A *Macho* held him on either side. He didn't see the sergeant. "Clean yourself," ordered one of the soldiers.

"Aaagh!" Hank cried out, as he tried to move his shoulder and back muscles. Bile surged up from his stomach and filled his mouth. He spat it into the stream.

The soldiers untied his wrists and eased him into the water, this time, keeping his head above the surface. The sharp rocks, gouging his abused back, and the stream, rushing over his body and through his clothes, brought back full consciousness.

The soldiers lifted him into a sitting position. Circulation returned to his arms and shoulders. The pain was intense, but now he could tolerate it. Then he saw the sergeant approaching from the command tent.

"Kill me," Hank rasped.

"Oh, no, my smart friend. We are not done with you yet."

"No more," Hank begged.

"There will be *much* more," the sergeant said, "but not here."

The soldiers lifted him to his feet. When they reached the muddy river bank, his water-saturated shoes slipped out from under him, and he fell onto all fours. The soldiers picked him up and dragged him toward the command tent. Hank saw the Jeep, and his hopes rose. But as they drew nearer, he saw that the tent was empty. Apparently the driver had returned without the lieutenant.

The soldiers let him slump to the ground. In front of him lay an empty body bag.

"Get in," the sergeant ordered.

"No," Hank moaned. Too weak to resist, he let the two soldiers force his feet into the bag. They pulled it around him and zipped it up to his chin.

The sergeant squatted down and put his demented face close to Hank's. "Major Mejías has sent for you," he hissed, then closed the zipper over Hank's face.

18. CAUSA JUSTA

Hank lay on his side in the rear of the Jeep, sealed in the heavy, rubberized body bag. They had left the zipper open just enough so he wouldn't suffocate. Hank's breathing came in labored gasps; his nose apparently was broken. The split in his lower lip had finally stopped bleeding.

He could hear two voices. One was the sergeant's; the other he didn't recognize. Early in the trip, they had prodded him with what felt like a metal rod. He had lain still, feigning unconsciousness, and eventually they had lost interest in him. He estimated they had driven for about an hour.

The Jeep came to a brief stop, and Hank heard the sound of traffic. He realized they must be in the city. They took off again, and a surge of fear rose in his chest. The beatings in the jungle had just been the prelude for the torture that awaited him in *La Preventiva*. He was going to die, as his grandfather had died, as if it had been predestined.

A few minutes later the Jeep stopped again, and Hank heard the men climb out. They grabbed the body bag and yanked it over the tailgate. Hank slammed to the ground, unable to move his arms enough to break his fall.

They dragged him feetfirst across the ground. The surface beneath him felt soft; he envisioned the dirt compound outside *La Comandancia*, where Major Mejías had shot the coup leaders. Then he felt himself being lifted into the air and carried for a short distance . . . then dropped again onto a hard surface. His legs were lifted. He was being dragged up a stairway, feetfirst. A long stairway.

Now they apparently were on a landing . . . turned a corner . . .

stopped. He heard a door open, then he was dragged forward again. Stopped again. The zipper came down, and a bright light momentarily blinded him. He heard the hiss of a Coleman lantern.

Hank painfully raised up on one elbow and squirmed out of the body bag. The sergeant stood near the open doorway, holding the lantern. The other *Macho* trained a rifle on him. Hank frantically looked around. The cell was empty. The stark concrete floor and the unpainted cinder block walls were blackened with age and humidity. There were no windows.

The *Macho* with the rifle spat in Hank's face, and the sergeant laughed. Then both men turned and left, slamming the door behind them. The cell was plunged into darkness, except for a flickering sliver of light beneath the door.

Hank struggled to his feet and limped across the room. He ran his hands over the door's hewn surface. There was no handle—no way to open it from the inside. He listened; the only sound from the corridor was the faint hiss of a lantern.

He returned to the far side of the cell and slumped into a sitting position, his back against the cinder block wall. The thin crack beneath the door was the only source of air. An acrid ammonia smell penetrated his clogged nostrils.

For some time, he stared at the sliver of light, his mind numbed by pain and fatigue, punctuated by stabs of fear. Then a shadow moved liquidly in front of the light, and disappeared into the dark. Suddenly the movement registered: Snake! He struggled to his feet.

Footfalls echoed in the corridor and the door flew open. The *Macho* soldier had returned alone. Hank blinked, trying to adjust his eyes to the light from the corridor.

The *Macho* kept his rifle trained on Hank and laid a canteen on the floor. "The sergeant wants you awake when he comes back with Major Mejías," he said, then kicked the canteen across the floor.

In the flickering light, Hank saw a two-foot snake crawling along the wall, away from the door. It had a triangular head and

X-patterned scales—a fer-de-lance, deadly and aggressive. The *Macho* turned to leave.

"Wait!" Hank cried in Spanish, stalling; he needed to see where the snake went before the cell went black again. "Is this La Preventiva?"

The *Macho* turned and said with a laugh, "No, *gringo*. This is Major Mejías' private place. You will beg the major to take you to *La Preventiva*."

The fer-de-lance disappeared into a small hole near the corner of the cell.

Unaware, the *Macho* said, "I would like to stay here and see what he does to you, but I must return to Portobelo. I think I will visit your girlfriend again."

Hank struggled to his feet, but the grinning *Macho* stepped backward into the corridor and slammed the door.

Hank felt his way along the wall to the corner where the snake had disappeared. He dropped to one knee, his back toward the wall, and blocked the hole with the sole of his shoe. He had the snake trapped, until he moved his foot.

His mind raced. It must be young to be so small. That meant there must be others. He felt the fer-de-lance nudge against his shoe. He took a deep breath. The snake was his way out, like the extra round he'd carried in Nam. He just had to put his wrist in front of the hole. Death would be quick.

He lowered his right arm, but then raised it again, gripped by fear. He clenched his fists. Do it now! he told himself, before Mejías gets here. Cold sweat drenched his body. He lowered his arm again and placed the inside of his wrist against the sole of his shoe. Do it now!

Suddenly the vision he'd had after his night in *La Preventiva* rushed back to him. In the dream, he'd been lying on a bed of snakes, needing to warn Andrea. "Oh, God!" he moaned. He'd told Andrea to come back to the city, and Mejías knew about her and Alberto!

Hank raised his arm and kept the sole of his shoe pressed firmly against the wall.

Time passed. The backs of Hank's legs quivered with strain and fear. Then he heard footfalls in the corridor. The door flew open. This time it was the black *Macho* sergeant who entered the cell, pistol drawn. Hank appeared to cower in the corner. The sergeant said something over his shoulder, and Major Mejías stepped into the cell, carrying a rope and a length of rebar.

Hank no longer felt the snake pushing against his shoe. *"¡Por favor!"* he pleaded and hysterically pounded the wall.

Mejías and the sergeant moved forward, grinning.

Hank felt the snake aggressively respond. He rose to a crouch; then with a quick first stride, he scurried along the wall to the next corner. He appeared to cringe. The sergeant and Mejías crossed the room, laughing.

The sergeant didn't feel the fer-de-lance strike the back of his boot, or notice it wrap around his ankle, or feel it begin to crawl up his leg. Mejías shouted *"¡Culebra!"* just as the snake struck through the sergeant's bloused trousers, burying its fangs into his leg. The sergeant screamed and frantically tried to hit the snake with the barrel of his pistol. Mejías dropped the rope and rebar, and stumbled backward, fumbling with the snap on his holster. Hank lunged between the two men, driving his right forearm under Mejías' chin and knocking him off to the side, then darted through the open door and slammed it behind him.

A shot echoed from inside the cell. Someone screamed—probably the sergeant. Then another shot and a shout: "Let me out!" This time, Hank recognized Mejías' rasping voice. Several more shots rang out in rapid succession. Apparently, they were shooting at the door, but their bullets couldn't penetrate the heavy wood.

Hank sagged against the cinder-block wall, his heart pounding. He was free, at least momentarily, but where the hell was he? He picked the Coleman lantern off the floor and held it above his head. At the end of the corridor, bats fluttered.

Inside the cell, the two soldiers began to plead. Hank looked back; his grandfather would never have left them like that. Hank took a few steps down the corridor, estimating the distance from the door to the snake hole. "Sorry, Grandpa." He bent over and pounded on the wall, hoping he was filling the cell with snakes.

Then he straightened up and hurried down the corridor. At the far end, decades of bat guano lay piled in the corner. That was the ammonia smell! Fort Amador! He must be in the old island bunker. He ducked under the fluttering bats and hurried down the long stairway.

At the bottom of the stairs, the barred door stood open. He paused in the doorway long enough to extinguish and discard the lantern. The night was clear. He saw a path through the underbrush; it had grown much higher since he was a boy.

He emerged from the dense foliage and saw a Jeep parked nearby in the sand; otherwise, the beach was deserted. He checked inside the Jeep—no keys. He had no intention of going back into the tunnel to get them. As he jogged across the sand toward the causeway, his entire body ached, but still functioned.

He turned onto the narrow asphalt road. A quarter-mile away, he could make out the silhouetted buildings of Fort Amador. He stumbled up the road in search of help.

Four helicopters rose suddenly from the midst of the fort. They sounded like Apaches. Were they on night maneuvers? The helicopters flew in formation due east, then turned back and hovered over the bay.

Hank's breath came in short gasps; the abuse he had received was taking its toll, and he had to slow to a walk. He passed the officers' club, where he and Andrea had dined the day of the failed coup. The club was dark.

A block farther, he stumbled onto the grounds of the Marine headquarters building; there were no lights here either. Then he realized the entire area was dark. He climbed the steps and pushed his way through the front door and into the dark anteroom.

"Halt!" rang out a woman's voice. "Who goes there?"

Hank heard a bolt slam a round into a rifle chamber. "My

name is Hank Duque!" he shouted, throwing up his hands. "I need help."

The room suddenly was illuminated, not by lights, but by a series of flashes. Hank caught a glimpse of two women Marines standing in front of him—one armed with a rifle. A split second later, shock waves rattled the windows. He and the women dived onto the floor. One of them, a heavyset technical sergeant, flipped on a high-powered flashlight and pointed it at him. The other, a slim PFC, aimed an M-16 at his face.

Hank shielded his eyes and shouted over the barrage, "Easy! I'm an American. I'm with the Associated Press. What the hell's going on? That sounds like artillery."

"Show some identification!" ordered the sergeant.

Hank reached into his back pocket. It was empty. "I don't have any identification. PDF *Machos* took me prisoner yesterday afternoon."

Before she could reply, heavy weapons erupted. A fierce battle seemed to have broken out all over Fort Amador. The front door flew open. The sergeant turned the flashlight in that direction, and Hank recognized the lance corporal from the officers' club. "Don't shoot!" he shouted. "I know her!"

"Get over here, Davis!" the sergeant shouted to the lance corporal.

Lance Corporal Davis dived onto the floor beside them.

"Do you know this guy?" the sergeant demanded.

Davis frowned and shook her head.

"The officers' club," Hank said. "I'm the former Marine. The lance corporal."

"Jesus, man! You look like shit. What the hell happened to you?"

Hank didn't even try to answer. An Apache now hovered directly overhead, as if protecting the building while it slammed rockets elsewhere into the fort. Finally it flew off.

Headlights flashed across the front window, followed by the sounds of a Jeep sliding up in front of the building. Another woman Marine, a black PFC, came running through the front door.

"They're coming this way, Gunney!" she screamed, diving onto the floor with the others.

"Who's coming?" demanded the sergeant.

"PDF soldiers. At least a dozen of 'em. I saw 'em slippin' through the fence near their barracks."

The sergeant turned to Davis. "You and Harrison, get rifles for the rest of us." Davis and the black PFC hurried through a door marked "Duty NCO". They each came back with two rifles and two cartridge belts. Davis looked inquiringly at the sergeant, who hesitated, then gave a curt nod.

Davis handed Hank an M-16 and a cartridge belt. "Lock and load, Marine."

They assumed firing positions—Hank and the sergeant on opposite sides of the front door, the other three women at open windows. They all peered down the dimly lighted street. The Apaches had ceased fire, and now hovered over another part of the fort. The artillery barrage also had let up; now there was only sporadic small arms fire.

"Do you know how to shoot that thing?" the sergeant asked Hank.

"Lady," Hank muttered, "I was shootin' an M-16, when you were sellin' Girl Scout cookies."

"Lady?" she exploded, turning the muzzle of her weapon toward him.

"My mistake . . . Sergeant. Now tell me what the hell's goin' on."

"Saturday night, the PDF killed a Marine lieutenant at a road block. Shot him in the back. President Bush must have decided he'd had enough. What you're seein' is the start of a full-scale invasion."

"An invasion?" Hank said in disbelief.

"Yeah, code name, 'Operation Just Cause'. It's going on all over Panama. The U.S. troops here on Fort Amador are fighting the PDF troops that share this installation. Only problem is, it started an hour early. Me and my people were supposed to be long gone from here."

"Here they come!" Davis said.

They all sighted down their rifles at a dozen or so figures, charging up the middle of the road.

"Stand by!" the sergeant ordered.

The PDF soldiers were now within fifty yards, running toward them.

"Hold it!" Hank shouted. "I don't think they're armed."

"What?" the sergeant exploded, then said, "I think you're right. Hold your fire, people!"

Hank stepped into the doorway and shouted, *"¡Paren!"*

The PDF soldiers stumbled to a halt about twenty yards away and threw up their hands.

"Put the light on 'em," Hank told the sergeant, then shouted in Spanish, "What do you want?" One of the soldiers responded, and Hank said, "I think they want to surrender."

The sergeant moved into the doorway beside him. "Tell 'em to come forward. Slowly."

Hank repeated the order in Spanish, and the soldiers meekly trudged up the walkway. "You women are gonna be heroes," Hank told the sergeant.

"Fuck you . . . what did you say your name was?"

"Hank Duque."

"Fuck you, Hank Duque," she said gruffly, but was unable to suppress a smile.

The surroundings were quiet now; apparently, the battle for Fort Amador was over. The sergeant told Davis to fire up the emergency generator. The lance corporal hurried outside, and moments later a diesel engine started and dim emergency lights came on.

The prisoner count turned out to be fourteen. Hank and the women herded them into the building's windowless galley, and the sergeant assigned the two PFCs to guard the door. Then Hank followed the sergeant and Lance Corporal Davis into the Duty NCO office.

"I gotta report in," the sergeant said. She sat down behind a desk and tried the phone. "Line's dead." She reached into a drawer and pulled out a two-way field radio.

As the sergeant established communication, Hank looked about the office. Emblazoned on the wall in red and gold were the Marine Corps emblem and the motto: *Semper Fidelis*—Always Faithful. The recollection of another Marine sergeant flashed into his mind: H. G. Taylor, who had given up his life on the grounds of the Tivoli Hotel.

The squawk of an incoming transmission brought him back to the present. Southern Command asked for an account of the events. Hank noticed a rest room at the far end of the office. He told Davis, "I'm going to the head."

Closing the door behind him, he leaned on the sink and looked in the mirror in disbelief at his bruised and swollen face. His nose obviously was broken, and his left cheek bone was swollen so badly that the eye above it was almost closed. His split lower lip had clotted, but needed to be sutured. No wonder Davis hadn't recognized him.

He turned on the faucet, leaned down, and gulped thirstily. Then he straightened up and gingerly wiped his battered face with a wet paper towel. It was like tending the face of a stranger. He went over to the toilet and relieved himself. Good, at least no blood.

Someone knocked on the door.

"Yeah?" he said.

"What size shoes do you wear?"

"Ten."

Davis opened the door and handed him a pair of combat boots. "I guessed elevens. These'll have to do. I got you something to wear too," she said, handing him a set of clean utilities.

"Thanks," Hank said gratefully. The shirt and trousers also were slightly large, but were a significant improvement over his own filthy rags.

A few minutes later, he walked out of the rest room, just as the sergeant signed off.

"Fort Amador's secure," she said. "Now the fighting's moving to the city. They're goin' after that bastard Noriega, right where he lives—the *Comandancia*."

"Sergeant," Hank said, "I've got to get into town. I need a vehicle."

"No way. Wait 'til this is over, and I'll take you in myself."

"My girlfriend and her little boy are out there. I told 'em to come back to the city. Her apartment's just a few blocks from *La Comandancia*."

"I'm sorry," the sergeant said, "there's nothing I can do."

"Let him have the duty Jeep," Davis said. She reached over to a pegboard and took down a set of keys.

"I can't do that," the sergeant said, grabbing the keys away from her.

"I gotta find 'em, Sergeant," Hank said. "They're . . . all I've got."

The sergeant studied him for a moment. Then she turned to Davis. "Report to the galley. Help Parker and Harrison guard the prisoners."

"But, Gunney—" Davis began.

"Move out, Marine!" the sergeant barked.

Davis reluctantly left the room. The sergeant returned the keys to the pegboard. She looked at Hank again, then deliberately turned her back on him and walked toward the rest room, saying, "I gotta make a head call."

Hank smiled. "Semper Fi' . . . Gunney," he said, addressing her for the first time by the nickname reserved for Marine gunnery sergeants.

The sergeant broke stride momentarily, but entered the rest room and closed the door behind her, without looking back.

Hank sped through the middle of Fort Amador in the duty Jeep. Several U.S. military vehicles patrolled the dimly lighted street, but no one challenged the Marine Corps Jeep, driven by a hunched-over figure in utilities.

A mile outside the fort, heading up *Avenida de los Mártires*, he had to pull over. Ahead, a convoy of M-113 armored personnel carriers had blocked the thoroughfare and appeared poised to enter *El Chorrillo*. *La Comandancia* lay only two blocks away.

Another Marine Corps Jeep pulled up beside Hank's. "Get your helmet on, Marine!" a lieutenant hollered.

"Aye, aye, sir!" Hank shouted, bluffing.

The lieutenant did a double-take, apparently having caught a glimpse of Hank's battered face, but then continued up to where the convoy was parked.

Overhead, Hank heard the drone of approaching aircraft. He looked back and saw two black AC-130 Spectre gunships lumber out from behind Ancon Hill. He recognized the stubby turbo-prop aircraft from Vietnam.

The two gunships cut loose on *La Comandancia* with a deafening barrage of rockets. Smoke poured from the main building, and the smaller structures were obliterated, but the walls around the compound withstood the salvo.

The Spectres made several passes, then withdrew. As they flew back behind Ancon Hill, the convoy of armored personnel carriers rolled off the elevated thoroughfare and down a side street into *El Chorrillo*.

A fierce ground battle broke out around the complex. Loyalists fought from the surrounding tenements with small arms, as they had during the failed coup. One of the tinderbox structures ignited.

Hank needed to get to the *Santa Ana* district before this onslaught did. He frantically looked about for a way off the clogged thoroughfare. Seeing none, he drove forward, weaving through the snarl of military and civilian vehicles.

Ahead, the Marine lieutenant who had shouted at him now stood on the shoulder of the road, surveying the battle below. Hank swerved onto the shoulder to get by the stalled traffic, and leaned on the horn. The lieutenant turned and signaled for him to stop. Hank kept coming. The lieutenant held his ground. At the last second, to avoid hitting him, Hank swerved down the side street.

Damn it! He was heading right into the firefight. However, he had no choice but to follow the path that had been cleared by the armored personnel carriers. Noriega must have received advance warning of the invasion, because the intersections were blockaded with abandoned cars. Scores of corpses lay strewn behind the barricades, most wearing the makeshift uniforms of Noriega's Dignity Battalion.

A block away from *La Comandancia*, Hank slammed on the brakes. A mob of PDF soldiers rounded the corner and ran toward him. The soldier in the lead saw Hank and raised his hands over his head. The others followed suit. Hank waved them away. The soldiers streamed by the Jeep, looking for someone else to surrender to.

Three members of Noriega's Dignity Battalion rounded the corner and opened fire on their retreating PDF allies. With a squeal of tires, Hank bounced onto the nearby sidewalk and turned left down a narrow alley. Flames engulfed the buildings on the right. Ahead, two Digbats ran from a tenement entryway, and flames exploded behind them. The paramilitary thugs were firing *El Chorrillo*! A bullet exploded the passenger-side windshield, and Hank leaned down as far as he could, as he plunged headlong through the blazing corridor.

He raised up again, just in time to swerve past an abandoned car and careen around the corner onto *Avenida A*. Refugees swarmed up the thoroughfare, fleeing the inferno with only a few meager possessions. As Hank passed, they scowled up at him, trying to determine if he was one of the Americans laying waste to their homes.

When he reached the *Santa Ana* district, he found the streets nearly deserted. However, the balconies were jammed with people watching the ominous orange glow approaching from the west.

Hank pulled up behind Andrea's apartment building. He hesitated. Please, God, let them be here. Then he forced his aching body out of the Jeep and limped into the building.

The apartment door was locked. He knocked and shouted,

but no one responded. His shoulders sagged and he slumped against the wall.

Down the hallway, a door opened. An old man stuck his head out. "Go away!" he shouted in Spanish.

Hank knew the neighbor only by sight. "Have you seen the woman who lives here? And her little boy?"

The old man set one foot in the hallway. He had a revolver in his hand. "Go away, *gringo!*"

"I live here! You've seen me before."

The old man peered at him.

"I am Enrique Duque. I live here with Andrea and Alberto." He pointed to his face. "*La guardia* did this to me."

The old man studied him for a moment, then said, "She has gone to the home of her uncle. She was very angry." With that, he turned and went into his apartment, slamming and locking the door behind him.

Hank hurried down to the Jeep. As he climbed inside, he noticed the left front tire was almost flat—probably punctured escaping from *El Chorrillo.*

He hurried down *Vía España,* the damaged tire causing the Jeep to pull to the left. As he entered the banking district, a power failure plunged the neighborhood into darkness. Security alarms echoed throughout the affluent shopping center. Shadowy figures scurried over the sidewalks, apparently the first wave of looters. Two hurled a trash can through a store window

Hank turned onto *Avenida Espinosa.* The rim grated on the concrete as he headed up the hill, then turned left, entering the *La Cresta* district. The affluent neighborhood was dark; he wasn't sure he would be able to find the Castillero home. Then on the next block, he spotted Andrea's van parked at the curb and pulled in behind it. The neighborhood security guard was nowhere in sight.

Hank climbed out of the Jeep and limped up the walkway. He pounded on the front door until finally it opened. Sr. Castillero stood in front of him, a hunting rifle in one hand, a lighted candle in the other. His eyes widened with fear at the sight of Hank.

"Arrgh!" Hank roared, lunging forward and grabbing the rifle. He drove the Panamanian backward across the tiled foyer until his feet went out from under him. Hank landed astride Castillero and with both hands pushed the rifle barrel against his throat, trying to choke him.

"Hank, stop!" Andrea screamed, dropping to her knees beside him. She held a candle close to his face and gasped at the sight of his distended features. *"¡Por favor, mi corazón!"* she begged, throwing her free arm around his neck. *"¡No mas!"*

Hank looked up and saw Alberto, standing in the living room, looking on silently. Hank relaxed the pressure and let Castillero breathe.

"Come," Andrea said. She helped Hank to his feet.

Castillero lay coughing on the floor. Then he moaned and rolled onto his side. He managed to pull himself into a sitting position, leaning against the wall. "They were only supposed to frighten you," he gasped, "to make you leave the country."

Sra. Castillero entered the foyer, and her husband held up a hand to her. She gazed down at him with loathing, making no effort to comfort or assist him.

"I will make it up to you, Andrea," Castillero moaned. "And to your parents. I swear it!"

Hank angrily stepped toward Castillero again, but Andrea moved between them. *"¡No mas!"* she said firmly.

The sun rose behind Ancon Hill. Alberto sat between Hank and Andrea on the back steps of the Castillero home. Two miles away, the *El Chorrillo* district still smoldered. Through the open kitchen door, they listened to the Canal Zone radio station. The PDF had been crushed throughout Panama, and Panamanians now filled the streets, hailing the U.S. troops as conquering heroes. The station had carried a brief statement by George Bush, who claimed the invasion had been necessary to protect American lives. And there were unconfirmed reports that the Vatican Embassy had given sanctuary to General Noriega, but within a short time would turn him over to the United States for prosecution on drug trafficking charges. All of the general's staff officers were already in custody, except for a Major Carlos Mejías, whose whereabouts were unknown.

Hank looked down at Alberto, who was staring at the far-off columns of smoke.

Andrea had her son's hands clasped between her own. She whispered to Hank, "He has not spoken since we left the farm."

Hank placed a fatherly hand on the boy's shoulder. "I'm sorry about your animals . . . *Hijo*."

Alberto emitted a heavy sigh, then looked up at Hank. Tears welled in the boy's eyes, and suddenly he threw his arms around Hank's waist and began to sob.

Hank and Andrea both held him. It was some time before he quieted. Andrea, who also had been crying, smiled down at her son and let him use her handkerchief. Then Alberto turned to Hank, and reached up and gently touched his swollen face.

"It will heal, *Hijo*," Hank said. "It will all heal."

EPILOGUE:
PANAMA 2000

Our lives teach us who we are.
—*Salman Rushdie*

It was almost noon. In just a few minutes, a ceremony would be held to celebrate the end of the United States' sovereignty over the Panama Canal Zone.

Hank parked his Associated Press van on a side street beside the former Ancon elementary school. "Don't forget the radio, Alberto," he said to his stepson, now nineteen.

"Edgardo has it, Dad," Alberto replied from the backseat. His nine-year-old half-brother was already out of the van and waiting impatiently on the sidewalk.

"And I have your camera," Andrea said, opening her passenger-side door.

As Hank joined his family on the sidewalk, he looked through the chain link fence at the old school building. "That was my school, when I was your age," he said to his younger son.

"I know, Dad," Edgardo said, "you've told me."

Hank turned to his older son.

Alberto smiled and said indulgently, "And your father before you . . ."

Hank turned to Andrea, who also smiled, saying, "I think this is the first place you took me."

Hank chuckled. "After you took me to a couple of riots, as I recall."

"You insisted on going," she said.

Hank gazed at the school for a moment, then turned back to her. "I was just thinking . . . I've spent exactly half my life in Panama—the first fourteen years, and the last eleven. The twenty-five in between . . . are just a blur."

His wife smiled affectionately. "This was where you belonged, *Enrique.*"

Hank returned her smile.

"Let's go!" his younger son said. "We're going to miss everything!"

They walked the half-block down Ancon Hill. A hundred or so spectators stood quietly at the edge of the thoroughfare that ran between Ancon and Panama City. Originally named *Fourth of July Avenue* by the United States in the early 1900s, it had been re-named *Avenue of the Martyrs* by Panama after the 1964 riots. Today, the Panamanian government was renaming it *Avenue 2000*, to symbolically lay to rest the century of ill will between the two countries. The street had been closed off for the ceremony.

A larger crowd was forming on the other side. "Let's watch from over there," Hank said. "We'll get a better view of the top of the hill."

They crossed over and found a good vantage point at the curb. Putting a hand on his younger son's shoulder, he pointed up the hill. "That's where the old Tivoli Hotel used to be. My grandfather, the one you're named after, stood up to Theodore Roosevelt there."

"Who's Theodore Roosevelt?" the boy said.

"He was . . ." Hank began, but then said, "I'll tell you about him, and your great-grandfather, tomorrow."

Andrea moved closer to Hank, taking his arm. "Tell him about 1964 also," she said quietly, so only he could hear.

"Think I ought to?" Hank said, looking up the hill, remembering what it had been like to be a frightened fourteen-year-old, pinned down in the cross fire.

She nodded.

"Okay," he said. Then he turned to Alberto. "Peaceful end to a troubled century, Son."

"Are you sure it's over, Dad? Look at those people across the street."

Hank looked. The cluster of spectators on the Ancon side were obviously Americans—remnants of four generations of dedicated Canal Zonians who, throughout the 20th Century, had imposed their sense of order on Panama's spontaneity.

Alberto said wryly, "Panamanians on this side of the street, Americans on the other. Where do you and I belong, Dad? In the middle?"

Hank looked at his stepson. Somewhere, there was a former American soldier, who had abandoned Alberto and his mother twenty years ago, and would never know the fine young man he had grown to be. Before Hank could reply, a crescendo of bells, sirens, and automobile horns sounded across the city.

When the din finally subsided, radios throughout the crowd carried a brief conciliatory message from former United States President Jimmy Carter. He concluded his broadcast saying, "In the spirit with which the French gave the United States the Statue of Liberty, we offer this flag to be flown over your city."

Atop Ancon Hill, an enormous Panamanian flag unfurled as it was hoisted to the top of a fifty-foot flagpole. The Panamanian national anthem echoed throughout the city.

Then there was quiet. The Americans across the street stood in stony silence. The Panamanians gazed up Ancon Hill, as if expecting Teddy Roosevelt and his Rough Riders to surge over it and revoke the accord. Hank smiled; he'd use that description in his AP release tomorrow.

Then, on the Panamanian side, someone began to sing an age-old song from Carnival, and others joined in:

"Panameño, panameño,
Panameño vida mía,"

A lump formed in Hank's throat. Like everyone who had lived in Panama during the 20th Century, on either side of the border, he knew the song. He looked at Andrea and said, "*Panameña*, you *are* my life."

Tears welled in Andrea's eyes, and she interlaced her fingers through his.

Hank turned to Alberto. "I think you're right, Son. We belong in the middle of the street." He stepped forward, and his family followed. The Americans on the Ancon side stared at them. Then one stepped from the curb . . . then another . . . then several.

The two factions met in the middle of *Avenida 2000*—first with awkward handshakes, then with ***abrazos***.

ISBN 978-1-4196-7621-5
90000 >

Made in the USA
Lexington, KY
29 November 2011